When the doctor had gone, Alexander lay back against the pillows, exhausted. Philip's medicine had only partly masked the pain.

In the far corner of the room shadows shifted momentarily, billowing outward like a curtain, then steadied. A figure stood there, a man in old-fashioned armor, heavy helmet pulled down to hide his face. The king opened his mouth to challenge the stranger, then stopped abruptly as he recognized the markings on the massive shield. The shape freed its sword arm from its heavy cloak and pushed back its helmet.

Its face was the face of Zeus Ammon, the god who had spoken at Siwah. The apparition stared back at him, perfect face showing neither praise nor blame.

The lamp flared then, and the figure was gone. Alexander took a deep breath and winced at the returning pain in his side. He could not guess what the god had wanted from him, and was too drained and weak to send for the augurs who could interpret the vision. There had been neither urgency nor comfort in the god's eyes, only an inhuman watchfulness. Still puzzling over it, Alexander slept.

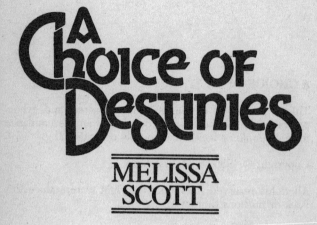

A CHOICE OF DESTINIES

MELISSA SCOTT

BAEN SCIENCE FICTION BOOKS

For my friends—D.S., T.G.A., M.M.,
B.^{3}, E.C., C.T., P.N., J.C., D.R.,
and, specially, L.A.B.

A CHOICE OF DESTINIES

This is a work of fiction. All the characters and events
portrayed in this book are fictional, and any resemblance
to real people or incidents is purely coincidental.

A Baen Books Original

Baen Publishing Enterprises
260 Fifth Avenue
New York, N.Y. 10001

First printing, June 1986

ISBN: 0-671-65563-9

Cover art by David Egge

Printed in the United States of America

Distributed by
SIMON & SCHUSTER
TRADE PUBLISHING GROUP
1230 Avenue of the Americas
New York, N.Y. 10020

THE MACEDONIAN CALENDAR

MACEDONIAN MONTH	GREGORIAN MONTH (Approximate)
Artemisios	mid-April—mid-May
Daisios	mid-May—mid-June
Panemos	mid-June—mid-July
Loios	mid-July—mid-August
Gorpiaios	mid-August—mid-September
Hyperberetaios	mid-September—mid-October
Dios	mid-October—mid-November
Apellaios	mid-November—mid-December
Audnaios	mid-December—mid-January
Peritios	mid-January—mid-February
Dystros	mid-February—mid-March
Xandikos	mid-March—mid-April

Like most ancient calendars, the Macedonian calendar was based on lunar observations, and thus is about ten days short of the solar year; thus the Gregorian months given above can be no more than approximate. To compensate, and keep the Macedonian calendar in line with the seasons, intercalary months were added, a second month of Xandikos in the third, sixth, eighth, eleventh, fourteenth, and nineteenth years of the cycle, and an extra Hyperberetaios was observed in the sixteenth year.

The Macedonian stadion is approximately equal to one-eighth of a Roman mile; 8.7 stadia equals (approximately) one English mile.

PROLOGUE:

Alexandria Eschate, winter (Peritios), 1855 imperial (1499 A.D., 2252 Ab Urbe Condita-A.U.C.)

It was snowing again. Jason of Sestos stared out the window at the swirling flakes obscuring his view of the surrounding hills. It was a depressingly familiar sight after three years in command of the garrison at Alexandria Eschate, and he turned away from the window, sighing his boredom. The Sogdians had been more or less civilized since Philip Alexander's reign; the Scythians and their Kievan allies had been quiet for nearly fifty years. Still, Alexandria Eschate, Alexandria the Farthest, the last of the eastern cities founded by Alexander III and I, retained its strategic importance, and Jason supposed he should feel flattered to hold such an important command.

He turned away from the window, glancing around the officers' mess. The servants had lit a roaring fire in the main fireplace, and a dozen oil lamps gave an added warmth in the dark afternoon. Most of the other garrison officers were present, except for Polemocrates, the junior infantry commander, whose Foot Companions had the watch: there was little for them to do in

this weather, except wait for spring. Alexander the
Thessalian, one of perhaps a dozen Alexanders in the
garrison—the name was, not surprisingly, the most
common in the empire—was bent over his daybook,
fingers flashing along the beads of his tallyboard as he
calculated the month's accounts. The senior infantry
commander, Amyntor son of Alexander, was sprawled
in a comfortable chair, feet stretched out to the fire. A
book lay open in his lap, but he did not seem to be
reading. Jason crossed the room to join him, glad of
the excuse for conversation.

"Not a very interesting text, I see," he said.

Amyntor started and looked up, a rueful smile crossing his face. "Very interesting, actually," he said.

"Oh?" Jason asked, more to break the monotony
than out of real interest.

"Flavius Arrianus, *History of Alexander III/I*,"
Amyntor answered, displaying the book's spine.

Philip Gellius, the garrison's Roman engineer, looked
up from his dice game. "That's the controversial one,
isn't it?"

Jason had long ago ceased to be surprised by the
variety of the engineer's interests. Amyntor nodded.

"Your move, Philip." Alexander the Lydian, commander of the garrison's tiny cavalry detachment, leaned
across the gaming board to touch the engineer's arm.
The earrings that had given him his second name
flashed in the lamplight, and Jason found himself wondering again why the cavalryman had adopted that
Lydian custom. He wasn't really a Lydian, but a citizen of Alexandria-in-Egypt, and God alone knew what
obscure races made up his bloodline. Mostly eastern
peoples, Jason thought, Persians and Asian Greeks
and possibly Egyptians; the Lydian was too darkly
pretty to have much western blood.

Philip tossed the dice and shifted his counters along
the board's curving track, saying, "I read it. What do
you think, Amyntor?"

"It is interesting," the infantry officer said, "but. . . ."

"What are you talking about?" the Thessalian asked, pushing aside the tallyboard.

Amyntor silently held up his book. Philip said, "It's another history of the great Alexander, only this one says the Greek rebellion was the greatest thing that ever happened to him."

The Thessalian snorted, and the Lydian said scornfully, "And how does he figure that?"

"He says that if Alexander had continued east the way he wanted to, there would've been an unstable, shifting frontier somewhere in the middle of India, and that not even Philip Alexander would've been able to hold it together. He says the Greek states would've rebelled and the end result would've been the fall of Alexander's empire and the rise of Roman power, at least in the West," Amyntor said.

"I know a Roman argument when I hear one," Alexander the Lydian said. He shifted his counters, frowning, and rolled the dice with a muttered invocation. Philip smiled and picked up the dice.

The Lydian shook his head, pushing the tiny pile of copper coins across the table toward the Roman. "What else does this Arrianus have to say?" There was a note of challenge in his voice and Jason sighed. Like most of the elite Companion Cavalry, who could trace their regimental history directly to Alexander's own cavalry, the Lydian was more than a little in love with the heroic conqueror. In his eyes, at least, the great Alexander could do no wrong. Jason smiled faintly. It was in part to discourage such romantic notions that the Companions required a year's service in a provincial garrison before a man could be promoted to squadron leader.

Amyntor grinned and gave Philip a quick, malicious glance. "He says the Greeks built everything important anyway, that any culture Rome built would've been sterile and imitative and barbaric—and he's Roman himself."

Philip shrugged, not letting himself be baited. "If I remember correctly, the word Arrianus used was pragmatic. There's nothing wrong with a little pragmatism, Amyntor."

"Pragmatism couldn't hold all those people together," the Lydian began, and Alexander the Thessalian said, "This doesn't sound much like history to me."

Philip nodded. "I thought that myself."

The Lydian said slowly, "I don't know. Why not speculate? This sort of negative history—or whatever you want to call it—might give some insight into what actually did happen, help you isolate what the important factors were."

"You can't test any of these things," the Thessalian said impatiently. "The past only happens once."

Jason sighed again, closing his ears to the rising argument, now diverted into all too familiar territory. Philip and the Thessalian would gang up on Alexander the Lydian—as they always did—argue him to mulish silence, and then would probably spend the rest of the night arguing the finer points of philosophy. There was one thing, though, he thought, glancing again at the snow that swirled ever more thickly outside the windows: if Alexander had gone into India, he might not have had to put a garrison in this godforsaken spot.

CHAPTER 1:

Bactra, winter (Peritios), 29 imperial (328 B.C., 426 A.U.C.)

It was a quiet night, so still that the soldiers standing watch on the city wall could hear the faint shrilling of flutes from the house taken over by their own brigade's commander. A few, shivering even under the layers of sheepskin and wool, glanced enviously toward the sound, then up at the sky, judging the waning hours of their watch. One, pausing to warm his hands at a brazier, mumbled the watchword to the man who held the next section of wall. Getting the proper response, he jerked his head toward the inner city and added, "What wouldn't I give to be down there."

The other man, a grizzled, bearded veteran of King Philip's day, laughed softly, so as not to attract the attention of their file-leader. He fumbled under the folds of his cloaks and brought out a wineskin. "Here, have a swallow of this."

The younger man, newly arrived from Macedon, drank gratefully. It was so cold that he could barely

5

taste the alcohol. He shivered and moved closer to the brazier.

"You don't want to be down there," the veteran went on. Glancing over his shoulder for the file-leader, he cradled his fifteen-foot sarissa against his shoulder and tipped a cooled brick out of the folds of his cloak into the brazier. A second stone was heating among the coals, and he retrieved it cautiously, wrapping his hand in several layers of cloaks. The younger man stared enviously, and did not hide his smile when the other burned his fingers.

"They don't have a brazier," the veteran said, hand in his mouth. "Or wine. And the officers're right there. You're better off up here, boy." He snapped his unburned fingers for the wineskin, which the other reluctantly returned, and turned away, shouldering his sarissa.

The younger man stared after him for a moment, then turned back to his own stretch of wall, wrapping his thick cloak even more tightly around his body. Even without a brazier, he thought, he would be warmer inside. He glanced over his shoulder, across the roofs of the low-lying, foreign buildings, toward the sounds, then turned resolutely away, looking east across the invisible hills. Nothing moved there, nor was any resistance expected from the Bactrian and Sogdian tribesmen after the victories of autumn and early winter. Remembering that campaign, the young man smiled. Those had been his first battles, and he had done well; with the gods' favor, he would do still better in the spring, especially if they went east as rumor said they would. The real veterans, the ones who had been with Alexander since the army crossed into Asia, were grumbling about that already—and let them, he thought. It was time for younger men to make their mark. The thought was almost as warming as the wine; he moved along the wall wrapped in its comfort, dreaming of glory.

It was warmer in the brigade commander's quarters, but not by much. Guests and host alike wore their heaviest tunics and kept their cloaks handy. Even the flute-girls were clothed, though they made great play with their heavy draperies. Craterus son of Alexander, brigade commander of the Foot Companions and the night's host, had ordered the dining couches drawn close around the hall's archaic central fire-pit. Slaves tended the leaping flames, but, though Craterus's face and shoulders were warm enough, his feet were icy in their sheepskin wrappings. He sat up abruptly, swinging his feet toward the fire, and shouted for more wine. A flute-girl smiled invitingly at him, and Craterus beckoned to her, pulling her close as much for her body heat as for her other charms.

The party, which had begun at sunset, was winding down at last. Coenus, the commander of the senior brigade of the Foot Companions, lay half asleep on his couch, staring into the fire. He roused himself with a start and shouted, "Craterus, good night to you. It's time we ancients were in bed."

That raised a sleepy laugh: Coenus was the oldest man present, with sons serving in his own brigade, but he was no ancient. It was his men, with Craterus's, who had borne the brunt of the winter's fighting. Coenus himself had been in the thick of it, and had the fresh scars to prove it.

"The night's still young, Coenus," the king protested, propping himself up on both elbows. He lay with his feet to the fire, his face in shadow, but everyone could hear the laughter in his voice.

"That's as may be," Coenus retorted, with dignity, "but I'm not." He hauled himself to his feet—like all the guests, he had been drinking since sunset—and made his way to the door, weaving only slightly. Conversation resumed, but sluggishly, and Craterus, watching with a host's eyes, sighed his regret. The party would end very soon now. Even as he thought this, he saw Hephaestion, commander of the Companion Cavalry, yawn openly. Craterus, who disliked the cavalry commander intensely, scowled at him, but to his surprise it was another of the Foot Companion's brigadiers who spoke next.

"Craterus, I'll follow the example of my elders." Perdiccas ran a hand through his sandy hair, dislodging a garland of wilted greenery, and rose with the assistance of a willing flute-girl. He favored the company with a cheerful leer, and staggered off toward the house he had commandeered.

Hephaestion, sitting on the end of a couch at the king's right hand, returned Craterus's scowl—he disliked the brigadier nearly as much as Craterus disliked him—and glanced sidelong at the king, wishing he would leave.

Alexander grinned back at him, knowing perfectly well what his friend wanted. He himself was not quite sober, but most of the others were very drunk; the pleasant conversations were long dead. It was time to leave, though he could cheerfully have talked the night away. He sat up, reaching for his cloak, and said, "Craterus, I'll leave you also."

Hephaestion gave an almost soundless sigh and stood easily, wrapping his cloak securely around his body. "And I."

Craterus rose, too, staggering a little as the wine hit him. He shouted for a slave to bring torches and walked with the others into the cold courtyard. It was very quiet; so quiet that the king's voice seemed to echo endlessly as he said his good nights. Craterus, cloakless, could feel the frost in the air, but stayed outside until he saw the king's party enter the tiny gatehouse. Then he turned back to the warmth of the hall.

The five men on duty at the gate had a small brazier going just inside the gatehouse, but it did little good. Their breath steamed in the still air, and Hephaestion, shivering, drew his cloak even more tightly around his shoulders. The king did not seem to notice the cold. He greeted the guards cheerfully by name, but was surprised when their answers came too slowly. "What's the trouble, Aeropus?"

The half-file-leader grimaced. "It's her, sire." He jerked his head at what seemed to be a pile of rags next to the brazier. Alexander glanced curiously at it, and the rags stirred, unfolding. Hephaestion took the torch from the slave and held it close. A woman crouched against the gatehouse wall, wrapped in layers of shawls and blankets against the cold. Her hair was streaked with grey, but her face was young and wild, and her eyes were mad. Like the eyes of a frightened horse, they showed the whites all around the iris. One of the guards whispered a charm against witchcraft as she rose to her feet, clutching blankets about her.

Aeropus went on nervously, "She said she had to talk to you, had a seeing for you, but she wouldn't let us take a message, or bring her in to you. She said she'd wait, you'd come."

"I'm here, mother," Alexander said, gently. "What was it you wanted?" The woman was shaking despite the layers of clothing; Alexander loosened his own cloak and swung it around her shoulders.

"Alexander," Hephaestion said, half a warning, half a plea for care. There had already been two attempts to kill the king; it was only too easy to picture this half-mad female as some plotter's agent. The king ignored him.

"What is it, mother?" he asked again, tightening his cloak around the woman. As he did so, she caught his hands in hers. Alexander stood patiently, waiting, as her shaking eased. He could smell the oil she wore in her hair, and, beneath its sweetness, the sour scent of her unwashed body.

"I'm sent, King Alexander," the woman said at last. "The god sends me. He tells me this is a chancy time, a bad time, this night and the days to come. Especially this night—it's a night to stay with friends, King Alexander, your luck's with them this time."

"What will happen?" Alexander asked. "Why is it a bad time?"

The woman shook her head wildly. "The god doesn't tell me. But he tells me it's chancy, balanced on the sword's point between one fate and another, and it's a night for friends, King Alexander."

Alexander nodded slowly, convinced in spite of himself by the absolute certainty in her voice. He had heard that certainty before, at Siwah and at Delphi, and trusted it. "Thank you for the warning, mother. I'll heed the god. Now, come back inside with me, and get warm. I want to give you a present."

"No!" The woman jerked her hands away. "No, I may not, not until it's over. Then I may, and I will ask, but not till then." She shrugged off the king's cloak and said, "Tonight and the days ahead, King Alexander. The god warns you." Then she was gone, darting out of the gatehouse like a startled deer.

Alexander took a step after her, but she had vanished already into the empty streets. Aeropus retrieved the cloak and Alexander put it on, suddenly glad of its protection.

Hephaestion said, "You believe her."

Alexander grinned at him. "And so do you." A strange, giddy mood was taking hold of him, growing from the awareness of his danger. He snatched the torch from Hephaestion, who had been holding it like a weapon, and caught the slave by the shoulder. "It's a night for friends, she said, so let's have them. You, run and fetch Peucestas, tell him what's passed and that I want him back. Erigyius and Laomedon, too, and Perdiccas and Coenus—Aeropus, send some of your men after them. And the rest of the Friends, by the gods." He glanced again at Hephaestion, who shook his head, laughing.

"They won't thank you for this," he said. "They're all home and asleep by now."

"Wake them, then," Alexander cried. He walked back toward the hall, where lights still showed under the heavy door. "Craterus, bring out more wine!"

"Are you ordering them to come?" Hephaestion asked.

"I'm inviting them," Alexander answered, still smiling. "Let them stay in bed if they want. Now, come on."

Ptolemy, by polite reckoning and official recognition the son of Lagus, was awakened by the noise of movement in the streets and his chamberlain's gentle knock on the bedroom door. He sat bolt upright, listening in momentary panic for the sound of fighting, then relaxed enough to shout, "Come in."

The chamberlain, a Greek from Alyzia, opened the door slowly, and sidled into the room. He was carrying a small oil lamp, and it sent strange shadows across the painted walls. Ptolemy was not in the mood for shadow pictures.

"What is it, Cleander?"

The chamberlain took a deep breath. "Sir, a message from the king—"

Ptolemy flung back the blankets, reaching blindly for his tunic, and Cleander added hastily, "Sir, it's not an emergency. King Alexander's sent a messenger to invite you to a party."

"What?" Ptolemy stopped reaching for his clothes, and slid back into bed, drawing the blankets up over the lower half of his body. "He *invites* me to a party—at this hour? It must be after midnight."

"The middle of the second night-watch, sir," Cleander said, stone-faced.

"Tell the king—" Ptolemy began, then paused. "An invitation, not an order?"

"So the messenger said, sir."

If the king had meant it as an order it would have been couched as one. With Alexander a man knew where he stood, always.

"Tell the king," Ptolemy began again, "that I thank him for the courtesy, but am in no disposition to join him."

Cleander's lips moved silently as he memorized the message, and then he bowed deeply. "I'll send that message, sir."

"Good night," Ptolemy said, and did not wait to hear the chamberlain's murmured response. Beside him, Thaïs, his Athenian mistress, stirred with curiosity.

"I wonder what that was about," she said.

"I have no idea," Ptolemy said grimly, "and until tomorrow, I don't care." He could tell, from the restored silence in the streets, that there was no emergency requiring his attention—and if there had been, the king would have sent orders, not an invitation. It was all very well for the king to drink the night away, he could—and probably would—sleep through the next day. The King's Friends, the core of officers and administrators that made up the royal council, had no such opportunity. Ptolemy himself, who bore the archaic title of Bodyguard, had the daily life of half a dozen infantry brigades to oversee. Chilled and grumbling, he burrowed deeper into the blankets, toward Thaïs's warmth.

The chamberlain's knock roused Ptolemy a second time just past dawn. The general swore at him, brushing away Thaïs's automatic caress, and shouted, "What is it this time?"

"Sir, three of the men beg an audience. They say it's an emergency." Cleander's voice was particularly sonorous, the tone he reserved for absolute disaster.

"Enter." Ptolemy threw back the covers, heedless of the chill, and reached for his tunic. Thaïs, her presence already forgotten, sat up slowly, clutching the blankets to her bare breasts. She, too, had recognized the chamberlain's tone, and had been Ptolemy's mistress long enough to guess its cause. Not an enemy attack—the Sogdians were placated by Alexander's recent marriage to one of their princesses and the Bactrians had been pounded into submission. In any case, tribesmen did not fight in winter. This had to be internal trouble: mutiny, trouble with the mercenaries, or, worst and most likely, Macedonians fighting among themselves.

The chamberlain coughed discreetly from the doorway, and Ptolemy said, "Well, what is it?" He was mostly dressed now, sword at hip, lacing his sandals over the heavy sheepskin leggings.

"I had them wait below, in your private chamber," Cleander said. "They say it concerns the king."

Ptolemy swore again, and jerked the last knot tight. Slinging his cloak over his shoulder, he said, "Who are they?"

"Eurylochus, sir, rear-rank man in Demophon's battalion," Cleander answered.

Ptolemy nodded, recognizing the name, and gestured for Cleander to precede him from the room. As they hurried down the narrow stairs that led to the inner courtyard, the chamberlain added, "Also a Foot Companion and one of the royal pages."

"Get Menedemus," Ptolemy said. Menedemus commanded his household guard. "But quietly, don't alarm anyone." There was still a remote chance that this was nothing serious, but it was not a risk Ptolemy wanted to run, not when the king's life might be at stake.

His private chamber was full of lamplight and shadow, the narrow shutters closed tight against the cold. At Ptolemy's nod, Cleander opened them, letting the early morning light into the room. Two men and a boy were waiting under the watchful eye of a household soldier. Cleander spoke softly to a second guard, then came to stand at the general's shoulder.

Ptolemy leaned back against the edge of the single

table. "Well?" he asked at last. "You have information that concerns the king?"

The shorter of the two men, a powerfully built, swarthy man, hunched his shoulders uneasily, but answered promptly enough, "Yes, sir. Eurylochus son of Arseus, sir, rear-ranker Demophon's battalion of Meleager's brigade, and a Macedon of Pella." Having identified himself, he was unable to go on. The boy, whose eyes were red and swollen from weeping, sniffled softly. Eurylochus cast a glance toward him and tried again. "It's really my brother, sir, Epimenes. Him. They came to me and said there was a plot to kill the king, so I came straight to you."

"Whose plot?" Ptolemy snapped.

Eurylochus hunched his shoulders again. "His, Epimenes's." He gestured at the weeping boy. His voice was bitter: he was facing not just the end of his military career, but probably his death as well.

The boy burst into tears, fist pressed to his mouth to choke the noise. He tried to speak, but could only shake his head silently.

"May I speak, sir?" That was the second man, taller and fairer than Eurylochus. He was very pale, and closed his hands into tight fists to hide their shaking.

Ptolemy nodded. "You are?"

"Charicles, sir, son of Menander. Pike-man in Demophon's battalion." He was younger than he had looked at first glance, not much older than the weeping boy, and coldly frightened. He swallowed hard, and said, "Epimenes is my beloved, sir. We've been together since the army came into Bactria. He had the night-watch at the king's quarters last night, and he came to me when he came off duty, like he always does. This morning, he seemed upset about something, and when I pressed him, he told me that last night the other pages on his watch had persuaded him to join them in killing the king. When the king didn't come home until after the watch had changed, they couldn't do anything, and Epimenes didn't want to go along with it anyway, not any more—" Despite his own fear—he knew only too well that he could be accused of complicity in the page's treason—Charicles reached out to touch Epimenes's shoulder, offering what comfort he could.

Eurylochus said, "They came to me, sir, and we all came here."

Ptolemy nodded, looking past them to the doorway. Menedemus was standing there, and had heard most of the pike-man's account. Catching the general's eye, Menedemus said, "Do I call out the guard, sir?"

"Not yet," Ptolemy answered grimly, and glared at the sniffling page. "Who's behind this—who put you up to it?"

Epimenes choked back a sob, and said, almost inaudibly, "No one, sir. Hermolaus thought of it. Because of Cleitus, he said."

Pages had planned—and committed—regicide before this in Macedon's bloody history, but Ptolemy hesitated briefly. It was possible that others were involved. Of the King's Friends, he knew he himself had not been involved, and of course Hephaestion's devotion to Alexander was absolute. As for the rest. . . . None of them were unambitious, but some made more believable conspirators than others. "Menedemus, double the household watch, but do it discreetly. Then choose a strong escort to take these to the king." Menedemus nodded, and vanished. "Cleander, send word to General Hephaestion and General Peucestas; tell them what's happened and that I've gone to the king. Who holds the walls?"

"Craterus's brigade has that duty," Cleander answered.

Ptolemy made a face. Alexander had begun the night at Craterus's party, and it was just possible that that party had been an excuse to get the king drunk, to make it easier for the pages. . . . He shook himself decisively. "Right. Warn his watch commander directly, and send someone to Craterus, too. And, Cleander—"

The chamberlain looked up alertly.

"After you've seen to those messages, inform Thaïs of what's happened, and tell her to stay indoors until she's heard from me."

"Yes, sir," Cleander said.

Menedemus reappeared in the doorway, somewhat breathless. "Sir, escort's ready."

"Good." Ptolemy waved impatiently at the others. "Move."

Alexander had taken up residence in the largest and most luxurious house in the city of Bactra; a two-storied building distinguished from the rest of the city by its painted columns and crude mosaic floors. The king's bedchamber was at the rear, connected to the rest of the house by an unsteady stairway running along the back wall of the large dining hall. Chares, the usher who had charge of the royal household, usually slept in the alcove under the stairs, and Ptolemy wondered sourly what the conspirator pages had planned to do about his presence. Two pages, gawky adolescents who showed little sign of their high birth, were standing guard at the bottom of the stairway.

Ptolemy glared impartially at them all, and said, "I want to see the king." His voice rang loud in the near-empty hall. In his alcove, Chares stirred, and dragged himself from his bed. The two pages exchanged looks, and then the braver of the two said, with a quick glance toward the alcove, "Sir, the king's asleep, he left orders not to be disturbed."

"I'll wake him," Ptolemy said. "It's an emergency."

By now, Chares had pulled himself out of his alcove and stood leaning against the stairs, rubbing at his temples. At Ptolemy's words, however, he gestured for the pages to admit the general, saying, "What's happened, general?"

"Treason," Ptolemy flung over his shoulder. "Double the watch here."

Chares froze, his aching head momentarily forgotten, then shouted for the nearest of the duty guards. Ptolemy turned away and hurried up the stairway. The other four pages who made up the day watch were waiting in the outer of the two rooms, eyeing each other nervously. They had heard the noise outside, as had the Persian servant who crouched silently in a corner, hoping to be ignored.

"You," Ptolemy said, and pointed to the pages. "Get out."

Their faces registered only honest confusion. The tallest opened his mouth to protest, but Ptolemy was in no mood to listen. "*Out*," he snarled.

The pages scrambled to obey, and at the same moment, Ptolemy heard footsteps on the stairs. A second later, Hephaestion's tall form loomed in the doorway. He had been running, but caught his breath enough to ask, "Alexander?"

Ptolemy nodded a welcome. "Still asleep. I was just about to wake him."

Hephaestion gave a sigh of relief, even though he had known from Ptolemy's message that the plot had failed.

"Hold them out here," Ptolemy said to his soldiers, and pushed through the second door.

It was very bright in the inner chamber: the servants had not dared to risk disturbing the king by closing the painted shutters. Alexander did not move when the door opened, or when Hephaestion spoke his name. Ptolemy grunted irritably and shook the king's foot.

Alexander woke instantly and sat up. There was a mark on one cheek where he had been lying on his seal ring. "I left orders," he began querulously, and then the others' expressions registered. "What's happened?"

Ptolemy grunted. "The night-watch pages planned to kill you last night," he said bluntly. "If you'd come home—but when you didn't, one of them got cold feet."

Alexander looked up sharply, and then a slow, thoughtful smile slid across his face. "So, her first prophecy's fulfilled. I wonder what the rest of it'll be."

"Prophecy?" Ptolemy asked, not certain he wanted to hear.

"There was a woman, a seer, waiting for me when I left Craterus's party," Alexander answered. "She told me I should spend the night with friends, so I went back to the party." His smile widened briefly. "I invited you, Ptolemy, you could've come."

Ptolemy muttered something blasphemous under his breath. He distrusted oracles as a matter of principle, especially ones that came true.

Hephaestion said, "She could've heard something of the plot, Alexander."

"However she knew, she saved my life," the king said. He looked around automatically for a page to bring his clothes, then frowned, realizing. Hephaestion brought a tunic from the nearest clothes chest, and Alexander put it on, still frowning. The Persian servant brought sword belt and sandals. Alexander pushed himself out of bed and allowed himself to be dressed, listening to the rising noise of voices from the outer chamber.

"Who have you told?" he asked.

"Hephaestion, Peucestas, Craterus," Ptolemy answered promptly. "Craterus's men had the watch. The boy said it was just pages, but. . . ." He let his voice trail off as Alexander's eyes narrowed dangerously.

"We'll see, won't we? That'll be all, Bagoas," he added, to the Persian, and stepped into the outer room.

The other generals Ptolemy had summoned were waiting there, Craterus unshaven and puffy-eyed.

Peucestas, who had not answered the king's invitation, looked more alert, Macedonian sword visible beneath his Persian coat.

"Thank the gods you're all right, Alexander," Craterus said.

"The gods are gracious," the king answered conventionally. His eyes were fixed on Epimenes, who stood trembling under the watchful gaze of two of Ptolemy's troopers. "Epimenes son of Arseus."

The boy bit his lip, and answered, very softly, "Yes, sire."

"Why?" Alexander asked.

Craterus said, "Never mind that now. Who else is involved?"

Epimenes looked wildly from king to general, then drew a shaky breath. "The other pages of my watch. They—we—worked it so we were all on duty together. Hermolaus and Sostratus, Antipater son of Asclepiodorus, Anticles, and Philotas son of Carsis the Thracian. Sire, truly, that was all. Charicles and Eurylochus didn't know anything about it until I told Charicles, and they went straight to General Ptolemy, I swear it."

"Eurylochus is your brother, I know," Alexander said. He glanced at the two men who stood under guard, trying not to show their own fear. Eurylochus was on the verge of promotion to file-leader, while Charicles was still young enough to hope for advancement. There was little motive for treason there. "And Charicles—what kin is he to you?"

"My lover," Epimenes answered faintly.

Ptolemy said, "They're both reliable, good soldiers, Alexander." He did not bother adding details, knowing the king's uncanny memory for his men.

Alexander nodded. Epimenes was telling the truth, of that he was certain, but this plot was serious enough even without outside involvement. And the seer had warned of days of danger to come. "Peucestas," he

said aloud. "Send a detachment of your men to arrest
the others."

"The royal pages Hermolaus, Sostratus, Antipater,
Anticles, and Philotas," Peucestas repeated. "At once,
Alexander."

"Wait," Alexander said. "When you have them,
turn them over to Hephaestion for questioning."
Macedonian law and tradition permitted torture in
treason cases. He glanced quickly at the cavalry commander, reading in his face the anger that would give
him the necessary ruthlessness. "Make sure they can
walk to their trial."

Hephaestion nodded grimly, knowing exactly why
he had been chosen, and followed Peucestas from the
room.

"And Epimenes?" Craterus asked.

Alexander looked back at the page. "You haven't
answered my question," he said. "Why?"

Epimenes looked away. Almost inaudibly, he said,
"We were seduced."

Craterus gave a short bark of laughter, and the page
flushed deeply.

"It was Hermolaus," he said. "He kept talking about
how you'd changed, become more like a Persian tyrant than a king of Macedon—never in so many words,
though—and then. . . ." Epimenes's voice trailed away,
and he shrugged miserably. "It seemed like he was
right," he said, almost in a whisper. "After Cleitus."

Alexander's face went rigid. He had not yet forgiven
himself for Cleitus's death, but he could not bear to
have anyone else throw that in his face. Into the
sudden silence, Craterus said, "That has an Athenian
sound to it."

"Or any of the other Greek League cities," Ptolemy
agreed, one eye on the king. "I wonder who's been
talking to this Hermolaus."

Alexander controlled his temper with an effort, staring at the page. The boy made a pitiful figure, snif-

fling, frightened out of his wits: not worth anger, or even contempt.

As if he had read the king's thoughts, Charicles said, tentatively, "Sire, I beg you. Spare his life."

The king stared a second longer, prolonging the moment, then said, "Very well, he lives." He glanced at Charicles, whose tensed body slumped fractionally with relief. "As for you, and you, Eurylochus, return to your duties. Epimenes will be kept under guard until this is settled—Ptolemy, you see to that—but when he's returned to you, see he follows your examples and not another's."

"Thank you, sire," Charicles said. "I will."

"King Alexander, thank you," Eurylochus echoed.

Alexander nodded, his mind already turning to other business. "You may go."

The two Foot Companions backed from the room. Ptolemy beckoned to Menedemus. "Take the boy away, find some place secure to hold him, and make sure no one speaks to him."

Menedemus nodded. "At once, general," he said, and jerked his thumb at the soldiers guarding the boy.

Alexander said, as the man hustled an unresisting Epimenes from the bedchamber, "Anticles. Anticles son of Theocritus." He glanced at Ptolemy. "Does the name sound familiar?"

The general frowned, racking his brains, but shook his head. "Not offhand."

"Theocritus is a battalion commander of hypaspists," the king said. "Currently commanding the garrison at Alexandria Eschate."

Ptolemy swore softly. The hypaspists were the elite infantry, even more so than the Foot Companions who formed the bulk of the phalanx. If a battalion of them were involved in the plot, especially holding that strategic fort. . . .

Alexander smiled without humor. "I see the same thought occurs to you." He pushed open the main

door of the bedchamber, and shouted, "Chares!" When
the usher appeared at the bottom of the stairs, the
king continued, "Send for the Friends. I want them
here now. Craterus, pass the word to your officers, no
one's to leave the city without my personal order. If
anyone gets out, they'll answer for it."

"At once, Alexander," the brigadier said.

"And, Chares!" Alexander had turned back to the
stairs. "Send for Menidas, as well." Menidas was a
Greek, commander of the mercenary cavalry, but had
other talents as well. If Theocritus were involved in
his son's plot, and it became necessary to get rid of
him, Menidas was the man to do it. He had proved
his worth before.

It took less than an hour for Chares's runners to
assemble the King's Friends; Menidas, dressed as carefully as if he were going to a symposium, arrived on
their heels. Alexander outlined what had happened,
not omitting the seer's warning, then invited them to
join him in a thanks-offering. Menidas—watching from
the sidelines as each general poured a few drops of
wine, muttered a prayer, and threw a pinch of incense
on the fire—saw how they eyed each other for signs of
guilt, and was hard pressed to hide his own smile.

It was mid-afternoon before Peucestas returned with
word that he'd arrested all five pages and turned them
over to Hephaestion as ordered. The evening was well
advanced before Hephaestion appeared. The cavalry
commander kept his face impassive as he took his
place at the king's right hand. His afternoon's work
had sickened and angered him in equal measure, but
he refused to show either.

Alexander waved for the Persian servants to pour
wine—the pages had been relegated to other duties,
at least until the conspiracy was fully exposed—and
said, "Well?"

Hephaestion took a gulp of his wine and answered,
"Well, what? They confessed. They were eager to

confess." He emptied his cup with two more swallows, beckoned for the nearest servant to refill it.

"Come on, out with it," Craterus said. "Was it just the boys?"

Hephaestion gave him a deadly look, and Alexander said, "Who else, then?"

Hephaestion's anger drained away suddenly, and he said, "Callisthenes." Callisthenes was Aristotle's nephew, allowed to teach the pages as a favor to the king's old tutor.

"I can't believe Callisthenes had the practical sense to plot against the king," Perdiccas said slowly.

Hephaestion replied, "Oh, I don't think he was behind the plot itself, but he gave enough philosophy lessons on republics and tyrannicides—and on the ethical and political inferiority of all things Persian—to make him morally guilty. I've got him under guard now." He shook himself, angry that he had wasted time on someone so unimportant. "But that's not the main thing. Anticles—son of the garrison commander at Alexandria Eschate. He claims he sent a letter to his father, Theocritus, telling him what he was going to do. By the time Theocritus got it, of course, it'd be what he'd *done*—so Theocritus would have no choice but to help him."

Heads nodded around the circle of couches—Macedonian law presumed that all a traitor's kinsmen were equally guilty of treason—and Alexander said, "A very clever boy, Anticles."

"Too clever," Coenus growled. He looked unusually aged in the uncertain lamplight, but his voice was still strong.

"When did he send the messenger?" Neoptolemus asked. He was a young man, only recently promoted to overall command of the hypaspists, and could not hide his unease at the thought of treachery from his men.

"Two days ago, he says," Hephaestion answered.

Everyone turned to look at the royal secretary, who was in charge of the surveyors. Eumenes said, in his unpleasantly precise voice, "Approximately two thousand, one hundred and seventy-five stadia to Alexandria Eschate. A man on a fast horse could do that in five days. If he had cause to hurry, of course."

"He was told it was urgent, but not told the message," Hephaestion said wearily.

Alexander said, "Menidas. Take a party of your best men, and your pick of the horses—my own, if you choose—and overtake that messenger. When you catch up with him, send him back here under guard, and go on to Alexandria Eschate. Sound out Philip—Philip son of Gorgias, he's Theocritus's second-in-command—" He did not glance at Neoptolemus for confirmation. "If he isn't in on the plot, and I doubt he is, inform him of what's happened, and together you can arrest Theocritus. If he is, kill him, and Theocritus. Eumenes, draft an order to that effect."

Menidas sighed deeply. Order or no order, it would not be easy if he, a mere Greek mercenary, had to kill a Macedonian officer. But the royal name worked a potent magic with these troops—and in any case, it probably wouldn't come to killing. "And if I don't overtake the messenger, sire?"

"Proceed to Alexandria Eschate anyway," the king answered. "Deal with Theocritus." He smiled suddenly, dazzlingly, as though he'd read the Greek's thought. "You'll have my order and my seal to give you authority."

Menidas nodded. From any other commander, that promise of protection would have been mere bluff, and the Greek, like any intelligent mercenary, would have started looking for a new employer. But from Alexander. . . . Menidas had cause to know how powerful the king's name could be. Three years ago, when General Parmenion, commander of the Macedonian army stationed in Ecbatana, had plotted against the king, Menidas had been sent with forces to break the conspiracy. The safest way of doing that was to kill the general; his troops, given the choice of believing the king or their immediate commander, unhesitatingly condemned Parmenion.

"And the pages?" Perdiccas asked.

"Get it over with," Coenus said. Despite his seniority, he didn't often speak in council, and the others glanced curiously at him. "What I mean to say is, put the case before the Assembly right away; let the men decide. That'll stop what the little bastards were saying, anyway."

Alexander's eyes narrowed. He resented the suggestion that he needed to prove the pages wrong, and doubly resented his sense that the brigadier was at least partly correct. None of which was Coenus's fault: the king would not be angry at a man who was merely speaking his mind in council. "I fully intend to put the matter to the Assembly," Alexander said. "They're Macedonians, all of them, that's their right. But not until Menidas gets back from Alexandria Eschate." He glanced again at the Greek, whose face was still remote, calculating the best way to do a difficult job. "I don't want to give Theocritus any warning. Craterus, you'll keep the city sealed until he returns."

"Let everyone in and nobody out," Craterus said, nodding. "What about Callisthenes? From what Hephaestion says, he started it all."

Hephaestion made a face. "As I said before, I don't think he was part of the plot itself. I do think he talked too much to be considered entirely innocent."

Craterus shrugged. "Either he's guilty or he isn't— and he sounds guilty enough to me."

"I thought he agreed with Callisthenes," Peucestas murmured to Ptolemy, but Craterus heard.

"I hate to see any Macedonian turning into a Persian, yes. But I'm the king's man."

Peucestas, who had adopted Persian coat and trousers and the Persian language with equal facility, swore at the brigadier in barracks Macedonian.

"Be quiet," Alexander said. "Craterus, guilty or not, Callisthenes is a Greek—of what city I don't know." He looked mildly surprised at his own lack of information.

"Stagyra, probably," Ptolemy said. That was Aristotle's city, it would make sense for Aristotle's nephew to be its citizen. "And since your father refounded it, Alexander, you're technically its patron now."

Alexander waved the suggestion aside. "That wouldn't do me any good with the Greek League—especially with Athens. And there's Aristotle to think of, whom I won't willingly offend." He glanced at Hephaestion, who had been Aristotle's pupil as well, and a favorite. The cavalry commander nodded his thanks, and the king went on, smiling slightly, "Besides, he's not that dangerous—his death isn't worth the political consequences. Put him under close arrest, Hephaestion; he'll keep until we return to Greece."

Which could be never, Hephaestion thought, with the Indian campaign in the spring and the projected search for the encircling Ocean. Close arrest forever . . . it suited Callisthenes. "Yes, Alexander," he said aloud.

Alexander glanced at Eumenes, who looked up quickly.

"Almost done, sire," the secretary said. He sprinkled the sheet of papyrus with fine sand, blotting the ink, then brought it to the king. Alexander read through it—four brief lines giving Menidas the king's authority in the matter of Theocritus's treason—then, rising, crossed to the secretary's desk to add his signature. There was wax already melting on the brazier; he poured a generous amount at the foot of the papyrus and added his personal seal. To Menidas, he added, "What horses do you want?"

Menidas accepted the order, careful not to touch

the still-soft wax. "My own are good enough," he said. He had never stinted on horseflesh, though he had starved himself and his men before this. "I'll leave at once?"

The king nodded. "The gods go with you."

From the king, the farewell was more than merely conventional. Menidas nodded his thanks and was gone.

The council broke up quickly then. Hephaestion, following the other officers from the room, glanced over his shoulder. The king was watching him, and, seeing that, Hephaestion paused with one hand on the painted door post. Alexander nodded.

"You stay."

Hephaestion had more than half expected the invitation, but he was gratified by it nonetheless. He came back into the room, and, at Alexander's gesture, seated himself in a chair by a large brazier. "I'm glad you decided not to try Callisthenes," he said.

Alexander shrugged, stretching his feet toward the brazier. "As I said, he's not worth the trouble it'd cause. He's no danger if he doesn't have an audience—and I trust you to deny him one."

"Oh, I will, believe me." Hephaestion finished the last of the olives someone had left on the low table.

Alexander stared at the nearest lamp, fixing his eyes on the brooding, brutal Pan-face that decorated the handle. It had come with him from Macedon, and, before that, had stood in his rooms at Mieza and at the palace at Pella. "I'm still sorry Aristotle didn't come with us," he said.

"So was I, the minute I met Callisthenes," Hephaestion said.

"It might have changed his mind about the Persians," Alexander went on, as though the other had not spoken.

Hephaestion sighed and replied, "Aristotle's getting too old for campaigning and in any case he's more use to you back in Macedon, teaching your son."

"It depends on what he's teaching him," Alexander said. He glanced thoughtfully at his friend. "You keep up your correspondence with him still. Has he changed his thoughts on barbarians yet?"

Hephaestion made a face. "Philip Alexander has other tutors, you know."

"Which means—?"

"No, he hasn't." Hephaestion sighed again. 'That's not fair, though. He doesn't say all barbarians should be our slaves any more, only real barbarians like the Sogdians. But he doesn't approve of your idea of giving the Persians equality with us."

Alexander swore softly, but without much passion. He had long ago realized that some of Aristotle's political theories were less than useless, especially when compared to his other teachings—but then, he had made it quite clear both to Aristotle and to his son that he had not hired the old philosopher to teach kingship. The boy would learn that from Antipater, the regent, who had been regent under Philip a dozen times before.

"If you want," Hephaestion went on, "I can remind him of his duty—I'll be writing anyway; he shouldn't hear of Callisthenes's arrest from someone else first."

"No," Alexander said, more sharply than he had intended. "They both know their responsibilities, Philip Alexander and Aristotle. Hermolaus was a trouble-maker from the day he left Macedon. And I'll tell Aristotle, Hephaestion."

Hephaestion glanced quickly at the king, recognizing the warning in his voice. Alexander was still too angry and too hurt by the pages' treachery to want to talk of it. To push further would be to invite one of his rages, of which he would be ashamed in the morning. And to be honest, Hephaestion thought, I'm grateful it's he who'll break the news to Aristotle. "Very well," he said, and added lightly, "If you believe the Pythagoreans, Aristotle must've committed quite a crime in some previous life, to be given a nephew like Callisthenes."

Bagoas appeared then, followed by a second servant carrying pitchers of wine and water. Bagoas set the tray of food on an unsteady table then turned to supervise the mixing of the wine. Hephaestion turned his attention to the food; a cold roast fowl, bread, cheese, and more olives.

Alexander said, "That will be all, Bagoas, we'll serve ourselves." The Persians bowed and edged away, Bagoas's beautiful face impassive. The king waited until he was sure they were out of earshot, then said, "If the seeress doesn't come to claim her gift, Hephaestion, I want you to find her."

Hephaestion tore a strip of meat off the chicken's side—he was well on his way to stripping it bare—and said, "She said she'd claim it when the danger was past."

"Whenever that may be," Alexander said quite calmly, "she ought to be rewarded before that."

Hephaestion grunted dubiously. He was not entirely sure he believed in the woman's prophecy—there were too many temporal ways she could have heard rumors of the boys' plot for him to be convinced of the warning's supernatural origins—but he had to agree she had earned a substantial present. "I'll find her, then. But I, for one, won't be convinced the danger's over until Theocritus is standing in front of the Assembly."

CHAPTER 2:

Bactra, winter (Peritios), 29 imperial (328 B.C., 426 A.U.C.)

After the alarms of the previous day—the summoning of the Friends, the hunt for and the arrest of the pages—the conspiracy could not be kept secret. Knowing that, Alexander summoned the rest of his officers, including battalion captains and cavalry squadron leaders, to the next morning's sacrifices, told them of the plot, and asked them to join him in special prayers of thanks to the gods of his house. The king spoke well, as always, and, like the Friends, the officers were eager to prove their own goodwill. The news spread rapidly, as Alexander had intended, and later in the day more sacrifices were made among the individual units, foreign and Macedonian alike.

The next day, one of Craterus's men caught a Persian merchant trying to bribe his way out of the city. He was the first of three such, all agents of minor Persian princes. All were handed over to Peucestas, who imprisoned them comfortably, promising in flawless Persian to release them to carry their message as soon as the king saw fit. There were no further signs of trouble, and the army rapidly returned to something approaching its usual routine. Even the royal pages returned to their duties. watched over by a more than usually careful Chares. Still, the seeress did not appear to claim her reward.

Following the king's orders, Hephaestion spent the better part of a morning searching for her. When he finally found the seeress, squatting comfortably on the doorstep of a house that had been taken over by some troopers of the Companion Cavalry, she was polite, but absolutely refused to see the king or accept any present from him. When Hephaestion would have pressed her further, she repeated her promise that she would claim her reward when the danger was over, and retreated hastily into the house. Shrugging to himself, the cavalry commander hunted out the senior trooper of that squad, a grizzled, responsible wing-rider, told him to treat the woman as someone under the king's personal protection, and headed back through the dirty streets to the royal quarters.

The king was busy with the secretariat, but dismissed them with thanks as soon as the duty page announced Hephaestion's arrival. "Well?" he called, even before the cavalry commander had reached the top of the stairs. "Is she provided for?"

Hephaestion paused in the doorway. The outer of the two rooms was very stuffy, the air heavy with the odor of singed bread and the stink of incense, both burned to disguise the stink of lamp oil. Apparently the pages had realized that neither tactic worked: the shutters stood open on the window that overlooked the stableyard, but the cold, lifeless air had not yet washed away the unpleasant smells. The cavalry commander shook himself and came fully into the room, saying, "Yes, she's provided for."

The king gestured to the hovering page, who brought wine. Hephaestion accepted a cup and a handful of dried fruit, and went on, "I made some inquiries as well. She has quite a reputation among the men." He looked inquiringly at the king, who nodded.

"Go on."

Hephaestion took a swallow of wine. "She's a Syrian," he began slowly, "and, as best anyone can tell, she's been following the army since we entered Babylon. No one knows her real name—she refuses to say if she even has one—but she answers to Pasithea. The men also call her Alecto, and she's been left strictly alone since she cursed a man who promptly died in battle. She's living now in the quarters of some Companion troopers, of Aristo's squadron—I understand she takes up with soldiers as she pleases, brings them luck so long as they do what she wants. From everything I've been told, there's not a man in the army who'd dare cross her, but I warned Socrates—Socrates son of Sathon, it's him she's living with—that she was under your protection."

"Good," Alexander said. "And her present?"

"She refused to take it until the danger is completely over," Hephaestion said. "Her god forbids it."

Alexander shrugged, but accepted the excuse. "Do you believe in her now?"

Hephaestion swirled the wine in his shallow, silver cup, and did not answer for a moment. There was less water in the mix than he liked for drinking in the middle of the afternoon, especially when there was good water available. "The stories are convincing enough," he said, reluctantly, "but I've heard the same things about other fortune-tellers."

The king grinned. "Whom you trusted less?" His eyes shifted to the door, and he said, rather irritably, "What is it, Adaeus?"

The page, a handsome, dark-eyed boy, bobbed his head in apology. "Your pardon, sire, but Metron son of Polystratus, file-leader of Nicomachus's battalion, and Machaon son of Alexander of Mieza request an immediate audience."

Hephaestion looked up sharply. "Nicomachus—that's part of Craterus's brigade, isn't it?"

Alexander nodded, frowning. "Admit them." Metron he knew, a reliable, undistinguished man, who had reached the rank of file-leader primarily by virtue of his herculean size, but the other name was unfamiliar. Then the door opened again, and Metron ducked into the room, looking even more ungraceful than usual. He was followed by a bearded man with the look of a merchant, a man whose clothes were badly travel-worn. Alexander eyed him uneasily, noting the outline of a dispatch bag beneath the stained cloak. "What is it?"

Metron hesitated, and the king, following the direction of his eyes, frowned even more deeply. "Heiron," he said, to the page hovering beside the wine table. "You may go. And you, Adaeus."

Both boys bowed and hastened away, exchanging glances, half frightened, half curious. Alexander gestured for the newcomers to seat themselves, and waited, leaning back in his chair.

"News from Greece, sire," Metron said at last, when the messenger said nothing.

The king studied the two faces. Metron was nakedly afraid; the messenger, Machaon, was too exhausted to show open emotion. "How bad is it?"

The messenger took a deep breath. "Very bad, sire." He shook himself. "My name is Machaon son of Alexander, citizen of Mieza. I have dispatches from Antipater: the Greek cities are in revolt."

Alexander made a soft sound between his teeth. "Which cities?"

"Sparta, Thebes," Machaon answered. "Athens almost certainly by now, and with her the rest of the League cities."

"Gods, what an unholy alliance," Hephaestion said. He jerked to his feet, unable to sit still any longer, and crossed to the window, pushing the shutters open even farther to drink in the cold air. "Has Antipater——?"

Seeing some flicker of emotion in the messenger's face, Alexander flung out a hand to silence his friend. "What else, Machaon?"

The first of his news told without an explosive mishap, the messenger grew suddenly talkative. "The regent fought a battle, sire, and took heavy losses. He's driven back into Thessaly. The generals in Asia have sent more men, but the allies are wavering, and the levies are too raw to be of much use." He reached beneath his cloak, and brought out the bulging dispatch bag. "The regent sends you these."

Alexander took the bag, snapping the brittle seal. "Who else knows of this?"

It was Metron who answered this time. "Only myself, sire, and maybe my file. But all they know is there are letters from the regent. I brought him here at once, not talking to anyone else, as soon as he said it was urgent."

The king nodded to himself. Hephaestion said, "So we have a little time."

Alexander nodded again. "Metron, you've done well. Go back to your file now, and see that they keep quiet about this. I know I can trust you not to repeat anything you've heard."

"By the Styx," Metron answered promptly, the most binding oath he knew.

Alexander smiled. "Good man." His smile faded abruptly. "Adaeus!" There was a sound of footsteps on the stairs, a pause as the page hesitated in the face of Metron's bulk, and then the boy appeared in the doorway.

"Sire?"

"Have Chares send runners for Craterus, Ptolemy, and Perdiccas. And Peucestas. They're to come at once, whatever they're doing." The page nodded, but Alexander was staring through him. "Then send

Proxenus to me." He would have preferred Polydamus, who was the most reliable of his agents, but Polydamus was currently employed inspecting the line of forts being built to hold the northern border against the marauding Scythians.

"At once, sire," the page said, and hurried away again.

Hephaestion leaned against the windowframe, watching the king unroll the first of Antipater's letters. In the sudden silence he could hear the sound of the Foot Companions at their interminable pike-drill, a battalion captain shouting the cadence. Beneath that, very faintly, came the sound of the Bactra market, a murmur of many voices, like the noise of distant waves. The news was very bad. If Antipater was really driven back into Thessaly, that was the war half lost already— and the letter had to be at least five months old. Hephaestion shook himself. Antipater had been one of Philip's chosen generals, he would know how to recoup his losses. . . . But Alexander had stripped Macedon bare of soldiers the previous spring. Antipater's troops would be the half-trained levies, while the cities would have the experienced men who had served as the League's troops to draw on. Hephaestion glanced quickly at the king, and saw from his face that it was true. The terms of the treaty that created the Greek League had been clear: each city was obliged to supply troops to the Hegemon Alexander only so long as the Persians remained undefeated. With Darius's death and the defeat of Bessus, Alexander was unquestionably Great King, master of the Persian empire, and had felt obliged to keep the treaty and send the majority of the foreign levies home. But those troops had been hostages for the good behavior of their parent states; with them home again, the cities had felt no compunction about rebellion.

Hephaestion pushed himself away from the window and poured a cup of wine for the messenger, who drank thirstily. One unit alone had been deemed too dangerous to allow to return, but that single act of good sense seemed not to have done any good. "It's the Thebans that worry me," he said aloud, and reached for the first scroll that lay discarded on the table.

Alexander nodded without looking up: as always, Hephaestion's thoughts had matched his own.

"Sire?" Adaeus stood in the doorway again, looking around nervously. "Proxenus is here."

"Admit him," Alexander said.

Proxenus shouldered past the page, a stocky, light-weight man who moved like a fighting-cock. He glanced quickly from king to messenger to hovering general, summing up the situation, but said only, "Trouble, sire?"

"Trouble enough," Alexander answered, setting aside the last of the scrolls. "I want you to pick out a couple of your men, men who know how to keep their mouths shut, and set a watch on the Thebans. They're not to know they're being watched, either. If there's anything at all out of the ordinary, I want to know about it. You lead them."

Proxenus nodded, thoughtfully. If there was time enough for secrecy, then things weren't desperate; still, he looked curiously at the scrolls discarded on the table.

Seeing the look, Alexander said, "There's trouble in Greece, Proxenus—which isn't public knowledge yet, and I don't want it to be."

Proxenus pursed his lips in a soundless whistle of comprehension. "I understand, sire," he said. "I'll get on it at once." Then he was gone, clattering down the stairs.

"Let's hope there's such a thing as a soldier who won't talk," Hephaestion said sourly. He remembered Proxenus from his own boyhood, and not fondly.

Alexander said, "He'll find some, or gag them himself."

Hephaestion grunted dubiously, but turned his attention to the scroll in his hands. The news was even worse than the messenger had said: not one defeat, but two. Antipater had tried to recoup the first losses by bringing out the levies, hoping to crush the Greeks by sheer weight of numbers. It should have worked— would have worked if it had been hoplite against Macedonian phalanx. But Antipater had found himself up against the regiments of the League, not trained to the phalanx themselves, but not afraid of it, either. Experience had told: the levies had broken, hundreds were killed fleeing, and in the aftermath Antipater had lost his hold on the Greek city-states. Mazaeus, the satrap in Babylon, reported that he and the commanders in Asia, Antigonus, Seleucus, and the rest, had sent reinforcements, but had few men to spare. "Gods," he said softly, "this must be three, four months old, too."

The king nodded his agreement. "But Antipater holds Thessaly, and will. Thessaly hates the League— and there are enough small cities who fear Athens and Thebes more than they fear us."

The door opened again, and Adaeus said, "Pardon, sire. The generals are here."

"Show them in." Alexander collected the last of the scrolls from Hephaestion and set them together on the wine table.

Predictably, it was Craterus, muffled to the eyes in a showily woven cloak, who pushed his way in first. "What's going on now, Alexander? That brat wouldn't say a word—"

"He wasn't supposed to," Hephaestion said, quite audibly, and was instantly ashamed of himself. By way of apology, he began to pour wine for the newcomers, first adding more water from the silver pitcher.

Alexander said, "News from Greece."

Ptolemy lifted his head sharply. "Bad news?"

The king gestured to the scrolls. "Bad enough. Sparta and Thebes have risen, and they've beaten Antipater."

Ptolemy's heavy eyebrows rose, and he reached hastily for the letters. Perdiccas whistled sharply, running a hand through his sandy hair.

Craterus, his annoyance abruptly quelled, tugged thoughtfully at his chin. "Where they go, Athens follows," he said, "especially with the old man beaten."

Peucestas's hand tightened visibly on the walking stick he affected along with the rest of his Persian dress. With an effort, he relaxed his grip and set the stick against the wall, wiping a suddenly sweaty palm on the skirts of his coat. "How old are the letters?"

Alexander glanced at the messenger, who was asleep, head resting on his folded arms. Craterus snorted, following the direction of the king's gaze, and stretched out a long arm to shake the messenger. The man started and sat up, looking around wildly.

"Sire—sirs. I—beg your pardon, sirs."

"Just a few questions," Alexander said. "Then you can rest."

The man looked desperately tired. Ptolemy looked up from the second dispatch long enough to push his own cup toward the man. "Here, drink up."

The messenger took it gratefully, drained the cup, and poured himself another without being told. The king waited until he had finished that before asking, "How long were you on the road?"

"Three months, sire, and a little more." The wine had brought brief color to Machaon's sunken cheeks, but it was clear the effect would not last. "But I came from Babylon. The man who brought these had come by sea, maybe two months' journey. . . ."

"Was there any other news?" Ptolemy asked, setting aside the first scroll.

The messenger shook his head. "No, sir, only rumors. They were saying Athens would join the rebels—"

"Probably already has," Craterus muttered.

"But Antipater was still in Thessaly," Alexander said.

"Yes, sire."

"He's surely back in Boetia by now," Perdiccas said, but his tone was less certain than his words.

Craterus picked up the scroll Ptolemy had discarded. "I told you you shouldn't send any of our so-called allies home, Alexander."

Hephaestion stirred, but Peucestas spoke first. "The terms of the League—"

"Be that as it may," Alexander said, rather sharply. "It's the allies still with us that worry me." He glanced at the messenger, who was drowsing again. "Metron—your man, Craterus, the file-leader in charge of the gate watch—had the sense to bring him here directly, without letting him talk to the file."

"I'm surprised he had the brains," Craterus muttered.

"And I've set men to watch the Thebans," the king went on as if no one had spoken.

Ptolemy grunted his agreement. "What about the other foreigners?"

Hephaestion said, "The Allied Horse have been brigaded with the Companions since we came into Bactria. I can vouch for them—so will Erigyius." Erigyius was another of the king's Friends, who held overall command of the mix of Greek mercenaries, Thracians, and Scouts who made up the light cavalry.

"You can't tell how they'll react when it's their city or Alexander," Craterus said. He looked at the king. "I'd've said the same thing about the infantry; I had them for six months against the damned Sogdians, but against their own city? It's not a chance I'd take, Alexander."

"I don't know," Perdiccas said. "The ones who stayed—it was their choice, and they're the young ones, anyway. They'd rather be lords of Persia. The ones to worry about have already gone home."

"Except for the Thebans," Peucestas said.

"Right," Craterus said. "You can't take chances with them, Alexander. That's the Sacred Band, they're for Thebes first, last, and always. I say, take a couple of brigades of hypaspists down there—now, before word can spread—and kill them all."

Hephaestion and Peucestas started to protest at the same moment, and stopped in confusion, each gesturing for the other to speak. Into the silence, Ptolemy said, "It might not be the worst thing, but if we did that, we'd have to consider the rest of the foreign troops."

"Thebes broke the treaty, and the Sacred Band was the hostage for their good behavior," Craterus said. "The king has a perfect right to kill them."

Perdiccas shook his head thoughtfully. "It's too dangerous. Suppose it got out of hand?"

Hephaestion said, "You really think the other mercenaries would listen to that sort of logic? We can't afford to frighten them into a mutiny."

"You're exaggerating," Craterus snapped. "Three hundred top fighting men—do you want to try keeping them under house arrest until they've proved their loyalty? Don't be ridiculous."

Alexander looked away from the argument, shutting out the rising voices. The Sacred Band, hostages for Thebes's good behavior, were the immediate danger, and, obstinately, he refused to consider the other obvious consequence of the revolt. The Band could be destroyed, despite its deserved reputation, but it would be a waste of good men, both the Thebans and his own troops. More than that, it would be an admission that he could not hold their love.

"Peucestas." The king did not raise his voice, but the wrangling stopped instantly.

"Yes, Alexander?"

"If the League cities are smart, they'll try to cause me trouble in Asia. I want Darius's kindred watched, very discreetly. You deal best with the Persians, you handle it." Without waiting for Peucestas's murmured acknowledgement, the king went on, "Craterus, inform your watch commanders of the rebellion, and have them keep a special eye on the foreigners in the city. I'll speak to the army as a whole in the morning. Perdiccas, I want your men under arms as well, just in case. I don't care what excuse you give them."

"Surprise maneuvers," Perdiccas muttered, and Craterus said, "I'll see to it at once, Alexander."

"Ptolemy, I want you to take care of him." Alexander nodded at the messenger, asleep again and forgotten. "See that he gets the rest he needs, and a good meal, but when he's rested I want everything he knows about the rebels."

"All right," Ptolemy said. He hesitated briefly, gauging the king's mood, then added, "And the Sacred Band?"

"I'll deal with them," Alexander said.

Hephaestion, recognizing the tone, looked up quickly, but the expression on the king's face silenced his half-formed protest. Alexander's normally ruddy complexion had gone pale, and his mouth was set in a familiar, grim line.

"Alexander," Craterus began, then, seeing the king's anger, shook his head slowly and beckoned to Perdiccas. Ptolemy shook Machaon awake, then, with Peucestas's help, eased the messenger down the stairs.

Left alone with the king, Hephaestion waited for a long moment before saying, "Shall I have Adaeus call the bodyguard?"

"No." With an effort, Alexander managed a lighter tone. "No need."

Hephaestion sighed. "I thought that was what you had in mind." No one had touched the plate of dried fruit since Metron had brought in the messenger. Hephaestion selected a piece and ate it, choosing his words with the same care. "It would be a foolish risk to walk into Theagenes's quarters alone, tell him Thebes is in rebellion, and wait to see what he says. At least take an escort."

Alexander shook his head, recognizing the logic of the cavalry commander's argument. "I'll take two of Proxenus's men, if that'll make you happy, but it has to be the two of us alone who speak to Theagenes."

Hephaestion ran a hand through his hair, disordering the short curls. The Sacred Band might well respond to a personal appeal from the king for their loyalty—Theagenes, their commander, was well known as a man of strict honor—but if they did not. . . . He put that thought aside. "I know what you want to do, and if anyone can do it, it's you, Alexander. But it's still a risk."

"I don't think so." Alexander drained his cup, and shouted for a page to bring his sword belt. He allowed the boy to arm him, then drew his cloak around his body. "Come on."

It was still light in the narrow streets, though there was a dank chill in the air that spoke of the approaching evening. There were not many people about: the watch did not change until sunset, and the soldiers' women were either at the closing market or already busy preparing the evening meal. Already the cooking fires were lit in or behind the commandeered houses, sending up thin columns of smoke that vanished against the smoke-colored clouds.

Theagenes had chosen his quarters with predictable caution. Like all of Alexander's officers, he had displaced one of the city's wealthier households; it had brought him and his men little in the way of comfort, but the shabby, single-story house did possess its own well-kept wall and a defensible gatehouse.

At the head of the street a shadow moved, detaching itself from the doorway of a poorer house, and Proxenus came forward to meet them, taking care to keep out of the line of sight from the gatehouse.

"Nothing stirring, sire," he said, without waiting to

be asked. He jerked his head toward the doorway, where a second armed figure could be seen. "Pithon's with me. I sent Timander and Melamnides around the other way, and they didn't see anything either. I'd stake my life the Thebans haven't heard a thing."

The king nodded thoughtfully. Hephaestion glanced along the curve of the street, could just see one of the Sacred Band standing outside the shadow of the gate-house. The Theban wore corselet and greaves, but had set aside shield and spear: Proxenus seemed to have guessed correctly.

"Melamnides," Alexander said abruptly. "You'll keep watch here. The rest of you will accompany me while I speak with Theagenes. If we don't return by the time the watch turns, Melamnides, inform General Craterus at once."

"Yes, sire," the youth said, with great determination.

The king rewarded him with a smile and a nod, then turned toward the Thebans' quarters. The others fell into step automatically, Hephaestion at his shoulder, the three soldiers in line abreast, a few paces behind. Proxenus's face bore its perpetual, disguising scowl; behind his back, the other two exchanged a speaking glance. They were both hypaspists of the spearhead battalion, the elite of the elite, the king's own infantry, but the Sacred Band was a formidable opponent. Proxenus, true to his orders, had said nothing more than was necessary, but the hint of trouble in Greece had been enough. Pithon loosened his sword in its sheath, then, grimly, both men disciplined themselves to their toughest swagger.

At the party's approach, the pair of Thebans who held the guardhouse straightened to attention, the clean-shaven one hastily picked up his spear. Then the other—he was bearded, but no older than his companion, breaking the Sacred Band's tradition that its sworn lovers be man and youth—recognized them and stiffened to the salute.

"King Alexander," he said, his voice more surprised than wary.

Alexander acknowledged the salute, and said, "I want to speak with Theagenes, now."

The Thebans exchanged quick, puzzled glances, and then the bearded one said, "At once, sire. Cleander, take the king to the general."

"Sir." The Theban spoke not to his companion but to the Macedonians. "This way, please." He led the way through the narrow gatehouse and out into the courtyard that stretched between the protecting wall and the house itself. There were more Thebans there, most of these unarmored, some clustering around a dice game, another group sharing a wineskin. A cluster of Asian women, spoils of the campaigns through Persia and Bactria, were busy at the cook fires. The flow of conversation checked at the king's entrance, but resumed again almost at once, the voices merely curious, not concerned.

There was another pair of soldiers at the main door of the house. Cleander nodded to the senior of the two, and said, "King Alexander wishes to speak with Theagenes."

"He's at dinner," said the younger of this pair, wide-eyed.

His companion said, rather irritably, "Tell him King Alexander is here, idiot."

The younger man set his spear aside and hurried into the house. The other said, "You can return to your post, Cleander. If you'd come with me, sire—sirs?"

Alexander nodded his thanks, and followed the man into the darkness of the house. It was an old-fashioned place, built around a central hall that was barely large enough to hold a dozen dining couches. The broad firepit gave off more smoke than heat, and the whole house smelled of its ashes.

Theagenes had established himself in the largest and most comfortable part of the house, a pair of rooms at the very back, separated from the main hall by a heavy curtain. Cleon was waiting there. At the king's approach, he pulled back the curtain and said, "The general bids you welcome, sir."

"Thank you," Alexander said. "Proxenus, you and your men wait here."

Proxenus nodded once, sharply. Cleon, who had intended to offer the newcomers wine, fell nervously silent in the face of unexpected hostility. Alexander spared the hypaspist one reproving glance, then he and Hephaestion entered Theagenes's quarters.

The small outer room was very dark, and a slave woman, a Greek this time, was busy with the lamps that stood in clusters in the corners. There was very little other furniture in the room, and what there was was crudely-made local stuff. As the Theban guard had said, Theagenes had been at dinner: a tray full of half-emptied dishes stood on a side table.

"King Alexander?" Theagenes emerged from the bedchamber, hooking back the curtain to let in a little more light from the inner room's narrow windows. "What can I do for you?" Without waiting for an answer, he prodded the slave woman. "That's enough. Go on, out."

In silence, the woman caught up the tray of dishes and fled. Hephaestion stepped quickly aside to let her pass.

"News from Greece," Alexander answered.

Theagenes's heavy eyebrows drew together in a thoughtful scowl, and his eyes grew wary. "I've sent for Menander," he said. Menander was his second-in-command, as well as his sworn companion. "Wine?"

"I'd be glad of a cup," Alexander said with a bleak smile, and seated himself beside the low table.

The slave had mixed the wine already, and the painted jar—Greek ware, brought with care all the way from Thebes—sat in the center of the table, a ladle and a set of worn silver cups beside it. Theagenes filled the cups and handed them round, watching the king. Alexander's face was closed, inviting no questions, and, seeing that, the Theban felt a cold touch of fear.

The silence stretched to breaking. Hephaestion shifted uneasily, but could find nothing to say. At last, footsteps sounded outside, and a new voice announced, "Menander, general."

"You sent for me—?" Seeing Alexander, the newcomer checked abruptly, uncertainty and then distrust flickering across his face. Theagenes frowned at him, and Menander hastily smoothed his expression.

"News from Greece," Alexander said again.

Hephaestion tensed in spite of himself at the change in the king's voice, then put aside his wine with studied casualness. Alexander spoke into the deepened silence.

"Thebes and Sparta have rebelled."

For a second neither Theban moved, and then Theagenes slammed his clenched fist against the table, making the wine cups rattle. Hephaestion started, then flushed deeply in embarrassment. Alexander ignored them both.

"Thebes has betrayed me; you haven't," he went on. "I have no reason to distrust you. But I can't ask you to make this choice, Theagenes. I won't force you to fight against your city, and I can't let you return to Greece to fight for her. And I won't waste good men. I'm asking you to garrison Bactra for me, until this rebellion is settled."

The little room was close, smelling of the lamp oil and the fire in the hall outside. The sound of their breathing seemed thunderous; beneath it could be heard, faintly but very distinctly, the sound of a woman wailing in another part of the house. A bad omen, the king thought. Let it be for Thebes. The sound stopped abruptly, and the quiet closed in again. Alexander stared at Theagenes, willing him to speak, to give the answer he wanted to hear, to take the opening he had carefully left for him.

Menander said, "What about Athens?"

Hephaestion and Theagenes jumped. Alexander said, "What of her?"

"Where does Athens stand in this? Is she allied with Thebes again?" Menander's tone was bitter: it had been Athens that persuaded Thebes to stand against Philip, and Athenian troops that had broken first at Chaeronea.

Hephaestion glanced at the king, willing him to say yes. It was almost certainly true—Athens never missed a chance to meddle in the politics of other states, and her demagogues bitterly hated Macedon. It would hardly be a lie.

Alexander could feel the cavalry commander's eyes on him, and shook his head almost imperceptibly. "When my messenger was sent, Athens was still uncommitted."

Menander grunted and was silent. Theagenes sat very still, his hand white-knuckled on the wine cup. It had been nearly eight years since he had, reluctantly, agreed to the oligarchs' decision to ignore Athens's proddings and obey the terms of their treaty with the late King Philip, supplying men and money for the invasion of Asia. Theagenes, knowing perfectly well he and his men were hostages, had expected nothing better than to be distrusted and ignored, or, more likely, to see his people systematically destroyed. Neither had happened; Alexander had accepted their presence at face value, assuming their loyalty, and, grudgingly, Theagenes had found himself giving it. Alexander had treated them as he treated his other units, Macedonian and foreign alike, as tools shaped for specific but different tasks, never committing them unless they were clearly the right unit for the job at hand, but then expecting nothing less than their greatest efforts. On the long march down the Asian coast, the Sacred Band had regained their pride. And now, Theagenes thought bitterly, the oligarchs had once again conspired to destroy that pride. They were men without honor; they did not know how to keep their given word, nor even have the intelligence to know when to break it. . . . He took a deep breath, mastering himself with an effort.

"You said Thebes betrayed you," he said abruptly. "They've betrayed us too, and after you kept faith with all of us, Alexander. We knew nothing of this, I swear it, we—I—would have voted against it if I could have. Let us keep our word. Let us stay with you."

"I will not ask you to fight against your city," Alexander said again.

"In the years since it was founded, the Sacred Band has never broken faith, or acted against honor," Theagenes said. Menander growled something, and Theagenes flung out a hand to silence him. His splayed fingers were shaking; Alexander was careful to look away.

"These oligarchs have dishonored us too often," Theagenes went on. "Let us stay." He drew a deep breath. "I swear to you, on Iolaus's altar, if you'll have us, we'll serve you to the death. Even—especially against Thebes."

Menander gave him a shocked glance. It was one thing, that swift look said, to disapprove of Theban policy, but something else entirely to offer to fight against the city. Theagenes said sharply, "They've left us no other honorable course this time."

Menander hesitated, then, reluctantly, nodded. "Very well."

Alexander said carefully, "I accept your oath, Theagenes, and I swear this, in my turn: I'll hold your honor as dear as my own."

Theagenes nodded jerkily. "Done." He hesitated for a moment, clearly marshalling his thoughts, then said slowly, "This plot of the pages, did Thebes have a hand in that, too, I wonder?"

Alexander's mouth tightened abruptly. The thought had not occurred to him, in the more pressing concerns of the morning, and the possibility angered him even further. Hephaestion, with a quick glance at the king's stiff face, said, "The two couldn't be connected. The timing's impossible."

Tardily aware of the king's anger, Theagenes murmured an apology, and repeated his promise of loyalty. With an effort, the king relaxed enough to respond graciously, and the two men parted in formal friendship. In the street, voice lowered to keep both the Thebans and the trailing hypaspists from hearing, Hephaestion said, "But will he keep that word?"

The king did not answer, and Hephaestion, watching the other's grim face, did not press the issue. There were other questions he wanted to ask as well, and did not dare—what would be done about the pages now that the situation in Greece made their treason even more dangerous; what, if anything, would be done to secure the loyalty of the satraps back on the Asian coast; and most important of all, would the army march to help Antipater? He himself could see no way to avoid it; and thus no way to carry out the planned Indian campaign. If the officer left behind in Asia had thought their reinforcements would be enough to quell the rebellion, Mazaeus's dispatch would have said as much; by the time a new messenger could reach Bactra from the mainland, it would be summer at least, and the army would not be able to relieve Antipater until the next year. Even starting as soon as possible, it would be hard to make the coast before the sailing season ended. And even Alexander would not move instantly when it meant the end of his cherished dream of reaching Ocean.

The courtyard of the royal quarters was unexpectedly crowded: Chares, acting under Ptolemy's orders, had doubled the household guard. Alexander eyed them dubiously—they were hardly inconspicuous—but continued on into the house.

Peucestas was waiting in the antechamber that gave onto the main hall. At the king's approach, he gave a sigh of relief and came forward quickly, saying in a low, urgent voice, "Alexander, Exathres requests an immediate audience."

Exathres was Darius's brother, who had joined Alexander in hopes of getting revenge on Darius's murderer. The king raised an eyebrow. "What does he want?"

"To offer his loyal assistance, he says," Peucestas answered, sighing. "Alexander, I don't know how he heard. He has his agents in the camp—all the foreign commanders do—and agents in Babylon as well. I'm trying to find out."

"Do what you can," Alexander answered. "Very well, I'll see him."

The Persian was waiting with his retinue in the main hall, the lamplight glinting from the gold borders of his luxurious coat. His fleshy, heavily bearded face was in shadow, hiding his expression as he turned to face the king. Alexander drew himself up to his full height—he was still nearly half a foot smaller than the other—and beckoned to the Persian. Exathres came forward gracefully, stooping to the prostration, then rose to receive a kinsman's kiss. The ritual greeting completed, the Persian stepped back, saying, in Persian, "Great King, Majesty, I am greatly grieved to hear of this rebellion in Greece. Am I correct in believing you will soon march to punish the traitors?"

The king's command of Persian was somewhat limited, though he understood it well enough. He answered, in Greek, "As I've only just heard of the trouble myself, Exathres, I've made no firm plans. I will be meeting with my officers over the next few days, and you will, of course, be invited."

Exathres bowed, switching smoothly to Greek himself. "I hope Your Majesty will permit me and mine to accompany you. Treason is a terrible thing."

Both Hephaestion and Peucestas looked up sharply at that. Persia and the Greek cities were ancient enemies; to land in Greece with Persian troops as any part of the army would be to throw away any chance of winning over the smaller League cities. Alexander hid his own grimace of distaste, and said, "I'm grateful for this proof of loyalty, Exathres. But as I said, my plans aren't certain yet. We'll talk more tomorrow."

Exathres bowed again. "I am honored to be of service to Your Majesty." With a graceful gesture, he collected his attendants, who also bowed, and then the group of Persians backed politely from the hall.

When he was certain they were out of earshot, Peucestas said softly, "I have men watching them."

Alexander nodded thoughtfully. "It's as well to be careful," he said, almost to himself, then beckoned to the others. "Come on, there's work to be done tonight."

CHAPTER 3:

Bactra, winter (Peritios) to Miletos, late summer (Hyper-beretaios), 29 imperial (327 B.C., 426 A.U.C.)

Despite attempts at secrecy the news of the Greek rebellion spread like fire in dry tinder. By the time of the morning sacrifice, some version of the news had penetrated every corner of the camp. By evening, it had reached the camp followers and petty merchants. There was little reaction from the camp followers—the Greeks among them were professionals, or slaves bought cheap before the army had left the mainland, and the few exceptions had come for the love of some soldier and cared nothing for politics—but the news sent ripples of panic through the traders' camp. Many of them were Greek, and half a dozen, citizens of the most prominent rebel cities, abandoned their goods and tried to slip away from Bactra. Ptolemy, whom the king had detailed to watch for any such attempts, took a certain grim pleasure in thwarting them. He was equally pleased to find that none of them seemed to be spies for the League; in the king's present mood it was unlikely even Ptolemy could keep spies alive long enough to provide any useful information.

Alexander was bitterly angry. After the first meeting with his officers, informing them of the rebellion, he refused to discuss any details for sending troops to Antipater's aid, or of returning to Greece himself. Instead, he turned his attention at once to the imprisoned pages, declaring that they should be tried at once, without waiting for Menidas to return from Alexandria Eschate. The Friends accepted his insistence without argument, and arrangements were made to clear the market square, the only place in Bactra large enough to hold all the Macedonians.

Like an amphitheater on the morning of a festival, the market square began filling well before dawn, but it was full light by the time the last of the Macedonian soldiers had filed into the broad square. A crude platform had been set up in front of the low building that normally housed the city's court. There the king and the Macedonians among the Friends—the others were not entitled even to hear the trial—took their places, listening to the mutter of conversation that made the market echo like a hollow shell.

It was an unexpectedly bright winter's day. The sun, rising at last above the low roofs of the shops that ringed the market, glittered from the sea of armor visible beneath the half-concealing cloaks. Every Macedonian who wished to attend was there. A mixture of trusted mercenaries and non-Macedonians who also acknowledged Alexander's kingship—Agrianians and Paeonians and Thracians—guarded the city walls, while beyond the shuttered, empty shops a detachment of the Sacred Band stood watch at the approaches to the market, turning away any curious foreigners.

At last, the door of the court buildings opened and a detachment of hypaspists appeared, escorting the accused pages. The noise of the crowd deepened as the first soldiers caught sight of them, a ripple spreading through the crowd as more and more soldiers craned to see. Then the prisoners had reached the platform, and Alexander held up his hand for silence. The sun, rising behind him, turned his hair to reddish gold, brighter than the royal diadem.

The noise stopped gradually, the conversations dying away into a shuffling and then to nothing. The pages showed the marks of questioning, but walked without help.

"Macedonians!" Alexander shouted in their language, his own mother tongue. His voice carried very clearly in the quiet air. "You already have heard most of the story that brings you here. It's your right to hear the rest, and your duty to judge and punish. I accuse these pages you see before you of plotting to kill their king. I accuse them on the word of Epimenes son of Arseus, who revealed the plot, and on their own confession."

Standing well back in the knot of officers that waited at the king's right hand, Ptolemy sighed, letting his eyes sweep across the attentive crowd. Alexander spoke well, as always, shaping words and gestures to match his audience. As always, the soldiers responded to the king's will, listening with rising anger to the slow unfolding of the plot. It was too much like the drama for Ptolemy's taste, though Alexander was unaware of the way he played the crowd—just as Ptolemy was unaware his king reserved a subtler magic for swaying him. The general looked away, shutting out the king's clear voice to concentrate on the testimony he himself would have to give.

Hephaestion caught the brief, unhappy movement but ignored it, watching the king instead. Alexander was more than merely convincing: even knowing the details of the plot perhaps better than the king himself did, the cavalry commander found his own emotions stirring in response. Then Alexander had finished, with only the briefest of allusions to the rebellion in Greece. Epimenes was brought forward to confirm what the king had said. He spoke very badly, mumbling and ashamed, so that the men at the far end of the marketplace could not hear at all, and had to have his words repeated to them by men closer to the platform. Ptolemy spoke next, gruffly adding his word to what Epimenes had said, and finally Hephaestion recounted the pages' confessions. Only then did Alexander turn his attention to the prisoners.

"What do you say in your defense?"

The group of boys shifted sullenly, glancing at each other without speaking, and then a blocky, dark youth stepped forward slightly, throwing a contemptuous glance at the spear automatically lowered to block his path.

"I am Hermolaus son of Cleon. I speak for us all." Hermolaus had a high-pitched, carrying voice, and a look of white-lipped fanaticism. One of the others glanced at him sidelong, like a nervous horse, and moved away a little. "Yes, we planned to kill Alexander—to free the Macedonians from the chains of a tyrant, a tyrant whose rule grows more offensive every day."

There was an angry murmur from the crowd at that, but the boy cried it down. "Yes! A tyrant! Haven't we all noticed how Alexander has changed since Darius was beaten? How he apes Persian ways, favors only Persians, marries a barbarian female—and does anyone dare speak against this, as a Macedonian should be able to speak, freely to his king? What happened to Philotas when he tried it? He was charged with treason, too, and executed."

"He had a fair trial, you little bastard," a hypaspist shouted, and there was a yelp of agreement from his neighbors.

"Did his father?" Hermolaus shot back. "Did Cleitus?"

The king's face paled slowly, and one hand contracted into a fist. The soldiers' roar of fury was reassuring, a sort of forgiveness. Alexander maintained his savage silence, waiting for the boy to finish.

Hermolaus's voice rose sharply, the words coming more and more quickly, so that the men in the back of the crowd shifted and strained to understand. Somehow the correctness, the pure philosophical logic of his argument, was not coming through. "These murders are just part of his tyranny," he shouted. "Look at how he plays at being Great King—and he'd like to turn us all into Persians—into slaves, which is the same thing. Didn't he ask us all, last winter, to bow down and adore him? Is that the way a man, a Macedonian, should act?"

The crowd stirred at that, angry voices blending into a vast mutter of discontent, and Hermolaus shouted them all down, his voice cracking painfully. "No free-born Macedonian could tolerate this. The democracies of Greece have taught us how to deal with tyrants—"

A new wave of shouting cut him off abruptly. Whatever chance Hermolaus had ever had of convincing anyone of anything was gone forever at the first mention of the Greek cities, and he knew it. He kept going, trying to outlast the torrent of abuse, but his voice was utterly lost in the noise. Alexander waited until he faltered, then held up his hand for silence. Grudgingly, the soldiers quieted.

"Hear him out," Alexander called, and waited until the last shouts died away. "Hermolaus, do you have anything more to say in your . . . defense?"

There was renewed jeering from the crowd and Alexander lifted his hand again. When the noise died down again, the page said sulkily, "I have finished."

"And the rest of you?" Alexander asked.

One, Sopolis, sighed and shook his head, and Anticles muttered bitterly, "What else is there to say?"

The king waited a moment longer, and then, when it was clear that no one else would speak, turned to the assembly for the final time. "Macedonians, what is your verdict?"

The crowd roared back, "Guilty!"

Alexander nodded gravely, though no other verdict had been possible, and held up his hand for the last time. The soldiers quieted, eager for the kill. "Macedonians, you have found these four guilty of treason. It remains to carry out the sentence—outside the city."

Perdiccas had chosen for the execution a hollow, just far enough outside the city walls to avoid pollution. It was the sort of place that in Macedon would have been made into an amphitheater. Ptolemy made a face, thinking again of the drama, and looked away. A detachment of Agrianian javelin-men, squat, barbaric-looking men, made up the perimeter guard. At the king's order, they saluted and backed away, revealing the waiting piles of stones.

Perhaps half the army had come to take part in the execution; there would not be stones enough for all of them. Perdiccas grimaced irritably, uncertain if it was his own lack of foresight or the execution itself that he disapproved of. The impassive hypaspists bound the pages' hands, then half shoved, half dragged them into the center of the natural amphitheater. The pages stood where they had been placed, huddling together as if that would protect them. Alexander waited until the hypaspists were clear, and said, "Begin."

The first rock landed far up the slope. As it passed him, Anticles instinctively dodged aside, as though it were one of the ball games the pages played off duty. The soldiers jeered, and Hermolaus snapped something at the other boy. Anticles froze, chin lifting proudly. A moment later a better aimed stone drove him to his knees.

Unspeaking, Alexander watched them die, his face as expressionless as a statue's. When it was over he ordered Perdiccas to see to the burning of the bodies, and turned back toward the city. Behind his back, the Friends exchanged looks and followed. Craterus said, softly, "Now maybe he'll attend to the Greek business. Hephaestion, you talk to him."

The cavalry commander, sickened by the executions, shot an angry glance in his direction, then lengthened his stride until he had almost overtaken the king. Ptolemy said, in the tones he would use to an importunate child, "Not now, Craterus. Let it go."

Craterus snorted, declining to acknowledge the insult. "If not now, when? If there aren't some decisions made soon, we'll miss the sailing season. And then where will Antipater be?"

Ptolemy said, in exactly the same tone as before, "Tomorrow, Craterus." The brigadier subsided, grumbling.

At the city walls, the group of Friends hesitated slightly, until it became clear the king had no further orders for them. Then the group began to break up, each officer returning to his own quarters. In the shadow of the gatehouse, Coenus put his hand on Hephaestion's shoulder.

"Walk with me."

Hephaestion gave the brigadier a startled glance— there was too great a difference in their ages for him to be a particular friend of Coenus's—but their quarters lay in the same section of the city. "If you wish."

Coenus nodded, setting a slow, deliberate pace toward the better houses, avoiding the marketplace. There were things that needed to be said, he knew, but he doubted he was the man to say them. Still, it was a matter of duty, and at that thought he straightened his shoulders like a younger man. Hephaestion saw the movement, and lifted his head warily.

"Walk ahead," Coenus said to the servants who escorted them. Hephaestion nodded for his own men to do the same, and waited, watching the brigadier.

Coenus sighed. "Craterus was right, you know." He knew it was not the cleverest of openings, but having made that beginning, he had to continue. "The king must come to some decision, and soon."

Hephaestion's face tightened again, then slowly relaxed. He would not be angry with Coenus, not when he was merely speaking what everyone knew was true. "I know that," he said, softly, "and when the king asks me for my opinion, I'll tell him that."

Coenus hesitated again, weighing the advisability of saying more, then shook his head thoughtfully. There had been enough said today; tomorrow or the next day would be a better time.

The two men parted formally. Once inside his own quarters, Hephaestion shouted irritably for his Egyptian body-slave. When the man appeared, Hephaestion ordered his best chair to be placed in the wedge of sunlight that streamed in through the open window, then sent the library slave for one of the precious scrolls that stood in their travelling cases along the inner wall of the narrow bedchamber. The young man returned quickly and settled himself beneath the window. He read well—it had been for that skill, and his beautiful, unaccented Greek, that Hephaestion had bought him—but Diagoras's words could not hold the cavalry commander's attention. When the light faded, Hephaestion did not order the lamps lit, but dismissed the slave with thanks and sat for a while in the growing dark.

There was a cough from the doorway, and Hephaestion looked up sharply. The Egyptian said, "Pardon me, sir, but there's a message from the king."

"What is it?" Hephaestion asked, and an unfamiliar voice answered, "General, the king would like your company at dinner."

Hephaestion sighed. After the executions, and with the Greek rebellion still hanging over them, dinner with the king would not be a pleasant experience. But he also knew why he had been invited, and accepted the obligation willingly. "Tell the king I'll be there directly."

The lamps were lit in the king's chamber, casting pools of dappled light across the floor and walls. The servants had cleared away the dinner dishes some time before, leaving only the massive wine bowl on the table between the couches. Alexander stared into the depths of his wine cup, face remote. Hephaestion watched uneasily, waiting for the other to speak, and put aside his own emptied cup.

After a long moment, Alexander said, not raising his voice, "Bastards." He used the Macedonian epithet, the barracks-word he had learned as a boy, and followed it with other choice terms picked up in a lifetime of soldiering, cursing pages and demagogues alike with unrivaled fluency. His voice lost the overtones of polite Greek, becoming purely Macedonian.

Hephaestion listened silently, as he had done from boyhood, half appalled by the outburst, half admiring. But this was not the time for admiration: it was this Alexander who killed Cleitus, and the shadow of that act was too dark. He said into the pause while Alexander drew breath, "I doubt that's anatomically possible."

Alexander glanced sideways at him, startled by the sheer irrelevance of the comment. For a moment, his reaction hung in the balance, and then, irresistibly, his mouth twitched upward. He sobered quickly, and said without heat, "And damn Antipater, too. What did he think he was doing?"

"He isn't you," Hephaestion said quietly, "or even Philip. And he's getting old."

There was another, shorter silence, and Alexander said, "I don't want to go back to Greece."

"You could send back part of the army," Hephaestion began, "an expeditionary force under Craterus—"

"Leaving me without the men I need to go into

India?" Alexander asked. "And Craterus might lose." The king glared blindly into the flame of a lamp, grieving for the campaign he had planned, as much discovery as conquest, across India to the encircling Ocean. "The League will pay for this."

"Let them," Hephaestion said. "Let them literally." He leaned forward, not sure if it were wine or inspiration speaking. "We're both young yet, not even thirty; there's time to settle things in Greece—and in Persia, by the gods—and *then* go on to the East. Fine the League cities a few dozen talents each, as much as they can bear, and let them pay for the campaign."

Alexander smiled and held out his hands. Hephaestion embraced him fiercely, offering that comfort as well. He rested his cheek against the king's hair, wondering why he did not feel Alexander's disappointment more keenly. He was angry at the rebels, of course, but did not grieve for the Indian campaign. Hephaestion locked that knowledge away with the few other things he did not share with Alexander, and bent to kiss the other's hair in mute apology. Alexander gave a small, contented sigh, and pulled away.

"It's only justice that the League pays for India," Alexander said at last. "Who would you choose for regent in Asia?"

Only a little startled by the abrupt change of subject, Hephaestion said, "Peucestas. Who else?"

"My thought exactly," Alexander said. He stared into space again, reviewing all the things that would have to be done, both to get the army safely back to Greece and to secure his Asian conquests. Supplies would have to be found, a practical line of march chosen, satraps selected for these eastern provinces, the Asian regency arranged and financed, his own marriage to Darius's daughter, which he had been putting off, would have to be celebrated at last. . . . "Find Pasithea again," he said. "See if the danger's far enough past that she'll accept a present."

To Hephaestion's surprise, however, there was no need to seek out the Syrian. She presented herself at the courtyard gate early the next morning, and, as Alexander had ordered, was brought immediately into his presence. The king, in the presence of his Friends, thanked her again for her warning, and asked her what gift would make her happy. She stammered and grew shy, but finally made her request: a servant to do her cooking. She asked for nothing more, but at the mention of a tent of her own her eyes grew wide. Tent and slave-girl, and a mule and male slave to look after the baggage, were all provided. Over the following weeks, Pasithea became less ragged, and her face lost its starved, feral look.

His painful decision made, and the seeress provided for, Alexander turned his attention to planning the march back to the coast. He garrisoned Bactra, gathered settlers and soldiers for the chain of cities along the Scythian border, and began then to gather supplies for the three months' march from Bactra to Ecbatana. The army's evident delight at the chance to return to Greece, and, not incidentally, to sack Greek cities, seemed only to spur him on. Menidas returned from Alexandria Eschate with a frightened and bitter Theocritus as his prisoner. Alexander listened to both men's stories, and seemed inclined to believe in Theocritus's innocence, but ordered him held under guard regardless. Only on the last day before the army was to leave Bactra did the pace ease.

As was his custom, Alexander spoke to the troops. going from unit to unit—Bactra had no single square large enough to contain all the army—accompanied by those of his Friends who had no other pressing duties.

To the Macedonians, the Companion Cavalry, the Foot Companions, and the hypaspists, Alexander was a Macedonian and their king, angry at the betrayal, and blunt in his promise of vengeance and plunder for his loyal subjects. To the light cavalry, Thessalians and

Thracians, the Greek mercenaries and the Scouts, he was very much their general, laying out the coming campaign; to the rest, the archers, the half-savage Agrianian javelin-men, the engineers and all the rest of the miscellaneous units, he was what each one wanted, compelling their consent. To the Sacred Band, Alexander spoke of honor and of pride and of his own sorrow; when he had done, the Thebans cheered him, swearing their eternal loyalty.

Under the cover of the shouting, Perdiccas said, "I swear they'd sack Thebes themselves and sell their sisters if they thought he'd like it." Release from fear sharpened his tongue. There were no more than a dozen men in the king's escort, even counting the Friends—and though no Macedonian was ever seen without his sword, the Friends were unarmored. Had the Sacred Band chosen to revenge Chaeronea, they could have done so.

Peucestas said, rather more sharply than he had intended, "It's a good thing they love the king."

Perdiccas sighed. "You know, that's the difference between Philip and Alexander."

Peucestas looked inquiringly at the other man. He himself was too young to have served under Philip, but Perdiccas had been made a battalion commander just before the old king's murder. "What do you mean?"

"Philip was a good king and a fine general, and the men loved him—but not in the same way. Look: Philip could have ordered a man to jump off a cliff, and probably would've been obeyed, right? Alexander could get a hundred volunteers: that's the difference." He gave Peucestas a quick, malicious glance, and added, "And you'd be one of them."

Peucestas, who had started to laugh, cursed instead, recognizing the kernel of truth in the other man's words.

*   *   *

The first stage of the march, from Bactra to the summer palace at Ecbatana, was the worst. Alexander had chosen to accept short rations and the possibility of Scythian attack in exchange for reaching Ecbatana before summer. Careful planning and judicious bullying of the local populations made sure that the army did not starve, though none grew fat. The new chain of forts along the Scythian border served their purpose, too; they saw no raiding nomads.

The army rested at Ecbatana for two weeks, officers and men alike savoring the luxuries of the royal city. For the king and the Friends, however, there was little time to rest. The royal treasury had been left at Ecbatana for safekeeping; now the entire sum, talents of coin as well as jewels and plate, had to be transported to Babylon to finance the coming campaign, and to make up a regent's treasury. Harpalus, the crippled treasurer, grumbled bitterly at the new demands, and Ptolemy began a discreet investigation of the royal finances. Harpalus had once been caught stealing from the treasury, but had been forgiven. This time, there were no missing funds, and Harpalus paraded his injured dignity for some days. Theocritus, still bitterly shamed by his son's treason, was formally pardoned, and restored to command of the hypaspist battalion that would remain as part of the regent's army. Peucestas, already informally accepted as Alexander's Regent in Persia, complained at being left Theocritus, but even he had to admit that it was the safest solution.

It was at Ecbatana, too, that Alexander became aware for the first time of the number of children among the hordes that followed in the army's wake. Some few were the products of legitimate marriages or long-term liaisons; most were the half-acknowledged offspring of the camp-followers. Something, plainly, needed to be done about them: he would not have them turned loose in Babylon to fend for themselves, nor could they be brought to Greece; half-Persian bastards would not find a life worth living in Macedon. After some thought, Alexander ordered the word spread that any son of a Macedonian could be enrolled in a new brigade: The boys would be fed and housed at royal expense and trained to take their fathers' places in the phalanx. By the time the army left Ecbatana, some three hundred boys of varying ages had been enrolled in the new corps. In that modest beginning were the seeds of greatness.

There were far fewer girl-children to be provided for—a soldier with no sons at home might well feed a boy-child, but in most cases a bastard daughter had only the inadequate resources of its mother to see it through. But some had survived infancy, and to the ones not already being trained as prostitutes, Alexander offered a place in the queens' household in Babylon plus a generous dowry. The neatness of the solution pleased him: not only did it fulfill the obligation he felt to his men and their offspring, but also, through the special status of the training corps, and the size of the girls' dowries, emphasized his own wish for a union of his two peoples.

The march from Ecbatana to Babylon, down from the mountains into the heartland of the Persian empire, was an easy one, marred only by the death of the king's ancient warhorse in the foothills of Susiania. Alexander wept bitterly over the animal's death— Bucephalus had been a treasured companion of his youth—and his men, responsive as always to the king's wishes, labored willingly through the three-day halt to build a memorial over the horse's tomb. The men of the hill tribes, still half savage despite generations of Persian rule, came, wondering, to see the temple the foreign king erected for his horse. Still grieving, Alexander offered to remit their taxes if the tribes would use that money to maintain Bucephalus's tomb. The tribesmen exchanged dubious glances at such incomprehensible behavior, but agreed readily enough. Craterus, who was himself the descendent of hill tribes and distrusted all such on principle, found the most prominent of their leaders and explained to him in detail what would happen to him if the tomb were not maintained. The tribesman swallowed hard, and swore on his father's grave that he would keep his promise. Craterus was still somewhat doubtful, but comforted himself with the thought that he had done his best.

Alexander had planned to spend less than a month in Babylon, but it quickly became clear that, despite the messengers he had sent ahead from Ecbatana, he would need more time in the city. Nearchus, a Friend and the king's chosen admiral, was dispatched at once for the coast with enough men and money to hire, buy or seize enough ships to carry the entire army to the Greek mainland. At the same time, Alexander sent his most skillful agent, Polydamus, to negotiate with the oligarchs of the little coastal town that Nearchus had chosen as the best landing place. Brauron had been friendly to Macedon before, if only out of hatred of the other cities: Polydamus carried enough coin to ensure her friendship once again.

Once those plans had been set in motion, the king turned his attention to securing the situation in Persia. In a ceremony that mingled Persian splendor and Macedonian ritual, Alexander conferred the regency on Peucestas; in an even more splendid ceremony two days later, the king married the elder of Darius's daughters. She and Alexander's second bride, a Sogdian—the first, Orestid, wife, mother of the heir Philip Alexander, had died in Macedon four years earlier—were installed in separate wings of the royal palace, ceremoniously bedded, and promptly forgotten. The ceremonies were followed by several days of feasting and celebration—payment in advance, said the cynics among the soldiers, for the coastal march ahead.

Just after midsummer, after a final day of sacrifices and prayers, the Macedonian army left Babylon. At the king's order everyone travelled light, without the horde of camp followers and merchants, and with a drastically reduced baggage train. Even so, the weather was changing by the time they reached Miletos, the sailing season giving way to autumn storms.

With his usual efficiency, Nearchus had assembled a massive fleet, large enough to accommodate even the Macedonian army. He had gathered the necessary stores and fodder in advance, too, speeding the embarkation enormously. A dispatch was waiting from Polydamus as well: Brauron would, for a price, allow the Macedonians to land. Pleased, Alexander set aside the talent agreed upon, and the crossing began.

It was very crowded aboard the flagship, the disciplined crew tangling with the chaos of the royal household in the low midships pavilion. At the stern, Nearchus watched the confusion from the commander's chair, while the pilot screamed himself hoarse trying to create some kind of order. Below decks, however, things were fully under control; the drum beat out a steady, conservative stroke, and the oars rose and fell easily, pulling the ship forward through the low swell of the harbor.

Hephaestion clung to the port rail, grateful that this was one of the cataphract ships with its full upper deck rather than an older trireme that had only a central catwalk running between the rows of oarsmen. He flattened himself against the racked shields to avoid a hurrying sailor, who promptly disappeared down the hatchway to the rowers' deck, and for the first time he saw the full fleet spread out behind them. The four other quinquiremes—the flagship was the first and best, with a crack crew commanded by Nearchus himself—were spread out in a great lambda, the flagship at the point. Their oars beat the water in a stately rhythm, as though all five ships were listening to a single drummer. The newly painted eyes on the bows of the great ships rode up and down together, though in the comparative calm of the harbor the bronze sheathing of the ram barely showed above the waves. Banners snapped from the curved sterns, as new and as bright as the painting. Beyond them, trailing back in the same line and filling in the center, came the triremes, smaller and less well-armed— carrying only one catapult as against the three cata-pults of the quinquiremes—but as bravely decked out in new paint and banners.

Scattered among the last lines of warships, their sails almost hiding the buildings along the shoreline, came the round-bellied merchant ships, bearing pro-visions and more troops and the horses. Himself a poor sailor, Hephaestion was worried for the horses; in part, perhaps, because they shared this his only weakness. He would have to rest them well after landing, he decided, and pray that Alexander made no immediate plans that demanded peak performance from the Companion Cavalry. But the king understood that horses could not be pushed as far as men, and would do his best to spare them.

The motion of the ship changed subtly, checking almost imperceptibly, then riding up at a new angle as the ship left the protection of the harbor. Hephaestion swallowed hard, and, though he was not a particularly religious man, made a silent offer of a bull to Poseidon, if only the voyage were smooth. The chains of islands would provide some protection from bad storms, of course, but it was late in the season and there was a long stretch of open water between Icaros and Myconos. Already, the new motion, a sideways tossing that al-ternately lifted and buried the banked oars, unsettled him.

Outside the midships pavilion, under the eyes of the page guarding the king, Ptolemy and Coenus had begun a dice game, tossing the counters carefully on the heaving boards. Ptolemy looked up from a particularly good throw, eyed the cavalry commander's pallor, and nudged Coenus. Coenus grunted sympathetically, and turned back to the game.

There was a flurry of action at the stern. Nearchus rose from his chair to reel off a string of orders while sailors ran forward to the sail and to the signal flags at the stern. The two helmsmen strained at their steering oars, and the ship heeled over slightly, turning north to avoid one of the outer islands. She straightened again almost instantly, but her motion was perceptibly rougher. Hephaestion swallowed again, tasting bile. He straightened cautiously, testing his balance, then lurched without dignity toward the pavilion. He caught himself on one of the guy ropes—Ptolemy grinned even more broadly, but, mercifully, said nothing—and ducked under the tent flap.

It was relatively quiet inside the pavilion, and much warmer. The pages had laid out beds for the Friends in the outer room. Hephaestion stretched out on a pile of familiar blankets, drawing his cloak around his shoulders, and closed his eyes. Alexander was asleep in the inner section of the tent, not seasick—Alexander was never seasick—but storing up sleep for the upcoming campaign. Despite his queasiness, Hephaestion twisted to reach the edge of the cloth that screened the inner room, lifted it a fraction of an inch off the decking. Through the opening, he could see the king sprawled on a pile of bedding, tunic disordered and sword belt discarded at his side. His eyes were closed, and his chest moved with the slow rhythm of sleep. Hephaestion let the curtain fall again, and settled himself on his own cushions.

After a while, the worst of the sickness passed, but he did not dare do much more than unfasten his sword belt and lay it on the deck beside his pile of bedding. After a while he loosened his cloak as well, and lay staring up at the sagging ceiling. Sick as he felt, he almost wished he had been the one left to rule Persia—the regency could have been his for the asking—but he knew he would change his mind as soon as they landed in Greece. In the meantime, there was nothing he could do but wait, and endure. With a sigh, he closed his eyes and tried to sleep.

In the stuffy inner room, Alexander lay with his eyes closed, halfway between sleep and waking. The plans that could be made in advance were already in motion. By now, the army should have been well into India, through the mountains as soon as the worst of the snow melted, then into the plains. Halfway to the Ocean. The League cities would pay dearly for their treason, in money, as Hephaestion had suggested, and in blood. Then he would return to the east, and the Ocean.

INTERLUDE:

Trans-Indus Province, summer (Loios), 191 imperial (165 B.C., 588 A.U.C.)

"So," the older man said, theatrically, "we stand in the heart of India. Alexander himself was never able to do as much."

"Lucky Alexander," his companion said.

The older man made a short, barking noise that might have been laughter, and turned back to the fretted window. Outside, the garrison town of Philippopolis—Philippopolis-trans-Indus—was slowly dissolving in the summer rains. A few native women moved laughing along the muddy street, heedless of the steamy downpour, their brilliant dresses plastered to their bodies. If he had been newly come to India, the older man might have watched with admiration; after nearly eight years' duty with the Trans-Indus brigade, he barely noticed the women's lithe curves, looking instead for any sign of his troops. He could not see the guardhouse from that window, but there should have been men on duty at the entrance to the stableyard. Frowning, he picked up the bell that stood on the nearest table and shook it sharply.

The runner, a stocky, shock-haired native, appeared almost at once. "General, sir?"

"My compliments to the watch commander," the older man said, without turning away from the window, "and I would be grateful if he saw to the stable guard."

"Sir!" The runner saluted sharply, and backed away.

"He's probably just gone round the corner," the younger man said, with Persian delicacy.

"The both of them, at once?" the older man snapped. He broke off instantly, regretting the loss of control. India was getting to him as well: Trans-Indus duty was a notorious breeder of mutiny and discontent. Perhaps it was time he asked to be reassigned. Then his eyes fell again on the scrolls lying on his desk, growing pulpy in the damp air. He could hardly do that, not with those messages still to be dealt with. And, once he had dealt with them, he would very likely not get the chance to ask for a new assignment before the native kings reassigned him permanently.

The other man saw the direction of his gaze, and sighed himself, rubbing at the scars on his chin. They were the sort of scars a rising young commander should have, turning nearly feminine beauty into masculine dash—except that they had been acquired in an Ephesian tavern brawl, when a prostitute swung a broken bottle across his face. "As bad as all that, sir?" he asked, tentatively.

The general grunted. "Read for yourself, if you want."

The other man made no move to pick up the crumpled scrolls. "It is said," he said carefully, the Asian notes suddenly prominent in his voice, "it is said, general, that the Scythians and some other, newer—even stronger—tribe are pushing at the Sogdian border. It is said Alexandr'Eschate's been refortified, and the border forts need new blood. It is even said, general, that we're the new blood."

The general shook his head at the accuracy of the Philippolpolis grapevine. "It is said—" he used the Persian phrase, mimicking the other's diction "—correctly."

"Then we'll abandon Philippopolis?" In spite of himself, the younger man was unable to keep the pleasure from his voice.

"We will not," the general snapped. "Though I grant you we ought. No, Hippostratus in Bactra orders me to send the best of my legion, leaving me with barely a battalion to keep the peace—I beg your pardon, Mithrenes, but your Scouts are hardly the kind of troops I need to keep down trouble—and tells me at the same time that the king orders me to hold the Trans-Indus borders inviolate. If Cleopatra were still regent, there'd be none of that nonsense, I can tell you."

Mithrenes nodded thoughtful agreement. The Queen Mother Cleopatra, daughter of the Sogdian branch of the royal family, had had her great ancestor's instinctive grasp of strategic necessity, as her treatment of the Rhodian pirates had proved. Her son, only newly come to the throne, lacked both his mother's genius and the experience that could in part substitute for it. But then, the Trans-Indus Province had never been a particularly wise venture, even if it had been an irresistible one. When the Maruyan Empire fell nearly seventy years before, Alexander VI had seen that as an invitation to go one better than the great Alexander, and extend the empire's borders to the encircling Ocean. To no one's surprise but his own, the feuding native kings had proved formidable opponents; the army had never been able to push more than a few hundred miles beyond the Indus, and had bought that steamy territory very dearly. It was not easily held, either: nearly every year, once the rains had ended, some local princeling raised an army and had to be put down.

"The great Alexander knew what he was doing, putting the borders in Bactria," Mithrenes said aloud.

The general grunted again. "Help me think of a tactful way to put that in dispatches."

Mithrenes grinned, his usual good temper reasserting itself. "I doubt there is one, sir."

The general doubted it himself, doubted too that the young king could be persuaded to see reason before he had lost many good men. Then he squared his shoulders resolutely. It was a question of duty—he was a Roman Ptolemy, Stoic by upbringing and temperament—and he would do his duty to his men and the empire, whatever the cost. Even, he thought, if it meant pulling back to the Bactrian border without royal orders and accepting the consequences.

CHAPTER 4:

Brauron, early autumn (Hyperberetaios) to Athens, early winter (Audnaios), 29–30 imperial (327/6 B.C., 426/7 A.U.C.)

The crossing went more smoothly than Nearchus had anticipated, without even the threat of a bad storm to contend with. Polydamus had done his work well: Brauron turned out to welcome the Macedonian king, and the inhabitants grew even friendlier once they saw the Persian gold the newcomers had to spend. The city oligarchs even blocked Athens's chief agent's attempt to flee, and presented the man to Alexander on the king's arrival in the city. Alexander eyed the sweating merchant, found that he owned one of the best houses in the city, and promptly appropriated it, confining the merchant and his household in what had been the women's quarters. Polydamus had done extremely well to secure that kind of cooperation; the king's reward was generous, and Craterus, who had never liked Athens or Athenians, quietly doubled the sum. A rich man for life, Polydamus retired to his tent to contemplate his fortune in discreet contentment.

Most of the army was billeted outside the city walls, as was the king's practice when he did not plan to

remain long in a place. The city and its attractions
were not off limits to the soldiers, however, and the
streets and markets were filled with Macedonians eager to spend their loot. For a few, it was a pleasure to
rob feisty Greeks instead of servile Persians. The commanders punished those whom they caught, and
watched carefully for any signs that Brauron was no
longer willing to tolerate the Macedonian presence.

However, the city was still friendly—and would
remain so, Perdiccas said caustically, until the money
ran out. Hephaestion was more dubious, but when,
already late for a meeting of the Friends, he was
delayed by yet another cheerful, mixed crowd spilling
out of an unrobbed wineshop, even he had to admit
the justice of the brigade commander's remark. He
cursed them all impartially, marking the presence of
one of his own troopers for a later reprimand, and
managed to force his horse through the crowd without
mishap.

At the royal quarters, he tossed the reins to a waiting slave, and hurried into the house, dodging a second slave at work sweeping up dirt and dead leaves in
the main hall. The pages on guard outside the king's
rooms stood aside smartly at his approach, but Hephaestion checked abruptly at the sound of angry voices
from within. From the pages' blank faces, the argument had been going on for some time.

"Announce me," Hephaestion said, as though he
had heard nothing.

The nearest page swallowed hard, but said, "Yes,
sir." He ran lightly up the stairs, Hephaestion following more deliberately, and tapped his spear against
the door. The angry voices stopped at once, and Alexander said, "What is it?"

"General Hephaestion, sire," the page answered
nervously.

"Admit him."

The page pushed open the door. Hephaestion set

his face in its most neutral expression, and stepped into the room. Craterus glared at him like a baited bull, then, finally seeing Eumenes's smirk, turned away, muttering to himself. Alexander was standing in the archway that led onto a narrow balcony, hands jammed into his belt, feet apart, glaring at the other two. Without turning his head, he said, "You're late."

"I know," Hephaestion said. "I'm sorry." In the king's present mood, there was no point in apologies. He glanced curiously at the others, wondering what had provoked this fury.

Craterus said, "Maybe you can talk some sense into him, Hephaestion, with your privileges. It's beyond me."

"It's not a question of talking sense," Alexander said, voice rising, "it's a question of you learning to take orders."

Craterus purpled. "Orders, is it, Oh-Great-King?" He ran the Persian words together into a single epithet.

Ptolemy said, carefully controlling his own anger, "I don't see the sense in splitting the army yet, Alexander."

Hephaestion looked quickly around the room, taking in the maps spread out in front of Eumenes, the flushed, angry faces, and said, "What's going on?"

Alexander turned on his heel, slamming one hand against the nearest pillar of the archway, staring out the narrow window. Ptolemy made a gesture of disgust.

"Antipater's sent word it's too dangerous to bring his troops out of Thessaly," Craterus said through clenched teeth. "The League army's just waiting for him, it's too big, too well trained, and his men won't face it—and Alexander wants to split our men—"

Alexander's hand contracted to a fist. Controlling his voice with an effort, he said, "I intend to besiege Athens, and Thebes, if the League doesn't turn to face me before I get there. And by the gods, Antipater will come south if I tell him to."

Hephaestion whistled softly and crossed to the desk,

swinging the top map to face him. It was one of Philip's beautifully drawn maps of Attica and Boetia, stained from travelling and heavy use. He studied it carefully, though the painted lines were thoroughly familiar, and said, cautiously, "Can we afford to split the army, if the League has as many men as Antipater says?"

"That's what I've been trying to say," Craterus began, and Alexander said, still keeping a tight rein on his temper, "I tell you, the League doesn't have that large a force. Not of trained men, in any case—I've the Scouts' reports to prove it. Which is why I'm also sending a man to Antipater, to make sure my orders are carried out."

"I pity the poor bastard," Craterus muttered, loudly enough to be heard.

The king turned on him. "If you haven't anything useful to say, keep quiet."

Ptolemy pulled unhappily at his stubbled chin, then rose and crossed to the desk, fumbling through the papers for the Scouts' report. Eumenes, with the faintest of smiles, handed it to him. The brigade commander glanced again over the lines of neat, secretarial handwriting, and said, "Alexander, to choose between these reports, and Antipater's—I'd tend to choose Antipater."

Alexander, sensing that the other was wavering, said, "You read the last three dispatches Antipater sent me in Asia. Did they sound like the man my father trusted? This defeat's shaken him badly, Ptolemy, he's not seeing clearly."

Ptolemy shook his head, but he had to admit the force of the king's argument. And if that were the case, and the Scouts' reports were the reliable ones, then Alexander's plan was the best.

Alexander said coolly, "Hephaestion, I'll want you to command the army that besieges Athens. I don't care if you take the city—I'd rather you didn't, in fact.

But I want the League army to *think* that Athens is in danger. I want them to have something to argue about."

Hephaestion frowned, then understood. The Greek League had always been plagued by disputes between the representatives of the various member cities. If Athens were under siege while Alexander advanced on Thebes and Antipater moved in from Thessaly, the League generals would tie themselves in knots trying to decide on a strategy. And whatever they did—move south to raise the siege, hurry to protect Thebes, turn north to meet Antipater, turn south to face Alexander, or, most likely of all, do nothing—there would be seriously discontented troops in the army that met Alexander.

Craterus said, less unhappily than before, "I still don't like it, Alexander. The League troops are good."

Alexander smiled slowly, offering an honorable peace. "I know that, believe me. But the Foot Companions are better, and you'll have command of them."

Craterus made a wry face, recognizing the king's tactics. "What can I say to that?"

"Nothing, I trust," Alexander answered, a fraction too sharply, and turned to Ptolemy. "I want you to go to Antipater for me. I need his troops to move south— that's a direct order from me, which you'll have in writing, as well as my authority to take command of the levies if necessary."

Ptolemy's bushy eyebrows flew up. Taking command of the regent's army, even with a royal order to back him up, would be a touchy business—merely persuading Antipater of the accuracy of the king's information would be difficult enough. "And how am I to get to Pherae?" he temporized. "It's three days' hard ride to Thermopylae alone, with the League army in my way."

"You can go by sea," Eumenes said helpfully. "It's not too late in the season for coastal travel."

Ptolemy shot an annoyed glance in the secretary's direction, even as he recognized that the man was right. "If you think it's really necessary, Alexander, of course I'll go."

The king nodded. "Good. Eumenes, draft the appropriate orders, and have them for me to seal by tomorrow morning."

"Of course, Alexander," the secretary murmured, gathering his papers.

The other officers stood as well and turned to go. Alexander said, "Hephaestion."

"Alexander?" Hephaestion paused just inside the doorway. Ptolemy, one hand on the latch, sighed and pulled the door closed behind him.

"You were late," the king went on. "Was there trouble?"

Hephaestion shook his head. "No trouble, just crowds in the streets. Brauron still seems content with us."

"At least until the money runs out," Alexander said.

Hephaestion nodded and came to join the king beside the window. It overlooked the street, and the cavalry commander gave the dusty, sun-baked ground only a cursory glance before turning back to face the king. Alexander leaned against the pillar, hands now clasped behind his back, staring blindly into the street and asked, "How badly do the men want to go home?"

Hephaestion blinked, momentarily nonplussed. "Badly enough," he said, after a moment. "A lot of them have family they haven't seen, and they all want a chance to act like heroes to their wives."

Alexander shrugged, still staring into the empty street. "And so they should," he said, after a moment. "When I've settled with the League, Hephaestion, that'll be the time to go home. I'll take the married men, go with them myself."

That was unlike Alexander, who had never expressed the least desire to return to Macedon. Hephaestion looked up sharply, and Alexander grinned.

"Yes, I have other reasons, two good ones, in fact."

The king's face sobered quickly. "You've seen the dispatches from Antipater. You've also seen the letters from my mother."

Hephaestion took a few steps back into the room, hiding his expression of distaste. He disliked and distrusted the Queen Mother Olympias and knew she returned the feeling. She also hated Antipater and her letters to her son were full of complaints about the regent's incompetence. "Do you really believe any of what she says?"

Alexander's mouth twisted wryly. "Any trouble in Macedon is more than half her doing, that I do believe. But there definitely is trouble—that's why I'm sending Ptolemy to speak to Antipater, to find out just what's really going on."

Hephaestion nodded. "Have you spoken to Ptolemy about the Queen's letters?"

"No," Alexander answered, "and I don't intend to. I want to hear what he makes of the situation, without any hints from me."

Hephaestion nodded again, more slowly. He didn't envy Ptolemy his assignment, going north without a full knowledge of the situation, but he could understand the king's reasons. "You said there were two reasons?" he asked, after a moment.

"Yes." Alexander paused a moment, thinking of his own childhood, then said, "After the pages' conspiracy—it's time Philip Alexander had some real experience. He's old enough; I intend to bring him with me on my next campaign."

As the king had ordered, Ptolemy left for the north as soon as Alexander and the secretaries could draft the appropriate letters and orders. Two were for public consumption, a long, polite letter from the king to his regent, and the formal order to bring the levies south; the others were private, to be used only if Antipater proved obstinate. The packet weighed heavily on Ptolemy's mind through the first days of the uncomfortable sea journey, until the seas grew too rough and even Ptolemy took to his bunk, quite seasick. Nearchus's chosen captain, a stocky, dark-skinned Cretan like the admiral, took an insane pleasure in the storm, but Ptolemy, who had cursed him roundly throughout the voyage, had to admire his skill as he brought the ship safely into the unprotected harbor north of Thermopylae.

The commander of the Thermopylae garrison was waiting for them, having seen the ship and its royal markings as it came up the bay, and greeted them all with effusive warmth, promising lodgings and all the comforts of home for as long as they wished to remain. The Cretan captain, whose insanity did not extend to chancing the return voyage, cheerfully and immediately accepted, and was soon installed with one of the garrison's better hetairas. Ptolemy thanked the man politely, explained that he was sent from the king to Antipater, and asked only for a few men to supplement his own escort. The garrison commander hesitated, a strange wariness showing beneath his effusive welcome, but agreed. Ptolemy slept a single night at Thermopylae and rode out the next morning in the rain.

It rained throughout the three days it took for Ptolemy's party to reach Pherae; it was raining still when they passed under the massive carved gates into the city. Damp and chilled to the bone, Ptolemy did not question his good fortune when he was met not by Antipater but by a younger chamberlain, who apologized for the regent's absence and escorted the bodyguard to a well-warmed chamber. By the next morning, however, dry and warm again, Ptolemy began to sense a new wariness, almost a veiled hostility, among the household servants, and braced himself for trouble when he met Antipater.

The regent did not make his appearance or send

any message until well after noon. By then, Ptolemy had had to put a tight rein on his temper: Antipater unquestionably was regent, and thus second only to the king, but Ptolemy was the king's messenger, and deserving of more courtesy. When Antipater at last summoned him, Ptolemy was only just able to give the messenger the polite answer he deserved.

The regent's quarters were close and musty-smelling, shutters closed tight against the rain, a dozen smoky lamps providing what little light there was. An Illyrian slave woman had just finished mixing wine; at Antipater's querulous order, she measured out two cups, and backed from the room.

Before Ptolemy could think of a polite beginning, Antipater said, "I suppose I should be flattered it was you Alexander sent."

Ptolemy controlled himself with an effort, managed to smile smoothly as he turned to face Antipater. "Indeed, sir, it was a coveted assignment. After seven years in Asia, it's good to be even this close to home."

Antipater grunted dubiously. "I can think of a few other reasons you might covet it," he muttered.

Ptolemy decided to pretend he had not heard, and reached for his cup of wine. Antipater had aged badly in the past years, skin falling in onto the bones as though all his muscles had wasted away, a half dozen teeth gone, the fierce eyes dimmed, hands swollen and crooked. He was not yet sixty, but looked twenty years older.

Antipater nodded grimly. "Oh, it's not a pretty sight, and it's all *her* doing—like your being here. I know that, so you needn't bother lying."

"Sir?" Ptolemy said carefully, trying to capture the tone of the old days, when he had served in Antipater's brigade. Then, watching the old man's face, he abandoned the effort. He was not under Antipater's command any more, and there was nothing he could do to recall the bond that had been between them. "Antipater," he said aloud, "Alexander sent me with orders for the army, to bring them south to support him against the League. I don't know what else you're talking about, but you owe me an explanation."

Antipater's anger collapsed with surprising suddenness, and he sank back into his chair. "That's what you say," he muttered, almost to himself. "Maybe you even believe it. But it's her doing all the same."

Ptolemy seated himself across from the regent. "Whose doing?"

"Is there any other *her* in Macedon?" Antipater asked bitterly. "Olympias, that's who. And don't tell me you don't know she's been plotting against me. I've seen the reports she's sending Alexander, I know what she says, what she thinks."

That made almost too much sense for Ptolemy's taste. Olympias was ambitious—that was common knowledge throughout Greece, from Epirus to Sparta; Olympias had sent weekly dispatches to Alexander throughout the Persian campaigns, though the king had confided their contents to no one but Hephaestion, and had shown no inclination to act on them. But now, Ptolemy thought, I can guess what they said, and I think if I were Antipater I would find it hard to believe that Alexander hadn't listened to his mother. Only Alexander would send me on a mission like this without telling me Olympias had been meddling in politics again.

Aloud, he said, slowly, "Antipater, I give you my word, I know nothing of all this. Alexander sent me north from Brauron to bring you his orders and to explain what he has in mind, nothing more. I landed at Thermopylae four days ago—and a lousy journey that was, too. But it was better than going overland and risking a run in with the League army. I rode straight here, expecting none of this."

Antipater sighed, and straightened slowly. "I'm sorry, Ptolemy," he said, a little stiffly. "I beg your pardon if

I've misjudged you. But you haven't been here, haven't had to contend with the things I've had to put up with. Gods, I'd rather have fought the Persians than have to put up with her ways. She has questioned my judgment, to my face and behind my back; she has undermined my authority with my men, especially in Macedon, and with her kinsmen in Epirus—" He broke off, flushing, and said more calmly, "I won't endure it any longer, Ptolemy, and you may tell the king that from me. Either I am Regent, and my word is as the king's, or I am not, and I will retire to my own lands—which the gods know need my attention after all these years of service."

Ptolemy took a deep breath. "You can tell the king yourself, Antipater. He wants you to lead the army south."

Antipater glanced suspiciously at him. "I thought that command would go to you."

Ptolemy shook his head. "They're your men, you trained them. Who else?"

"And your position in all this?"

Ptolemy shrugged. "I'm the messenger, primarily." It was a lie, but he judged it safe enough to tell. "If you'll give me a brigade command, I'll take it, or whatever you want."

Antipater hesitated again, testing the suggestion. "Yes," he said at last, sounding almost like his old self, "I'll need you—the more experienced officers the better. So Alexander wants me to bring the army south . . . while he marches north, catch them between the two forces?" He nodded to himself. "Good enough. When does he start?"

"He'll have started already," Ptolemy said. "So how soon can your men be ready to march?"

Antipater hesitated a moment, lips moving as he calculated, then answered, "Ten days. Two weeks at the most." He saw Ptolemy's look of surprise, and added defensively, "They're scattered across Thessaly now, to spread out the demand for supplies. I wasn't anticipating a winter campaign."

Ptolemy shrugged, hoping his expression of innocence would convince the regent. Philip had campaigned in winter often enough, and Antipater had served with him then. "Who could have? Ten days is plenty of time."

Antipater nodded and rose stiffly. "I'll get my officers on this right away—and it would oblige me if you'd accept a command."

"Of course," Ptolemy murmured, and breathed a silent prayer of thanks. A brigade command would let him keep some control of the coming campaign, without constantly having to worry about offending Antipater.

"But one thing, Ptolemy." Antipater turned with his hand on the door latch. He raised his voice slightly, as though to reach some unseen listener. "I want you to know—I call on you to witness that I intend to speak to the king about the queen mother's interference in affairs that are no concern of hers. If I should die on this campaign, of sickness or of wounds, I demand you remember what I've said."

Ptolemy opened his mouth to demand an explanation, but Antipater cut him off. "And that's for *her* information as well," he said, more quietly. "You've not forgotten what a powerful witch she is."

Before Ptolemy could think of anything to say to that, Antipater nodded politely and was gone, closing the door gently behind him. Left to himself, Ptolemy leaned back in his chair and whistled soundlessly. He had not forgotten Olympias's reputation—no Macedonian could—though he was not entirely sure he believed it. But the atmosphere in the town, the sense of distrust, of anticipating disaster, even the constant, steady rain—it all had the feel of a spell, like a trail of soot from an ill-regulated lamp.

Then he shook himself again. Spell or no spell,

Olympias was much to blame for the atmosphere pervading Pherae—and for Antipater's decline. She had done her best to destroy him and he would say as much to Alexander. Ptolemy smiled rather bitterly to himself. It would do him no harm to say so, in any case: the queen mother had never liked him, suspecting—like half of Macedon—that Philip, not Lagus, was his father. He drained his wine cup, untouched until that moment, and his smile grew wider. Yes, something would have to be done about Olympias— and he was very glad that it was Alexander who would have to do it.

The main part of the army left Brauron toward the end of the month Dios, leaving only a skeleton force under Nearchus to protect the ships still in the harbor. The inhabitants of Brauron seemed genuinely sorry to see them go, and perfectly content to provide for the remaining troops. At Alexander's order, the Athenian agent was allowed to escape, to give the city plenty of time to try to recall their share of the League's army.

Two days after the agent's hasty departure, the third of the army under Hephaestion's command, including two brigades of Foot Companions, the Thessalian heavy cavalry, engineers, and most of the foreign infantry, split off from the main body, heading west and north by easy stages toward Athens. Despite their leisurely progress, Hephaestion's force reached Athens without opposition, and faced only a token force outside the city walls. It was routed with the loss of perhaps a dozen Macedonians, and Hephaestion settled in for the siege. Diades, the short, balding senior engineer in charge of the siege machinery, had protested vehemently at not being allowed to mount a proper assault, and he took a bitter pleasure in selecting the most spectacularly useless sites for his engines. Hephaestion finally had to warn him not to be

quite so ironic in his choices, for fear of giving the
game away—after all, the Athenians had to believe
their city would be attacked.

The main part of the army moved north into Boetia,
meeting no resistance until they were two days' march
short of Thebes. A troop of Acarnanians, that city's
contribution to the League, ran headlong into a squad
of Scouts. The Scouts, outnumbered, fought their way
free, but the next day Craterus's brigade, supported
by six squadrons of Companion Cavalry, made contact
again. The Acarnanian commander, himself badly
outnumbered this time, made a stand nonetheless,
and was decisively beaten. From the prisoners, Alexander learned that the League was behaving exactly as
he had hoped—the Acarnanian commander spoke with
real bitterness of councils devoted to insults and poli-
ticking rather than strategy—and was moving its army
slowly southeast to cut him off from Thebes. Alexander slowed his own progress even further, and sent
more parties of Scouts out ahead of the main army.

The League commanders chose to make their stand
in a broad plain some twenty stadia north of the river
that marked the border of Boetia, less than a day's
march from Thebes itself. Alexander's advance guard
had held the fords for some days; now the king brought
the main body up quickly, before the League could
shift to some more advantageous ground. The chosen
field was harvest stubbled, but flat enough to let cavalry maneuver easily—and the Companion Cavalry
was far superior to anything the League could muster.
It was the perfect battleground for Alexander's pur-
poses, and he accepted the League's stupidity as a gift
from the gods.

Gathered in the outer section of the king's massive,
three-roomed tent, the generals studied the hastily
amended maps and listened for a final time to the
Scout commanders' descriptions of the League's chosen ground. The reports were more than satisfactory;

the clipped voices began to take on a note of pleased anticipation. Listening, Alexander smiled and leaned across the map, gathering their attention with a glance.

"Craterus, you'll have overall command of the phalanx," he began. "Advance obliquely, left flank refused; outflank them on the right if you can—I want to draw the Athenians out of line, make an opening for the Companions. The Scouts and the Agrianians will screen our advance."

Heads nodded all around the table, recognizing familiar tactics, and Coenus reached for another cup of wine. His brigade would be in the center of the phalanx, with nothing to worry him but the necessity to keep formation and kill Greeks.

"I'll take command of the Companions myself," Alexander went on. "Neoptolemus, the hypaspists will anchor our left flank. You'll be facing the Theban line, so I expect you'll see some hard fighting."

Neoptolemus nodded, his sun-browned face very sober. This was only his second campaign as the hypaspists' commander, and his first major battle under the king's eye. He leaned forward again to study the map, as though a perfect knowledge of the land would still his fear. Alexander gave him an encouraging smile—the hypaspist had proved his worth a dozen times over as a battalion commander—and turned his attention to the cavalry. "Menidas, Erigyius, your men will screen the left flank."

Erigyius, who commanded the ethnically diverse, lightly armed Allied Horse, stirred faintly, and said, "The League cavalry is better armed than my men."

Before the king could answer, Menidas said, "You screen the hypaspists. My men can hold the cavalry." He tugged at his scented beard, and did not add the rest of his thought: his mercenaries could hold the League horse, but could not break it. Erigyius nodded, not happily.

Alexander, reading their thoughts, said, "That's all I

ask." He glanced again around the circle of faces, picking out the infantry brigadiers. "Craterus, Meleager, your brigades will hold the center of the line. Polyperchon, your brigade will link with the hypaspists on the left." He paused theatrically, anticipating the reaction he knew his next order would produce. "Coenus, you'll link with Theagenes on the right. The Sacred Band will hold the right flank."

There was a sudden, profound silence in the dimly lit compartment, a silence so deep that the generals could hear the challenge of a sentry somewhere on the perimeter. The Macedonians exchanged disbelieving looks, but before any one of them could decide to speak, Theagenes cleared his throat.

"I thank you, King Alexander, for the honor you show us. We will not fail you."

Craterus rolled his eyes at that. "Alexander," he said abruptly, and made a disgusted face as the other generals shifted away from him, visibly disassociating themselves from whatever he was going to say. "Alexander, I don't doubt Theagenes's loyalty—" he saw the king's face darken, and added grudgingly, "—or the rest of his men. If they wanted to betray us, they'd've done it already, I grant you that. But they're not Foot Companions, and they're not trained to the phalanx. I doubt the wisdom of asking them to hold the right flank."

Theagenes said, stung, "We've been following your tactics since we joined you."

"Seven years," Polyperchon said, neutrally, his eyes on the king. Alexander valued Craterus for his willingness to say the unspeakable, but sometimes the brigade commander went too far.

Alexander said, "The Sacred Band has earned the right to the place of honor. This is as much their fight as mine." There was a note of finality in his voice that silenced all further opposition. He waited a moment, and then, satisfied, calmly began to outline possible contingencies, sketching out his orders for each situation. Slowly, and then with increasing concentration, the generals gave their attention to the problem at hand, each one forming his plans for his own men. The commanders fought in line with their men; once the battle was fully joined there would be no opportunity for further orders. Alexander had the double gift of knowing what orders to give and then knowing how to trust his men.

The morning of the battle dawned cool, with a brisk wind that blew scraps of clouds across the sun. The wind would make it impossible for the archers to do much damage to the League line; Alexander stood in the doorway of his tent for a long moment, testing its strength before deciding against any changes in the battle order. The soldiers, hunching over a cold breakfast, felt the wind, too, and prepared themselves for an even harder fight.

The last squad of Scouts rode in as the king was snatching a hasty breakfast. Alexander listened to their captain's report—the League troops had stood to arms all night, as afraid of mass desertions as they were of a Macedonian surprise attack—and ordered the good news passed along to his generals while he himself made the requisite sacrifices. When he was done, and the omens had been judged favorable, trumpets sounded to begin the march. The men formed up by unit, grumbling to take the edge off their fear, but as the king rode the length of the column to take his place at the head of his own squadron of Companion Cavalry, the complaints turned to cheers. Alexander acknowledged the cheering as he spurred past, the sound sparking the familiar excitement, an ecstatic joy almost indistinguishable from terror.

As the Scouts had reported, the League army was already drawn up in battle array, letting the Macedonians take the initiative. Well screened by cavalry and the light infantry, the Foot Companions shifted ponder-

ously from column to obliquely angled phalanx, the
Sacred Band on the right flank leading the way. Alexander eyed the League cavalry massing against his
left, and dispatched two more Companion squadrons
to reinforce Menidas.

The light infantry, their work done, fell back against
the phalanx, which opened ranks slightly to let them
through, then closed up again and moved on. For a
moment, the League line held steady, and then, almost imperceptibly at first, the Athenian battalions
began to shift to their left, trying to keep from being
outflanked. The commander of the Leucan battalion
immediately to their right cursed them soundly, and
lengthened his own line in a vain attempt to keep
contact.

The Athenian cavalry, which had been hanging back
in some confusion, rallied at the sight of the danger to
their fellow citizens, and swept in toward the Macedonian flank. Alexander had been waiting for that
move. He lifted his lance in signal and gave the war
cry, setting spurs to his horse in the same instant. The
Companions exuberantly picked up the cry, surging
forward after the king. Alexander shouted again, giving himself up completely to the terrible excitement
of the battle. He forced his own horse in among the
Athenians, stabbing at their leader. The lance's heavy
point slid uselessly across armor; the king shortened
his grip and struck again. This time the point sank
home, wedging itself deep in bone. With an effort,
Alexander wrenched it loose and struck again, hardly
noticing when something struck his armored shin. The
lance point skittered across an Athenian shield and
shattered against its metal rim. Alexander threw away
the broken shaft, and drew his sword.

In the center of the phalanx, Craterus heard the
king's first shout, and raised his own war cry. The
Foot Companions surged forward all along the phalanx, forcing the League line back a few paces before

the hoplites steadied. Craterus, cursing steadily under his breath, could see gaps developing in the League line where the flanking maneuver had pulled the Athenians away, but could not risk breaking his own line to exploit them. He hunched his body to take a Megaran spearpoint on his own shield, and thrust hard with his fifteen foot sarissa. The point slid, then caught. Craterus pushed hard, grunting with the effort, and felt something give. He stumbled forward a step in spite of himself, the Megaran spear snapping under his weight, but recovered in an instant, wrenching his sarissa free. To either side, the Foot Companions shifted to keep contact. Then there was a sudden flurry of movement to his left: the hoplite whose spear had broken darted under the Macedonian spears, sword drawn. Instinctively, Craterus lifted his shield to parry the blow, but he wasn't quick enough. The sword smashed into his helmet, slicing away the cheekpiece and carving deep into his jaw. Half stunned by the blow, Craterus fell back into the shelter of his shield, barely managing to keep his sarissa lowered at the enemy, and saw the file-leader to his left drop his own sarissa to hack at the Megaran. The Megaran went down, and a spearpoint from the rear ranks made certain of him. Blinking away the tears of pain, Craterus steadied himself, and thrust again at the enemy line.

Then, as suddenly as it always happened, the Athenian cavalry shattered, first the rear-rankers and then the point-men throwing away their weapons in a blind rush to get away. Alexander shouted hoarsely for the nearest squadron leader to pursue, and turned his own attention back to the locked infantry. For a moment, his vision was blocked as the pursuing squadron swirled past him, and then he saw, quite clearly, how the battle lay. The Sacred Band, fighting with almost superhuman fury, had failed to turn the Athenian flank, but their effort had opened gaps in the League line. Neither Craterus nor Polyperchon, hard pressed to support the hypaspists on his left, had been able to exploit any of the breaks. Alexander raised his sword again, gathering his squadron, and drove for the nearest gap. The League troops held for a few moments longer, then broke, the line fragmenting into its component parts. The Macedonians surged forward in pursuit.

The battle itself took less than two hours, but the pursuit lasted until sundown, and it was fully dark before the last of the Companion squadrons straggled in, wearing the expressions of men both drained and sated by the killing. Torches still moved across the plain: the remainder of the League army searching for its dead. The Macedonian army had lost only a hundred men, both dead and wounded; the League had not yet begun to count its losses.

Alexander waited in his tent to receive the delegations from each of the League cities. Now that the battle was over, the slaughter disgusted him—it had been a waste, completely unnecessary if only the League had kept its treaty.

"Corinth, Megara, Leucas, Euboea, a couple of Laconian towns," he said aloud, to kill his own thoughts. Those were the contingents whose commanders had appeared to ask for their dead, acknowledging defeat, and to beg preliminary terms for their cities. "And Athens has asked for her dead. That leaves—who?"

Erigyius, whose men had been as involved in the pursuit as the Companion Cavalry, did not seem to hear, staring into the flame of the nearest lamp. Both Meleager and Polyperchon looked uncomfortable, and Neoptolemus managed a lopsided grin. Craterus, still holding a bloodied cloth to the sword cut that had nearly broken his jaw, jerked his head toward the corner where Theagenes sat, Menander waiting at his shoulder.

"Them," Craterus said indistinctly, and relapsed, wincing, into silence.

"Do what you want with Thebes, Alexander," Theagenes said, without looking up. "Burn it; we'll help." Despite his effort to sound merely angry, the words came out anguished, betraying the bitter loyalty beneath his fury.

The Theban's words seemed to fill the tent. Craterus looked away, embarrassed, and Coenus mumbled something incoherent, his voice trailing off as he realized how inadequate his words would be. Alexander said, gently, "Theagenes—"

Before he could finish, a page pushed back the doorway of the tent, coughing apologetically. "Beg pardon, sire, but another delegation's here. From Thebes."

"Show them in," the king said.

The Theban commanders were still in their armor, clothing torn and stained beneath it. The leader, a stocky, greying man with a dirty bandage wrapped around one arm, gave Theagenes a single bitter glance, then turned his attention to Alexander.

"King Alexander," he said formally, "I am Xenoclides son of Hipparchus, commander of the Theban brigade of the Greek League." He did not introduce the two younger men flanking him, and Alexander did not ask their names. "I have come to concede the field and to beg for the return of our dead."

"You shall have it," Alexander answered.

Xenoclides took a deep breath, his eyes again straying to Theagenes, still sitting motionless in his corner. "I am also empowered to ask terms for the city."

Alexander paused, following the direction of the Theban's gaze. "I have said before," he said slowly, "that I am not the only one who has been hurt by Thebes's treachery—nor am I the one who has been worst injured. The Sacred Band, who came willingly with me to Asia, believing the city that bred them to be as honorable as themselves, has had its honor called into question by your actions. I ask Theagenes what should be done with Thebes."

For a long moment, Theagenes sat frozen, staring at the king. Alexander was not the man to pose impossible choices, not when a man had served him well, so the question had to be precisely what it seemed, a mark of trust, a gift, and a chance for revenge.

"Alexander," he said slowly, "if it were my choice alone, I would say burn the city, do with it what you will. But I recognize that not everyone in the city—certainly not the women and children, probably not my kinsmen, or my men's—supported breaking the treaty, and I doubt they should be punished. Nor, in all fairness, should Thebes be punished worse than any other city—and never more than Athens!" He took a deep breath. "Therefore, I ask you, King Alexander, to spare the city—on terms that they hand over the men who broke the treaty, which is no more than you've asked of other states, and that you garrison the citadel with your troops." He glanced at the Macedonian generals, and added, more urgently, "I don't ask to hold that garrison myself—in fact, I beg you to give it to someone else. I am afraid I would be too harsh on my countrymen."

Alexander nodded slowly. The Theban's words had crystallized something that had been in the back of his mind for some days, a possible solution to the constant danger of revolt in Greece. It would take a Greek to deal properly with the city states—Antipater had proved that he could not, whether or not it was because of interference from Olympias. Theagenes, with the Sacred Band to back him, was a logical choice for the part—and the answer he had just given should be enough to convince even Craterus of the Theban's loyalty.

"I find the terms wisely chosen," he said aloud. "And Thebes?"

Xenoclides said bitterly, "Thebes has little choice in the matter. Yes, we accept."

"So be it," Alexander said. "Xenoclides, take your dead. I will send to the city tomorrow, to settle the terms more permanently. Is that agreeable to you?"

Xenoclides nodded jerkily. "Yes, King Alexander, it will do."

The next days were spent in a whirl of activity. The League cities, warned by fugitives of the defeat, sent representatives to settle the peace terms. Alexander, who had been expecting them, asked only for money beyond the terms he had already settled with the field commanders. Megara alone saw this as a sign of weakness, and showed an inclination to repudiate her general's agreement. Alexander sent Craterus south with several battalions of Foot Companions, and the city hastily came to terms. At the same time, the king sent messengers south and east to Athens, informing Hephaestion of the victory and of his own plans for the future. Hephaestion read through the scroll, filed Alexander's long-term plans in a distant corner of his mind, and ordered Perdiccas to release the Athenian runner captured three days previously. The Athenians let the man into the city, jeering half-heartedly at the Macedonians escorting him, and Hephaestion settled back in his tent to wait for Athens to ask for a parley.

The signal came even more quickly than he had expected—the Athenians had had other messengers as well, bringing word of the defeat—but Hephaestion left the preliminary arrangements to Perdiccas. It would never do for the Athenians to guess that this capitulation—and a few demagogues' heads—were what Alexander was really after, not the destruction of the city.

It seemed an age before there was a cough outside the cavalry commander's tent, and one of Perdiccas's troopers appeared in the doorway.

"Beg pardon, general," he said, "but the Athenians have asked for a parley. General Perdiccas wants you."

Hephaestion nodded, tucking his helmet under his arm. "Lead on."

Perdiccas had chosen to confront the Athenian messengers on the siege line itself, almost in the shadow of the largest of the stone-throwers set up opposite the main gate. Hephaestion raised an eyebrow at that. It was a nice touch, keeping the envoys in mind of what could happen if they refused to make peace, but unnecessary—almost certainly so unless either he or Perdiccas made some serious blunder, since the Athenians themselves had come to ask for peace.

Perdiccas lifted a hand in greeting as the cavalry commander approached the line. His thin, mobile face was still, kept so only with an effort. Hephaestion returned the gesture, wondering what the brigade commander found so amusing.

"Hephaestion," Perdiccas said. "These are the Athenian envoys: Lysias son of Philoneus, Nichomachus son of Antiphon, and Asteius son of Phrynion, some of whom you may know already."

Hephaestion murmured a polite acknowledgement, trying to remember. He had only been in Athens once before, and that had been during Philip's reign, on Philip's business, but one name did sound familiar. Philoneus had been one of the politicians who had opposed Demosthenes, and therefore supported alliance, or at least accommodation, with Philip. This Lysias looked young enough to be that Philoneus's son, but there was no way to be certain of that.

"General Hephaestion," the oldest of the three—Asteius—said gravely. "We are here with the approval of the people of Athens—"

"At the request of the people of Athens," Lysias murmured gently, and Nichomachus grumbled something under his breath.

"—to sue for peace with Alexander," Asteius finished smoothly.

That little exchange defined the three of them neatly, Hephaestion thought. Lysias was part of an anti-Demosthenes faction, all right, and probably the son of Philip's agent; Nichomachus was a member of a faction that still supported the demagogues; and Asteius, then, was some grave, politically neutral elder, chosen for his ability to keep the peace between the other two members of his embassy as well as for his abilities as a speaker.

"As you surely know," the cavalry commander said carefully, "the king himself is elsewhere, but I have his authority to speak for him."

Asteius nodded slowly, a gesture that was almost a bow. "We accept you as his lawful representative and we ask for terms."

"These are the terms I am empowered to offer," Hephaestion said. "Alexander offers to respect the rights of Athens, under the terms of the Greek League as agreed at Corinth in the first year of his reign; to return any Athenian prisoners in exchange for due compensation; and to return any Athenian dead—on the condition that Athens herself punish those politicians who have been open enemies of Alexander and of Macedon—Demosthenes in particular—or turn said demagogues over to the king to be punished. Alexander asks this knowing that the people of Athens are not his enemies, but they have been misled by power-seeking politicians." That was something of a lie—the people of Athens, lately, were easily swayed by any plausible orator—but it would allow the more reliable factions within the city to save face.

"We would be glad to see our prisoners returned," Asteius said sadly. He looked and felt suddenly very old: he had sons with the Athenian army, and the messengers had brought no word of either. "And our dead."

Hephaestion nodded.

Nichomachus made a disgusted face. "We've no choice but to agree to terms," he said irritably. "Though what you mean by 'open enemies'. . . ." He glared at the Macedonians, challenging them both with a look. "I've spoken against Alexander, and against Philip, for a dozen years now. Does that make my head a trophy for Alexander's tent?"

Before Hephaestion could answer that, Lysias said, "And spoke against breaking our agreement with the League, once it had been made." He fixed his eyes on Hephaestion, the illusion of youth dropping away. "General Hephaestion, let's be plain. It's Demosthenes you want—maybe one or two others, but most of all Demosthenes. Well, we don't have him. He was with the army—though I doubt he stayed with them for long—but when word came that Alexander was in Greece, he and his closest associates fled, no one knew where." He took a deep breath and reached into the folds of his himation, ignoring both the whispered curse from Nichomachus and the sudden tension in Perdiccas's shoulders, to produce a crumpled roll of papyrus. "This arrived three days ago—how the messenger got through your lines, I don't know, but I think you'll find the information of use to you."

"How can you betray him, Lysias?" Nichomachus demanded.

"He's always wanted to die for the city, hasn't he?" Lysias answered. "Now he gets his wish." He glanced again at Hephaestion. "Demosthenes's head for Athens's safety is a good bargain for us."

Hephaestion accepted the battered scroll, unrolled it carefully, and scanned the crabbed letters. The message was not addressed to Lysias—and I won't ask how he got it, the cavalry commander thought—but the intended recipient, one Simmias, was obviously in Demosthenes's confidence. Hephaestion skimmed through the text of the letter, then let the scroll fall closed again. Perdiccas, struggling to read over the cavalry commander's shoulder, cursed him in a whisper.

"I thank you for this, Lysias," Hephaestion said, and turned to Asteius. "Sir, if you allow, I will take this as evidence of Athens's willingness to make peace with Alexander, and to rejoin the Greek League."

Asteius nodded slowly. "As you wish, General Hephaestion. We accept, for Athens, the terms you outlined for us—but as it grows late, may we defer the discussion of which of our people Alexander considers his open enemies until tomorrow?"

"Of course," Hephaestion answered. Perdiccas nodded impatiently, his attention still on the scroll.

The envoys took their departure formally, and then, as soon as they were out of earshot, Perdiccas demanded, "Let me see the letter—and what was in it, anyway?"

Hephaestion ignored him, beckoning to the nearest trooper. "Find Polydamus, have him meet us in my tent," he ordered. Handing the scroll to Perdiccas, he said, "There wasn't a chance, was there? Demosthenes has gone to Syracuse—apparently he's made connections there, had this plan all worked out in advance, expecting the League army to lose once Alexander came back. A truly noble man."

"Syracuse," Perdiccas said, and whistled.

"Exactly," Hephaestion answered. The Athenian envoys had reached the shadow of their own gate; there was no need, even in the strictest etiquette, for the Macedonians to remain waiting any longer. The cavalry commander turned away, drawing his cloak about his shoulders. Perdiccas followed, shaking his head unhappily.

"Syracuse," he said again. "That'd be worse than Tyre to take."

"If we have to besiege it," Hephaestion said. He smiled suddenly, with more confidence than he felt.

"Do you think the Syracusans will have much love for a stray Athenian demagogue?"

"He has a knack for popularity," Perdiccas said dryly.

The trooper had done his work promptly; Polydamus was sitting in the antechamber of the tent, the Eyyptian body-slave pouring wine. Hephaestion nodded a greeting, and extended the scroll toward the slave. The Egyptian set aside the wine jar and took it, glancing curiously at his master.

"Make me a fair copy of that," Hephaestion said, "no, two fair copies, as quickly as you can." He did not need to add the usual injunction to silence. The slave nodded, and settled himself in a corner of the tent, balancing a writing board on his lap.

"What's happened, general?" Polydamus asked.

Hephaestion grimaced. "Demosthenes has fled to Syracuse and seems likely to be welcomed there with open arms. I want you to ride to Alexander at once—leave as soon as you can, as soon as Psintaes finishes making your copy of the letter."

Polydamus nodded, and Hephaestion went on, thoughtfully, "You might also make plans to go to Syracuse yourself, see if you can't persuade them that sheltering Demosthenes—the gods forbid they should consider making an alliance against Alexander—might be hazardous for the city. That might ultimately prove as effective as a siege, and a lot cheaper."

"Send him with a few talents, that'll get the job done," Perdiccas said.

Hephaestion nodded. "That had also occurred to me," he said. "If Alexander doesn't mention that possibility, Polydamus, tell him we suggested it—but I think he will."

Polydamus nodded again. "This'll be hard on the men," he said quietly. "They were counting on an end to the fighting."

Hephaestion made a face, but before he could say anything the slave had risen from his corner, holding out a fresh piece of papyrus. Hephaestion accepted it, glancing quickly at the text, then handed it to Polydamus, who took it cautiously, careful not to smudge the ink.

"Go now," Hephaestion said.

"At once, general," Polydamus answered, and was gone.

Perdiccas said, after a moment, "He's right, you know, the men won't like it."

"Alexander was planning to go with the married men to Pella once things were settled with Thebes," Hephaestion said. "This needn't stop him—any of us can handle collecting an invasion fleet, especially if Syracuse is willing to talk. And as for our people— they aren't stupid. They'll be able to see as well as we can that we can't say Greece is pacified until Demosthenes is dead."

The other man shrugged. "I suppose you're right."

"I'd better be," Hephaestion answered, and Perdiccas nodded, grinning.

"Yes, you had."

The king received Hephaestion's message and the captured letter philosophically. He had expected further trouble from Demosthenes when interrogation of the Athenian prisoners revealed that the demagogue had abandoned the League army as soon as it became clear Alexander himself was marching north to meet them. He had not, however, expected anything quite so dramatic as an attempt to ally with Syracuse, and could not accept the threat as a serious one. Syracuse, with its long tradition of rule-by-tyrant, was not likely to listen to any democrat, and especially not an Athenian one. Nonetheless, he ordered Polydamus to join the force sent south to assure Corinth's cooperation. If Demosthenes had reached Syracuse safely, someone in Corinth was likely to have heard of it. Once the sailing season opened, Polydamus would cross to Sicily and open negotiations with the city.

Antipater's belated arrival with the northern levies brought more important matters to the fore. Demanding an immediate audience with the king, he poured out his complaint against the queen mother, accusing her of every crime from political meddling and malice to witchcraft. Alexander listened, shocked in spite of himself by the regent's decline, then consulted Ptolemy. The bodyguard told him bluntly what he had seen in Pherae, sparing no details; the king took less than a day to make the inevitable decision. Hephaestion and Ptolemy could easily handle what was left to do to reestablish harmony in the League and to set up Theagenes and Antipater as joint regents. Only the king could correct the problem in Macedon. Regretfully, Alexander announced that he would personally bring the married men back to Macedon to spend the last months of winter and the early spring with their families.

CHAPTER 5:

Pella, late winter (Dystros) to Syracuse, late summer (Gorpiaios), 30 imperial (326 B.C., 427 A.U.C.)

The king's decision was a popular one. The army returned to Macedon in triumph, collecting a train of followers on the way. On the last stage of the march, from Aegae, where Alexander sacrificed at his father's tomb, to Pella itself, the column disintegrated into a Dionysian procession. It took five days to cover a distance that should only have taken two days' travel, as families who had not seen their soldier-kinsmen for six or seven years came to celebrate their return. Anticipating their arrival, the king had ordered stores of food, and especially of wine, brought in the baggage train from Aegae. He issued both freely to all comers, and the wine, at least, eased the shock as families met again as strangers.

More than that, the wine fueled the celebration. The soldiers decked themselves in the plunder they had taken from Persia, and gave still more away, to their own women and to the women who came to join the festival procession. As the straggling column came within sight of Pella's gleaming walls, the crowds grew

larger still. The country people lined the roads, bringing food and more wine and flowers, cheering the
army as it passed. More people spilled from the main
gate of Pella itself, and others leaned from the walls,
shouting their welcome, some chanting the old hymns
of rejoicing and thanksgiving. The noise was like a
solid wall; the horses, battle-hardened though they
were, snorted uneasily, flattening their ears against
their skulls. Alexander reined in, absently soothing his
nervous gelding, smiling at the waiting crowd. Coenus
watched the crowds with less pleasure. Philip, to whose
memory the king had sacrificed not a week before,
had been murdered during just such a triumph. Then
he shook away the thought. Today, at least, the king
had no enemies in Pella.

"Alexander?" Meleager forced his horse through the
crowd, grinning hugely. Seated on the saddle pad in
front of him was a boy of seven or eight, whose wide
mouth and slightly tilted eyes marked him unmistakably as Meleager's son. The boy had been born while
he was on campaign, and had never been formally
acknowledged. His mother, well-dressed but with a
rather plain, wary face, pushed her way through the
crowd after him; seeing her, Meleager added, "My
son Amyntor, Alexander."

The woman sighed deeply, the worried lines easing
from her face. There could not have been a more
public acceptance of paternity.

"A brave horseman already," Alexander said.

Coenus said, urgently, "Alexander, let me take a
squad, clear a path for you. They're blocking the gate
completely."

The king shook his head. "They'll let me pass," he
said, and spurred forward. His gilded body armor and
the double-ribboned diadem he wore in place of a
helmet were unmistakable even at a distance. At his
approach, the crowd set up another cheer and surged
forward, pressing close around the horses' legs. Alex-

ander smiled, and reached out to accept the wreath offered him by a pretty, dark-haired girl, giving himself up to the adulation.

Coenus cursed, and shouted, "Neoptolemus."

The hypaspist commander fought his way through the crowd, his mare dancing skittishly, completely unnerved by the friendly shouting. He had made the mistake of choosing a horse not yet battle-hardened. He curbed it savagely, and said, "What is it?"

Abruptly, Craterus had joined them, his horse under perfect control. "We've got to help Alexander," he began, and gave the grimace that passed for a grin since the Megaran laid open his face. "Whether he wants it or not."

Coenus nodded. "My thought exactly."

"Neoptolemus, if you can't keep that mare in hand, sell her," Craterus snapped, swinging in his saddle to assess the resources at hand. "Meleager, I need you."

The hypaspist commander flushed deeply, but had to admit the justice of Craterus's complaint. The mare would panic if he tried to force her into the crowd and do more harm than good. Meleager tightened his hold on his son, and said, "Very well, Craterus." He did not look back as his wife was swallowed by the cheering crowd.

At Craterus's gesture, the other three officers began to work their way into the crowd that surrounded the king, using the weight of the well-trained horses to force a passage. At last Craterus had forced his way to the king's side. He shouted, his words swallowed completely in the uproar and reached for the king's bridle. Alexander started at the movement, his eyes wide and excited, and automatically began to swing his horse away before he realized who was beside him. Then some of the excitement faded from his face, and, very slowly, the column began to move forward again.

The crowds were just as thick in the city itself. The king and his officers moved forward at a snail's pace,

their progress frequently halted altogether by the press
of people. They were deafened by the shouting and
half buried in the hail of flowers thrown from windows
and roofs, but at last they reached the palace itself.
The crowd pressed close there, too; it was all the
palace guard could do to keep the steps clear. Craterus
swore loudly—there was no place for the king to
dismount—and began to turn to clear a space, but
Alexander waved him back. With a shout half of warning and half of sheer pleasure, the king kicked his
horse forward, urging it through the line of palace
guards and up the stairs to the broad porch. There
was a renewed outburst of cheering, and the gelding
danced nervously, its unshod hooves clattering loudly
on the marble tiles. Alexander quieted it, and one of
the guards came running to hold its bridle. The king
dismounted easily and came forward to greet his son.

Olympias waited with the boy, radiating disapproval.
She had dressed imperially, as always, her gold-
bordered himation pulled tight over a crimson gown
spangled with tiny gold stars. Even at the age of fifty
she still had a maenad's figure. The sunlight glittered
from her jewelry, from the huge carved garnet that lay
in the hollow of her throat, whitening her skin by
contrast, and from the diadem, a heracles-knot on a
double band of woven gold, that confined her high-
piled hair.

Alexander took a deep breath, surprised by such an
open challenge, and embraced his mother. There were
more cheers from the crowd; under the cover of the
shouts, Alexander said, "I want to talk to you, Mother."
Their embrace was what it had always been, Olympias's
iron will tangible beneath the incongruous softness of
a woman's body.

"And I want to talk to you, Alexander," Olympias
answered, pulling away. "But you're forgetting your
son." She smiled as she always had when hiding a

rebuke, and Alexander turned his attention to the boy.

The boy looked back at him with hugely solemn eyes. He looked younger than the eleven years Alexander knew he possessed, dwarfed by his princely clothes, and the king was unaccountably disconcerted.

"Philip Alexander," he said aloud. "I'm glad to see you, now you're grown. You wouldn't remember me, I think. You were not yet two when last I saw you."

"No, Father," the boy said in a colorless voice.

"His name is Alexander," Olympias said, in the same moment, still softly.

Alexander glanced sharply at her. "It was Philip Alexander when I acknowledged him," he said, and could not keep an edge out of his voice.

"But he prefers to be called Alexander," Olympias said, and set a jeweled hand on the boy's shoulder. Philip Alexander darted a single glance at it, and looked away again, only his eyes moving in his solemn face. "Don't you, Alexander?" Olympias went on, and the king saw her hand tighten fractionally.

The boy's eyes lifted in sudden adult appeal. It was like a scene from his own childhood, Alexander realized, and felt a sudden rush of sympathy for Philip. This was what Olympias had done to him all those years, to them both, pitting father against son to her own ultimate advantage. "It's my wish that Philip Alexander bear both names," he said, forestalling any answer from the boy, "honoring Philip as well as me. But in any case it's a matter we'll settle between us, Philip Alexander and I. For now, we'll go in."

Without waiting for Olympias's answer, he lifted one hand in a final acknowledgement of the crowd's cheers, gathered his officers with a glance, and turned to pass through the carved doorway.

"As you wish, Alexander," Olympias answered, still smiling slightly, and stood aside to let him precede her through the door. "There's wine and a light meal waiting in my chambers. I thought you might like to join me there, and tell me everything about your conquests. The chamberlains will see to your friends."

"Of course, Mother," the king answered, grimly. "I'm sure we have a great deal to say to each other."

The women's quarters were much as they had always been. The afternoon sunlight streamed in from the central garden, falling just short of the loom that filled one wall. The frame was never empty, though Olympias herself never set hand to it. One of the women had begun an intricately patterned piece, but it had barely progressed beyond the first few rows of rosettes and waves. The door of the inner room stood partly open, just enough to offer a glimpse of the painted cabinet that was said to house the queen mother's magical paraphernalia.

Alexander took his seat opposite his mother as one of the slave girls poured wine, studying Olympias's face. She had aged well, visibly disdaining any attempt to conceal it; her skin fell in on strong, proud bones. There was no grey at all in her dark hair. Olympias smiled slowly, well aware of his scrutiny, and gestured toward the table a second slave set between them.

"I hope you'll find these still to your taste, after the delicacies of the Persian court." She was watching the king as closely as he watched her, assessing the changes. Alexander's face had hardened and thinned, revealing the strong bones beneath the boyish roundness. There was a new maturity in the set of his full lips, and new shadows in his deep-set eyes.

"I haven't changed much, Mother," Alexander said, politely acknowledging her examination. "I have a great many things to settle with you, so many that I'd prefer to start now."

"Of course, Alexander," Olympias said. "What is it you want?"

"These are private matters, Mother," Alexander said.

"You will want to dismiss your women." Before she could answer, he added, "You may go, too, Philip Alexander. I will see you again at dinner."

Olympias gestured sharply at her attendants, then got herself under control. "Give your grandmother a kiss before you go, Alexander, and be sure you come to me before dinner so I can dress you properly."

Philip Alexander gave his father a swift, unreadable glance, but submitted dutifully to Olympias's embrace. When both he and the women were gone—and Alexander felt reasonably confident that none of the women were lingering behind the closed doors—the king leaned forward in his chair.

Olympias forestalled him. "What is all this nonsense about business, that you can't even have a bite to eat before you begin? And after all the effort Elaphion made to please you."

Alexander refused to allow her to seize control of the conversation so easily. "You know perfectly well what I'm talking about, Mother," he said. "You've done your best to undermine Antipater's authority— which I granted to him, and not to you."

Olympias leaned back in her chair, her back still very straight, both hands resting on the arms of the chair. She looked like a statue of Athena seated in judgment, though Athena was not one of the gods she worshipped. "Antipater is an old woman, more so than I am, incompetent, and jealous of anyone cleverer than himself. He's never liked me, so naturally he blames his failures on me, and not his own stupidity."

"He's a good general," Alexander began.

Olympias laughed. "Who lost everything you'd won in Greece—and then blames that on me. I understand he's asked to be relieved of his responsibilities; I think you should do it."

Alexander raised an eyebrow, wondering who had informed Olympias of Antipater's decision. "Did you have someone in mind for the post?"

Olympias shook her head. "No. That is the king's decision." The lines at the corners of her dark eyes tightened slightly, a faint betrayal of an inner laughter. There were very few suitable candidates for the post of regent; she knew them all, and how to control each one.

"I'm relieved to hear you say so," Alexander said, guessing her thoughts. "It's my decision, then, to keep Antipater as regent, though I shall appoint Theagenes to help him keep the peace in Greece itself."

"A wonderful pairing," Olympias jeered. "An old woman and a Greek to rule Macedon."

"Better than an old woman alone," Alexander answered. Olympias flushed angrily and the king went on, "Antipater remains my regent, and I won't have his authority questioned by anyone. If necessary, Mother, I will give my commanders instructions to ignore any orders from you." Such an order would do no practical good—Olympias was adept at working through others when she had to—but the threat of such humiliation might at least make her act more circumspectly. "Now, to more important matters. I intend to take Philip Alexander with me on the coming campaign."

Olympias looked up sharply. "He's a child—he's not yet ten."

"Eleven at the new year, Mother," Alexander answered. "Old enough."

"I'm surprised you remember his age," Olympias said spitefully. "But then, you've overcome your aversion to women—or at least to marriage, since then."

Alexander ignored the jibe, and said, shrugging, "It's necessary to secure the succession."

"Half-Persian brats to rule over Macedon? Unlikely."

"They could rule very well in Persia, I think," Alexander observed.

Olympias waved a hand in dismissal. "You've yet to get them," she said, "and I doubt you shall." There was something about her voice, less taunting than contemplative, that made Alexander look up quickly.

"Don't threaten me, Mother."

Olympias merely looked at him, all innocence except for her unreadable eyes. Alexander matched her stare for stare, and for the first time, it was Olympias who looked away first. "I intend to bring Philip Alexander with me to Syracuse," the king said after a moment. "At least for now, he is my heir—"

"All the more reason not to risk him," Olympias said, feebly.

"—and it's time he began learning to rule," Alexander went on as though she had not spoken.

"You didn't learn to be what you are from Philip."

Alexander smiled. It was a creditable imitation of his mother's expression of triumph, startling on his younger face. "Nor did I learn it from you, Mother." He rose to his feet, forestalling Olympias's bitter answer, and bowed politely. "I'm glad we've had this talk, Mother, I think we understand each other much better now. We will be some months in Macedon—my chamberlains will see that Philip Alexander has what he needs for the campaign." Without waitng for any response, he stalked from the room.

Olympias remained sitting for a long time, watching the sunlight drain from her rooms. Alexander had neatly taken most of her power from her: not even she could rule Macedon without a male heir to speak for. It had simply not occurred to her that Alexander would be prepared to do that to her, and the taste of that miscalculation was bitter in her mouth. For the first time in her life, she felt old.

A burst of cheering from the main hall roused her. It was just sunset. The king and those of his Friends who had come north with him would be feasting tonight, celebrating his triumphs. Olympias's mouth thinned. Alexander had won a single battle, but she had the means at hand to negate it, and to make hers the ultimate victory.

* * *

The army spent three months in Macedon, the men dispersing across the hills to their families. Alexander remained in Pella, putting his own house in order. Olympias's agents in the royal household were quietly replaced with men of Alexander's choosing. They were all men who had served with the king in Asia, mostly trusted junior officers too old or too badly injured for further campaigning, men who would remember Alexander as their commander, not as an untried boy.

Dispatches arrived regularly from Hephaestion in the south. The battle near Thebes had broken the League's resistance completely; the smaller cities, never fond of their larger neighbors, competed with each other to demonstrate their friendship with Macedon. Even Sparta sent envoys to discuss a new treaty. Hephaestion, who had always had a good sense of political realities, sent them on to Pella, where they were received with appropriate ceremony. The envoys were practical politicians beneath their mask of Spartan bluntness. Alexander came to terms with them quickly enough, and enlisted a battalion of Spartan mercenaries, commanded by the son of the elder envoy, to compensate for the garrisons he would have to leave behind with Theagenes.

Only Syracuse remained silent, neither openly hostile nor offering any tokens of friendship. Craterus, scratching at the beard he was growing to hide his scar, muttered irritably about bad sailing weather and advised the king to wait. Alexander agreed that the sailing season was over, but sent orders for Polydamus and a strong escort to sail for Syracuse as soon as the weather moderated.

It was an early spring. By the middle of Xandikos, Polydamus had found a captain willing to make the crossing. He was received with all courtesy by the Syracusans, but it quickly became clear that the oligarchs who controlled the city were divided, and Demosthenes was gaining in power. Syracuse had good reason to fear tyrants, having only in the past twenty years recovered from the devastating cycle of tyranny, revolution, and anarchy that had left her a broken, depopulated city, with grass growing in her streets. Demosthenes fanned those fears, and evoked the memory of Timoleon, the moderate Corinthian democrat who had single-handedly rebuilt the city. Polydamus's only weapons were fear of Alexander and fear of Carthage. Alexander was still in Greece, and Dionysius's walls, the greatest in the known world, still defended Syracuse; the Carthaginians were quiet beyond the river Halycus. Slowly, the balance began to shift in Demosthenes's favor.

Alexander received Polydamus's information with outward calm and immediately ordered Nearchus to begin assembling another fleet. By the beginning of Daisios, when the reassembled royal army left Pella, Nearchus's work was already well underway. When the army, joined now by the better part of Hephaestion's troops, reached the coast at the end of Panemos, the fleet was waiting. It was too soon after the great reunions at Pella and throughout Macedon for the officers even to think of separating the soldiers from their women, and they turned a blind eye as men struggled to buy places for their lovers on the already crowded merchantmen. Despite the complications, the fleet sailed as planned on the third day of Loios, preceded by a single fast trireme bearing Alexander's final offer to the city.

At its arrival, Syracuse panicked. The Council of Six Hundred met in haste to consider the king's letters, failed to come to a decision, and threw the matter before the popular Assembly. The townsmen, plagued by rumors from the moment the Council opened, were in no state to consider anything calmly, and the chief magistrate was too old and frightened himself to control the orators adequately. There was a riot in the

Assembly itself, the worst of all possible omens. The
city militia subdued that disturbance, but as night fell
more rumors filled the city. Alexander had sworn to
kill anyone who had ever supported the demagogues,
some said; others, that he had vowed the death of
every third man unless the city surrendered. The cry
went up that Alexander was already at the gates, and
the militia had joined him, betraying the city. A mob
surged to the harbor, and was beaten back by the
militia, but the brief calm did not last.

By midnight, most of the townsmen had taken to
the streets in a frenzy of terror, feeding on each
other's fear. A mob of artisans broke into the house
belonging to Demosthenes's most prominent local sup-
porter, and butchered him and his wife in their bed.
His son, a boy of ten, was thrown from the houseroof;
he survived the fall, but lay bleeding until some cob-
blers noticed him and kicked him to death. The militia, arriving too late to save anyone, was driven back
by the mob. The watch commander, panicking, gave
the order to fall back into the fortress of Ortygia, and
lost the last chance to stop the riots.

All night the mobs coursed through the streets of
Syracuse, hunting out and killing anyone who had the
slightest connection with Demosthenes. By dawn the
crowd had grown to number nearly three thousand,
and a grocer named Periander had emerged as leader
of the mob. In Ortygia, those members of the Six
Hundred who had managed to reach the comparative
safety of the inner city debated what to do. But Ortygia's
walls had been drastically weakened during Timoleon's
rule, to prevent further tyranny, and Periander forced
a breach. The militia fled and the mob took control of
Ortygia.

Polydamus, knowing there was nothing else he could
do, barricaded himself in his rented house, and waited,
praying that the inevitable fires would not reach him.
Two young Athenian women, daughter and wife of

one of Demosthenes's lesser allies, struggled through Polydamus's garden to beg sanctuary. The mob had dragged Demosthenes and the other Athenians from their beds, they said; they had escaped through an upper window when the mob broke down the main door. The younger woman clutched her three-year-old son to her breast: she had been forced to leave her infant daughter sleeping with her nurse. Polydamus brought them in, and waited tensely for other refugees. There were none; the women crouched, too terrified to weep, in the center of the house, listening to the screams from the street.

After two days of rioting, the mob wore itself out. The violence lessened, then turned against the mob's original leaders. Polydamus, recognizing the signs, took half of his hypaspist escort and ventured out into the battered city. There had been fires, one wiping out the poorest quarter, where the rioting had begun; bodies lay in the streets, already beginning to stink. Grimly, the Macedonian sought out the survivors of the Six Hundred. The chief magistrate, who was also chief priest of Olympian Zeus, lay dead beside his polluted altar. Polydamus rounded up what was left of the militia and together they began to put things in order.

There was no question now of anything but submission to Alexander. The Six Hundred gathered the mutilated bodies of Demosthenes and his allies and left them on the Ortygia docks, mute testimony to the riots and the decision of the people of Syracuse to support Alexander. When at last Alexander's fleet was sighted from Ortygia, Polydamus himself sailed to meet it, to try to offer some explanation.

Alexander, balancing himself against the guy ropes that supported the quinquireme's mast, eyed the tendrils of smoke still curling up from the city proper, and shook his head. "You did what you could."

Polydamus sighed. "There are also two women who survived, Athenians," he began.

Alexander said, "They're under my protection." His voice was harsher than he had intended; he moderated his tone with an effort. "They can be returned to their families, if that's what they want. But they'll be provided for."

Hephaestion said, watching the king, "Syracuse will do this sort of thing, for all their fine talk of Timoleon."

"Is it safe to go ashore?" Craterus asked abruptly.

Polydamus nodded.

Alexander said, "We will land."

There was no further argument from the Friends. One by one, the quinquiremes made their way into the great harbor, the crews hastily covering the catapults in the bows of each ship. They docked at the long wharves that served Ortygia; the triremes and the round-bellied troopships landed along the north shore of the harbor, just outside the city suburbs. Most of the army would camp there, Alexander decreed, to avoid straining the city's already limited resources any further. The speaker for the Six Hundred accepted the king's wishes gracefully, and then, gesturing vaguely at the heaped bodies, asked what the king wanted done with them.

Alexander's face tightened. There was no identifying the individual bodies now, not without a sickeningly close examination, but Polydamus was sure of Demosthenes's death. "Give them their rites, in the gods' names."

The army spent nearly a month in Syracuse: there was much to be done. The news of the riots encouraged the Carthaginians to try raiding across the Halycus again. At the Six Hundred's request, Alexander sent a flying column of Companions and hypaspists west to supplement the force sent by the other Sicilian cities. The Carthaginians were driven back, but everyone knew that it was merely a temporary victory.

Syracuse itself began quite patiently to rebuild its civic life. The temple of Olympian Zeus was cleansed, Macedonians and Syracusans alike attending the ceremony, and a new chief magistrate was chosen from the three eligible families. Perdiccas swore the judges had manipulated the choice, and even Alexander, usually willing to give the gods the benefit of the doubt, had to admit that the brigadier's suspicions seemed justified. The lot fell on one of the most vocal of the pro-Macedonian faction, a man who was quite young for the post, with little political experience. Demonax proved, however, to be a shrewd, practical man. After their first meetings, Alexander recognized a competent administrator, and began to talk of leaving Syracuse.

It was hot in the king's tent, and very stuffy: the tent was wrongly sited to catch the occasional sea breeze. No lamps had been lighted in the stifling outer chamber, but it was still so hot that the heavily watered wine stood untouched in the center of the table.

"Demonax has asked that we leave a supporting garrison," Ptolemy said. His tone gave no hint of whether or not he agreed with the Syracusan.

"If we're going back east," Craterus said, tugging at his beard, "we'll need all our men ourselves."

Alexander did not answer, twisting the massive bracelet he wore on his left wrist. In the dim light, the central garnet, framed by coiling snakes, looked like a pool of ink. The conversation faltered and died.

Hephaestion stared out the open tent flap, wishing he were in his own somewhat cooler quarters. Beyond the narrow line of a drainage ditch, light glinted painfully from a line of stone, the remnant of a hundred-year-old counterwall. Another such course of stones backed one side of the king's tent. Twice in a hundred years, Syracuse had been the death of Athenian pretensions: the words trembled on his lips, but it was too hot for philosophy.

There was a mutter of voices outside the tent. Alexander looked up sharply, but before he could shout a question, one of the pages stuck his head into the tent. "Your pardon, sire, but there's a runner from the harbor. A delegation has arrived from Taras and Heraclea, and some other cities."

"The old Italiote League!" Ptolemy said, startled.

Alexander frowned. The Italiote League had been the creation of his maternal uncle, Alexander, the king of Molossia; it had also been that Alexander's death. Eight years before, the same year he himself had invaded Asia, the Greek city-states of the Italian peninsula had applied to Alexander of Molossia for help in dealing with encroaching Samnite and Lucanian tribesmen. Alexander of Molossia had united the cities in an efficient League and had driven back the tribesmen, taking control of southern Italy. Taras had promptly revolted, and in the ensuing fighting, Alexander of Molossia was killed.

"I'd like to know what they want first," Craterus said.

Perdiccas said, "Alexander's help against the Samnites, of course."

"They wouldn't have the gall," Neoptolemus said. "Would they?"

Perdiccas laughed, and Ptolemy grunted reluctant agreement.

"Those cities haven't any shame," Craterus muttered.

Alexander held up a hand to silence them, and said to the page, "Bring this delegation here at once."

"Yes, sire—" The page's voice was abruptly cut off as a figure darted past him, closely followed by a second page. It was Pasithea. Ptolemy sighed audibly, and sheathed his half-drawn sword.

The second page said, "I'm very sorry, sire, truly, but she wanted to see you regardless, and I didn't like stopping her—"

Alexander nodded, cutting off the flow of words, and said, "What is it, mother?"

"You must not see these people," Pasithea said. She was out of breath, her clothes disordered, as though she had run all the way from the harbor. "King Alexander, you must not. It is most unlucky, a witchcraft, and you must not."

Neoptolemus made a gesture to ward off evil. Ptolemy and Hephaestion exchanged looks, and then Ptolemy said, "Alexander, bad luck or not, there's no reason not to see them."

The king frowned at them, commanding silence, and took Pasithea's hands. She was trembling perceptibly. Cautiously, Alexander touched her hair, smoothing it as he would soothe a frightened animal. "Why mustn't I see them?" he asked, very gently. "Tell me about this witchcraft."

Pasithea shook her head wildly, making her jewelry clatter. "I cannot, it's hidden. But there's witchcraft in it, and you must not see them."

"Why not?" Alexander said again. Pasithea shook her head, but said nothing.

There was a long silence, and then Craterus said, explosively, "Gods below, they're only envoys. What can they do—what harm could there possibly be in seeing them?"

Neoptolemus made his warding-off gesture again, saying, "The omen's clear, Alexander. Don't see them."

"On what grounds?" Perdiccas asked sweetly. "The king's afraid of—what?"

"Shut up, Perdiccas," Hephaestion said. "You can always tell the truth, Alexander, you had a warning from the gods to transact no business today."

Alexander gave no sign of having heard any of them. Pasithea was a tall woman: they stood eye to eye, the king staring at her face as though he could read some further omen in its lines. Then, abruptly, the woman pulled away from him, crying, "You will not heed me."

It was not a question. Before Alexander could move to stop her, she had darted from the tent, running blindly toward the shore. She stumbled once, nearly falling, and just managed to save herself. Alexander said, "Heiron! Go after her; make sure she's all right." The page nodded and was off. Alexander went on, "When the envoys arrive, Adaeus, admit them."

It seemed an age before Adaeus at last appeared in the doorway, saying, "Messengers from Taras, Heraclea, Thurii, Consentia, and Metapontium, sire."

Alexander did not move as the envoys filed into the tent, blinking in the sudden dimness. The silence stretched out for a dozen heartbeats, and then Alexander said, "You are welcome, gentlemen, be seated. Adaeus, wine for the envoys."

"I thank you, King Alexander," the leading envoy said, and found a seat in the circle of chairs, gathering his long gown with a dramatic gesture.

At the sound of his voice Hephaestion sat up sharply. He knew that voice, and fought to place the memory. It was at Pella, at the marriage of Alexander of Molossia and Philip's daughter Cleopatra—Mentor, his name was, and he was an Epirote noble, distant kin both to the Molossian Alexander and to Olympias. For no good reason, Hephaestion felt a chill of fear.

"I am Mentor son of Amathus," the envoy went on, and Alexander said, "I know you. What does an Epirote prince have to do with the cities of Italy?"

"I speak for Consentia, King Alexander," Mentor answered. "After your uncle's untimely death, the citizens asked me to lead them, to protect them against their enemies."

Ptolemy snorted audibly, his face a study in polite disbelief. He knew Mentor, too: if Consentia had asked for protection, the citizenry almost certainly regretted their choice of protector.

"But I also speak for the Italiote League," Mentor went on, and gestured to the other envoys who still clustered nervously at his back.

"The Italiote League's dead," Alexander said. "Your rebellions killed it."

Ptolemy lifted an eyebrow at the king's dismissive tone, and Craterus and Perdiccas exchanged uncertain glances. It was not like Alexander to be so abrupt with any embassy, even one led by a man with a reputation as bad as Mentor's, and even more unlike Alexander to refuse help to anyone.

"That's true, King Alexander," a second envoy said, "and we've had cause to regret it ever since. Your pardon, sire, I am Hippodamus of Taras. The League was the one thing that kept our lands safe against the tribes, and when it was broken—" He hesitated, then said, firmly, "—when we broke it, we broke our own strength. We can't stand alone, King Alexander. We've come to beg you: accept the hegemony of the new Italiote League, defend us against these barbarian tribes. You will have our absolute loyalty."

"As my uncle did?" Alexander began, but his voice was drowned in the envoys' murmured agreement. He waited until that died away, and said again, "My uncle had the same assurances, Hippodamus. Will yours be worth any more?"

"We will swear to whatever terms you like, King Alexander," the Tarentine answered promptly. "Only help us."

Alexander sighed, recognizing the desperation in the envoy's appeal. From all accounts, Hippodamus had reason enough to be afraid—the Samnite tribesmen were no match for hoplites in a pitched battle, but they were canny enough to refuse such a battle, and they were deadly raiders—but Mentor's presence warned of hidden meanings. "Gentlemen," he said slowly. "It's late in the day to make such a decision, and I will also wish to discuss this with my Friends.

We'll talk more about this tomorrow; in the meantime, you'll dine with me tonight."

Alexander ordered a separate, open-sided pavilion set up to hold the dinner couches, but the usual evening breeze did not appear, and the diners lay sweltering in the hot, still air. The envoys, knowing their business, lost no opportunity to talk of the injuries they and their cities had suffered at the hands of the Samnites and Lucanians, and even from the citizens of Rome, who were slowly extending their influence to the south. The king listened impassively, and ended the dinner as quickly as he could.

Outside the pavilion, the guests dispersed to their beds, the generals to their tents, and the envoys collected their horses for the short ride back to the city. Alexander put his hand on Hephaestion's arm. "Walk with me a while."

The cavalry commander nodded, falling into step at the king's side. Alexander did not turn toward his own tent, but kept walking toward the sea.

The narrow beach was crowded with the ships that had brought the Macedonian army from Greece, each one lit by a single lantern hanging from the bow. A ship's watchman called a soft challenge as they passed. At Hephaestion's gesture, the escorting page gave the watchword, for good measure holding up his torch to show the king's impassive face. It was dead low tide. Alexander led the way between the ships, out onto the sand past the heap of debris that marked the tide line.

"Wait here," he said to the escort, and walked on toward the water. Hephaestion followed silently. The escorting troopers leaned against their sarissas, yawning; the page planted his torch in the sand and sat beside it, resting his head on his knees.

The king did not pause until he reached the water's edge. Small beach creatures, disturbed by his presence, scurried out of his way, their scuttling noises blending with the sound of the waves. On the horizon, the white stones of Ortygia glowed faintly in the starlight. Hephaestion waited, watching the king.

"I haven't any choice in this," Alexander said at last.

Hephaestion said, "Accept the hegemony, but send someone else—me, Craterus, Ptolemy—to lead the campaign. Any one of us could deal with these tribesmen. You can go east again."

The king shook his head, his face a pale blur in the darkness. "You know better than that. I don't have the men to split the army—if I gave you enough men to beat the Samnites, I wouldn't have enough for India, or the other way 'round. Better I make an end to the threat once and for all."

Hephaestion sighed. Alexander was right, of course; the garrisoning of Asia and Greece had left the core of the army intact, but without the manpower to create two separate armies. But that knowledge would not ease the king's disappointment. Before the cavalry commander could say anything, Alexander went on, "This is my mother's doing, I'm sure of it. I should have listened to Pasithea—the omen was clear enough."

"Clear?" For a moment, Hephaestion's anger on the king's behalf threatened to overwhelm him. He calmed himself with an effort, and said, "She gave no reason. Alexander, even if you'd waited until tomorrow, nothing would have been changed. They would have asked exactly the same thing. What difference could it have made?"

Alexander shrugged. After a moment, he said again, "I can't refuse."

Hephaestion made a face, glad of the darkness. Any other king could refuse—there were a dozen different excuses that would work, all legitimate—but not Alexander. The Greek cities were in danger, that much was clear, and, with the probable exception of Mentor, their envoys had made an honest appeal for help. Alexander was not the man to deny them and it was that generosity that made him loved. "No," he said aloud, "*you* can't."

"And what's the shame in that?" Alexander flared.

"None," Hephaestion said. "Only honor."

Mollified, Alexander put his arm around the other's waist. "I'm not pleased, though," he said. "I feel my mother's hand in this."

"Oh?"

"Witchcraft, Pasithea said, and what other sorceress knows me so well?" Alexander smiled without humor. "And Mentor is her kinsman. Witchcraft or not, I think he'd do her bidding."

Hephaestion nodded in spite of himself. Olympias was no politician, but she was clever enough to see the possibilities of her Italian kinsman and his troubles, and use them to keep Alexander from returning to the east.

"The gods blast them all," Alexander said bitterly, and turned back toward his tent.

INTERLUDE:

Egyptian Alexandria, autumn (Dios), 1440 imperial (1084 A.D., 1837 A.U.C.)

It was hot in the Square of the Whispering Hermes. Theon son of Hermaïscus settled himself on the rim of the central fountain, leaning companionably against a carving of a dryad, and reached into the breast of his tunic for the fruit he had purchased earlier. At his side, Ursulina of Tyre hiked up the skirts of her dress, heedless of maiden modesty and the censorious stare of a passing Reform-Christian priest, and dangled dirty feet in the waters.

"You really should not do that," James of Kano said, in his precise, accented Greek, and accepted the pear that Theon offered him. He was the son of a Hausa resident alien, and a recent convert to unreformed Christianity; the freedom demanded by—and given to—the once-cloistered women of St. Hypatia's college both disturbed and intrigued him.

Ursulina made a rude noise, well aware of the other's interest, and examined the pear Theon handed her. "It's bruised."

Instantly, James said, "Take this one, Ursulina, I haven't touched it yet."

The girl made only a token protest, and rewarded the other's insistence with a brilliant smile and graceful surrender. Theon rolled his eyes and sighed with audible disgust. "What did you think of the lecture?" he asked.

Ursulina's hand went involuntarily to the overfold of her gown, confirming the presence of the tablets on which she—and every other student at the various Universities of Egyptian Alexandria—made her daily notes before transferring the important facts to papyrus or the even more expensive parchment. Reassured, she said, "I enjoyed it. I think it's very plausible that Olympias was responsible for the great Alexander's going into Italy."

Theon said, "I think you're overstating her influence."

"No, I do not think so," James said slowly. "After all, there was no sound tactical reason to go there. The Italiote cities were of no value, and still are of no value. Yet the great Alexander went there."

"I think he just couldn't turn down a request for help," Theon said.

"Yes, but who made the request?" Ursulina asked. "Mentor of Consentia, the queen's cousin." James nodded in solemn agreement.

Theon eyed them both with disgust, recognizing an alliance he could not possibly break. "Maybe," he said, "but was it witchcraft?"

"No," Ursulina said promptly, and at the same moment James said, "Yes."

A belief in witchcraft and the powers of magic was a firm tenet of Old Christianity, as well as a part of Hausa culture; Ursulina, only tenuously a Reform-Christian herself, was notorious among her friends for her interest in radical materialist philosophies. The two looked at each other, romantic interest for the moment submerged in the greater passions of scholarship and philosophy, and Theon leaned back against the dryad to enjoy the fun.

CHAPTER 6:

Southern Italy, late summer (Gorpiaios) to Campania, late autumn (Apellaios), 30 imperial (326 B.C., 427 A.U.C.)

Two days later, Alexander accepted the hegemony of the Italiote League, demanding only token safeguards against betrayal. The Friends protested vehemently, even as they recognized the futility both of any safeguards and of their protests, and were ignored. The fleet was already assembled and supplied for the short voyage to Italy proper; all that remained was to settle matters in Syracuse. Demonax begged for a garrison, both to protect himself and to protect the city. After much debate, and over the Friends' protests, Alexander left not only a garrison made up primarily of Greek mercenary infantry, but also Philip Alexander as its nominal commander. Nearchus would have the actual command, and both the chief engineers would remain until Dionysius's walls had been rebuilt around Ortygia. Even so, it was something of a risk, and Craterus in particular was vocal in his opposition. Alexander pointed out sharply that the boy would be in more danger in Italy with the army, and that, in any case, Syracuse only gave trouble when the city sensed weakness. No one suggested returning the boy to Macedon, and Alexander carried the day. At the end of Gorpiaios, the bulk of the army crossed to Italy, leaving Philip Alexander in nominal command of the forces in Syracuse.

The next two months were spent in the Italian hills, chasing Samnites. The tribesmen had learned long ago that they could not stand against well-trained troops in a pitched battle. At the first word of Alexander's approach, they retreated to their hill fortresses, ready to resume raiding as soon as the Macedonians moved on. Alexander had faced the same tactics in Sogdiana and Bactria, and methodically proceeded to neutralize them. Leaving Craterus in command of the main body of the Foot Companions, Alexander divided the more lightly armed, fast-moving troops—hypaspists, Agrianians, Thracians, and the archers—between himself and Ptolemy, and the two groups struck deep into the mountains, attacking the Samnites on their own ground. Hephaestion, with a strong cavalry force, patrolled the foothills. The Samnites were completely unprepared to respond to these unexpected attacks. Alexander and Ptolemy took three of the hill fortresses almost without loss to themselves, taking hostages and forcing several major tribal chiefs to sue for peace. When at last the remaining tribes united to attack Metapontium, Craterus brought his troops across the peninsula by forced marches to support Hephaestion, and together the two generals utterly destroyed the Samnite army. By the middle of Dios, Alexander was camped on the southern borders of Campania, hammering out the last of the treaties with the Samnites.

Alexander's campaigns had not gone unnoticed in Rome. As his troops moved closer to Campania, an area Rome considered Roman property, the senatorial debates grew more and more acrimonious. Alexander's reputation had preceded him: a majority of the Senate wished to establish good relations, but the specifics of the embassy were hotly debated. The more nervous wished to negotiate an entirely new treaty; others—older senators unaffected by the new fashion for things Greek—pointed out sharply that Rome already had a perfectly good treaty with the Italiote League, and that a change of hegemon did not invalidate it. The latter view prevailed, and the embassy that went south to Campania carried a tart reminder of the old treaty. Alexander, annoyed, reminded the senators of Rome's breach of that treaty, and demanded that Rome return the city of Neapolis to his Samnite allies, from whom it had been taken a year before. After a week's debate, there was no agreement. The two ambassadors, following their instructions from the Senate, declared Alexander the aggressor in a just war and returned to Rome. On the first day of Apellaios, Alexander marched into Campania, heading for Neapolis.

Marcus Fabius Caeso, the junior of the two newly elected consuls, had opposed the Senate's ultimatum, proposing instead an alliance with Alexander against Carthage, Rome's perennial and most dangerous enemy. He was unwise enough to remind the jittery senators of his opposition; in a nearly unanimous vote, Fabius Caeso was granted the command of the army assembling to stop Alexander's advance. The consul shook his head in disgust, and began to plan his strategy. Slowly, the Roman forces began to move, heading south by easy stages toward Neapolis.

The Macedonians moved cautiously in Campania, wary of both its hostile population and of their nominal Samnite allies. Alexander chose his campsites with an eye to defending them against either a surprise attack from Rome or an attack from "renegade" tribesmen. The men of the phalanx, seeing that, kept an obtrusive, unofficial watch on both the hundred or so Samnites who escorted their chief, and on Mentor's Consentian levies. Mentor, wisely, pretended he did not notice, but made arrangements to take himself and his men back to Consentia. The Samnite chief protested and was told to provide the excellent guides he had promised or put up with it. The Samnite, who controlled only half the men he had claimed to rule, was forced to back down. The guides remained unreliable, and progress was slow.

Six days into Campania, Thaïs presided over a dinner in her tent, watching the guests and the level of the wine with equal care. Ptolemy had suggested she hold the entertainment, hoping it would help ease the growing tensions, and Thaïs had accepted the veiled order without demur. Now, as she glanced from under lowered lashes at the men's faces, she could see that she had failed. To be fair, though, neither the food nor the wine were up to her usual standards—the greater part of her household, including her expensive Sicilian cook, had been left behind in Taras—and the entertainment, two flute-players and an Italian acrobat, was distinctly common, as were the other women present. While most of the king's Friends had current mistresses who could be produced at parties, and Craterus was perfectly content with the company of the rangy blonde known to most of the army as the Amazon, Thaïs had been unable to find suitable companions for either Hephaestion or the king. The best she could find were two rather ordinary Megaran courtesans, uneducated, pretty things, who did their best to ape the manners of their betters. Thaïs eyed them fiercely, reducing the bolder of the pair to blushing silence, and glanced at Ptolemy, who reclined beside her, staring into the depths of his wine cup.

"More wine?" Thaïs asked softly, and crooked her finger at a slave.

Ptolemy roused himself enough to glance 'round the circle of couches, and shook his head. The army had barely covered fifty stadia, less than half a normal day's march, and tempers were short. Too much wine would only fuel that anger. Thaïs shrugged to herself and waved the slave away.

Craterus sat up abruptly, dislodging the Amazon from her comfortable sprawl, and beckoned for a slave to bring more wine. "Fifty stadia," he said, as the slave filled his cup, "fifty stadia up and down these hills, and we're still how far from Neapolis?"

"The guides say, about three hundred and fifty stadia," Laomedon son of Larichus said, grimacing, and shrugged his thin shoulders. He was no great soldier, was not even properly a Macedonian, being the son of one of Philip's Mytilenean allies, but he had the gift of tongues. That talent was more of a curse these days: he was responsible for communicating with the Samnite and conscripted Latin guides, and the strain of that responsibility showed in his eyes.

"The guides," Craterus said contemptuously.

Alexander said, "The surveyors say the same, Craterus. Five or six days, given the ground."

"Six days' march, then, and then a siege," Craterus said. "It's getting on toward winter, Alexander."

"We've campaigned in winter before," Hephaestion said. "Even you've had a few successes after snow was on the ground."

Craterus bristled at that and Ptolemy roused himself hastily. "Winter campaigns, yes," he said loudly, riding over Craterus's attempt to continue the quarrel, "but not like this. How far can we trust the Samnites—or the Leaguers, for that matter?"

"Is now the time to discuss this?" Coenus protested thickly. He had drunk heavily all evening, trying to drown the ache that had settled deep in his bones.

Alexander sat up and ran his hand through his hair, dislodging the wilted garland. The Megaran courtesan retrieved it mechanically, but did not dare replace it. "There's no one but the Friends here," the king said. "And we're in Thaïs's house. You can speak freely here."

"I thank you, King Alexander," Thaïs said loudly, hoping to divert attention, and snapped her fingers for the acrobat. The Italian ignored her, listening with wide-eyed fascination.

Coenus ignored her, leaning forward, hands planted on his knees. "Very well, then, Alexander," he said, "there's something I've been wanting to say."

The brigadier had spoken in Macedonian; Alexander answered in the same language. "Go ahead, say your piece."

"My men are unhappy about this campaign," Coenus said, "and I'm not happy about it myself. They ask—and I ask—what good this Samnite bargain does us? All it does is get our men killed. Why should we do their dirty work, when they've never been friends of Greece—by the gods, Alexander, they killed your own uncle. It's not territory we can hold easily, the damned Italiote League's useless, the Romans're bad enemies—" He broke off suddenly, frowning, then remembered the thread of his argument. "So why don't we just go back to Macedon and let them kill each other?"

Craterus nodded slowly. He had drunk just enough to make himself careless; before he could think about what he was saying, he said, "There's sense to that, Alexander."

Hephaestion hissed an obscenity and Perdiccas kicked him hard, just above the ankle. The cavalry commander took the blow without flinching, eyes fixed on the king. Alexander ignored them, staring at the two Foot Companion brigadiers. "Well?" he said, after a long moment. "Are there others who agree?"

"No," Hephaestion said at once. "There's a treaty to keep. I say we go on."

"You would," Craterus snapped. "This is a matter of strategy, boy, not your pretty feelings."

"You wouldn't know strategy from—" Hephaestion began, furiously, and Alexander said, "Enough." He did not raise his voice, but Hephaestion sank back onto his couch. Craterus paled and was silent.

"Enough," Alexander said again. He stared a moment longer, daring either man to say another word, then relaxed a little. He had drunk as heavily as the others, and when he spoke again he was a little too eloquent. "You've raised a fair question, Coenus, I understand your concern. But listen to me, then. The Greek cities along the coast have been fighting one tribe or another since they were founded. If we're going to protect those cities we have to settle things with the tribes once and for all. There's no solid frontier, either we take it all, or we abandon the cities—that's what happened to my uncle, he didn't see how much he could win with an alliance. As for Rome—Rome declared war on me, remember? I'd've preferred some alliance. And, yes, they're good fighters, but we're better." He paused, and went on more naturally, "Much better. Neapolis is a Samnite city, we're bound by our treaty to recover it for them. We'll winter there, and see if Rome is more willing to treat."

All around the circle of couches, heads nodded solemnly, ready to be convinced. Thaïs sighed almost soundlessly, and signalled for the flute-players to begin again.

As the first notes shrilled out, the door of the tent was whisked back to admit one of the pages. Alexander frowned, but said nothing as the boy hurried over and murmured something in a low voice. The king's face hardened, and he stood up abruptly.

"Amyntas son of Arrabaeus has made contact with the Roman army," he announced. "All of you, come with me."

The Friends scrambled to their feet, wine and women forgotten, and followed the king from the tent, shouldering each other aside in their haste. Thaïs, left to herself, exchanged wry glances with Perdiccas's current favorite. It had not been one of the Athenian's more successful parties and both women knew it—and its ending had been a spectacular disaster.

"We'll be on the move tomorrow," the Amazon said. Her voice was flat-voweled, uncultured. She was no high-class hetaira and made no pretense of being one.

"And a battle to come," Perdiccas's mistress said. "The gods protect us all." Her prayer was mechanical: like all the women who followed the army, she had long ago come to terms with all the possible permutations of victory and defeat. She rose in a flurry of draperies, and hurried away to her tent. The other women followed.

Thaïs echoed the prayer, already clapping her hands for the household slaves to begin clearing away. If Ptolemy dies, she thought, I'm still young, there will be other men. I have wealth enough, in coin and in jewelry, and I have fast horses that will take me out of range of the Romans, if Alexander should lose this battle. The litany did little to still the knowledge that she would miss Ptolemy if he were killed. She shook her head angrily. Alexander had not lost a battle in his life, and would not begin now.

Amyntas was waiting in the antechamber of the king's great tent, sitting in a chair drawn close to the brazier. He was a swarthy man, unshaven, and still filthy from days of riding. In his faded tunic and cloak—like all the Scouts, he wore no body armor—he looked more like a Thracian bandit than a soldier. Only his plumed helmet, discarded beside his chair, gave any hint of his rank. He looked up as the king entered, one hand going to the dirty rag looped above his right knee in a vain attempt to hide the wound.

Alexander raised an eyebrow at the movement. "Timander, have Chares send for Philip the doctor," he said. "You had fighting, Amyntas?"

"We did that," Amyntas said grimly. Hephaestion gestured for the nearest page to pour the scout a cup of wine. Amyntas accepted it gratefully and took a deep swallow before saying, "This is nothing, though, not worth a doctor. One of their short javelins grazed me, that's all. The important thing is, they're on the move."

Alexander nodded. Amyntas had earned command of a squadron of scouts during the Persian campaigns, and had proved his reliability a dozen times since then. If he said the Romans were moving, he was right. "And your men?"

Amyntas made a face. "I lost eight, Alexander, and another four, wounded not too badly. We ran right into their scouting column; we had to fight. My mistake; I wasn't expecting them. But after we got free we tracked them back to their camp, and I got a pretty good look at them."

He broke off as a page returned, escorting the doctor, and said urgently, "Sire, it's only a scratch."

"Let Philip see to it," Alexander said, and nodded to the doctor, forestalling further protest.

Ptolemy said, thoughtfully, "Twelve men dead or wounded, out of thirty. That's a strong advance party."

"Very strong," Amyntas agreed. He gave a grunt of pain as Philip unwound the rag from his leg and fell silent, biting his lip.

Hephaestion gestured for the nearest page to bring the map case, then sorted through the rolls of papyrus himself. The map of Campania was not as good as the maps of Greece or Asia, being based more on guesswork and the Scouts' reports than on the surveyors' work, but he unrolled it anyway, shaking his head at the blank patches. Perdiccas came to lean over his shoulder, muttering to himself.

When the doctor had finished his work, the king dismissed him with thanks. Amyntas lurched to his feet, most surprised when the bandaged leg bore his weight. Before he could join the group around the map, the tent flap was pulled open again.

"Sire, Tyrimmas son of Aretes has returned from patrol."

Before the page could say anything more, Tyrimmas had shouldered his way into the tent. He checked a little on seeing the assembled generals, and said, "I beg your pardon, sire, sirs. But my patrol's found the Roman army."

Amyntas looked up sharply—Tyrimmas's Scouts had been nowhere near his men—and Alexander said, "Where?"

The Friends made way for the raw-boned Thracian, who stared for a long moment at the map, translating ink and charcoal lines into familiar countryside, before saying, "Here."

"Gods below," Amyntas said, in spite of himself.

The king glanced at him. "And you met your Romans—?"

"Here," Amyntas said, and touched a point a hundred and thirty-five stadia to the north and west of the place Tyrimmas had indicated. That was better than a day's march, even over good ground, and the crude map showed a range of hills separating the two points.

"Two armies," Craterus said, half to himself, and tugged furiously at his beard.

There was a sudden silence in the tent. There could be no question in anyone's mind that they were facing two Roman armies, one blocking the best road to Neapolis, the other threading the narrow band of open ground between the hills and mountains to the south, in an obvious attempt to break the Macedonian line of communication with the Italiote League cities.

Alexander said, "What's their strength?"

Amyntas looked up, startled, and got control of his thoughts with an effort. "We hit the patrol about here, say forty men, cavalry. We got free, followed them, and found the main army about twelve stadia back.

From the size of the camp alone, I'd say they had a full six brigades."

"That's three of their legions," Laomedon said quietly. "According to everything the Samnites have said, their total strength is about four legions. There are two allied legions, too, based at Neapolis."

Alexander nodded. "Cavalry?"

"I don't know, sire," Amyntas answered. "They'd half-fortified their camp, with that and the dark, I couldn't be sure. But the ones we met weren't Roman, that I can tell you."

"They've always relied on their allies for cavalry," Laomedon said.

"And the force you met, Tyrimmas?" Alexander asked. His face showed nothing but a sort of professional admiration for the Roman commanders.

"Another three brigades, sire," the Thracian answered. "Only a few squadrons of cavalry, though, maybe five hundred men."

"Did they know they were seen?" Alexander asked.

Tyrimmas shook his head. "No, I'm sure they didn't."

That was better news than any of the officers had expected, though Campania was hardly ideal country for a cavalry fight. Hephaestion nodded to himself, already working out the best ways to deploy his Companions. Craterus's lips moved silently, calculating. Before he could finish, Ptolemy said, "That's six thousand men on our tail, Alexander."

"And twelve thousand more ahead of us," Craterus muttered. He could feel a trap closing on them and shook himself angrily. More loudly, he said, "I say we deal with them first, mop up the rest later."

Disconcertingly, Alexander smiled. "If we meet either one of those armies, it's on their chosen ground. The Scouts have been telling us how scrubby it is, bad for cavalry—we may outnumber them both, but any battle would be too costly. No." He leaned over the map again, tracing a line from the Macedonian camp directly across the hills to Neapolis. "How far would you say that is, Amyntas?"

The scout hesitated, then said, "Two hundred stadia, maybe?"

The king looked at the other scout. "Tyrimmas?"

"I'd make it two hundred and ten stadia," the Thracian said, warily.

The Friends looked at each other, already able to guess the king's plan. Ptolemy said, "Even with a forced march, the infantry would have a hard time covering two hundred stadia—and there's the baggage and the women to consider."

"And there's nothing to say Neapolis has been stripped of troops," Perdiccas said. "If we arrive and find it fully garrisoned. . . ." He did not need to finish.

Hephaestion said, thoughtfully, "Laomedon said four legions at Rome and two at Neapolis, the Neapolitan ones being allies. There are about four thousand men in a legion, if it's two of our brigades, and the Scouts can account for, say, eighteen thousand? That's five legions right there. Neapolis can't be that strongly held."

"Exactly," Alexander said. "Ptolemy, I know the whole army couldn't cover that ground in a single day. I will take two brigades of Foot Companions—yours, Perdiccas, and yours, Coenus—all the Companion Cavalry, the hypaspists, the Agrianians, the horse archers; that force can easily reach the city and throw up a siege line. The rest of the army—Craterus, it's your command—will follow at the best speed you can. It doesn't matter if you don't reach Neapolis in a single day, my force can hold a siege for two days if we have to. All that really matters is that you avoid the Romans. Hephaestion's right, the Neapolitan garrison has to be depleted, and the city itself doesn't like Rome. We can take it—and its harbor—before the main army can relieve them. And with Neapolis for a base, we'll be in a perfect position to bring the Romans to battle on our terms."

One by one, reluctantly, the Friends nodded. Not even Alexander's enthusiasm could hide the fact that they were in a dangerous situation, caught between two strong Roman forces. On the other hand, the king's solution, though it carried its own risks, was exactly the sort of plan that had worked before. Alexander smiled again, sensing their acceptance, and said, "Good. We'll ride at dawn."

Fabius Caeso received the information that his scouts had made contact with the Macedonians with outward calm, and closeted himself at once with his officers. An hour later, a scowling centurion emerged from the consul's tent to fetch Caius Maelius Mesala, the half-Neapolitan commander of the allied cavalry. Two hours later, a chastened Mesala was on his way south, accompanied by a small escort, riding hard for Neapolis. The sky was growing light with dawn by the time the exhausted troop passed through the gates of Neapolis.

Lucius Cassius Nasidienis, the military tribune in command of the Neapolitan garrison, heard the consul's message through once while he dressed, then had Mesala repeat it once more before the garrison's other officers arrived. The second, smaller force swinging south and east to cut off Macedonian communications was as yet undiscovered. Fabius was gambling that Alexander would try to close with him at once and ordered Cassius to take most of the Neapolis garrison to reinforce the second army. Cassius grunted dubiously—he had been in Neapolis for six months now, and knew only too well how his Neapolitan allies would react to the idea of any risk, calculated or not—and braced himself to override the Neapolitans' inevitable arguments. He lacked the consul's age and rank, and Fabius's acid tongue, to goad them on. The sun had been up for hours before the first cohorts grudgingly formed up for the march.

The Companion Cavalry and about half the hypaspists —there were not enough spare horses to mount the entire battalion—rode for Neapolis at the first brightening of the sky. Perdiccas's and Coenus's Foot Companion brigades went with them, escorted by the horse archers and the Agrianians. Alexander, riding at the head of the lead squadron, set a moderate pace at first, moving warily over the uneven ground. The infantry kept up easily, abandoning the neat marching columns to make better speed through the hills. As the sky grew brighter, the king picked up the pace. By the time the last of the Companion Cavalry squadrons made its way out of the hills and into the broad valley that led to Neapolis, the infantry was a good hour's march behind. Alexander slowed his march to hold that distance, but kept on toward the city.

The centurion in command of a Roman scouting party saw the Macedonians first, as they emerged from the long valley, and dispatched a pair of runners to warn the main column before the nearest horseman saw his group. The Companion gave an excited yelp, wrenching his horse around and lowering his heavy cornelwood lance. His squad leader echoed the shout, spurring his horse to the charge. The Companions rode over and through the little party of Romans. The squad leader reined in, breathing hard, and turned to stare at the bodies lying in his wake, wondering if he had made a mistake in killing them all. The deed was done; he shrugged to himself, sent one trooper back to warn the king, and spurred on in search of the main Roman force.

Alexander received the squad leader's warning with outward calm. When the squad leader himself returned with the information that nearly two brigades of Romans were blocking their path, the king swore once, bitterly, and said, "We go on. Send a rider to warn Perdiccas."

Hephaestion said, "Do you want the hypaspists dismounted?" He did not need to ask why they could not wait for the rest of the infantry. They were committed; the Foot Companions would catch up soon enough, and the cavalry could hold the Romans until then.

"They'd be cut to bits," Alexander said, and shouted for a page to gather the squadron leaders.

Cassius Nasidienis reined in gently, seeing the first of the returning advance guard, and felt the first stirring of fear in the pit of his stomach. He could not see the rest of the ten-man squad. The rest of his suite, the Neapolitan officers, runners, aides, and signaller, slid to a stop behind him, whispering nervously to each other. The man—Roman, reliable—fell into step beside the tribune, one hand resting on Cassius's saddlecloth.

"Well?" Cassius asked quietly, still searching the distance for the rest of the advance guard. The second man, breathing heavily, slid to a stop at his companion's shoulder.

"Trouble," the first man answered, and could not refrain from glancing nervously over his shoulder.

"Alexander?" Cassius asked.

"Alexander's cavalry."

Cassius twisted in his saddle to look back along the line of soldiers, straggling a little in spite of the best efforts of the centurions. The sweat was running under his corselet, soaking the coarse wool of his undertunic. With a real legion, made up of Roman troops rather than half-trained allies, he might have hoped to hold off even Alexander's cavalry, but he doubted the Neapolitans would stand against a charge. "How many? And what about infantry?"

"Maybe fifteen hundred, two thousand," the second man said. "I didn't see any infantry." He eyed the tribune's unlined face, and added, "They'll cut us to pieces, without horses of our own."

Cassius recognized the trooper's thought—it was common enough, for all that he had served in the army for eight years, and had earned his appointment— and said only, "How far?"

"About a mile, and coming fast."

Cassius glanced over his shoulder and waved for the rest of his suite to join him. "Alexander's cavalry is in sight, a mile off," he said without preamble. "Horatius, put the two Roman cohorts on the flanks. Hector, Lynceus, make sure your centurions keep your people in the line. We'll withdraw toward Neapolis." He looked around the circle of faces, seeing nothing but panic, and said urgently, "They don't have any infantry with them; the cavalry won't be able to touch us if we just hold our line. We'll retreat in drill order."

Horatius Regulus, a stocky, balding veteran of a dozen or more campaigns, saluted smartly. "At once, tribune," he snapped, and glared at the officers to either side of him, until they, too, mumbled agreement. Privately, he shared Cassius's doubts, but knew better than to let them show.

Lynceus son of Androtimes, the younger of the Neapolitan commanders, said faintly, "As the tribune wishes. But shouldn't we send a warning to the consul? And to General Gabinius?"

Mesala pushed back his helmet and rubbed his stubbled face with both hands, trying desperately to regain some alertness. He had asked to come with the tribune, even after his all-night ride, and was just beginning to regret his rashness. "The horses are mostly fresh," he said slowly, as much to himself as to the tribune. "We could make it to Fabius's camp, or to Gabinius, by sundown."

Cassius hesitated, then nodded. He had too few horsemen—Mesala's dozen troopers—to do any good against Alexander's men; if he tried to use them against the Companions, he would only lose them all. "Go, warn Fabius."

Mesala nodded again and wheeled his horse away, shouting for his men.

Hector son of Demetrius, who had been given a command only to conciliate one of the Neapolitan factions, said, "Shouldn't we just escape while we can, tribune?"

"No," Cassius snapped. "If we run now, we'll all be slaughtered. We will withdraw toward Neapolis in good order, and with our face to the enemy, and we may get out of this yet, if it's only cavalry. And if you don't panic."

Hector muttered something about being slaughtered in any case and Horatius said, "Stop wasting time, Greekling."

"Move," Cassius said, and was at last obeyed.

Horns sounded along the column, and the standards flashed as the centurions maneuvered their maniples into the line of battle. The line solidified slowly, centurions cursing their reluctant men into close order. The centurions left only the smallest of gaps between the first- and second-line centuries. Seeing that, the third-rank men exchanged nervous glances, and their centurions stood poised to stop any flight.

The Macedonians, advancing at a steady trot, did not waver at the sight of the solid line of infantry. At the head of the leading squad, Alexander lifted his lance, signalling the troopers to close up behind him. All along the rough line, the other squad leaders did the same, abruptly transforming the mass of riders into a disciplined line of wedge-shaped formations, like the teeth of a saw. The king gave the war cry, echoed instantly and terrifyingly by the Companions. The horses lurched to a canter and then to a gallop.

On the Roman left, a Latin recruit, completely unnerved by the shouts and the approaching horses, threw away his shield and turned to run. The nearest centurion blocked his way, swinging his sword back-handed. The recruit fell, his head nearly severed from his shoulders. The centurion stepped silently into the recruit's place. The rest of the century stood firm.

As the Macedonians came within javelin range, Cassius shouted, "Loose!" The trumpeters sounded the two-note call, and the deadly spears flashed from the line. The Companions faltered. One animal went down, tangling the following horses; the squads to either side veered away, cursing, and pulled their own animals out of range. Alexander swore to himself—the Romans were not going to be frightened into breaking their line—and wheeled his own horse away again.

"Gods," Horatius said softly. "We held them."

Cassius grinned fiercely at him, then beckoned to the nearest runner. "So we did. You, pass the word. We'll withdraw, in drill order. Third-rank by alternate centuries, then first-rank, then second. Tell each commander, and the senior centurions, and get back to me when you've done it. They're to wait for my signal."

"At once, tribune," the runner said, and dashed off down the gap between the cohorts.

Cassius turned back to Horatius. "Don't you see? Not even Alexander can make a horse charge a line of spears head-on. And he's left his infantry behind. We've got time, Horatius. We may make it back to the city yet."

Horatius grunted agreement, but said dourly, "It's a long way, tribune. A very long way."

Sobered, Cassius nodded, scanning the ranks for his runner. He stared out past the milling cavalry, even now planning for the next charge. At last the runner returned, bringing the acknowledgements. Cassius beckoned to his signaller. "Sound the withdrawal."

The man set his horn to his lips, braced himself, and produced a braying three-note call. It echoed up and down the line, and the third-rank men began to move. Alexander caught the movement at once, and raised the war cry, pointing toward the potential gap in the Roman line. His squad swung close again, forcing the horses toward the spearpoints. The third-rank men grounded spears and stood firm. Swearing, the king let his horse have its head, swinging away from the line. As they turned away, the Romans loosed a flight of javelins, downing three of the Companions. A fourth javelin, nearly spent, grazed the king's leg between the skirt of the corselet and the top of his shin piece, leaving a long, bloody scratch. Alexander hardly felt it, staring first at the Macedonian bodies, and then at the Roman line as it shifted ponderously backward. They had not gained much ground, but enough small gains could keep them away from the infantry. Shaking his head, he shouted for the nearest squad leader, and then for Hephaestion. When they appeared, he said, "We have to hold them here."

Hephaestion winced, thinking of the men it would cost them, but understood the necessity. And cost them it did. Three times more the Romans sounded the retreat; three times more the Macedonians charged and were driven back. They left dead men and horses behind them, a few more each time. A young squad leader, thinking he saw a gap, charged headlong between the Roman lines, and was promptly cut down. A dozen of his men died with him, caught on the spears or hacked to death with the deadly Roman short swords. Each time the Romans gained a few more yards of ground.

It was not enough. As the Romans began to retreat for the fourth time, there was a cheer from the Macedonians, starting at the rear of their line, and moving rapidly forward. It could mean only one thing, Alexander's infantry had arrived at last, and the Roman line wavered. Cassius cursed them hoarsely, and shouted for the signaller to sound "form line". The man raised his trumpet, but the notes wavered and cracked, and only a few of the other signallers answered his call.

"Sound again," Cassius said, but the signaller was staring over his shoulder, face distorted in terror. Cassius turned, too, and saw the third rank disintegrate. First one man, then another, than two more, and finally whole groups and files threw away their weapons and ran toward Neapolis. The signaller threw away his horn and ran. Cassius lifted his sword but the man was too quick for him.

"Horatius!" he shouted, and then, when the commander did not answer, "Romans! Stand fast!"

The cavalry swirled past him, shouting their war cry. A single cohort of Romans stood firm on what had been the right wing. Cassius fought his way toward them, knowing only that he would rather die with them than be cut down fleeing. The centurion still in command shouted something that sounded welcoming and gestured to the tribune's horse. Cassius leaped free then, abandoning the animal to its fate, and the centurion pulled him into the momentary safety of the line.

On either side, the Companion Cavalry surged past, ignoring the knot of Romans in favor of easier prey. Cassius choked back a sob of sheer fury. He had won only a temporary respite, until Alexander's infantry could close with them—and if the Neapolitans had held their ground, they could have made it safely back to the city. But they would see how Romans died.

Alexander saw the disintegration of the Roman line with savage satisfaction. Glancing over his shoulder, he could see the two Foot Companion brigades advancing inexorably toward the single cluster of Romans who still put up an organized resistance. Ahead, the rest of the Roman force streamed toward Neapolis, just visible now on the horizon, closely pursued by the Companion Cavalry. Alexander reined in sharply, shouting for a page. A boy appeared almost at once, thin face very white, but with his horse well under control.

"Tell Neoptolemus to join Coenus, and deal with what's left of their wing," the king ordered. "Then they're to follow me. I want Neapolis." Without waiting for the page's acknowledgement, he spurred after the Companions. Hephaestion followed, grim-faced.

It was slow work dragging the cavalry away from the blood sport of the pursuit, but together the two commanders managed to gather nearly a full squadron before catching up with the main body. The ground was growing rougher; here and there they passed the piles of bodies where desperate Neapolitans had made their final stand. Hephaestion cursed softly, and spurred his tiring horse hard, driving it to greater efforts. If this kept up, there would be no prisoners left either to bargain with Neapolis, or with the main body of the Roman army. Alexander saw that, too, and urged his horse on, talking gently to it in a voice that did not match his grim face.

They reached a broad stream, its water barely deep enough to cover the horses' hooves. Hephaestion made a face, and let his horse pick its own path down the low bank, made muddy and treacherous by the passage of hundreds of men and horses. Alexander followed, then reined in abruptly in the center of the stream, holding up his hand for silence. The others paused, listening, and then they heard it, too: a man's voice, shrill with fear and pleading.

Alexander swore once and turned his horse down the stream itself, heedless of what might lie beneath the surface.

Hephaestion said, "Alexander, wait!" The banks rose steeply further down the stream, making it the perfect place for an ambush. The king did not turn and Hephaestion gestured to the nearest squad leader. "You, and your men, come with me. The rest of you, ride along the banks."

There was a scramble for the banks as the Companions sorted themselves out. Hephaestion, wincing at the thought of what the riverbed would do to his horse's hooves, followed the king.

The stream curved south, the banks becoming higher and steeper. Bushes grew along the edge, screening the stream to either side. The troopers riding along the bank cursed as the trailing branches caught at their mounts' legs and at their own feet, but kept station. At the bank's highest point, four Companion troopers sat their mounts in the middle of the stream, staring up at the bushes. A fifth, dismounted, perched precariously halfway up the bank, pulling himself up by the protruding roots. He carried a dagger in his teeth. One of the others stuck his lance thoughtfully into the brambles above his friend, producing a shriek of pain and fear.

Alexander shouted wordlessly and spurred his horse forward along the stream. Great plumes of mud and water spurted from beneath the horse's hooves. The rest of his party spurred after him, and there was a great splash and cursing as one of the horses stumbled, throwing its rider. The king did not turn, reining in to confront the five troopers. They swung 'round to face him, half startled, half chagrined. The man who had been climbing the bank dropped back into the stream, missed his footing, and went sprawling in the mud. He scrambled to his feet, not daring to curse, and took his horse's bridle from the rangy youth who held it for him.

"What do you think you're doing?" Alexander asked, without raising his voice. He had few qualms about the casual killing that inevitably followed a victory but he objected to pointless cruelty.

There was a momentary silence and then a trooper riding an ugly brown gelding said, with some embarrassment, "Sire, we've caught a Neapolitan."

Alexander eyed them for a moment longer, knowing

perfectly well what they had had in mind, then said, "So I see." He looked up at the bank then, seeing a faint glimmer of white among the dark leaves. "You there, come down. Your life's safe."

There was a scurrying noise, and the bushes churned wildly. A figure, weaponless, without armor, dropped from the bank and threw himself to his knees in front of the king. Alexander's horse tossed its head and danced sideways, momentarily startled. The king soothed it automatically.

"Alexander, Great King, spare my life," the Neapolitan wailed.

"He's already done that," Hephaestion said, quite audibly. He was beginning to dislike the Neapolitan.

"You will not regret it, Great King, I can be of use to you," the Neapolitan babbled, still on his knees in the mud. "I am Hector son of Demetrius; I am of importance in the city, and no friend to Rome. They forced me to join them; there were many like me on the field today, who'll welcome you to Neapolis."

"Get up," Alexander said. Cocking his head to one side, he considered the Neapolitan as he scrambled to his feet, scraping futilely at the mud. The man's tunic had once been a good one; its woven border still showed exotic colors and metallic threads through the mud. The man who chose to wear such an expensive tunic into battle was at the very least a rich man and rich men were influential in any city. "Hector son of Demetrius," he said aloud. "I have no quarrel with Neapolis, only with Rome."

"And the gods know Neapolis has no quarrel with you," Hector said fervently. "You will be welcomed with open arms, as our liberator."

Hephaestion snorted dubiously at that, having heard such promises before, but Alexander said, "Thank you." He pointed to the nearest of the five troopers. "You, Glaucias, give him your horse, and be glad you didn't kill him."

Glaucias dismounted with very poor grace and handed his horse over to the Neapolitan. One of the king's troopers boosted the shaking man onto the saddle-cloth. Alexander swung his horse downstream again. "Follow me."

It was late afternoon, the shadows deepening between the overhanging banks. The king's party retraced their path down the stream, and left the water as soon as the horses could make their way up the bank. Neapolis was visible in the distance, starkly outlined by the setting sun. Alexander squinted thoughtfully at it for a few minutes, then sent most of the Companions he had collected back to Coenus and Perdiccas. The two brigadiers would already have dealt with the remains of the Roman forces; one last effort was needed from them now to secure the city. Hephaestion protested briefly at the loss of the cavalry, pointing to the line of scrubby trees that half blocked their line of march. Alexander answered tartly that they would collect the rest of the Companions as they went, and rode on before the cavalry commander could respond.

The pursuit had gone further than the king had expected. By the time the horses drew level with the little wood, only a dozen troopers had joined the king, and most of those rode wheezing, exhausted horses. Alexander gave Hephaestion a quick look, and waved for the troop to swing well clear of the trees. The cavalry commander grunted his approval, but too softly for the king to hear.

"Sire! King Alexander!" The youngest of the troopers pulled up his horse at the edge of the wood, pointing in among the trees, then whistled. A riderless horse emerged from the wood, responding to the boy's familiar call. Its trappings and bloodied saddle-cloth were Macedonian. The nearest troopers drew their swords.

Alexander urged his own horse closer, letting it walk a little way into the trees. A few yards in, the

wood opened up again into a shaded clearing. A body
in a Macedonian cloak was crumpled at the far side of
the open space, the broken stump of a javelin protruding from between two segments of the corselet. Alexander beckoned sharply to the nearest troopers and
drew his own sword as the men moved into the wood
beside him. It seemed suddenly very quiet, so that
the sounds of the horses, the soft, metallic rattling of
harness and bridle, sounded very loud. One of the
troopers, seeing the body, gave a quiet exclamation.
The other dropped his lance, useless among the trees,
and drew his sword.

Alexander said, "Get the others. We go in."

Hephaestion, coming up behind him, cursed softly
to himself, less at the inevitable decision—if there
were still a pocket of Romans in the wood, rather than
one lucky straggler, they could hardly be left there—
than at the thought of hunting through forest in the
fading light. He drew his sword and edged forward
until he was riding at the king's left.

Alexander acknowledged the other's presence with
the merest flicker of a smile and said, "Sathon, you
and your men dismount, fan out with me."

"At once, sire," the squadron leader answered.

Alexander twisted to look over his shoulder at the
Companions crowding into the wood behind him, and
lifted his sword to wave them forward. In the same
instant, a javelin flashed from among the trees ahead.
It struck the king high in the side just at the edge of
the corselet, ripping through the leather outer skin
and tearing away the metal plates before slicing deep
between the king's ribs. Alexander fell backward, grab-
bing left-handed for the horse's mane. The frightened
animal reared, throwing him under the hooves of the
following horse, which danced backward, shrieking.
The king rolled free, and was up in an instant, one
hand pressed to the broken corselet. There was blood
on his fingers.

Hephaestion kicked his horse forward, putting its body between the king and the trees from which the javelin had come. "Sathon, Aristo, get them, ride them down."

To either side, troopers kicked their horses into motion, diving into the woods. A dozen men, veterans all, pulled their unwilling horses to a stop halfway across the clearing, forming a line between the king and the unseen enemy. They waited nervously, swords ready, but there was no further attack. Hephaestion dropped from his own horse, tossing its reins to the nearest Companion, and took the king's shoulders, easing him gently to the ground. Alexander was very pale, eyes wide and not quite focussed. He breathed in short, painful gasps.

"Let me see," Hephaestion said.

Alexander spread his fingers slightly and shook his head. Hephaestion hissed softly between his teeth at the sight of the welling blood and began loosening the ties of the corselet. The javelin had sliced through one of the cords that held the shoulder piece in place; Hephaestion loosened the other, and then, very carefully, cut the laces that held the chest pieces together. He lifted the king slightly, and a trooper appeared from nowhere to take Alexander's weight. Together they eased away the broken corselet. Alexander winced visibly but made no sound.

The young trooper who had found the riderless horse dropped to his knees at the king's side. The boy's face was stricken, but he had kept his wits about him: he held out a strip of cloth torn from someone's undyed tunic. More such strips were bundled in his hand. Hephaestion nodded his thanks, too coldly afraid to remember the boy's name, and glanced up at the trooper supporting the king's shoulders. The man nodded reassuringly and tightened his hold on Alexander. Very carefully, the cavalry commander eased aside the king's hand, and put the wadded strip of cloth against the wound. Alexander twitched in spite of himself, left hand contracting into a painful fist.

Hephaestion felt his own muscles tighten in sympathy. The wound was an ugly one, a deep slash that ripped away a triangular piece of flesh along and below one rib, baring the bone.

The first piece of cloth was soaked through already. Hephaestion snapped his fingers for another, and the boy gave it to him, too frightened to ask questions. The bleeding slowed gradually. Hephaestion left the last sodden pad in the wound and added two more on top of that, binding them all in place with longer strips cut from his own cloak. Alexander winced again as the bandages were tightened, but breathing was less painful. He whispered, "Help me get the corselet on."

Hephaestion gave him a startled look, and said, "Alexander, I—"

"Put it on," Alexander said. With an effort, he sat up fully, bracing himself with his left arm. "I can ride. And I want Neapolis."

Hephaestion still looked rebellious, but caught the king's hand as he reached for the nearest piece of the corselet. "All right," he said, a little too loudly. Alexander was right, unfortunately: only his presence would be enough to overawe the Neapolitans, and get them possession of the city without further fighting. And the corselet would hide the bloodstains well enough. "But wait for Perdiccas?"

Alexander nodded, pain throbbing in his side with every breath. Hephaestion shook his head, but together he and the older trooper got the king to his feet and put the corselet back together around him. Awkwardly, Alexander twitched his cloak forward, hiding the torn leather and broken scales. Then the two troopers helped him back into the saddle. He collected the reins, trying to ignore the sudden weakness

sweeping over him, and there was a cheer from the
forest. The pursuing troopers had returned.

The first trooper shouted over his shoulder, "You
see? They can't kill the king."

A second man, a blond Illyrian, shouldered past
him, holding up two dripping objects. Alexander blinked
at them, momentarily unable to focus. Then the Illyrian
tossed the severed heads to the ground in front of the
king, saying, "There're two of the bastards that did it,
sire. We'll get the others, too."

Alexander nodded and managed to say, in something approaching his normal voice, "Thank you. A
golden cup for each of you." It was the traditional
Illyrian reward. The blond man whooped his pleasure,
turning to his companions with delight. Alexander
turned his horse away, steadying himself against the
animal's neck. Hephaestion pushed close and Alexander straightened with an effort.

"I'm all right," he said aloud. "On to Neapolis."

In the heart of the forest, Horatius Regulus crouched
unmoving in the limbs of a tree, hoping the branches
would hide him from the troopers still combing the
wood. His whole body ached with the effort of keeping absolutely still: the slightest unnatural tremor of
leaves would betray him. Resolutely, he set himself to
ignore the pain, to wait patiently for full darkness so
that he could slip away to warn the consul. His mouth
twisted bitterly. He would have two failures to report
now, besides the battle. He had missed his chance to
kill the Macedonian king and in doing so had signed
the death warrant for what was left of his century. But
there had been nothing else to do and if he hadn't
missed. . . . He put that thought aside with an effort.
Alexander was hurt, which could only help the Roman
cause. And there was always the chance of fever,
perhaps even a mortal one: on balance, that was worth

the death of all his men, and his own, if it came to that.

The sound of horses crashing through the underbrush was moving away at last. Cautiously, Horatius shifted his grip on the nearest branch, then drew his leg up until it was braced more comfortably against the treetrunk. Despite his care, the dead leaves rattled alarmingly and a handful sifted down to join the others carpeting the base of the tree. Horatius tensed and shifted his grip on his second pilum. There was no sign that the Macedonians had heard, and, slowly, Horatius relaxed. It sounded almost as though the last of the horsemen were moving out of the wood. Still, it was not until after midnight that the Roman dropped painfully from his hiding place and struck out northwest toward the consul's army.

CHAPTER 7:

Neapolis, late autumn (Apellaios), 30 imperial, to Latium, winter (Peritios), 31 imperial (326/325 B.C., 427/428 A.U.C.)

A Neapolitan delegation was waiting at the city gates to offer Alexander their submission. The king roused himself to accept it with appropriate ceremony, letting Hephaestion and Hector son of Demetrius do most of the talking, and then ordered his men to take immediate possession of the town's citadel. Only when he was certain that all the Macedonians were safe within its walls did he allow the Friends to persuade him to bed. Hephaestion, swearing unhappily to himself, dispatched messengers to Craterus explaining what had happened, and asking the brigadier to send Philip, Alexander's Acarnanian doctor, ahead to treat the king.

When Philip arrived, only half a day ahead of Craterus's force, he clucked angrily over the wound, and spent the better part of the afternoon cleaning and rebandaging it. Alexander, too weak to protest, accepted a drink containing poppy syrup, and submitted without complaint to the doctor's ministrations.

When the doctor had gone, Alexander lay back

against the pillows, exhausted. Philip's medicine had only partly masked the pain, but the king had been too proud to complain. In the far corner of the room, shadows shifted momentarily, billowing outward like a curtain. Alexander frowned at them, willing the movement to stop. Then the shadows steadied. A figure stood there, a man in old-fashioned armor, heavy helmet pulled down to hide his face. The king opened his mouth to challenge the stranger, then stopped abruptly as he recognized the markings on the massive shield. He had half memorized that section of the *Illiad* as a boy, dreaming of the day some god would give him armor as fine. The shape freed its sword arm from its heavy cloak, and pushed back its helmet. Its face was the face of Achilles, familiar from statues and embellished by a boy's imagination, but the helmet rested easily on the ram's horns that curled back from the forehead. Alexander shivered: not Achilles, then, who was after all his ancestor, but Zeus Ammon, the god who had spoken at Siwah. The apparition stared back at him, perfect face showing neither praise nor blame.

The lamp flared then and the figure was gone. Alexander took a deep breath and winced at the returning pain in his side. He could not guess what the god had wanted from him, and was too drained and weak to send for the augers who could interpret the vision. There had been neither urgency nor comfort in the god's eyes, only an inhuman watchfulness. Still puzzling over it, Alexander slept.

The Friends were waiting in the antechamber when Philip emerged from the king's bedroom. The doctor eyed them warily, reading the signs of recent quarrelling, and said, "Sirs, the king will be well enough, if he rests."

Craterus, bearded face still showing the dirt of the forced march, said shortly, "The gods send he can."

Philip frowned without understanding, and Hephaestion said, "Never mind, Craterus. Go on, Philip."

Craterus grumbled something and the doctor said hastily, hoping to avert a quarrel, "As I said, general, he will be well enough, if he lets it heal. The wound in itself is not so bad, but he lost much blood, and there is always the danger of fever. The rib itself is cracked, too, and that will take time to heal."

Ptolemy said, "How soon will he be up and about?"

"He should stay in bed for three or four more days," Philip said austerely. "He's asleep now, but I'm sure he'll be able to see you in the morning."

Ptolemy grunted, glancing at the other generals. "Good enough," he said. The others nodded. Once their first fears were stilled, and there was a promise of a morning conference, each man had to attend to his own troops. The group broke up quickly, Perdiccas muttering something about the king's charmed life. Only Hephaestion remained behind. Philip eyed him curiously but waited.

"You said a cracked rib," the cavalry commander said, after a moment. "The way the javelin caught him, it ran along the bone. It would be more— chipped—than cracked, wouldn't it?" It was hardly a question.

Philip sighed. Aristotle's medical lore might be some-what old-fashioned, but Hephaestion had remembered at least the rudiments of what he had been taught. And no one had ever called the cavalry commander a fool. "Yes, general, and there were chips of bone in the wound. I removed all that I saw, but there is always a danger that I did not get all the pieces, or that other bits will break loose if he doesn't let this heal. But I did the best I could."

Hephaestion forced a smile. "I never doubted that. I just hope he has time to recover." At the doctor's puzzled frown, the cavalry commander laughed softly. "Philip, we beat one legion. There are five more waiting for us, and their commander would be a fool not to take advantage of the king's injury."

Philip nodded and mumbled to himself, "Let's hope he is a fool, or we could lose the king."

Alexander beat the doctor's predictions by two days. On the third day after the battle, tightly bandaged and carefully dressed in a dark red tunic that would disguise any fresh bleeding, he joined the Friends in the large, cold room that had served as the council chamber since the citadel was built. The servants had done their best to make the place comfortable, but even three smoking braziers did little to warm it. At Hephaestion's order, the pages had brought a massive, high-backed chair for the king—Persian spoils—as well as the usual light Greek chairs for the generals. Alexander settled into it, nodding his thanks to the cavalry commander, and carefully arranged his feet on the low stool.

The Friends exchanged nervous glances—the king's face was still very pale, an indefinable shadow of illness around his eyes—and Alexander frowned. "To business, then," he said. His voice was almost normal.

Craterus cleared his throat. "The Scouts have returned," he said, without preamble. "The two Roman armies have joined, and they have a fortified camp here, about a hundred and ten stadia due north of us. So far they haven't made any move to besiege the city, I don't know why not."

"Maybe they're interested in a treaty," Perdiccas muttered.

Alexander leaned back against the stiff cushions, suddenly grateful for their support. He would have to face the Roman army sooner or later—at the moment, it blocked the land road to the Greek cities in the south, and controlled a large part of the countryside that fed Neapolis—but he could make use of any delay. "Maybe they are," he said aloud, "Perdiccas, your people captured the Roman commander, didn't you? Let's see if he'll take a message to this Fabius."

Craterus said, "They don't seem the kind to make

treaties, Alexander. Remember what their envoys were like."

Hephaestion said, looking at the ceiling, "Of course, if we're negotiating—"

Alexander silenced the cavalry commander with a look and beckoned to the duty page. "Send for the Roman commander. And for the Neapolitan magistrates."

The boy bobbed his head and vanished. The Neapolitans appeared almost at once, as though they had been waiting for an audience. The page returned a few moments later, followed by a pair of hypaspists and a slight, brown-skinned man in a dirty cloak. "Lucius Cassius Nasidienis, Tribune of Rome, sire," the page announced.

"Come forward," Alexander said. He tilted his head to one side, studying the Roman. Cassius Nasidienis had a clean-shaven, cheerful, boyish face—deceptively boyish, if the way he handled the retreat were a true indication of his abilities, and not the work of more senior officers.

Cassius returned the king's stare openly, noting the signs of illness. Alexander nodded slightly, acknowledging the other's scrutiny. "So, tribune," he said. "The Neapolitans have asked me to—arbitrate in their quarrel with Rome."

Cassius drew himself up, uncomfortably aware of the multiple undercurrents in the conversation. "Neapolis had no quarrel with Rome three years ago," he answered, "when they begged us to protect them against their own kin."

Alexander smiled, very slightly, and one of the civilians said hastily, "Great King, not all the city chose to invite the Romans to be our allies. Even he will tell you that."

"I've yet to see a Greek city that ever agreed to anything unanimously," Ptolemy murmured, just loud enough to be heard clearly, and Perdiccas laughed. The Neapolitan flushed angrily.

"Is that so, tribune?" Alexander asked.

Cassius said, choosing his words carefully, "Certainly Anytus's faction never supported Rome. But they were very much in the minority here." He could not resist a pointed glance at Hector son of Demetrius, who stood with the other magistrates, his gilt-embroidered gown glittering in the lamplight. "Unlike the ones who accepted Roman aid and office, and then deserted us."

"You betrayed us," Hector son of Demetrius snapped back, "leading us against them." He glanced hastily at Alexander, and added, "No one could expect to defeat the great Alexander, conqueror of Asia and Greece—"

"I had my orders," Cassius said, unable to keep his temper any longer. "And if you hadn't broken, coward, we could have saved more than your miserable life."

"Whore's bastard, how dare you—" the Neapolitan began, and Hephaestion snapped, "Hold your tongue, you, do you always brawl in council?"

"Enough, all of you," the king said.

"I ask King Alexander's pardon," Cassius said, stiffly. "I forgot myself." There was something perversely senatorial about this Macedonian council, he realized suddenly, a crude resemblance between the freedom—the license—Alexander allowed his men, and the polished debates of the senators. The thought, true or not, freed his tongue. He had been trained for the Senate and its debates; he could handle this. He took a deep breath, and let it out slowly, waiting for the next chance to speak.

"Granted," Alexander murmured, and Neoptolemus said clearly, "The Roman had provocation, the gods know." Craterus snorted his agreement.

"In any case, tribune," Alexander went on, ignoring his officers' comments, "we have other business, you and I. There is the matter of ransom for yourself, and for the other prisoners. And the possibility, at least, of some peaceful arrangement for Neapolis."

"Alexander, Great King," Hector cried. "You can't make peace with Rome."

"Be quiet," Alexander said, raising his voice for the first time. The sudden exertion sent a wave of pain through his chest. With an effort, he kept his face expressionless, but his left hand closed slowly into a white-knuckled fist.

"King Alexander," the Roman said abruptly. "I fear I've forgotten myself again. I am—I was—the commander of the garrison here, but I am only a military tribune, under the consuls' authority. I cannot speak for Rome; only the Senate, or the Senate through the consuls, may do so. I am not really empowered to arrange ransom, that is the commander's right as well. If you will allow it, I will send one of my officers— under escort, of course—to speak to Fabius, so that my people can be ransomed. Fabius himself will have to decide if he can treat with you on behalf of the city."

Alexander drew a careful breath. "You are honest to tell me so. Very well. Will you take my message to your—consul?"

Cassius nodded, waiting.

"Tell him first I want to come to terms over the prisoners—and you may tell them, too, the dead had all their rites." Alexander paused again, eyeing the Roman warily. For all his apparent youth, Cassius had the unreadable face of a seasoned diplomat. "You may also tell him I have no quarrel with Rome." In spite of himself, the king's voice took on a hint of irony. "I am here only to protect my allies' rights and I wish to come to some reasonable solution. Polydamus will escort you." He beckoned, left-handed, to the messenger, who came forward quickly, taking the king's hand in a ritual gesture. "Polydamus is a Friend. He has authority to speak for me."

Cassius sighed slowly. Alexander had used the Macedonian word for "friend", which seemed to indicate it was a title like the more familiar "companion", but Polydamus had the look of something more than a mere ambassador. Abruptly, Cassius was overcome with the desire to refuse to be Alexander's messenger— there was nothing to like and everything to distrust about this embassy—but he had left himself no choice. "Very well, King Alexander," he said. "I will speak to Fabius."

Fabius received the embassy with his usual courtesy, sparing no formality in his reception of Polydamus. After Fabius had accepted Alexander's assurances that the Roman dead had been given their rites, the Macedonian was treated to a dinner conducted with solemnity. The consul refused to discuss business during the meal, promising that he would attend to Polydamus's other messages in the morning, after the Romans had made their own preparations for their dead. Polydamus, knowing perfectly well why the consul wanted a delay, soon returned to his own tent, leaving the Romans to talk among themselves.

Cassius waited in the chill half-darkness of the consul's tent, staring at the flame of the single lamp. The flame flickered as the tent flap was drawn back, and the tribune leaned forward quickly to protect the flame. Fabius drew the tent flap tightly closed behind him and said to his body-slave, "Get out. Wait in Gabinius's tent until I send for you."

The wizened Greek did as he was told. Fabius waited until he felt sure the man would be out of earshot, then, cautiously, opened the tent flap a few inches. No one was in sight. Satisfied, he came back into the circle of lamplight, and seated himself opposite his tribune. Cassius regarded him steadily, bracing himself for either praise or censure.

Fabius said, "Horatius tells me Alexander is wounded."

"Horatius is alive?" Cassius exclaimed. "I beg your pardon, sir, but I thought he'd been killed. Yes, Alexander's been wounded, but he's already up and about again."

Fabius grunted. "Alive, well, and very angry he missed his shot at the Macedonian."

Cassius smiled. It did not surprise him that it had been the veteran Horatius who had finally succeeded in damaging the seemingly unstoppable Alexander.

Fabius went on, "How badly was he hurt, could you tell?"

Cassius hesitated, then said honestly, "I don't know. There were a lot of rumors flying around, and, while I speak Greek well enough, Macedonian is another matter. He was in pain, but not incapacitated, when I saw him."

Fabius nodded, then rose from his chair to pace the length of the little tent and back again. Cassius watched him with a growing unease. Then he straightened his shoulders. He was the consul's protégé, as well as the son of Fabius's closest friend; he had a right to know what was going on. "Sir," he said, "is there trouble?"

Fabius started. He had half forgotten the tribune's presence, caught up in his own bleak thoughts. "Trouble enough," he said, and returned to his seat. "I received a dispatch from the Senate today."

"Oh?"

Fabius smiled grimly. "The Senate informs me that I now have allies in my fight. They've signed a treaty with Carthage, against Alexander."

"No," Cassius said involuntarily, though he knew perfectly well the Senate was capable of such an action. "Are they out of their minds?"

"Not entirely, I suppose," Fabius answered. "But I

confess I don't see the sense of it. What can Carthage do to help us?"

Cassius said, bitterly, "Nothing and they never will." His father had been killed by raiding Carthaginians.

Fabius smiled again. "Ah, but you're prejudiced, dear boy, because of your father's death, and I am also suspect—no, that's too strong a word. Let's say my judgment's not to be relied on, since I was so strongly opposed to insulting Alexander in the first place."

"Poppaeus Piso?" Cassius asked, naming Fabius's most important senatorial rival.

"Oddly enough, the very man who sponsored this treaty," Fabius said. Abruptly, the lightness left his voice. "Gods hear me, what am I supposed to do? Our numbers are roughly even, and I think our legions are as good as his phalanx any day, but I'm not Alexander. I'm no Greek-lover, I was brought up before this fad for Greek education, but I'm not ashamed to admit he's a better general than I am."

Cassius sat very still, unnerved by the frustration in Fabius's voice. After a long moment, he said, "You'll think of something, sir. . . ." His voice died away, and he felt himself flush painfully.

Fabius shook himself. "Oh, I've thought of a few things, Cassius, never fear. It's winter now. For all that he holds the Neapolis harbor, the seas are still too rough for him to be supplied that way. And I control the farmlands. I'm going to make him come after me, and then I'm going to retreat, and burn everything behind me. It may not stop him, but at least he'll come to battle hungry."

Polydamus met with the consul the following day, and again the day after that. Fabius was impeccably polite, but it became clear even without a definite refusal that there would be no negotiation except for the return of the prisoners. Recognizing that, Polydamus spent two more days obtaining a firm offer from Fabius for the prisoners, and a third day extricating himself from the other talks, and returned to Neapolis.

Alexander heard his agent's report with some disappointment, but in truth he had expected no more. He accepted Fabius's offer for the prisoners, pointing out, when Craterus objected violently, that two hundred men would make little difference to Fabius's force, and would be that many fewer mouths to feed. Supplies were growing short in Neapolis—the city was not prepared to feed nearly twenty-five thousand men, or their accompanying animals, in addition to its own population—and roving Roman patrols made it hard to live off the surrounding countryside. That left only one real alternative. Overriding Philip's predictions of disaster, and the Friends' cautious objections, Alexander began preparations to leave Neapolis in pursuit of the Roman army.

The main problem was supplies and there was no guarantee that Fabius would allow them to live off the countryside. Ptolemy took a certain grim pleasure in stripping Neapolis of every ounce of grain it could spare. It was paid for in full, but the city magistrates complained bitterly that they could not eat gold. Craterus suggested dryly that in that case payment could be omitted and the complaints ceased: the city was leaner for its contribution but it would not starve.

The Macedonian army left Neapolis at the full moon. Fabius, well informed of their movements by his agents still in the city, withdrew slowly toward Rome, using his knowledge of the land to keep about a day's march ahead of the Macedonians. The two armies between them had pretty much stripped Campania bare already, despite that land's reputation for abundance. As the consul moved into Latium, as yet untouched by the armies' passage, he did his best to strip towns and countryside, burning everything he could not carry off himself. The senior consul, Marcus Hirtius Fimbria, objected strenuously to the tactic, but Fabius contrived to ignore his protests.

Alexander, struggling to overtake the Romans, was forced to send his foragers farther and farther afield, slowing his progress even further. There was much grumbling and complaints of corrupt practices among the few merchants who still followed the army. To prevent trouble, the king sequestered those supplies, promising double payment later, and began issuing them as a supplement to the already reduced royal ration.

Fabius continued to avoid battle, falling back into Latium toward Rome itself. However, his orders were to keep Alexander away from the city, and not even he could evade the explicit wishes of the Senate. After much consideration, and consultation with his officers, he abandoned his policy of withdrawal, and moved directly north toward the little Roman town of Lanuvium, on the slopes of the Alban Mount. A sluggish river ran south from Lanuvium toward the allied city of Ardea some ten miles to the southwest. The true ford lay only a few miles from Lanuvium, less than a quarter of a mile beyond the swelling shoulder of the Alban Mount, though the river was passable even in the rainy season for at least a quarter of a mile above and below it. Farther downstream, the channel swelled and deepened, impassable even in the driest weather. Fabius took up his position on the far side of the river along the passable stretch, and set his troops at once to pitting the ford, leaving only a few disguised safe paths for his own skirmishers. Others worked to improve the already steep banks, cutting timber for crude breastworks.

Alexander's scouts, shadowing the Roman army at a discreet distance, pushed close enough to see the signs of fresh-dug earthworks and raw timber, and turned at once to warn the king, still a day's march to the south. Alexander listened to the scouts' reports and cut off Craterus's curses with an impatient gesture. "We push on," he said, and smiled grimly. "We can't give them time to finish their defenses."

Other scouting parties had reported a good, defensible campsite a few stadia south of the Roman position. It was just within reach of a long day's march and Alexander ordered the army to push ahead.

It was a hard march, as the king had expected. The Foot Companions and the three brigades of mercenary infantry struggled to keep the pace their officers set them, cursing the Romans and their own officers impartially. The cavalry, marching on foot to spare the horses, complained as bitterly. The sun had set before they reached the spot the scouts had selected. In the gathering dusk, many of the soldiers threw down their bedrolls where they could, not bothering to wait for the baggage carts and their tents, or even to establish a perimeter. Alternately cursing and cajoling them, the king shamed the front-rank men of Meleager's brigade into setting a perimeter guard. Under the lash of Craterus's scorn, his brigade took up the vanguard's job of patrolling the campsite itself, shunting each new arrival into his unit's traditional place. The Companion Cavalry, under Hephaestion's iron control, set up its picket lines with more efficiency, but the other cavalry was less disciplined. A few foreign troopers tried to insinuate their horses into the Companions' line, and quarrels and a knife-fight followed.

It was fully dark before the worst of the confusion was brought under conrol. By then, all but the last stragglers had made their way into the camp. A gang of slaves and servants unloaded the baggage carts while file and half-file-leaders waited impatiently to retrieve their tents. Eumenes's men had thrown up a cordon around the supply wagons, and the issue of rations was proceeding in a relatively orderly fashion. There would be no bread tonight— there had been no time to bake during the past week's march—only grain for the universally detested porridge, supplemented by a handful of olives or a wedge of strong-smelling cheese. The soldiers grumbled, but took what they could get.

Alexander, accompanied by only a page and a pair of troopers, made a final circuit of the camp, pausing at every campfire to tease the men into a better humor, consulting quietly with every officer he found, junior or senior. The march had tired him, too, and the weeks-old wound in his side ached abominably. By the time he had reached the Agrianians' precinct, and spoke with Pithon, their gap-toothed commander, he could feel an oozing dampness, like sweat, beneath tunic and bandages.

A fire was already burning in front of the king's tent. A pair of pages tended it, supervising the slave who cooked for the royal household. The rest of the watch stood to attention under the outstretched flap that screened the doorway, and the senior page said quietly, "The generals are waiting, sire." The words came out as a reprimand rather than the polite warning the boy had intended. Alexander gave him a sharp look, but nodded his thanks, and ducked into the tent.

A few of the Friends were still missing—neither Hephaestion nor Menidas was present and Pithon had not yet settled his men to his satisfaction—but the rest of the generals had drawn their chairs into a wide circle around a cleared spot of ground. Amyntas and a second scout commander knelt between the chairs, scribbling in the dirt with lengths of stick. Two oil lamps gave an uneven light to their work.

The pages had set out the high-backed chair the king had favored since being wounded. Alexander settled into it gratefully, murmuring a response to the generals' greeting, and accepted a cup of watered wine from a slave. He kept his cloak pulled close around his shoulders, hiding any sign of fresh bleeding. The scouts, after a quick glance in the king's direction, went on with their work, overturning an empty wine cup to represent Lanuvium.

"Where are the others?" Alexander asked.

"I don't know," Ptolemy said, and Perdiccas looked up, blinking even in the dim lamplight.

"Last I saw, Hephaestion was down by the horse lines."

"I'm here," Hephaestion said, from the tent flap. At the same instant, the senior page said, "General Hephaestion, sire, and General Menidas."

Both the newcomers were scowling as they found empty chairs, and the other generals eyed them warily. Craterus said, "Trouble?"

Hephaestion made a face, and beckoned for the slave to bring wine. Menidas said, "Nothing too serious, just a fight on the horse lines that we had to sort out."

Craterus sneered faintly, but he was too tired to make a quarrel. Pithon arrived a few moments later, and, last of all, Polyperchon, whose brigade had had the rearguard. The scouts had nearly finished with their crude map, disputing in whispers over the placement of a few final lines. Once, Laomedon, who had been in charge of interrogating the few prisoners—mostly peasants pressed into service as guides—leaned over and made a low-voiced correction. Amyntas looked up at last.

"This is what we saw, sire."

Alexander leaned forward, holding his cup in both hands. The movement set off a new pain in his ribs, as though he had been stabbed again. His hands tightened around the cup, the fragile gold bending under his hands. He took a careful breath, and the pain struck again, so sharply that it was an effort not to cry out. Across the circle of chairs, Hephaestion saw the convulsive movement of the king's hands, and looked up. Alexander had gone suddenly pale, muscles of jaw and neck starkly apparent. The cavalry commander opened his mouth to ask what was wrong and Alexander stared him down. The pain eased, very slowly. After a moment, the king loosened his grip on the wine cup—it was no longer perfectly circular, but a slightly dented oval—and took a cautious breath. The pain was there still, but not as badly, and he forced himself to concentrate on what the scouts were saying.

The other generals had noticed nothing. Amyntas swept his hand toward a cluster of pebbles that extended to both sides of the line marking the river, saying, "The hills aren't too steep at first, but they look to rise pretty sharply once you're in among them."

"We couldn't get too close," interjected the second scout, Tauron of Larisa. "The ground's very open all along the river, until you reach the hills."

Amyntas nodded. "The Romans are camped along the river here." His hand swept out again, indicating two lines of twigs stretching from just below the pebbles almost to the end of the line that marked the river. "I assume that's the ford, they were crossing freely along it. The banks looked fairly steep, and it looked like they were adding palisades on the low parts."

Craterus muttered a curse, tugging at his beard, and leaned forward to study the plan more closely. Alexander said, "Laomedon?" His voice sounded odd in his own ears, hoarse and strained, but none of the others seemed to notice.

Laomedon, who had been trying to get a word in, gave the king a grateful smile. "The ford is only about a quarter of a mile wide—that's a hair more than two stadia—but the river is passable for two stadia to either side of the ford."

"What do you mean, passable?" Craterus growled, and at the same moment, Perdiccas said, "You got this from those peasants we took? Were they telling the truth?"

Laomedon said, with some dignity, "Each one told

me the same thing, and they had no time to invent a common story. I think they were telling the truth." He looked at Craterus. "I meant passable, Craterus. A man on foot can cross there, without too much risk of drowning. Downstream, the water runs waist-deep instead of knee-deep, and gets deeper. One old man said there were a crooked tree and a white rock for markers: you can cross below, but not above. Upstream of the ford, it's no deeper, but the channel is narrow and rocky, and the current is fairly fast, coming out of the hills."

Craterus shook his head slowly, but said nothing more. A crossing under those conditions would be murderously difficult, impossible for the phalanx to keep the line. And with the Romans waiting in prepared positions, there would be fierce fighting to secure a foothold on the bank before the real battle could begin. It would be like Issus, where he had lost nearly a hundred men from his brigade, only worse: the river here was deeper, and the Roman commander, unlike Darius, did not seem the kind of man to run away before the battle was over.

Ptolemy rubbed at his forehead. "Is this the right place to meet the Romans?" he wondered aloud.

"Is any place the right place?" Perdiccas jeered.

Alexander, instead of answering, gestured for Eumenes to speak. The secretary smiled faintly, saying, "If we try to avoid battle now, and go southwest, we're still blocked by the river, which doesn't become any more fordable. And, of course, the Romans would simply follow along the river."

Ptolemy flushed angrily at the secretary's tone, and Craterus said, "Get to the point, pen-pusher."

"North and east, we have to skirt that damn mountain," Eumenes went on, a spot of color high on his sallow cheekbones betraying his own anger. "Not to mention a Roman city—or at least a Roman ally—and a second allied city somewhere on the northern side of the hills. Our best estimate is that it's nearly four hundred stadia to Rome by that road, and only a hundred and seventy-five stadia from the Roman camp—"

"I see," Ptolemy said, still angry. The Romans could swing around the shoulder of the mountain, or even go through the hills—there were bound to be usable tracks—and intercept the Macedonian army at almost any point they chose. But another commander would have taken that chance. He looked at Alexander. "We'll lose a lot of men here, Alexander. They're bound to have pitted the ford, just for starters."

The king nodded, his face grim. "I know. But there's also the supply problem." His voice was still strained. Both Craterus and Ptolemy heard it this time, and looked oddly at the king.

Hephaestion said, cutting off any comments, "What's the river like farther down? Could a small party cross below their lines?"

Amyntas said, "There's not much cover along the banks, you'd have to go a long way to cross unseen."

Laomedon shook his head. "They say it's been a dry winter," he said slowly. "I suppose the horses could swim it, but the men would need rafts, or at least something to cling to. And the current is strong."

Hephaestion nodded, unobtrusively watching the king.

Alexander took another careful breath, feeling the pain bite deep into his side. "Let that be a last resort, then," he said. He started to lean forward and checked himself abruptly. "Ptolemy, you'll have overall command of the phalanx, and the central brigade. Neoptolemus, the hypaspists will have the right wing, supported by the Companion Cavalry. I'll ride with them myself. We'll force a crossing, Neoptolemus, and establish a foothold for you."

The hypaspist commander nodded and the king went on, "I expect they'll concentrate their light infantry in

those hills—Pithon, it'll be your responsibility to drive
them back before we try to cross. The Paeonian horse
will support you in that—in driving them back."

Ariston, the Paeonian commander, nodded cheerfully. It was generally agreed among the Friends that
he was too stupid to know when an assignment was
difficult or even impossible. He simply did exactly
what he had been told, no more, and no less. Such
stupidity—heedless bravery, the kinder called it—
brought its own rewards: he had not only survived the
Asian and the Greek campaigns, but had prospered
from them. Alexander, who was well aware of the
Paeonian's faults, eyed him closely before continuing.

"Craterus, you'll have command of the left wing,
which will be your brigade and the mercenary brigades. The rest of the line, left wing to right: Craterus,
Meleager, Perdiccas, Ptolemy, Polyperchon, Coenus.
The Companion Cavalry will also have the left wing.
The rest of the light infantry and light horse—and
your archers, Ombrion—will screen the phalanx as we
advance." Alexander glanced around the circle again.
"Amyntas, I'll want reports as soon as it's light enough
to see their line. The rest of you—this is only a
preliminary disposition, I'll probably want to change
things when I see what the Romans have done, so be
ready. We'll take the advance very slowly, half the
battle pace."

Ptolemy was nodding to himself, studying the plan.
Craterus said, with a sort of grim satisfaction, "So the
phalanx does the dirty work again."

Perdiccas snorted audibly, but said only, "It looks
to me like our line might extend further than the
passable area. What then?"

"Deepen the files and cross upstream of Laomedon's
mark—"

"A white rock, the old man said," Laomedon
interjected. "He said you couldn't miss it."

Alexander nodded. There were other questions, more

comments, but not many: the plan was clear enough and its dangers were enough to sober even the most optimistic commanders. One by one, the generals retired to their tents to brief their officers, and then to get as much sleep as they could before the battle. The Friends were the last to leave, Hephaestion lagging behind the others. Perdiccas held the tent flap open for him pointedly and Hephaestion said, "I've business with the king, Perdiccas."

"Oh, indeed," the brigadier said with a knowing leer, and let the tent flap fall closed behind him.

Left alone with the king, Hephaestion studied the other intently, noting how he held his right arm immobile, pressed tight against his side. Alexander leaned back against the back of his chair, grateful for its support. After a moment, he said, "What business?"

Hephaestion said, "You're bleeding again."

Before the king could answer, the tent flap was pulled back again, and a page entered carrying the king's dinner. The corners of Alexander's mouth turned down almost petulantly, and he gestured for the boy to take the tray on into the inner chamber. "Then leave us," he added. When the page was gone, he said, "Yes, I think so."

"I'll send for Philip."

"No." Alexander stood up, wincing, then managed a pained smile. "It just needs to have the bandage changed, I'd rather you did it for me."

It was an appeal Hephaestion had never been able to refuse. Against his better judgement, he followed the king into the dimly lit bedchamber. Bagoas was busy with the steaming dishes, trying to present the stewed mess of porridge and onions and the slab of unpleasant-looking cheese as appetizingly as possible. He turned as the king entered, reaching for the wine jug, but the king waved him away and seated himself on the foot of the bed.

Hephaestion said, "Bring fresh bandages." Try as

he might, he was never able to be anything but abrupt to the Persian. Bagoas gave him a cold glance from under delicately lowered eyelids, but did as he was told. Hephaestion unclasped the king's cloak—there was only the faintest of stains on Alexander's tunic, a good sign—then unfastened the pins that held the tunic's shoulders together. Alexander grimaced irritably as the cloth fell free, revealing the bandages that circled his chest. There was a red stain about the size of a man's palm on the cloth over the wound. Hephaestion shook his head.

"I didn't have time to have it seen to," Alexander began, and broke off as Bagoas returned, carrying an armful of clean linen strips.

Hephaestion grunted, unwilling to rebuke the king in the Persian's presence, and very carefully began to loosen the layers of bandages. Alexander, wincing, lifted his right arm, supporting its elbow in his left hand. The last pad of cloth was stuck to the wound. Alexander's expression did not change, but he hissed very softly between his teeth. Wincing in sympathy, Hephaestion turned to ask for a bowl of warmed water. Bagoas had it ready. The cavalry commander nodded his thanks, and, as carefully as possible, soaked the bandage loose. Alexander gave a short exclamation of pain, his whole body going rigid.

Hephaestion cursed softly to himself and bent to examine the wound. Alexander's side was heavily bruised; the wound itself was partly closed, the scabs new and shiny. It had broken open in two places, one of which had already begun to close again, a new, dark scab forming on top of the older surface. The second break still oozed blood, and something white showed through the scab. Hephaestion sat staring at it for what seemed like a very long time, knowing perfectly well what it was. Philip's warning—and his own fear—had come true. A piece of bone had broken loose from the cracked rib and had worked its way to the surface of the wound.

"What is it?" Alexander demanded, between clenched teeth.

"A bone chip," Hephaestion answered flatly. "It'll have to come out."

Alexander muttered something of startling obscenity, then said, bracing himself, "Do it, then."

Hephaestion braced himself as well, and took careful hold of the protruding sliver. There was barely enough showing above the surface for him to get a good grip; he squeezed it tightly between thumb and forefinger and tugged sharply. Alexander's whole body jerked convulsively, but the king didn't utter a sound. Hephaestion swallowed hard, overcoming his own revulsion, and pulled again, harder. The splinter stayed fixed for a moment longer, then, quite suddenly, tore free, bringing a piece of the scab with it. The wound was bleeding freely again, and Hephaestion whispered a curse, groping for the clean bandages. Bagoas put one in his hand, and Hephaestion wadded it hastily against the wound.

The bleeding slowed fairly quickly, and Hephaestion hurriedly rewound the bandages, his eyes on the king's face. Alexander was very pale, his mouth a tight, colorless line, eyes staring straight ahead at nothing.

"Get some wine," Hephaestion said to Bagoas, and gently eased the king's tunic back up over his shoulders. "Neat."

The Persian did as he was told, returning in an instant with a cup of the syrupy liquor. Alexander drained it in two swallows, and whispered, "More."

Bagoas brought a second cup. Alexander took another swallow, then set the rest aside. Color was returning to his face, staining his broad cheekbones. Seeing that, Hephaestion said, "You should have Philip to see to this."

Alexander shook his head and managed a rueful

smile. "And have him tell me I shouldn't fight tomorrow? It would only worry him."

"Maybe you shouldn't fight," Hephaestion said.

"How can I not?" Alexander asked, smile widening.

Hephaestion shook his head, but returned the smile. Other kings had avoided battle when they were wounded, but not Alexander—never Alexander. The suggestion had hardly been worth making.

He remained with the king a little while longer, until Alexander's face returned to its normal ruddy color, and the king seemed to be moving with less pain. Only then did he start back to his own tent.

Pasithea was crouched beside the doorway of the king's tent. Hephaestion, heedless in his own exhaustion, nearly tripped over her. A page's soft exclamation warned him and he just managed to avoid her huddled form. The sudden noises woke the Syrian and she blinked at the cavalry commander, smiling sleepily up at him. Hephaestion stared back at her, overcome by nameless fears. To quiet them, he said, "No trouble, is there, mother?"

The Syrian blinked at him and Hephaestion was suddenly aware of the pages, hanging on every word. He waved them off, glaring, and dropped down beside the seeress. She sat up fully then, drawing her layers of clothing around her. She looked a little cleaner than she had in Asia, but a sharp, animal smell still rose from her.

"Have you had more warnings, Mother?" Hephaestion asked again, lowering his voice discreetly.

Disconcertingly, Pasithea giggled. "And if I had," she whispered, "you would not believe in them, I know." Then her feral face softened slightly. "No, no warning, not for the king. But I'll watch the night out and that will be for luck."

"The gods send us luck," Hephaestion said, more devoutly than he had spoken in a long time, and pushed himself to his feet. "Gods know, we'll need it."

CHAPTER 8:

The scouts were on their way well before dawn, so that they would be in a good position to take a final look at the Roman lines by first light. The rest of the army was roused a little later, file-leaders and half-file-leaders kicking their protesting men out of tents and bedrolls. The men armed themselves in the half-light, exchanging grim estimates of the probable Roman strength, and ate the meager, cold breakfast issued them. Even before they had finished, the file-leaders were moving among them again, ordering the tents struck and returned to the baggage carts. Infantry and cavalry obeyed, cursing. The carts and the camp followers, already grown to a fairly sizable train, would remain at the campsite, guarded by a skeleton detachment made up of the engineers, most of the royal pages, and a scratch battalion of older soldiers and semi-invalids.

The king was awake early, too, snatching his own breakfast while the pages armed him. He was wearing a bell corselet now, front and back each cast in a

187

single piece, rather than the segmented corselet that had broken outside Neapolis—the old-fashioned bell corselets were enjoying a sudden vogue in the Macedonian army—and he settled the increased weight more comfortably across his shoulders, shifting his own weight automatically to help the pages pulling on the sock-like underboots and fastening the stiff greaves. His wound was less painful now that the splinter had been removed, settling to a nagging ache that he could easily ignore, but there was an odd, indefinable weakness. Alexander stood very still for a few moments even after the pages had finished arming him, trying to analyze it, then shook himself and shouted for a groom to bring his horse.

The army was slowly sorting itself out, the soldiers milling about in the open space between the king's tent and the portable altar where the sacrifices would take place. As the king emerged from his tent, there was a cheer from the nearest squadron of Companions, quickly echoed up and down the line of soldiers. Alexander acknowledged it with a wave of his hand and beckoned for the groom to follow him. The two senior pages chosen to accompany the king into battle, as bodyguards and messengers, exchanged proud, frightened glances, and flung themselves onto their saddlecloths. Other pages handed them the king's helmet and lance, then stood staring enviously after their fellows.

As was only fitting, Alexander approached the altar on foot, his escort following at a discreet distance, but nothing could prevent the battalions' cheering as he passed. The king acknowledged the shouts with a lifted hand and called his own greetings to those within earshot. The excitement was contagious. The rush of emotion, joy and terror mixed, drove away any lingering remnants of the odd weakness that had gripped him earlier. Hephaestion, trying to gather his personal squadron and listen to the complaints of other squadron leaders, saw the change come over the king, and shook his head in fond amazement. He himself was coldly terrified—as always before a battle—and controlled his fear only with an effort. For Alexander it was different, incomprehensibly so. Hephaestion shook his head again, and turned his attention to his own people.

Aristander, the chief augur, was waiting beside the altar, several lesser seers hovering respectfully at his shoulder, but there was no garlanded sheep waiting for the sacrifice. All the captured livestock had gone to feed the army. There was wine, however, and incense in quantity. Alexander poured generous quantities of both—the incense sending thick, blue clouds into the augurs' faces—making the ritual prayers to the gods of his house, to Zeus the King, to Athena the war goddess, then to his own god Zeus Ammon and the ancestors of his house. He stepped back from the altar then, and in that instant the sun rose over the horizon, highlighting him against the smoke still billowing from the altar.

There was an awed murmur from the watching soldiers, and Aristander shouted into it, "The gods show the sign of their favor. The gods are pleased."

The murmuring swelled to a full-throated cheer. In the center of the column, Perdiccas caught at Hephaestion's foot. The cavalry commander leaned close and Perdiccas said, "I hope Alexander pays him what he's worth." Even his voice was less skeptical than usual.

Hephaestion, despising himself for the sudden shiver of superstitious fear, shrugged, and shook himself free of the brigadier.

After such a favorable omen, it took less time than usual to form the army into marching columns. Alexander and his personal squadron of Companions rode at the head, the king and his suite riding a little apart from the rest of the troopers. As they approached the river and the Roman position, scouts began to trickle back in. Some of the squadrons had seen hard fighting already; all brought bad news. The Romans had worked like slaves through the night, and had come very close to finishing their defenses. There were lightly armed troops throughout the hills on both sides of the river—it was those troops who had inflicted such losses on the scouts—but most of those men did not seem to be Romans. Amyntas, who had lost nearly half his squadron and been wounded himself, had nevertheless managed to secure a prisoner and bring him back alive. Under rough questioning—there was no time for subtlety—the man admitted to being an Ardean and that two legions were made up of troops from the smaller Latin cities dominated by Rome, but either would not or could not tell anything else of use. Alexander, already contemplating altering his dispositions, filed the information.

The Romans were well aware of the Macedonian advance. Fabius waited until he had heard that the scouts' probes had been driven off, then made a final circuit of his own lines. Roman and allied legions alike seemed ready, waiting at ease behind their rough palisades. The light infantry, a mix of allies and poor Romans who could not afford the heavy panoply of a true legionary, were ready, too. They set up a quick cheer at the consul's approach, and Fabius, touched by the unexpected show of affection, spent some minutes reminding them to be careful passing through the pitted ford. His own right wing extended some distance beyond the passable section of the river, in hopes of luring unwary Macedonians into the deep water. Before he could reach those troops, however, a gasping runner overtook him and informed him that the Macedonian skirmishers were in sight. The consul ordered that message passed to all the commanders, and hurried back to his own place with the central legion.

The Macedonians advanced very slowly, well screened

by the light infantry and cavalry. Alexander listened to
the reports brought by the runners who marched with
those troops, and then made his own necessarily brief
reconnaissance. The Roman position was even stronger
than he had expected, particularly on their left wing,
where a horde of skirmishers and light cavalry anchored the Roman line against the foothills of the
Alban mountain. The generals, gathering for the last
time to listen to the scouts' final reports, drew the
same conclusions. They stood murmuring together,
shaking their heads, and watched the king.

Alexander barely seemed to hesitate. His right wing
could not strike the decisive blow, as planned, until—
and unless—the Roman skirmishers were cleared from
the hills to let the cavalry and the phalanx cross the
river. The left wing, then, would have to carry the
weight, for all that the terrain was against it. He lifted
his arm, beckoning to the waiting officers. "Erigyius,
Hephaestion," he said. The two men spurred close,
waiting for their orders.

"The Thessalians will take the right wing," Alexander went on. "Hephaestion, the Companions will have
the left."

Both commanders nodded—there was still time to
make those changes—and waited for the rest. Alexander smiled unexpectedly, and Hephaestion bit back an
exclamation, recognizing that expression. Craterus,
crowding close to demand more of Ombrion's archers
to deal with the Romans in the hills, recognized it too,
and fell silent, one hand lifted absently to ward off
Erigyius's excited bay.

"Pithon," Alexander began, and looked around for
the Agrianian. "Ariston?" A moment later, Pithon shouldered his way through the cluster of officers, but the
Paeonian commander was nowhere to be seen. Alexander shrugged to himself—it was unlikely Ariston
would be capable of appreciating the minor change in
his orders in any case—and turned to the Agrianian.

"There're more skirmishers than we thought. It'll be a hard fight to clear them but it's more important than ever."

Pithon gave the king a broad smile, showing broken teeth. "Never worry, sire, we'll deal with these barbarians, too."

Alexander nodded his acknowledgement and turned his attention to the cavalry surrounding him. "Tyrimmas," he said, and, when there was no immediate response, said, "Pass the word for him. The rest of you, everything else stays the same—except, Hephaestion, I am taking three squadrons, my own, Hegelochus's, and Peroecles's, to cross the river below their battle line, and take them on their right flank."

Hephaestion began, "That leaves me only seven squadrons, Alexander—" and then Tyrimmas appeared, forcing his dun gelding through the crowd.

"Sire?" the scout asked.

Craterus said, "Alexander, the river's impassable."

"Not for horses," Alexander answered, still smiling, and glanced at the scout. "You said horsemen could get across below Laomedon's mark?"

"Yes, sire," the scout said, his face suddenly impassive beneath his helmet.

"Then we do it," Alexander said. He looked around at the waiting faces, staring down any possible opposition. "Is that clear?" There was a murmur of agreement, and the king beckoned to one of the pages. "Fetch Hegelochus and Peroecles."

"At once, sire," the boy answered, and rode away.

Craterus nodded slowly to himself, not daring to exchange looks with the other infantry commanders. It was a dangerous move but at least it would take some of the burden off his own men. Everything would depend on Alexander's party being able to cross without attack from the Romans: if the Roman cavalry spotted his move and brought their own horsemen downriver to counter it, not even Alexander would be able to force a passage.

The pages returned with the two squadron leaders. Hastily, Alexander explained the change in plan, not minimizing the risks, but infecting them with his own enthusiasm and certainty of success. "We'll go now," the king finished, and glanced for a final time at the other commanders. "Take your time getting into position. We'll cross as quickly as we can to relieve you."

There were neither protests nor comments, only grim agreement. Alexander smiled brilliantly at them all, then held out his hand for his weapons. The older page, Adaeus, instantly produced the king's double-plumed helmet. Alexander settled it into place, and took his lance from the second boy. It was a new lance, and seemed heavier than it should be. Alexander hefted it curiously, then put the thought aside.

"Tyrimmas, you'll guide us," he said. "The rest of you, follow me."

The horses moved off at a walk, Hegelochus and Peroecles shouting for their squad leaders to close up and join them. As the horsemen sorted themselves out, and the squadron leaders passed the word of their new mission, the king picked up the pace, until the horses were moving at a bone-jarring trot. They swung wide to the south, keeping well out of the Romans' sight.

Hephaestion watched them go, shaking his head unhappily. After the king's wound had broken open the night before, he wished that Alexander had sent some other commander—himself, for instance—to manage the crossing. There was too much danger of tearing it open again, of fresh bleeding. . . . The cavalry commander shut that thought away with his other fears, and wrenched his horse around, heading back toward the rest of his men. Erigyius gave him an ironic salute as he passed, shouting, "I don't envy you my job, Hephaestion."

Hephaestion returned the gesture. He himself did not envy Erigyius the job of forcing a crossing on the right wing, but was not about to say so. The Companion squadron leaders were waiting for him, already warned that something was up. Tersely, the cavalry commander explained the change in plans, and the squadrons began to move, swinging around behind the coalescing phalanx. They marched in parade order, horses prancing excitedly. The Thessalians, passing behind them with the same parade-ground precision, lifted their lances and shouted cheerful insults. Then the maneuver was complete, the depleted Companions now stationed on the left flank, the Thessalians on the right.

From his place in the center of the phalanx, Ptolemy saw the signals that indicated the cavalry was in place again, and signalled for the phalanx to speed up its advance. He did not dare move too slowly, least the Romans learn that something was up, but at the same time he had no desire to close too quickly. . . . From the front ranks of Roman skirmishers came a sudden shouting, and, faintly, the musical sound of metal against metal: the battle had begun. There was more shouting from the far right wing as the Agrianians made contact with the Roman skirmishers in the hills.

The phalanx continued its steady advance in silence. The skirmishers pressed forward ahead of them. Then, almost at the last minute, the Thracians' commander gave the signal to retire. The phalanx opened ranks to let them through, the movement precise as a drill, then closed up again. The light cavalry wheeled right as planned, moving to reinforce the Agrianians and Paeonians. The Roman skirmishers, raggedly-clothed men armed with spear and shield, with only a wolf-skin cloak for protection, gave way slowly before the phalanx. At the river's edge, they paused abruptly to release a flight of javelins, sowing gaps all across the Macedonian front. Craterus ducked behind his shield as a spear whistled past, and heard a shout of fury from the man at his left. He turned quickly, and saw the file-leader tugging frantically at the spear embedded in his shield. The metal shaft bent under his tugging, and the man stopped abruptly, cursing, fumbling with the straps of his shield. His sarissa wavered wildly, a danger to his neighbors.

"Get out of the line, you," Craterus shouted. "Second-rank man, take his place."

The file-leader dropped back, still cursing vilely. Ahead, the Roman skirmishers darted back through the water, dodging this way and that to avoid the pits that half blocked the ford. Perdiccas, whose brigade faced the ford itself, cursed bitterly to himself, and shouted, "Watch where they go, men, and follow them."

The shout was echoed by the battalion commanders of the brigades that faced the pitted ford, less as a real order than to reassure themselves that there were safe passages left. Ptolemy glanced up and down his line. The second- and third-rank men had closed the gaps opened by the Roman javelins; on the right, the Agrianians and Thracians seemed to be holding the Roman light troops, clearing the river banks for the hypaspists and the Thessalian cavalry. There was nothing to be gained by waiting. He took a deep breath and gave the war cry. The phalanx surged forward, dropping down the low bank and into the water, knee-deep only at the ford. The formation wavered and loosened as men floundered in the water, stumbling and cursing as they fought to avoid the pits.

On the left wing, Hephaestion urged his horse into the water, careful to keep upstream of the white rock—as Laomedon had promised, it was impossible to miss that landmark—and shouted for his squadron to follow him. The horses fought their riders, snorting and blowing as the chill water rose over their knees. The current tugged at the riders' feet; upstream, the first file-leader stumbled and fell in the waist-deep water, was swept downstream to fetch up, gasping, against the legs of Hephaestion's horse. The Romans, watching from the far bank, gave a derisive cheer. Hephaestion cursed them bitterly, and bent from his saddle to drag the trooper to his feet.

"Stay where you are," he shouted to his men. "Don't let them be swept away." This was not a cavalry battle, not yet; for now, his men could do nothing but support the infantry.

On the right wing, the Agrianians, already heavily engaged, heard the war cry, and redoubled their efforts. The Roman skirmishers gave way reluctantly, leaving bodies huddled in their wake. The Macedonians, too, left bodies behind them, mostly killed by stones from the deadly Ardean slings. Pithon, his light shield shattered by a Roman sword, threw it away, shouting hoarsely for his men to go on. A moment later, a stone struck him in the neck, and he dropped without a sound. Balacrus, his second-in-command, sprang to take his place.

Ariston saw the Agrianian fall and gave a shriek of pure fury, spurring his horse at the nearest cluster of Romans. The rest of the Paeonians, conditioned to blind, tribal obedience, followed him, screaming. Under that unexpected, impossible assault, the Romans gave way, falling back toward the hills.

Menidas, edging his cavalry forward in the narrow gap between the hypaspists and the Roman forces in the hills, saw the sudden charge with a blind disbelief that changed quickly to delight. Only the Paeonian would have tried such a thing and succeeded: a new gap was opening, wide enough to take the right-wing cavalry across the river. Shouting for Erigyius and the Thessalians to follow, he plunged into the water, driving hard for the opposite bank. The Roman cavalry was waiting for him. Menidas thrust hard with his spear, horse dancing beneath him, throwing up great plumes of spray. Then other Greeks were beside him, lances working. One man fell, speared through the body, his screaming horse struggling to turn and run away, and then Menidas had forced his own horse up onto the bank, striking desperately at everything ahead of him. A spear grazed his shoulder, but he was too terrified to feel the wound. Then there was a shout from his left, and more horses scrambled onto the bank. The Roman cavalry fell back to gain room for the charge, and more Macedonians fought their way onto the bank. The Roman charge drove them back a little, but could not dislodge their foothold.

All along the phalanx, the Macedonians struggled grimly to gain a foothold along the bank. In the center, along the ford itself, where the Roman palisades were strongest, the fighting was worst. The Macedonian line, already thinned and made ragged by the unavoidable pits, stood in the knee-deep water, thrusting up at the well-sheltered legionaries. Twice, three times, the sarissas opened a gap large enough for three men to spring up under the walls; three times the Romans drove them back again, battalion commanders ordering the retreat to keep from breaking the line. Bodies began to fill the shallows, their armor holding them below the surface to add another hazard to the crossing.

Further downstream, where the water ran deeper, Meleager's and Craterus's brigades fought their way onto the banks at last. That success opened a gap between Meleager's and Perdiccas's men, a gap that the Romans were quick to exploit. The third legion, made up, in part, of the survivors of Cassius's legion, and commanded by Cassius himself, surged forward. Meleager turned his battalion quickly, the men dropping back into the water to meet the new threat; the fighting, awkward and doubly dangerous in the rapid current, floundered back and forth along the channel. Hephaestion, already hard-pressed to hold off the Roman right-wing cavalry and at the same time provide some protection against the rear-rankers' being swept downstream, saw the flurry of attack and managed to detach three squads to support Meleager. The Macedonian line stretched dangerously, then held firm, but Meleager's red-plumed helmet had disappeared from view. Hephaestion cursed, glancing rapidly along the river, but could spare no time for a fuller search.

The king's party reached the riverbank at the point Tyrimmas had chosen for the crossing just as Ptolemy raised the war cry. Alexander grinned at his officers, then rose slowly along the bank for a few paces, judging current and depth. There was no sign that the Romans had spotted their maneuver, which was just as well: the river itself looked to be a formidable enemy. The dark waters swirled past at a dangerous speed, their true depth unguessable. Thoughtfully, the king pulled loose a piece of grass that had become entangled with his saddlecloth and tossed it into the water. It was swept instantly away, but at least the current flowed straight and true. With a shout, he spurred his horse forward, urging it over the shallow bank.

The water was barely knee-deep at first, but grew rapidly deeper. The king's horse whinnied its unease and fought the reins as the water rose higher, tugging hard at Alexander's legs. The king took a tighter grip on his lance and wrapped his left hand in the horse's mane, letting the reins lie loose along the animal's neck, urging it forward with knees and voice alone.

Abruptly, the horse was swimming, striking out desperately for the opposite bank. The current carried it rapidly downstream, so that by the time the horse felt bottom under its hooves again and scrambled ashore, snorting, they had come nearly a stadion further down the river. Alexander shook himself—he was soaked to the skin, and already shivering despite the winter sunlight—and turned to watch the others across.

The Companions had followed without hesitation. Their horses fought the current together, swimming strongly for the far bank. The riders clung to the horses' backs, trying to keep control of animals and weapons alike. Abruptly, there was a shriek from one of the riders, instantly cut off as Adaeus lost his grip on his horse and was swept away. Alexander tensed, urging his own horse back into the water, but the trooper riding next to the boy was quicker. Before the boy could sink too far, dragged under by the weight of his armor, he had leaned from his own horse and caught Adaeus by the skirt of the tunic, pulling him across his own thighs like a drowning calf. The page's horse, relieved of its burden, reached the shore easily, and was seized by one of the Companions.

Adaeus and his rescuer were the last to come ashore and willing hands reached to help the boy slide from the trooper's lap. The page had lost his helmet and his face already showed the beginnings of a massive bruise, where the trooper had accidentally kicked him. Nevertheless, he professed himself ready and willing to go on. Alexander nodded, listening to the distant sounds of battle, and waved for them to move on.

The king's party moved up the river at a steady trot, the shouting and noise growing gradually louder. At last the Roman flank came into view, an indistinct mob of horses milling around on the river bank. Alexander lifted his sarissa, and urged his own horse to greater speed, the Companions copying him. For a long moment, the Roman horsemen did not turn. Then the unexpected sound of hoofbeats penetrated to an Ardean trooper, who turned without haste, expecting reinforcements from his own city. The sight of the Macedonian king's double-plumed helmet struck him dumb for a moment. Recovering, he shrieked a warning, wheeling his own horse to face this new threat. All around him, the Roman cavalry turned in panic, abandoning their defense of the banks.

Alexander shouted his own war cry and spurred forward recklessly. The Companion squadrons struck the mass of the Roman cavalry before it had time to form up to meet the attack, driving deep among the enemy horses and pushing the rearmost squadrons back into their own infantry. Hephaestion, seeing the familiar double-plumed helmet leading the attack, waved his own squadrons forward.

"One more time, men," he cried, "once more." His men obeyed him, driving their tired horses into the central channel again, and this time they gained the bank.

Fabius, watching the fresh attack from his place in the center of his line, cursed sharply and ordered his last cavalry units, held in reserve in hopes of victory and pursuit, to his right wing to shore up the allied cavalry. The fresh troops forced their way into the melee, driving the Companions back momentarily, but they were driven back themselves by the sheer ferocity of Alexander's attack.

In his narrow beachhead, Craterus recognized the moment for a final effort. Shouting, he and his men pressed forward a final time, the left-most battalion curving around to attack the Romans already disordered by their own cavalry. The rest of the phalanx commanders saw the king's attack and pressed forward. Perdiccas's men at last closed the gap between their brigade and Meleager's, then, with a titanic effort, forced their way past the Roman palisade. More slowly, the other brigades followed, their lines reforming to take full advantage of their longer sarissas as they finally broke past the Roman defenses. On the Macedonian right, the Thessalians smashed through the last allied squadron, and the Roman line began to crumble.

Alexander forced his way past a last enemy cavalryman, stabbing almost blindly with his lance, then turned to survey the battle. The Romans were crumbling, some of the battalions on the wings disintegrating into a mob of fleeing men, others fighting now only to disengage and draw off in good order. He took a deep breath to signal the pursuit, and a Roman soldier broke suddenly from cover, dashing under his horse's hooves to slash at legs and belly. Alexander wrenched the terrified animal away from the danger, stabbing awkwardly with the too-long lance, and hastily shortened his grip. His second blow slid harmlessly along the Roman's corselet. Then the page Theodatus was at his side, crowding the Roman away as he hacked ungracefully with his sword. Alexander had one glimpse of the boy's white face, terrified and exhilarated, before boy and horse and Roman went down together in a kicking heap. Then the horse was up and running, bleeding from a long slash along its withers. A second later, the boy rolled free, and the nearest Companion planted his lance in the Roman's body.

"Machatus!" Alexander shouted. Theodatus was holding his right arm in his left hand, face white now with pain. "See to the boy. The rest of you, follow me!"

The king ended his pursuit a third of the way to Rome, leaving the rest of it to the Thessalians. Now that the excitement of the battle was gone, the strange weakness he had felt in his tent that morning returned. He shivered painfully. His tunic was still damp beneath his corselet, but he could not tell for certain if that was blood or river water. He lifted his right arm experimentally. There was a new, sharper pain, cutting through the steady ache, but he did not think the wound had opened again.

Hephaestion, returning with his own squadron of Companions, overtook the king well behind the former Roman position, riding slowly back toward the battlefield. Alexander sat his horse badly, slumped forward, body slack. The declining sun threw a humpbacked shadow across the grass. Seeing that, one of the troopers muttered a charm to avert the evil omen. Hephaestion, urging his tired horse up the slight incline to join his king, bit his lip to keep from echoing the man. The king was mercifully unaware of his shadow, and Hephaestion was careful to approach from the sunward side.

"The Thessalians chased a few hundred of them to the very gates of Rome," the cavalry commander said without preamble, "but Fabius brought off a good part of the rest in decent order. There was a great slaughter."

Alexander looked up and nodded, his face very pale. Hephaestion looked instinctively for a fresh wound. There was a long scratch along Alexander's left arm, deep enough to draw blood, but nothing more serious. Hephaestion sighed, urging his horse closer, and reached for the wineskin slung at his knees. Alexander shook his head, and Hephaestion said, "It's wine, not water. You need it."

The king made a face, but took the proferred wineskin. He took a cautious swallow, then another, and handed the skin back to Hephaestion. The cavalry commander took a long drink. The drink lay warm in his stomach, blurring the ache and fatigue of the fighting.

The women were already moving on the battlefield when they returned. Some were looking for their men—though very few could have heard of a death so soon after the fighting ended—but more had come to strip at least the foreign dead. Too many Macedonian bodies littered the plain and both commanders exchanged a quick glance, wondering which of the Friends had fallen.

"Let's go," Alexander said abruptly. Hephaestion looked up, startled, and the king said, "There's nothing more to do here."

"To the camp, then?" Hephaestion asked.

Alexander nodded but his attention was already elsewhere. "I sent you to the doctors an hour ago, Menestheus. Why are you still here?"

There was a nervous shifting among the troopers of the king's squadron, as though the horses themselves were shuffling their feet in embarrassment. A stocky figure detached himself from the rest, managing his rangy bay right-handed. His left arm, wrapped in a bloody rag, was slung across his body, bound to his corselet with a leather thong.

"The battle wasn't over, sire," he protested. "I was needed."

Alexander shook his head but he was smiling. "What good is a half-squad leader who can't hold a sword? You did well today, Menestheus, I don't want to lose you. Will you go now, or must I send someone to escort you?"

Menestheus ducked his head again. "I'll go now, sire." Without waiting for an answer, he wheeled his horse away, and set out at a trot for the camp.

"Idiot," Hephaestion said involuntarily, and Alexander nodded agreement.

"Pantordanus, go with him, see he doesn't kill himself on the way."

The trooper addressed grinned and sketched a salute, then wheeled his horse to follow the younger man. Alexander watched them out of sight, then produced a rather white-lipped smile. "Is there more wine, Hephaestion?

The cavalry commander offered the wineskin and the king drank deeply. A little color returned to his face, and he collected his reins with renewed assurance.

It was not a long ride back to the campsite, but it took twice as long as usual to reach the king's tent, pausing every half-stadion or so for Alexander to deal with various subcommanders. He stopped at the doctors' tents as well, and stayed to speak with every wounded man still capable of speaking. The list of the dead was rising as well, as soldiers reported the deaths of friends and squadron mates. Already the Foot Companions could number two hundred dead, most of those from Meleager's and Perdiccas's brigades, and there would be more. Meleager himself was missing; though no one had found the body yet, his second-in-command reported grimly that he was sure the brigadier was dead. The Agrianians had brought in Pithon's body, too, and nearly a hundred Paeonian bodies. Ariston, his good humor finally dimmed, rode with them, weeping softly. Alexander ordered the Thracians, who had suffered the least, to search along the river banks in the morning, in hopes of recovering more Macedonian bodies.

By the time they reached the royal tent, Alexander had emptied the wineskin. He dismounted without grace and without assistance, tossing the reins to a page. Hephaestion followed him into the tent without being invited, and waved away the pages who came to take Alexander's armor, loosening the pins himself. For a moment, Alexander didn't seem to notice, but then he said, "Let the boys do it, I'm all right."

Hephaestion ignored him, pulling apart the breast and back pieces, and said to the nearest page, "Bring wine, and don't bother mixing it."

"I'm all right," Alexander said again, rather irritably.

Hephaestion ignored him, and kept working at the fastenings of the armor. Alexander winced as the corselet was pulled away. His tunic was filthy with sweat and the river water, a few spots of dried blood showing above the wound.

Hephaestion said, "Let me call Philip."

"Absolutely not," the king said fiercely. "Gods below, he has work enough tonight. You can do it."

The cavalry commander shook his head, but had to admit the justice of the other's argument. He sent the hovering page for fresh bandages, then shouted toward the inner room for someone to fetch a clean tunic. Bagoas brought one at once, and together he and Hephaestion eased away the filthy tunic.

The wound had not bled much, was already nearly closed. When the page brought the fresh strips of linen, Hephaestion carefully rebandaged it, then poured a cup of neat wine and pressed it into his friend's hand. Alexander accepted it without looking and drained the cup. Hephaestion refilled it, but the king shook his head.

The three sat in silence for a long moment, and then the king shivered convulsively. Bagoas vanished instantly into the inner chamber, to return a moment later with the king's best cloak. Alexander accepted it with murmured thanks and the Persian hurried to build up the fires in the twin braziers. It was not that cold in the tent. Hephaestion eyed the king warily, but before he could say anything, the tent flap was pulled back, and one of the pages on guard duty said, "King Alexander?"

The king looked up quickly, visibly shaking away exhaustion. "Enter."

The page pushed back the door flap just enough to admit his head, and said, "Beg pardon, sire, but General Ptolemy is here, with a Roman delegation."

Alexander grinned. "We've got them," he said quietly. He drained the cup of wine, and said, "Admit them, by all means."

Hephaestion rose quickly, fumbling with his armor. It would be in bad taste to meet the Romans—who could only intend to acknowledge their defeat and ask for permission to collect their dead—in arms. He snapped off his greaves, then slipped loose the pins that fastened his own bell corselet. At the king's nod, Bagoas moved to help him. With the Persian's help, the cavalry commander wrestled awkwardly out of it at last. Bagoas bundled all the armor together and vanished into the bedchamber.

Hephaestion reslung his swordbelt just as Ptolemy

pushed through the door curtain. He was closely followed by four men muffled in heavy cloaks.

Ptolemy said formally, "Alexander, these are the Roman consuls. They request an audience."

The king nodded, not moving from his chair. "Of course, consuls. Heiron!" A page appeared instantly. "Chairs for my guests."

The boy hastily dragged five more chairs and couches into place, forming a rough semi-circle in front of the king's couch, then, without being told, mixed the wine.

"Please be seated," the king said. "What can I do for you, Fabius Caeso?"

The consul took his time answering, methodically loosening his cloak, which had been pulled tight around his face, then carefully choosing the chair that stood directly opposite Alexander's couch. His companions copied him, Cassius sitting cautiously at Fabius's left, the smaller, stockier man taking the couch to the consul's right. The fourth man took his place last of all, throwing back his torn cloak with an arrogant gesture that revealed the mail coat he still wore beneath it.

"King Alexander," Fabius said deliberately. "I have come to ask for a truce, to recover our dead. I have brought these men with me to add their voices to mine: Marcus Hirtius Fimbria, my co-consul, Caius Domitius Mela, his tribune, and Lucius Cassius Nasidienis, my tribune, whom you know already."

Hirtius Fimbria, a dark and stocky man, murmured a nervous greeting, pinching at his unshaven jowls. Caius Domitius Mela gave him a swift, contemptuous glance, and nodded, unspeaking. Unlike his consul, he looked like a soldier: he had the corded muscles of a fighter and long hands that should have been delicate but were calloused and knotted from long hours of drill. His face was almost expressionless, but the taut muscles that bracketed his thin mouth betrayed his anger.

Hephaestion, who had been going to sit slightly apart from others, where his filthy tunic would be less offensive, took one look at the steely, fanatic face, and took the chair that stood between Domitius and the king. Ptolemy glanced warily at them all, but said nothing.

Alexander took another long swallow of his wine and gestured for the page to serve the others. "I am more than willing to set a truce for recovering the dead," he said, almost amiably. "I would wish to show all honor to so gallant an enemy."

Domitius sneered faintly and waved away the drink. Fabius glared at him and Hirtius made a choked, disapproving noise. The king continued without noticing, "Will two days be sufficient for your ceremonies?"

Fabius nodded but the stocky Hirtius said, diffidently, "Three days would be better, King Alexander."

Alexander said, "I see no difficulty in that, consul. Do you, Ptolemy?" There was an odd note in his voice, one that the Macedonians recognized uneasily. Alexander was playing king in his father's style; he had something planned, and there was nothing anyone could do but wait to see what would come of it.

Ptolemy glanced warily at Hephaestion and answered cautiously, "No, Alexander, I see none."

The king glanced at Hephaestion, who shrugged fractionally. "There is one question you could answer, consul," Alexander went on. "Why have both consuls and their tribunes come to make a request that any one of you could have made with perfect propriety?"

"Like you, King Alexander," Fabius said, "we wish to honor our respected foe." There was a hint of irony in those words, which Alexander chose to ignore. Ptolemy hid a smile behind his hand.

"I am grateful for that," Alexander said, and beckoned for the page, at the same time giving an order in a low voice. Heiron refilled the king's cup directly from the wine pitcher. Alexander drank thirstily before continuing, "And I truly regret we're at war."

Fabius looked up at that, but Hirtius said wearily, "As do we all, King Alexander."

It was Alexander's fourth cup of neat wine, on top of the wine he had drunk on the way back to tent. He was growing flushed, color showing hectic on his broad cheekbones. Again, the Macedonians exchanged uncertain glances.

"Then perhaps we can come to some further agreement," Alexander said, "a truce, at least."

Hirtius opened his mouth to speak, and the other consul unobtrusively motioned for him to be silent. "King Alexander," Fabius said slowly, "I do not think we have the authority to make such an agreement."

"You're the two consuls of Rome, are you not?" Alexander asked. "How can you lack that authority?"

Domitius shifted in his chair, and a fleeting smile crossed his thin face. Hirtius glared at him.

"As consuls," Fabius said slowly, "we have the authority to negotiate, but the Senate and people of Rome must approve any treaty that would end the war."

Domitius said, with vicious formality, "I wish to remind the consuls of the Senate's decision the first time a truce was debated."

Hirtius turned on him suddenly, heavy face taking on new dignity. "And I remind you, tribune, that Poppaeus won by damn few votes, and the wise men— like you, Fabius, I admit it—all voted against it."

"Hirtius." Fabius leaned forward, touched his coconsul's knee. "Not now."

Hirtius took a deep breath. "No, of course not, I'm sorry." He looked up at Alexander. "I ask your pardon, too, King Alexander."

"Granted," Alexander said. He took a deep breath, choosing his words carefully. "I respect what I have seen of Rome and Romans, and I have no unresolvable quarrel with the city. But at the same time, I must protect my other allies, either by a truce, or by—other means. No, I'll be blunt: I can either destroy Rome—"

"You could try," Domitius interjected.

"I could do it," Alexander said, anger flaring abruptly. "I took Tyre; I could certainly take Rome." Ptolemy cleared his throat gently, eyes fixed on the king's face. Alexander paused and then, with an effort, mastered his temper. "Consuls, I suggest you find a more diplomatic tribune, or come alone. In any case, I have a proposal for you. As I said, I do not wish to destroy Rome, but I must settle things, for myself and for my allies. I propose this: we enter into an alliance, by which Rome will pledge to keep the peace with me and my allies. In my turn, I'll turn my troops against Carthage, which is no friend to either of us."

The two consuls exchanged wary glances, and Cassius could not suppress a soft, startled sound. Clearly the Macedonians did not yet know of the Senate's treaty with the Carthaginians. Fabius cleared his throat and said, cautiously, "That offer is most generous, King Alexander, but I fail to see how it guarantees your security. I'm not so naïve as to think you are foolishly generous, sir."

"Nor am I," Alexander agreed. "I will want two things. First, I wish to hold one of the two consulships—"

"It can't be done," Domitius said, and Alexander glared at him.

"I have held magistracies in the Greek cities in Asia," the king said, silkily. "I'm certain something could be arranged." He glanced at the consuls, measuring their reactions. "I would also want to seal such an alliance by marriage with a Roman woman of suitable family."

Fabius drew a nervous breath, glancing again at his

co-consul. "King Alexander, the offer is generous, and it will be considered. But I'm afraid you underestimate the difficulties of obtaining the consulship. Marriage with a girl of senatorial family would be easy in comparison." He broke off as Alexander shook his head.

"I must have the consulship if this is to work. No, I don't want any answer now. Take the time you need—three days, you said, to give your dead their rites?"

Hirtius nodded slowly, heavy face gone suddenly pasty.

"Then at the end of those three days, tell me your decision, if we can continue to talk, or if an alliance is impossible."

The note of dismissal in the king's voice was unmistakable, and Fabius rose slowly to his feet, collecting the others with a glance. "King Alexander," he said slowly. "We accept the three days' truce to bury our dead. At the end of that time, we will give you an answer to your other proposal."

"Very well," Alexander answered. "Heiron! You and the rest of your watch, escort the Roman gentlemen to the edge of the camp."

When they were all gone, pages and Romans together, Alexander leaned back in his chair and closed his eyes. His face was very flushed.

"That's a dangerous game to play with them," Ptolemy said abruptly. "What do you think you're doing?"

"Bluffing," Alexander answered, without opening his eyes. "I know it's dangerous, Ptolemy, but I don't want to face a siege, not of these people. It would be a waste to destroy them. If it doesn't work, we're no worse off than we were." His voice trailed off wearily.

Ptolemy eyed him narrowly. This bald threat—and it was a threat, and everyone knew it, no matter what was said about alliances—was the sort of thing Philip had done to win his hegemony over Greece, only Philip had usually been a good deal subtler about it.

This was a time for cunning and that was a quality Alexander conspicuously lacked.

Hephaestion said, "Alexander?" There was no answer, and the cavalry commander leaned forward to prod the king's shoulder. Alexander's eyes flickered open briefly, but closed again almost at once. Worried, Hephaestion laid his hand on the king's forehead. The skin was frighteningly hot beneath his fingers.

Hephaestion said, "Get Philip."

"What?" Ptolemy looked at him for a moment in complete confusion, before the fear in the cavalry commander's voice registered. Then the brigadier shouted for the duty page to fetch the doctor, and came to stand beside the king. "What's the matter?"

"Alexander's—" Hephaestion took a deep breath, getting himself under control with an effort. "Fever, I think—I'm sure. He's burning up."

The two men looked at each other with perfect understanding. If the king were incapacitated now, it could easily mean disaster for the entire army. When Philip arrived, they helped to move the king's unresisting body into the bedchamber, then waited outside until the doctor had finished his ministrations. Philip emerged at last and shrugged in answer to the unspoken questions.

"The king is resting now," he said simply. "He's very feverish—there's nothing to do but let it run its course."

"How long?" Ptolemy asked hoarsely.

Philip shook his head. "That's in the god's hands, generals. I will stay with him." He turned and went back into the bedchamber.

"So what now?" Ptolemy asked softly, less in anticipation of any answer than to break the sudden silence.

Hephaestion took a deep breath, conquering his fear with a visible effort. "We carry out his bluff," he said. "If we can."

CHAPTER 9:

*Latium, winter (Peritios) to Rome, late spring (Daisios), 31
imperial (325 B.C., 428 A.U.C.)*

The king grew no better over the next few days,
still feverish, hovering between fitful sleep and even
more fitful waking. The Friends did their best to hide
the severity of the king's illness, but when Alexander
was unable to preside at the funeral rites for the
Macedonian dead, even the most optimistic of the
soldiers had to admit that something was wrong. Grimly,
the generals moved to stamp out the worst of the
rumors. It was announced that the king was ill, that
he was recovering, and sacrifices were offered for his
restored health; this was nothing unusual, and the
ritual seemed to restore some of the army's confidence.

The Friends had other things to deal with, too.
Laomedon's questioning of the Roman prisoners—it
seemed a pity not to make use of their presence,
when it was unclear if the city would ever ransom
them back—brought out references to a Roman alliance with Carthage. Craterus, his temper already
strained to the breaking point, swore that this proved
that the Romans were completely untrustworthy, and

213

demanded that the army move to besiege Rome before it was too late. Hephaestion, with Ptolemy already deeply involved in informal negotiations with Fabius, lost his temper at that, and the two nearly came to blows before the rest of the Friends managed to restore peace.

After twelve hours of acrimonious senatorial debate, Rome finally agreed to allow Fabius to continue negotiating, though the consuls were unable to obtain the Senate's approval of the terms suggested by Alexander. The senators also decreed that, for now, all talks would take place outside of Rome. The men of Fabius's party argued in vain against such a gratuitous insult, but the majority remained adamant. These limited concessions did not arrive until the morning of the fourth day, Alexander's deadline for the Roman answer. Fabius cursed the senators for the delay and the vagueness of their answer, and sent riders of his own to the Macedonian camp to inform the king that he was ready to talk.

The Friends had been waiting for Fabius's decision, and had taken precautions to keep the Romans from discovering the severity of the king's illness. The messenger was met by an escort of select men and brought at once to Craterus's tent. There, Ptolemy announced unblushingly that Hephaestion and he had been appointed by the king to handle the negotiations, and that they would return at once with the messenger to speak with the consuls. The messenger, flustered by his reception, could think of no way to refuse, asking only to send a runner ahead to warn the consuls of their coming. The Friends agreed, with more flowery declarations of courtesy, and Perdiccas himself walked the runner to the camp perimeter and saw him on his way.

Three days after the battle, the Roman pyres were still burning. Ugly plumes of smoke rolled across the plain, sickening even the old soldiers with the stench.

Cassius, ordered to meet the Macedonian embassy, was very glad to be able to turn over the supervision of the rites to his centurions and his fellow tribune—in fact, he wished Domitius the joy of it. At the very least, it gave him the chance to bathe and change into fresh clothes, ones that did not smell of the fires.

The Macedonian party drew rein just outside the perimeter of the Roman camp and Hephaestion advanced to meet the Romans, throwing back his cloak to show that he carried only a sword. "Tribune," he said gravely.

"General," Cassius said, as soberly.

"Alexander sends us—myself and Ptolemy son of Lagus—with authority to speak for him," the cavalry commander went on.

Cassius nodded stiffly, and said, "The consuls will speak to you. If you will come with me?"

"Of course," Ptolemy answered, and Hephaestion nodded. Most of the troopers, Companion cavalrymen of Hephaestion's personal squadron, dismounted at that, leaving their mounts with the remaining pair of Companions. They formed a loose column at the generals' backs. Cassius's face tightened at the sight, and he repressed an angry comment. Instead, he turned toward Fabius's tent, and started walking without waiting to see if the Macedonians would follow.

The consul's tent was not nearly as elaborate as Alexander's massive pavilion, and at the moment looked positively threadbare: neither consul had been able to save much of his baggage after the battle. Cassius glanced at the Macedonians, daring them to notice. Hephaestion met the tribune's look with a bland stare. Ptolemy, more tactful, noticed nothing.

Fabius rose to meet them. Hirtius rose with him, looking even bulkier by contrast. The four exchanged formal greetings, eyeing each other, then took their places around the central table. Cassius, acting in place of Fabius's son, served wine and offered a plate of fruit, then sat unobtrusively in the shadows where he could hear everything.

Ptolemy spoke first. "Your messenger said you were willing to continue negotiating," he said bluntly.

Fabius nodded slowly. "That is correct. We wish to come to some agreement to end this war. I assume that is possible?"

Hephaestion shrugged slightly, watching the Romans. "That's the king's wish, certainly."

Ptolemy said, "Let's get to the point. Alexander named certain conditions he believes necessary for a permanent peace. Have you come to any further decision on those matters?"

The consul's shoulders tensed beneath his sober cloak. "In part. Allow me also to speak plainly. Your king's demands are understandable, but impossible. If we cannot discuss them, then however much we may all regret it, there can be no peace between us."

Hephaestion lifted his head at that and Ptolemy gestured unobtrusively for him to be quiet. "You say you understand them," the brigadier said patiently, "so why are they impossible?"

"The marriage isn't impossible," Hirtius said hastily, "it's just the consulship."

"Rome is a republic," Fabius said, overriding his co-consul. "Alexander is a king, twice a king, in fact. Our history—Romans could never accept a king ruling them, especially not as a consul. That is the impossibility."

"There are practical problems with Alexander's being consul," Hirtius interjected. "After all, the consul really has to stay in Rome, except during a war, and the people would never elect someone who was going to be off in a foreign country for his entire term."

Ptolemy nodded. "I know a little of your history," he said. Hephaestion gave him a sidelong glance at that bald lie, and Ptolemy continued blandly, "and I respect your traditions. Yet at the same time you must understand Alexander's position. He needs to be certain of Rome, particularly at first, when we've been such recent enemies. But he does not want to interfere with your city's government. What better way to gain both objectives than by holding your chief magistracy?"

Fabius spread his hands. "I understand that, and I appreciate his desire to spare us as much as possible." Irony tinged his voice, and Ptolemy smiled in knowing response.

"There is another option," Fabius went on, "or at least I see another option. Must Alexander himself be consul, or could he delegate the responsibility to one of his generals?"

Hephaestion's eyebrows rose almost comically, and even Ptolemy seemed taken aback. The older Macedonian recovered quickly, however, and said, "Wouldn't that be too easily construed as an insult to Rome and her people?"

"It could be presented as tact, unexpected in one unfamiliar with our ways," Fabius said dryly.

Hephaestion smothered a slightly hysterical laugh. Ptolemy's mouth twitched, but he said calmly enough, "I don't see any inherent impossibility in it."

Hephaestion shrugged again. "Nor do I."

"Did you have a candidate in mind, consul?" Ptolemy went on.

Fabius, who had hoped to reserve that point for later discussion, hesitated briefly. "We had discussed it," he said at last, "Hirtius and I. You, General Ptolemy, seem the logical choice."

Ptolemy's thick eyebrows rose, and he leaned back in his chair, one hand caressing his chin. When he did not speak, Hephaestion said, "Why?"

Fabius shrugged, an accurate imitation of the cavalry commander's gesture. "The general says he is somewhat acquainted with our customs and history, unlike other of Alexander's officers. More important, he is of high rank, but not a king himself, or in any way connected with kings."

Ptolemy passed his fingers quickly over his mouth as though to erase a smile, but sobered quickly. If he agreed to this solution, what would happen when the Romans heard the speculation—common talk throughout Greece—that King Philip was his real father? Hephaestion had an odd look on his face: clearly he, too, had worked out the ramifications of the offer.

Fabius eyed the Macedonians warily, but, when they said nothing, continued apparently without noticing the strange reaction. "You would also find it easier to remain in or near Rome, as a consul must, than would your king."

"True enough," Hephaestion said. "Consul—consuls, I see no immediate objections to this plan, and we'll gladly carry it back to Alexander. I assume that he would be able formally to propose Ptolemy's candidacy?"

Hirtius nodded eagerly. "It could be arranged."

"Then I can't think of anything objectionable." Hephaestion glanced at his companion, who stood ponderously.

"Nor can I, though I can hardly speak for or against." Ptolemy tucked both thumbs into his belt. "We will put your proposal before the king, consuls."

"At least as a base for further negotiations," Fabius murmured, but politely, and Ptolemy nodded.

"Of course. And of course any treaty with us would supersede any treaty with Carthage."

Hirtius began some incoherent answer at that, glancing in panic to his fellow consul for help. Fabius sighed—it had been obvious that Rome's alliance could not be kept a secret forever—and said, "Perhaps that will not be necessary, general. In any case, we can discuss that further at our next meeting."

The two consuls accompanied the Macedonians to the edge of the camp; on their return, Cassius had the slaves pour fresh wine and bring more fruit. Fabius settled into the nearest chair, sighing, and waved away both food and drink. Hirtius nibbled morosely at a fig, glaring at nothing.

After a moment, Fabius looked up. "Well, Cassius? You look displeased."

"How can I be pleased, Rome's beaten—" Cassius broke off abruptly, biting back the anger and grief of the past three days. "I beg your pardon, sir."

Hirtius plucked another fig from the platter. "You should be pleased, boy, you're getting what you argued for. Alliance with Alexander, and most likely against Carthage."

"Not like this," Cassius said, voice rising, and Fabius said, "Shut up, Hirtius." The heavyset consul made a face and continued nibbling at his fig.

To Cassius, Fabius said, "We've lost a battle, my boy, but at least we've preserved the city."

Cassius took a deep breath, controlled himself enough to say, almost calmly, "By making Rome a vassal of the king of Macedon, sir. I wanted an alliance of equals, not this. I could almost agree with Domitius that it would be better to go down fighting."

Fabius said, "You would agree that we can't beat Alexander in battle? That he could take the city if he tried?"

Cassius, recognizing the familiar, tutorial note in the consul's voice, nodded reluctantly. "Yes."

"And why can't we beat the Macedonians, when we've beaten every other invader?" Fabius went on.

"Because Alexander is the best general around—and the luckiest," Hirtius said through a mouthful of fig. "We don't have anyone his equal. Get to the point."

"That is the point," Fabius said. "We can't beat Alexander—but Alexander won't live forever." He looked almost coyly at his folded hands. "It is rumored even now that he's very ill, maybe even dying."

Hirtius snorted contemptuously. "I wouldn't count on it, Fabius."

"Even so," Fabius said. His voice was suddenly, fervently insistent. "He is not a god, for all his pretensions; he won't live forever. Do you think he's the man to build anything that will outlast him? Rome, Rome is immortal. If nothing else, we have time."

Cassius shook his head unhappily, swayed in spite of himself by the consul's certainty. It went against the grain to have to feign surrender, to wait for freedom until Alexander's death—which could be many years away, the man was only thirty-one—but there were no reasonable alternatives.

Hirtius said, almost mildly, "You'll have a time persuading the Senate of that, Fabius."

"My party will agree," Fabius answered, "and with your support, and your party's, we will be able to convince the rest."

"We'd better be," Hirtius muttered, shaking his head. "The gods send you're right, Fabius, or you'll have doomed Rome."

The king was sleeping normally when the generals returned from the Roman camp. By the next morning, he had recovered enough to listen to their report and to give his consent to their negotiations. That evening, however, the fever returned, and the king sank slowly into a sort of waking dream. All of Philip's remedies had no effect, and rumors of impending doom circulated wildly. On the second day, there was nearly a riot when a battalion of Foot Companions became convinced that the king had died. The trouble was only stopped when Alexander was carried to the doorway of his tent for them all to see. He revived briefly then, managed to speak a few words, and collapsed again as soon as the soldiers had dispersed. Craterus cursed everyone, and threw a tight cordon round the camp, hoping to keep the Romans from hearing exactly how sick the king really was.

Four days after Alexander's second collapse, the Friends gathered in Ptolemy's tent to discuss the latest dispatch from Nearchus in Syracuse. The Carthaginians, the admiral reported, were raiding in force across their old boundary of the Halycus River, and he asked for extra troops to help repel them. The decision to send reinforcements would normally have been an easy one, but under the circumstances it sparked an angry debate.

"Craterus has been saying all along that we shouldn't split up the army," Neoptolemus said at last.

"Let Craterus make his own arguments," Ptolemy snapped.

The hypaspist commander subsided, muttering, "Well, I agree with him."

In the same moment, Perdiccas asked, "Where is Craterus, anyway?"

There was an irritable mutter in answer, each general disclaiming any knowledge of the brigadier's whereabouts. Hephaestion pushed himself to his feet, suddenly impatient with everyone and everything. Alexander could be dying, and yet the Friends continued the same stale routines. He crossed to the open doorflap and leaned out, keeping his back to the others until he had controlled himself.

A group of women, soldiers' wives and slaves and common whores, clustered together by the embers of a fire, bending close over something in the dirt. One of them stooped, collected the irregular objects, and held them close to her lips. She muttered to them, and Hephaestion realized at last what it was she held. There could be no uncertainty about her question, either, and Hephaestion suppressed a shiver of superstitious fear. The woman opened her eyes and tossed the divining bones into the air. They fell softly and the women bent close over their pattern.

"No sign of him, then?" Ptolemy asked.

Hephaestion shook his head and returned to his place, saying "We'd better tell Nearchus about the king, whatever else we do, and send that at once."

The others nodded their agreement, reluctantly—no one wanted to cede any authority to any other officer, just in case the king did die and there were opportunities for ambitious men—but they had to admit that the cavalry commander was right. The message itself proved surprisingly easy to draft, a plain statement of the king's illness and a promise to consider the admiral's request. Eumenes produced a fair copy and passed the slip of papyrus to Ptolemy, who read it and handed it back.

"It'll do," he said.

Hephaestion nodded and reached for the seal he wore on a thong around his neck. A lump of wax waited in its metal dish, but the wax had congealed in the cool air. The cavalry commander made a face and set the dish on the brazier.

There was a sudden commotion outside the tent, and one of Ptolemy's slaves said quickly, "General Craterus, sirs."

Craterus swayed slightly, caught himself on the tent rope, and lurched through the doorway. He was royally drunk and knew it, and didn't care. He pulled himself up with an effort, turning his head owlishly to survey the company.

"Greetings, Craterus," Ptolemy said, a warning in his voice, and was ignored.

The brigadier's bloodshot eyes fixed on Hephaestion. "Hard at work, Hephaestion?" he said loudly, and stumbled forward, fetching up against the secretaries' table. Eumenes caught the rolls of papyrus without taking his eyes off the scene.

Hephaestion said, "Go sober up, Craterus." He turned his back on the brigade commander, poured the proper amount of wax on the foot of the rolled papyrus, then set the dish aside and slipped the seal from around his neck.

Craterus mumbled something, and Ptolemy said, "Shut up." Perdiccas laughed openly. Hephaestion ignored them all and started to set his seal to the cooling wax. Craterus caught his wrist, forcing the seal away.

"Who do you think you are?" Craterus hissed, and suddenly the drunkenness was gone from his voice. Hephaestion shoved back, forcing the bulkier man to step back from the table. Craterus's question seemed to echo dangerously in the quiet tent. None of the Friends was unambitious, but until now their desire for power had been leashed, subservient to Alexander's greater ambition. But if the king died . . . The unspeakable question seemed to hover in the air, on the verge of an answer.

Coenus said sharply, "What are we, barbarians? Fighting in the council, indeed. Sit down, the pair of you, and be civil." He was old enough to have fathered either man, and the acerbic paternalism of his words shattered the spell.

Craterus mumbled something incoherent. Coenus said, not unkindly, "Go home and sober up, son. Council's over, anyway."

Craterus made a face, but turned unsteadily and stalked away. The rest of the Friends exchanged wary glances, and then Ptolemy said, "Thank you, Coenus. I think you're right, we should end this."

"Nearchus needs to be informed," Perdiccas said.

Ptolemy said, rather sharply, "So we'll seal the dispatch."

The wax had solidified on the end of the scroll. Hephaestion managed a nod, not daring to speak, and reached for the scraper. He removed the hardened wax, then poured a second careful pool and set his seal to it. "Eumenes," he said, and despite his efforts the tone was still angry, "see that the messenger leaves at once with this."

The secretary took the papyrus, considering further comment, but decided against it. "As the Friends wish," he said, with delicate emphasis. Before anyone could answer, he collected his scrolls and slipped from the tent.

The council broke up quickly after that. Ptolemy gestured unobtrusively for the cavalry commander to remain behind, and, when the others had gone, extended a long arm to snare a cup of wine from a sidetable. He raised a questioning eyebrow at the other general. Hephaestion nodded wearily and accepted a cup.

"Drunk and stupid," Ptolemy said after a moment, "but mostly drunk. Alexander wouldn't thank him for it."

"No," Hephaestion said shortly, and took a long swallow of his wine. Ptolemy was watching him closely, and the cavalry commander made a face, knowing exactly what the other was waiting for. "As you say, he was drunk, and I don't carry tales. Am I a schoolboy?" Hephaestion controlled himself with an effort. "And anyway, the king's too ill to be bothered with trifles."

"Craterus isn't the only one to be thinking along those lines," Ptolemy said.

Hephaestion looked up, momentarily puzzled, then snorted agreement. "Yes. 'If Alexander dies, what can I get for me?' I know."

"It's a pity the boy isn't here."

"It would've been too dangerous to bring the heir on this campaign," Hephaestion said. "You know that. Nearchus can be trusted—I trust him."

"As do I," Ptolemy said.

The two men looked at each other in perfect understanding. They would defend Philip Alexander's rights against any of the Friends, and against each other, if it came to that.

"However," Ptolemy said, and smiled suddenly, "we're not likely to have this to worry about. Alexander heals quickly."

"True enough," Hephaestion said, but he could not bring himself to return the smile. Alexander had always healed quickly before, that was true enough, but he had never been this sick before, either. Philip did not seem to be able to do anything for him. Hephaestion closed his eyes tightly, tasting fear. More than anything else, he wanted to be at Alexander's side, to give what help he could, but there was no time to waste on such self-indulgence. He opened his eyes again and saw Ptolemy nodding at him.

"He'll be all right," the brigadier said softly, as much to convince himself as to comfort Hephaestion. "He will be."

Alexander was aware of the tension filling the camp but could not muster the strength to do anything about it. Still feverish, he drifted from waking to something like sleep, and was not always certain which was which. Philip, growing steadily thinner himself, remained constantly in attendance, but even he finally had to admit that there was nothing to be done except to allow the disease to run its course. Alexander accepted the doctor's presence and the regular visits from various of the Friends, but there were other, less definable figures that lurked in the shadows and sometimes whispered to each other in strange, foreign voices. Most often the shadows vanished as soon as the king looked straight at them; other times they remained visible for an instant before they disappeared, giving Alexander a glimpse into their shadowy world. With the cunning of illness, he refused to mention the shapes to Philip or to anyone, and set himself to learning how to see the phantoms. Over the days he mastered the gift of it, the steady sidelong glance that brought them into focus. Philip watched worriedly as the king grew more and more remote, lost in a half dream. Alexander was dimly aware of the doctor's concern, but obstinately refused to enlighten him.

Most of the shadow-figures were unfamiliar to him— shapes like odd, hybrid animals, or distorted characters stolen from the theater—but occasionally he caught a glimpse of one that he thought he recognized. Those figures were the hardest to see and the ones on which he expended the most effort. For the most part, he was not successful: he often saw an old woman whose jutting chin and scrawny figure seemed familiar, but her name remained unknown. There was a shape in Persian dress, too, who kept his face forever turned away. Alexander fought constantly to see it, not afraid of Darius's ghost but wanting to know the reason for such a visitation, yet he never could quite see the face. And once, Olympias sat for a moment beside the great loom in her rooms at Pella. She looked up and smiled, as though aware of Alexander's regard, and then the shadow faded.

There was another familiar shape, too, lurking just out of the range of Alexander's vision. He fought grimly to bring it into focus, struggling impatiently with his weakening body. He caught brief glimpses of the shield, the cloaked figure, once the head, helmet pushed back to rest on the god's horns, but no more. Exhausted, he sank back into sleep.

He was roused one night by a strange noise, clear and musical. In the light of the single lamp, he could see Bagoas asleep on his pallet by the doorway, and Philip drowsing in his chair. A third figure stood by the closed doorflap, cloaked and helmeted, shining with an uncanny light of its own. The king stared at it unafraid, trusting in his god. To his surprise, the figure did not speak, but drew his closed fist from beneath his gold-trimmed cloak. For a long moment, he stood frozen in that position, then, decisively, tossed something into the air. The ivory dice twisted lazily in the air, leaving trails of fire behind them, and bounced twice across the king's bed. They were weightless, entirely without substance. Even as Alexander struggled to sit up, to read their message, the cubes became transparent and faded altogether. The god vanished with them. Alexander lay back against his pillows, puzzling over the strangeness of it all. He was not afraid even now; he was curious, and, if anything, annoyed that the god had given him so ambiguous, so nonsensical, an omen. After a while, he slept, and this time there were no dreams to plague him.

Philip woke to find the king's fever had broken, and the king was sleeping easily. The doctor was not greatly encouraged—the fever had abated before, only to return—but when by midmorning the king showed no signs of the restlessness that had previously marked a relapse, Philip allowed himself a cautious optimism. The king slept out the rest of the day, a natural, healing sleep, rousing himself around sunset to demand food. Elated now in spite of himself, Philip had a light broth brought and fed it to the king with his own hands. Alexander ate eagerly and fell asleep again. He woke the next morning with a moderate appetite and for the first time in weeks showed a real awareness of his surroundings. Philip, vowing massive sacrifices to Asclepius if the king continued to improve and equally massive vengeance against the nearest shrines if he suffered a relapse, cautiously informed the Friends that the king was showing definite signs of improvement.

The Friends declared a formal thanksgiving sacrifice, followed by celebrating games. Alexander was furious at missing the latter, and it was the outburst that followed Philip's absolute refusal to allow him to attend that finally convinced his generals that the king was really on the mend. Coenus and his three sons held solemn sacrifices of their own, paying up vows. Ptolemy, predictably, shared his celebration with Thaïs. Perdiccas and Craterus, in a sudden burst of good feeling, hosted an expensive party, and one of the battalion commanders nearly died of the cold he caught sleeping dead drunk under the tables. In the privacy of his own tent Hephaestion wept briefly from sheer relief, then emerged again to watch the festivities with a philosopher's eye.

By the time the new moon brought in the month of Dystros, Alexander was on his feet again, disdaining Philip's last words of caution. He had lost a great deal of weight and still tired easily; both, he proclaimed buoyantly, would mend with time and food. As he grew stronger, he took more and more of a personal interest in the Roman negotiations, demanding solid answers. Fabius was forced to give ground and, with the reluctant support of Hirtius's party, managed to get a preliminary agreement to the general terms Alexander had outlined. Alexander accepted that agreement gracefully, not yet pushing for more, and Fabius pressed his own advantage, at last securing the Senate's consideration for a proper treaty. Between them, Fabius and Ptolemy worked out formulae that would please and protect both sides, and at last the consul was able to put that formal statement before the senators. Reluctantly, the Senate agreed to debate the treaty. The two consuls and their parties between them controlled enough votes to assure that the treaty would pass. In the Senate house, Fabius breathed a soft sigh of relief. The first part of his work was over. He straightened his shoulders, then, gathering his toga about him, invited Cassius to accompany him on the long walk back to his own house. The tribune eyed him warily, wondering what Fabius was up to, but agreed.

The horned moon was rising when Fabius finally reached his house. Cassius waited while Fabius exchanged brief words with the slave doorkeeper, then stepped forward to take his leave of the consul. The older man stopped him with an abrupt exclamation.

"Nonsense. Surely you'll take a cup of wine with me, after all the good we've done today?"

There was no refusing that invitation, and Cassius had to admit that there was something to celebrate.

That afternoon, the Senate had voted at last to consider
the treaty in formal session, and Fabius and Hirtius
between them controlled enough votes to win the
voting that would follow. Rome would be spared—at a
cost. "It would be my pleasure, sir," he said, and tried
to force some warmth into his voice.

"Excellent," Fabius answered. For a fleeting moment, his smile seemed forced, and then it eased into
something more genuine. "Jason," the consul went
on, "have chairs brought into the garden, and torches.
Have the wine served there."

The elderly slave, who had appeared behind the
doorkeeper, bowed deeply and vanished into the depths
of the house. Cassius followed the consul through the
stygian entranceway and into the atrium. Fabius avoided
the central pool blindly, then paused beneath the
broad archway that gave onto the garden. Cassius
followed more slowly, stepping cautiously across the
polished tiles that ringed the pool.

Slaves moved among the rose bushes and the low
banks of flowers, Some carrying torches, others bringing chairs and the wine table. Under Jason's direction,
they placed torches along the narrow strip of pave-
ment that ringed the central fountain, and set chairs
and table inside the ring of light. "Excellent," Fabius
said. "Pour the wine, and then you all may go. Come,
Cassius."

Cassius took his place opposite the consul, and accepted a cup from the grey-haired slave who poured
the wine. Most of Fabius's slaves were older, and had
been with his household for some years. The consul
was notorious for the simplicity of his habits since the
death of his wife and son. Fabius took a cup too,
smiling thanks and dismissal, then sat staring at the
fountain, wondering how to begin.

"It was a good day," Cassius said after a while.
"Even Domitius Mela couldn't sway them, and if he

can't, with his soldier's airs, then Poppaeus certainly can't."

Fabius sighed deeply, and set aside his untasted wine. With an attempt at cheerfulness, he said, "Yes. They'll give Ptolemy citizenship. I don't think even Alexander himself can destroy that agreement, and I have to admit he's deft enough when sober. Hirtius and I can deliver the popular vote."

"When sober?" Cassius asked, startled.

Fabius smiled, rather bitterly. "After Lanuvium, my boy. He was drunk when he threatened us, couldn't you see?"

"He was feverish," Cassius said, and was surprised by the warmth of his own defense.

Fabius looked curiously at him. After a moment, the consul shrugged and said, "Probably you're right. Put it down to an old man's cynicism." He shook himself, and said, briskly, "In any case, I think he'll speak well enough not to undo what I've done."

"So all that remains is a suitable marriage," Cassius said.

"Yes," Fabius said, and looked expectantly at the tribune, "a suitable marriage."

Cassius's eyes narrowed. "You have someone in mind, then, sir."

Fabius nodded. "I do," he said, "and you'll have guessed who already."

"Tell me," Cassius said.

"Your sister Cassia," the consul said.

"No," Cassius said flatly. She was his sister, aside from all the considerations of rank and status, and much loved; she deserved better than to be thrown away on a foreigner, on a barbarian king.

"Hear me out," Fabius said. "I have no daughters— no children at all, now—or I would offer my own kin. You are of rank, your family has a good reputation in Rome, but most of all I know I can trust you. You fought at Lanuvium, you know what's at stake. And you've met Alexander, you know he won't—abuse Cassia."

"No," Cassius said again, with less vehemence. "Sir, I can't sell off my sister, not even to Alexander. In any case, she'd never agree to it, and I wouldn't marry her to anyone without her consent."

"But she would listen to your advice," Fabius pointed out. "Cassius, think. Is there anyone else in Rome whom I could ask without having to pay too high a price for their help?"

Cassius shook his head mutely, momentarily too angry to speak. He hated the logic of the consul's argument, resented the very real necessity of the sacrifice even as he recognized both. After a long moment, he sighed, shaking his head again. "I can't promise Cassia will agree, sir."

Fabius nodded. "I know that. All I ask is that you make the offer, and give your consent as head of the family."

Cassius still looked mutinous, but said, "Very well, sir, I will do that."

Fabius bowed gravely to him. "I thank you, Lucius Cassius. I hope—I beg you to stay a little longer, I wouldn't have you leave here in anger."

Touched to the core by the older man's appeal, Cassius returned the bow, saying passionately. "Sir, you've been like a father to me and Cassia. I don't blame you for this at all. You're right, it's the only way."

Despite his brave words, however, it took two more days for Cassius to nerve himself to put Fabius's request before the women of his family. Cassia herself, a quiet, studious girl of sixteen, accepted her brother's announcement without apparent emotion—she was not promised to anyone as yet, though she was certainly old enough to be eligible, and had never expected to be consulted in the matter. Their mother Gratidia, on the other hand, protested violently, and was only silenced by the repeated reminder of the disastrous battle at Lanuvium. When at last Cassia herself was able to get a word in edgewise, it was only to say that she would follow her brother's advice, and then, almost as an afterthought, to ask what Alexander was like. Cassius floundered badly in his attempt at a description, but Cassia seemed satisfied enough.

Fabius passed along the news that Cassius had agreed to his sister's marrying Alexander, and the king promptly made a formal offer for her hand. Cassius unhappily accepted the general terms, but did his best to delay the negotiations on the actual contract. Alexander, who had both the Senate's final vote on the treaty and renewed trouble on Sicily to deal with, was happy enough to let the tribune make excuses. On the first day of Daisios, the Senate accepted Fabius's treaty by a respectable margin, at the same time formally repudiating the earlier agreement with Carthage. Alexander had agreed readily enough to the suggestion that Ptolemy rather than himself was the more logical candidate for the consulship. Fabius moved at once to have the brigadier made a citizen of Rome.

The more conventional senators were bitterly opposed to the idea, and Fabius was forced to abandon his first plan—to find a senator willing to adopt Ptolemy—and fall back on a simple decree of the Senate. This was more unusual and more difficult, and it took nearly a month of patient work before Fabius was able to acquire the votes needed to pass the measure. The Macedonians watched the complicated maneuvers with reactions ranging from amazement to frustration. Craterus, predictably enough, was both infuriated and disgusted by the Roman system; Ptolemy, who was slowly developing an odd sort of liking for the stubborn city, answered sharply that Macedon could profit from Roman ways. Alexander silenced the

quarrel with a look: he was intrigued by the machina-
tions of Senate and senators, he said drily, but not
when it was done at his expense. Fabius reported the
remark in select quarters in Rome, and obtained the
grant of citizenship for Ptolemy.

CHAPTER 10:

near Rome, early summer (Panemos), 31 imperial (325 B.C., 428 A.U.C.)

After five months in the same place, the original conglomeration of tents had begun to take on the outlines of a small city. Farmers from the surrounding towns had joined the merchants who followed the army to set up a real marketplace. Beyond that open space the more enterprising of the camp followers had set up their own quarter. Less-professional women were in evidence as well, and their children: there had been plenty of time for the individual soldiers to look to their own comforts.

The Macedonians had also spent some of their time in fortifying the area, replacing the original shallow trenches with a more permanent wooden palisade. Some of the senators had questioned its erection, claiming this was a hostile move from Alexander. Ptolemy, who first received the complaint, answered blandly that the building gave the soldiers something to do with their time, and kept them from harassing the natives. That silenced the most vocal objections. Still, not all of Rome was reconciled to the Macedonian alliance, and Fabius privately urged his tribune to come to an agreement over the contract as soon as possible. The tribune did as he was told: ten days after Ptolemy had been made a Roman citizen, Cassius made the short journey to the Macedonian camp to finish the arrangements for his sister's marriage.

The guards at the main entrance to the camp had been warned of Cassius's arrival, and a page was waiting to escort him to the king. The royal tent stood rather apart from the rest, near the river, but well upstream from the horselines. The two pages on duty at the tent door had also been warned to expect the tribune. They passed him in instantly, the younger of them murmuring a shy Latin greeting, the older announcing self-importantly, "Lucius Cassius Nasidienis, sirs."

The king had been hard at work when the Roman's arrival was relayed to him, and his table was covered with rolls of papyrus. At the Roman's entrance, Eumenes snatched protectively for several of them. Perdiccas, lounging in one of the several chairs, rolled his eyes, and Hephaestion sighed.

The king ignored them both. "Welcome, Cassius," he said, in Greek. His Latin was still very limited and likely to remain so: he had no particular gift for languages. He nodded to the shaven-headed slave who waited patiently in his corner to take dictation. "That's enough, Phaedrus, you may go."

The slave gathered his tablets and vanished. To Cassius, the king said, "I assume you've come about my offer for your sister?"

It was a reasonably tactful way to express it. Cassius suppressed a last, momentary bitterness, and nodded. "Yes, King Alexander. Cassia has accepted your offer, and I am willing to give my consent."

Eumenes raised an eyebrow at that—who had ever heard of a woman refusing an offer of marriage when it was presented by her male kin?—and he sneered faintly. Hephaestion said, "We're not in Athens, Eumenes."

"Thank the gods," Perdiccas added, grinning.

"There are a few matters that must be dealt with first," Cassius said firmly. "Chief among them, King Alexander, your previous marriages."

Alexander nodded, the corners of his mouth curving upward in a knowing smile, and waved the Roman to a chair. "It's common practice for a king of Macedon to have several wives—I only have two living. I don't see the difficulty."

Cassius seated himself opposite the king. "It is customary among Romans to take a single wife," he said austerely. "A subsequent marriage is invalid under our law."

"My queen—my chief wife, mother of my son—has been dead for four years," Alexander said. Somewhat to his own surprise, he was enjoying himself. "Surely, under law, that changes the situation somewhat."

"Yet you have two other living wives. The ideal solution," Cassius said, bracing himself, "would be to renounce your other wives."

Perdiccas laughed softly, turning his head away, even as the secretary said disapprovingly, "Impossible."

Alexander struggled to repress his own grin. He liked the Roman the better for the suggestion. "I could hardly divorce Darius's daughter," he said, with an attempt at severity.

"Roxane," Hephaestion observed, "is another matter entirely."

"I won't divorce her, either," Alexander retorted.

Perdiccas snorted, and Hephaestion said, quite audibly, "Pity."

Alexander gave both men a sardonic look, and turned back to Cassius. "But I don't mean to joke about such a serious matter," he said. "These other marriages aren't contracted by Roman law; your sister would be my only wife under your law, and would be treated as such in Rome, and with all honor in my household. The latter would be true regardless of law."

"If you marry Cassia without divorcing these other wives," Cassius said slowly, "I suppose the law could stretch a point." He paused, pretending to consider, though he and Fabius had worked out all the implications some days before. "But their children could not inherit in Rome, since those marriages would be invalid under our law."

Alexander's eyes narrowed, but he said, mildly enough, "Philip Alexander is the son of my first wife, now dead. That marriage would be valid, surely."

"Certainly, King Alexander," Cassius answered, "provided that you describe yourself in the marriage contract as a widower, and provided that Cassia steps into the place of the dead woman."

This time he had gone too far. The two generals exchanged a suddenly wary glance, and Eumenes said again, "Impossible."

Alexander's face hardened. "I cannot favor any of my wives above the others," he said. "Politically, it's impossible. But with Euridice dead, I'll have no other queen, and we can put that in the contract, if you like."

Cassius bowed, willing to back down gracefully if he could gain his other points. "I would want that," he said. "And also assurance, as a part of the contract, that Cassia would have at least the same rank and status as the—other women of your household."

"That," Alexander said dryly, "I would do for my own sake. But, certainly, we can put that in the contract as well—if in your turn you will formally acknowledge my right to have other wives."

"Maintain other women in your household?" Cassius asked apologetically. "To admit other marriages would prejudice this marriage in Roman eyes."

"To maintain other households, then," Alexander

said. "That describes the situation more exactly, anyway."

"In consideration of your foreign birth and customs," Cassius murmured as though thinking aloud. Hephaestion chuckled softly. The king nodded.

"Thank you, King Alexander," Cassius said. "Then there's only a dowry and the specifics of Cassia's rights of maintenance—"

Before he could go any further, the tent flap was pulled back. Alexander frowned deeply, and said, "Theodatus—"

"I'm sorry, sire," the page said hastily. "But there's a messenger from Syracuse."

The king's expression changed. "Show him in," he said. "Cassius, your pardon." Cassius nodded politely, but Alexander didn't see him, his attention already focussed on the newcomer. The page pulled the tent flap back further, admitting a sun-browned, strikingly handsome man.

Alexander's frown eased a little, and he said, "Timander, isn't it, son of Hellanicus?"

"Yes, sire," the man said, nodding. His faded blue cloak was mottled with salt stains: it had been a hard passage from Syracuse, the sailing season only just open.

"What's the news, then?" Alexander asked softly, fixing his eyes on the messenger's face.

"Good news, sire," Timander said hastily, and Perdiccas said, "Thank the gods." Hephaestion nodded agreement.

"Nearchus and the Sicilian cities brought the Carthaginians to battle," Timander went on, proffering a leather-wrapped cylinder. "They send this."

Alexander snatched at the cylinder, snapping the seals and letting the wrapping fall to the ground in his haste to read. Hephaestion edged close to read over his shoulder.

"Well?" Perdiccas demanded. Eumenes affected disinterest.

Alexander tossed the roll of papyrus in the general's direction. "Nearchus beat the Carthaginians after all," he said, in Macedonian, and then, remembering Cassius's presence, repeated the words in Greek. Perdiccas skimmed the scroll, then handed it to Eumenes, who read through it quickly.

"Do you think they'll stay back beyond the Halycus?" he asked.

"I don't know why not," Perdiccas said.

Alexander reached again for the scroll. He read through it again, Hephaestion still leaning over his shoulder. After some months of suffering constant small-scale raids from the Carthaginians, Nearchus had managed to force a battle, and had won a bloody victory. It had been a neat bit of maneuvering, and deserving of praise, but the admiral had not yet had to face the full resources of Carthage. "What about reinforcements from Carthage proper?"

"Nearchus has the fleet," Eumenes began, then stopped, reconsidering he's own words. The Carthaginians were too great a sea power to be dismissed so lightly.

Timander cleared his throat nervously. "It'll take some time to gather replacements for the men they lost," he said. "They suffered heavy casualties, sire."

"So Nearchus thinks that by the time they can assemble another army," Alexander said, "the sailing season will be nearly over?"

Timander nodded.

"That might not stop a Carthaginian fleet," Perdiccas said.

Cassius cleared his throat gently, strangely reluctant to intrude on this strategy conference. But the Macedonians were Rome's allies now, and Carthage was an old and hated enemy. "With respect, King

Alexander, there's another thing Carthage will have to consider. They no longer have an ally on the mainland."

Alexander nodded.

Hephaestion said, "Do you think they would try diplomacy, then, Cassius—treat with Nearchus, I mean?"

The tribune said apologetically, "General, they might, but certainly they wouldn't mean it."

Alexander shook himself abruptly. "For now, we have other obligations. First to the gods, to thank them for their favor. Then—Timander, the bearer of good tidings is to be rewarded, and doubly so when you did as much as any man to bring those good tidings to pass. Nearchus commends you highly for the flanking attack by the head of the Symaethus. Name your reward."

Timander blushed and stammered incoherent thanks, but could seem to get no further. Alexander smiled gently at him, and said, "If you can't name it now, you'll have to take coin, my friend. Will a talent suffice, do you think?"

Timander stared, speechless—a talent was more money than a common man saw in a lifetime, the price of a king's horse or the most exotic of slaves—and Alexander, still smiling, turned to the Roman. "Cassius, I must ask your indulgence. I'm afraid Carthage is the more pressing matter—and we've made a good start on the marriage contract, in any case."

"Of course, King Alexander," Cassius said politely. It was all he could do to keep a calm expression on his face. A Carthaginian defeat was always good news, but *this* time. . . . It meant Alexander would turn his attention there, and away from Rome. "The remaining parts of the contract are trivial enough," he said. "I'm confident of your honor."

When the Roman had gone, Alexander gave orders for a thanksgiving feast to be held that night, and sent for the rest of the Friends. As they arrived, Nearchus's

dispatch made the rounds, and one by one the commanders moved to the desk to study the map of Carthage that Eumenes had been able to acquire. There
was no question that Carthage had to be dealt with—it
was past time that their raids on Sicily were stopped—
but there was equally no question of its being an easy
campaign. Even Eumenes's map showed the city walled
on all sides, and triply walled on the single land
approach: it would be a long siege, in difficult territory. Despite that, Alexander was prepared to order
Nearchus to raise a fleet, and make the crossing to
Africa at the end of the main sailing season. The
Friends, to a man, announced that they could not
field an adequate army by then, even if the Romans
were prepared to offer their own troops—the Macedonian army, though it had only lost four hundred
men, had had nearly three thousand wounded. Reinforcements would have to be summoned from Macedon,
if Antipater thought he could spare the levies. Alexander sighed at that, knowing what the regent's answer
was likely to be, and ordered the discussion closed.

For the thanksgiving feast, a temporary pavilion
large enough to hold fifty couches was set up beside
the king's tent. Like the tent, the pavilion was Persian
booty. The guests, arriving at sunset, were blinded by
the sun glinting off the gilded tent poles. The pavilion
itself, just a long roof without walls, was made of a
rich, blue material, and sewn with silver disks that
would shine like stars when the torches were lit. The
food, when it arrived, would be served from golden
dishes.

Slaves were waiting with wreaths of flowers at the
entrance to the pavilion. Ptolemy accepted the first
that he was offered, made of some unfamiliar yellow
flower, and teased Thaïs into wearing a wreath of roses,
the pale pink a pleasant contrast in her dark hair. The
chamberlain was waiting for them inside the pavilion;
bowing deeply, he led them the length of the tent to

their couch just below the royal dais. Alexander was already present, Hephaestion, as always, seated at his left. Seeing Ptolemy, the king raised his cup in cheerful greeting. Timander had the couch to the king's right, and was already drinking deeply to still his nervousness at such an honor. An expensive hetaira, another gift from the king, shared his couch.

The other guests, the Friends and the unit commanders, perhaps fifty men in all, were arriving slowly, a laughing, contented crowd decked out in festival clothing. Already, flute-girls moved among the couches, and a female acrobat, naked except for thick bands of gold on her wrists and ankles, postured and danced in the open space between the rows of couches.

As the sun went down, a pair of slaves lit the torches, while others moved among the couches, staggering under the weight of the heavy trays, serving the first course. The wine flowed freely; by the third course, conversation was equally free, and the commanders' voices had risen cheerfully, shouting to be heard above the laughter and the squeal of flutes. Craterus acquired the company of the girl acrobat at some point during the final course. By the time the after-dinner wine was carried 'round, she sat giggling on the foot of the brigade commander's couch, wrapped in a chiton improvised from Craterus's cloak.

The king was in good spirits, quite recovered from his wound and fever. He reclined comfortably on his couch, talking to Hephaestion and Timander, or raising his voice to carry on a conversation with someone farther down the line of couches. He had drunk enough wine to bring a high color to his face. Hephaestion had matched him cup for cup: he reclined now on his own couch in a sort of companionable silence, watching the king.

By the time the wine bowls made a second round, the gathering had grown louder still, Greek and Persian manners disappearing. Some of the Greek Friends, still not entirely used to Macedonian customs, looked overwhelmed. Eumenes was asleep, face down on his couch. The hetaira whom he had hired for the evening sat placidly beside him, sipping at her wine. A new relay of slaves appeared, bearing yet more wine, and the woman prodded discreetly at the secretary, rousing him.

The slaves placed the fresh bowls on the cleared tripods and moved to refill the guests' cups. The king accepted his newly filled cup and raised it high, signalling for the toasts to begin. The guests were not too drunk to respond to that cue. The more sober nudged the rest to silence, and all eyes turned to the dais.

"Macedonians!" Alexander's voice silenced the last pockets of talk. "We have much to celebrate tonight, as you all know well."

At that, there was a laughing cheer from the listening soldiers, starting at the far end of the pavilion. Alexander waited it out, grinning. He was not precisely drunk, but he wasn't sober, either. "Yes, we've enough to celebrate," he repeated. "A victory, and the start of a good peace. I ask you to drink to that peace—and to the success of the marriage that will seal it." Without waiting for his listeners' response, he tipped the cup sharply, allowing the wine to fall in a thin stream to the dirt of the pavilion floor.

The answering cheer was more ragged as the guests struggled to take in the meaning of the king's announcement. Hephaestion poured a seemly libation, watching the others. The possibility of a Roman marriage had been an open secret, but this blunt statement of purpose was unusual in the king. Ptolemy, startled—he had expected first an announcement to the Friends in council, and then an announcement to the army—spilled nearly half his wine into the dirt, the purple liquid splattering Thaïs's gown. She didn't seem to notice, watching the king.

Most of the younger men, the squadron leaders and

the battalion commanders, seemed happy with the idea, cheerfully trading the traditional lewd jokes. Craterus, shocked into sobriety, had pushed the acrobat to the foot of the couch and was sitting up fully, eyes fixed on the dais. Eumenes, flushed and stupid with wine, was frowning as though he hadn't quite understood, or was still looking for the punch line.

"Alexander!" Neoptolemus sat up straight on his couch, putting aside his pair of flute-girls. "What is this marriage—who is the woman?"

"Her name is Cassia, sister of the tribune Cassius," Alexander answered. "A girl of excellent family. I intend to marry her to strengthen the alliance, and to prove to Rome that I intend to keep my word."

The hypaspist commander nodded owlishly. "The gods bless this, then."

"Alexander!" Craterus lurched to his feet, steadying himself against acrobat's shoulder. "You know how I feel about this Roman alliance—"

"We all know that," Hephaestion said.

"Shut up, boy," Craterus said. "If the king chooses to make a treaty with these people when the only way to deal with them is to burn the city, that's the king's business." He broke off abruptly, and went on, with surprising self-control, "But it doesn't matter, I said. What matters is, this girl isn't anything. What does marrying her get us, if—when their Senate decides to repudiate the treaty?"

It was an unexpectedly good question, from a man as drunk as Craterus. Hephaestion's hand closed over one of the apples lying by his plate, and he said, "If you can't see that, Craterus—"

"I'll speak for myself, Hephaestion," Alexander said. He did not raise his voice, but the cavalry commander flinched back as though struck. The king rose from his couch and came slowly down the pavilion to stand facing Craterus. The two men locked eyes, and after a moment, the brigadier looked away.

"Cassius is of rank, his family has high status in the city," Alexander said. "Even their Senate will think twice before shaming him by repudiating his sister's marriage. And Rome doesn't know me: it's only reasonable to offer them something."

Craterus said, "Alexander, the treaty won't last."

Alexander said, "Enough." He paused a moment, and then said, quietly enough that the men on the couches to either side could not hear, "Craterus, I respect you and your opinions. But the decision is made." He smiled, without much humor. "If I'm wrong, you have my permission to tell me so, and as often as you like. But not until then." His smile vanished as quickly as it had appeared. "Will you drink to my wedding?"

Craterus took a deep breath. This was a new Alexander, more like Philip in his dealings with his men, and the brigadier was uncertain of how far he could push this new persona. The king waited patiently.

"As you wish, Alexander," Craterus said at last. "The gods send it prospers." He picked up his cup from the table where he'd left it, then squared his shoulders. "Macedonians!" he shouted. "The king's wedding!"

The rest of the guests echoed his shout. Alexander touched Craterus's arm lightly, and smiled. Craterus returned the smile almost sheepishly, and the king turned away, moving to soothe Hephaestion's wounded feelings. The celebration resumed.

The king did not return to his own tent until well after midnight. Hephaestion, his good humor restored, returned with him, and the two settled companionably onto the king's bed, Alexander leaning against the other's shoulder. After a while, he said, thoughtfully, "The Carthaginian campaign is going to be interesting."

"It will be that," Hephaestion agreed. "We'll have to have reinforcements from Antipater."

Alexander nodded. "And Peucestas, if he can spare them. There's no reason to worry about using Persian troops in Africa."

Hephaestion gave a grunt of agreement. "They can't arrive until the end of the summer, though, and that doesn't leave much time to raise a fleet for Africa."

"I doubt there will be time," Alexander said. "I was thinking we'd cross in the spring." He tilted his head back to watch the cavalry commander's reaction.

Hephaestion whistled softly. "That's taking a risk." he said, after a moment. "Especially for the horses." The spring sailing season was notorious for unpredictably bad weather.

Alexander nodded again, and said, "I think Nearchus could find the captains to handle it."

"You'll have a time convincing Craterus," Hephaestion said.

Alexander laughed softly, but sobered quickly. The pages had forgotten to refill the single lamp. In its fading light, which flickered now and then in an errant breath of air, the furniture cast monstrous shadows that moved uneasily across the fabric of the tent wall. The king studied them warily, reminded in spite of himself of the dream-figures that had haunted him during his illness. Hephaestion felt the sudden tension in the other's body, and said, "What is it?"

Alexander hesitated, then said slowly, "Twice now, I've seen Zeus Ammon. He had Achilles's face. . . ." The first time, he just watched, but the second. . . ." His voice trailed off again.

Hephaestion glanced sharply at him, recognizing the sudden remoteness in the king's voice. Alexander's face had the expression he had worn at Siwah, the ear tuned to an inner voice, the heart given to something immortal, and the cavalry commander suppressed his frown of distrust. Part of that distrust was founded in jealousy, and Hephaestion was honest enough to admit that to himself—the words Zeus

Ammon had spoken through his oracle at Siwah were one of the few things Alexander did not share with him—but a good part of it was grounded in practical philosophy. Zeus Ammon had done his best to lead them into India, and, when that failed, he brought them into Italy: no reason, in Hephaestion's very private opinion, to trust the god's tactical sense. But Alexander believed utterly, and the cavalry commander could feel that belief tightening every muscle of the king's body.

"What, the second time?" he asked gently.

Alexander shuddered slightly, and the cavalry commander slid his arm around the other's waist, pulling him close.

"He never spoke," the king said, after a moment. "He threw dice, but I didn't see the numbers. 'The die is cast,' I suppose—but I don't know what that means."

Hephaestion tightened his hold. "Have you spoken to Aristander?"

The king shook his head.

"Pasithea?"

Again, Alexander shook his head. Hephaestion held him close. Whatever else the omen meant, it spoke of finality, of a decision made. If it heralded ultimate defeat, Alexander did not want to know. Alexander said nothing further, but he did not relax. His very silence demanded an answer.

"I don't know," Hepheastion said. "A man can see many things in a fever, you know that as well as I do."

That was not the answer Alexander wanted. He shrugged one shoulder, and said nothing.

Hephaestion said, "I'm not an augur. If you pushed me—"

"Yes," Alexander said fiercely.

"If you pushed me, I'd have to agree with you, it means your destiny is decided already. But if it were a curse, a tragic ending, you would know it. Achilles knew his fate, and chose it." Hephaestion hesitated, then added, "Unless that was what was said at Siwah."

Alexander shook his head, and said, in a more normal voice, "Maybe it means it's time to stop, to consolidate."

That was returning to solid ground again. Hephaestion breathed a sigh of relief, and said, "You knew that anyway."

Alexander smiled rather wryly. "You think I don't know what was happening while I was ill?"

This time, it was Hephaestion who tensed. Alexander went on, "If I were to die tomorrow, do you mean to tell me that Craterus, Perdiccas, all the rest of them would sit back and let the boy have it all?"

"If Ptolemy and I have anything to say about it," Hephaestion said, "yes, they would."

Alexander smiled then, and returned the other's embrace. After a moment, the king continued in a thoughtful voice, "There has to be a way to bind them to what I want, but I don't see it yet. And there's still Rome to deal with."

"The treaty's a good start on that," Hephaestion said.

"For as long as it lasts," the king said, and pulled away slightly. "Fitting Romans into the empire won't be easy—Persia was simple by comparison."

Hephaestion said, "Carthage will make it easier—a common enemy never hurts. And our people will take things from you, for love, they'd never accept from anyone else. You can use that."

"I know," Alexander said. "Still, sometimes I think Craterus's way would have been easier."

Hephaestion smiled, and, after a moment, the king returned the smile. "That's hardly Alexander's way," the cavalry commander said. "Come to bed, my friend."

INTERLUDE:

Syracuse, early autumn (Hyperberetaios), 1895 imperial (1539 A.D., 2292 A.U.C.)

The young man glanced over his shoulder, in the same instant pushing his black beret, badged with the Companions' wagon-wheel star and the lean Eastern Command lion, even deeper into his hip pocket. He should not have brought it with him at all, but he had trained himself from the age of seventeen to snatch up that beret as he left his quarters, and he had not been able to break the habit even now.

At least in Syracuse, carrying the beret was only dangerous if someone had gotten wind of the commanders' plot. Further north and west, an Eastern Command badge or even the hint of a Greek accent could mean a man's death. The Latin-speaking provinces were tired, they said, of paying to defend the eastern borders against the Islamic kingdoms in Arabia and the encroaching Kievan vassal-states, when the east did nothing to help against the Germans and Scandinavians who troubled the west. The emperor, old and sick and a confirmed easterner in temperament, could do nothing to calm the westerners, and the empire trembled on the verge of civil war.

The interior of the bar was very cool and quiet after the hot noise of Syracuse's streets. The young man paused to let his eyes adjust to the dimness and nodded in answer to the bartender's murmured greeting. It was safe to go up: he crossed the main room, empty except for a couple of old men slumped over the chessboard in the far corner, and took the rattling stairs two at a time.

The second door leading off the upper hallway had been fitted with a new lock when the commanders began their meetings. The plate was still very shiny, conspicuous in the light from the single unshaded bulb, and the young man grimaced at it as he knocked lightly on the door. He knocked twice, then paused, and knocked again. Instantly, the door opened a fraction of an inch and the British engineer-captain peered out, his square face contorted into a suspicious frown. He recognized the newcomer at once, however, and opened the door fully, the frown easing from his face. The young man followed him inside, murmuring a greeting. The engineer-captain slammed home the last of the door's three bolts, and returned to his place.

Maximian Brennus, the big Gaul who commanded the Third Special Auxiliaries—the Western Empire's equivalent of the Eastern Hypaspists—said sharply, "You're late, Dymas."

"I'm sorry, sir," the newcomer answered.

"Trouble?" That was Agathon son of Neoptolemus, colonel of the Third (Successor) Foot Companions, and the senior eastern officer involved in the plan.

Dymas shook his head, and took his place at the table. "No, sir. My relief was late, that's all."

"You're sure it was nothing?" Agathon pursued. "You weren't followed?"

"No, sir," Dymas said again, woodenly. He could understand the colonel's nervousness—they had all

gone too far now to back down, and the treason laws
had not been modified in any essential detail, except
in the method of execution, since the founding of the
empire—but he resented having his judgment questioned.

Across the table, Laurentius Sergius Catalina sighed
softly and pushed himself upright in his chair. The
others instantly swung 'round in their chairs to face
him, and the Roman smiled to himself. He had retired
from his colonelcy of the Twentieth Legion of Foot
the year before—it was either that or be cashiered by
the Western Command for his unpopular, easternizing
politics—but he was pleased to see he had not yet lost
the knack of command.

"Gentlemen," he said softly, "I've received word
from my agent in Egyptian Alexandria. The emperor
will fly to Syracuse tomorrow, and then head north to
Rome to address the Senate."

There was a brief murmur, half of disapproval, half
of satisfaction. The engineer whistled softly, and
Phraates of Susa said, with unfortunate emphasis, "Well,
I just wonder what he'll say."

Brennus gave the Susianan a disgusted look—it was
hard to remember, when enduring Phraates's airs and
graces, that the effeminate major was commander of a
much-decorated squadron of the crack Persian Lanc-
ers, on long leave from the nasty job of patrolling the
Euphrates border against the Islamic natives of Arabia
Major—and said, "My men are ready. I've already
been warned for escort duty."

"Good," Sergius said. "And you, Agathon?"

The Foot Companion commander took a deep breath.
"We're ready. All my battalion captains but one are
with us in principle—the one's an Egyptian, and you
know how rabid they've been against the west. I didn't
think I could take the chance." He paused to recover
his train of thought. "But the rest I'm sure of. They'll
join us."

Sergius nodded, though he would have preferred a more definite commitment from the battalion captains. "Alan?"

The engineer said, "I've been taking the work very slowly, like you ordered, sir. We'll be at it tomorrow, emperor's arrival or no." He grinned companionably at Dymas and Phraates. "Any fences too big for your little toys, my bulldozers'll handle."

"I hardly think it will come to that," Phraates said.

Sergius said, "Dymas, I've been reliably informed your squadron will be picked for the ceremonial escort, which will make our jobs a lot easier if it's true."

"I can probably get the assignment anyway," Dymas said, thoughtfully. "Cassander will trade duties."

"Excellent," Sergius said. "Is everyone clear on what they are supposed to do tomorrow?" He glanced around the circle as the others nodded, one by one. "And we're all agreed on Alexander of Rhagae as our candidate, once we've forced the election?"

Again, there were nods, and Brennus growled, "There's no one else with even a chance of holding it together, Persian line or not."

Sergius nodded himself, looking around the table a final time. Dressed as they all were in civilian clothes to avoid notice, the officers looked oddly uncomfortable rather than unmilitary. Brennus's checked trousers and Dymas's gaudy African-striped shirt did nothing to disguise their military bearing. But the same thing could be said about Sergius's Persian coat and trousers, and the ex-colonel was well aware of it. He straightened himself anyway, and said, "So, gentlemen, it's settled. We will seize the emperor tomorrow at the airfield, force him to abdicate and call an election, and throw our support unanimously behind Alexander of Rhagae."

Put so baldly, the plan sounded like the treachery it was. The easterners, still under the spell of Alexander I and III and his obsession with absolute fidelity,

looked away, unable to meet each others' eyes. Even
Sergius, who prided himself on being a hardheaded
Roman, felt the same twinge of guilt. To exorcise it,
he said, "Our duty is to the empire—all the empire.
This is the only way to preserve what the Great Alexander built. I will not say that he would have approved, no man can know that. But I will say he
would respect our motives."

"The Great Alexander would never have let things
get like this," Dymas said, bitterly.

"Alexander of Rhagae has the charisma," Agathon
said. "He can—he will pull things together again."

Phraates smiled and said, "You had better pray to
all the faces of God that he can, my friend. Or the
empire splits, and then everything will fall apart."

Sergius nodded in spite of himself. "Gentlemen,"
he said aloud. "Until tomorrow."

CHAPTER 11:

Italy, summer (Loios), 31 imperial, to Carthage, summer (Loios), 32 imperial (325/324 B.C., 428/429 A.U.C.)

Antipater proved surprisingly reasonable about releasing the latest levies for the Carthaginian campaign: clearly, he and Theagenes had matters well under control in Greece. The ships carrying the new men sailed from Macedon at the end of Gorpiaios, landing at Metapontium a week later. Their officers marched them north in easy stages, joining the main army just in time to witness the king's marriage to Cassius's sister. Philip had taken a new bride with each new war; the levies accepted this Roman marriage without dissent, and their commanders began the winter-long task of fitting them into the phalanx and the cavalry squadrons.

Throughout the late summer and the autumn, Fabius and his fellow consul fought to secure the consulship for Ptolemy. The election proved more difficult than the grant of citizenship had been. Fabius pushed his friends and political allies, called in favors done nearly twenty years before, and managed to produce a more than respectable following for the Macedonian brigadier during the inescapable ritual of the campaign. Ptolemy did his part with a good grace—he had a sharp sense of the ridiculous and knew perfectly well what he looked like in a chalk-smeared toga, courting the voters in the Forum—but after some weeks of campaigning against an increasingly vocal opposition, even he began to show the strain. As the election approached, the less obligated of Fabius's supporters found excuses not to send their dependents to wait on Ptolemy in the Forum, and the consul, correctly diagnosing those signs of defection, grew gaunt with worry. But, in the end, there was no need for his concern. His influence held firm, the bought voters stayed bought, and Fabius's rivals, already discredited by the army's defeat, were unable to muster a workable coalition. Ptolemy was chosen as one of the consuls by a reasonable margin, and Fabius himself was reelected.

Alexander expressed his formal pleasure at the results of the election, and the rest of the Friends teased the brigadier unmercifully. The Senate, having heard some of the cruder jokes, became unexpectedly stubborn, and only the combination of Fabius's most outrageous threats and blandishments kept the senators from repudiating the second part of the treaty. As it was, the Senate voted to fund only a single legion to accompany Alexander against Carthage, and Fabius's opponents managed to get Caius Domitius Mela appointed as one of the two military tribunes who would have command under Ptolemy. Cassius Nasidienis was to be the other, but Fabius still braced himself to report that failure to Alexander.

To the consul's surprise, however, Alexander accepted both the small number of troops and Domitius's appointment with equanimity. In private, the king was positively delighted by the turn of events: he had the hostages he wanted, in the persons of the Roman officers, and Domitius's presence gave him good reason to mistrust the Roman levies.

From midsummer, Nearchus had been hard at work in Syracuse, assembling another fleet large enough to carry the Macedonian army to Africa. By the beginning of winter he reported that he was ready, down to the merchant ships that would carry the siege machinery and the extra supplies. He also expressed his willingness to turn over the Syracusan command to anyone the king cared to name, in order that he himself might command the invasion fleet. Alexander promptly appointed Coenus regent in the admiral's place, and ordered the protesting brigadier to turn his brigade over to his son Amyntas. That silenced Coenus's protests briefly, until the king announced that he intended to sail for Africa at the beginning of the spring sailing season. All of the Friends raised loud objections at first—even Coenus was moved to quote Hesiod's description of the unsuitability and general foulness of the early sailing season—but Alexander gradually won them over, pointing out that such an early crossing would earn them the advantage of surprise and, more important, would probably trap a good part of the dangerous Carthaginian fleet in its winter harbor. As soon as the weather began to moderate, Nearchus brought his fleet from Syracuse to the newly founded port of Ostia. The Macedonian army, now supplemented by a single Roman legion, made its sacrifices to Poseidon—Hephaestion in particular, made a magnificent gift in hopes of an uneventful voyage—then filed aboard the ships. At the end of Xandikos, the fleet sailed for Africa.

The crossing was not an easy one, though luckily there were no major storms. In good weather the voyage took four or five days, though a fast merchant ship could make the journey in three. It took the Macedonians seven days to make the crossing, their ships delayed by adverse winds and a series of squalls that held the fleet almost motionless for a day and a half. As the weather moderated again, Nearchus slowly regained contact with his ships. The warships, all sturdy quinquiremes, had survived the storm, but two of the supply ships had vanished completely, without any witnesses to say whether they had been sunk or merely forced by some accident to turn back to Sicily. Nearchus sent one of the quinquiremes back along the fleet's course to search for wreckage but, after battling the waves for hours, the ship returned with nothing.

Near noon of the seventh day, the leading warship spotted familiar landmarks on the African coast, and the fleet hove to, to check their bearings. Despite the storms, they were not too far from their planned landfall, the headland opposite the city of Carthage itself. As planned, Nearchus split the fleet, taking most of the warships toward Carthage in hopes of trapping the Carthaginian fleet at anchor. The great ships turned ponderously, pitching against the waves so that the bronze rams alternately showed clearly and were buried in the foam. As the ships steadied to their new course, the drumbeat quickened: the Carthaginians had surely seen the fleet by now, and would be struggling to bring their own ships out of the harbor to meet it.

As the leading ships of Nearchus's fleet approached the entrance to the harbor, they shifted formation to line abreast, just as the first Carthaginian ship emerged from the narrows. Two more Carthaginians followed in single file. Without waiting for a signal from the flagship, Proteas son of Andronicus, whose quinquireme was on the left of the Macedonian line, ordered his drummers to sound the battle cadence. The ship leapt forward, sailors running to secure the mast and sail—never abandoned until the last moment, to give as much speed as possible at the moment of impact—while the marines ran forward to man the three bow catapults. The soldiers got off two shots before the ships closed, but did little damage.

The Carthaginian ship fought to turn away, out of

the line of the ram, and was half successful. The two ships scraped past each other, snapping oars and throwing the lower decks into confusion, before Proteas ordered his steersman to sheer off. The damage was worse aboard the Carthaginian ship; Proteas was able to bring his own ship around to ram before the Carthaginian captain was able to recover control of his vessel. The Macedonian ship struck the enemy squarely amidships, locking the two vessels together. The marines, mostly Greek mercenaries, poured forward, dropping over the curving bow onto the enemy deck. The Carthaginian soldiers, also including Greek mercenaries, were waiting for them. There was a short, fierce fight before it became clear that the Carthaginian ship was sinking under them, and Proteas sounded the recall. The marines fought their way back aboard their own ship, then cut free the last of the grapples that held the ships together. As the drum sounded a new cadence, the Macedonian ship slowly began to move backward, disengaging itself from the mortally wounded Carthaginian.

The ram pulled free with a great shriek of tearing wood, and the Carthaginian ship began to break up, wallowing deeper and deeper in the waves, surrounded by an ever-widening ring of wreckage. Lines trailed over the side into the water, and bodies, Macedonian and Carthaginian alike, littered the deck. There were swimmers in the water already, and the surviving oarsmen fought their way out of the sinking hull to join them. On deck, a gang of soldiers fought to work the single remaining catapult. Seeing that, the Macedonian mercenaries' commander ordered his archers forward and offered a prize for the best shot. Disputing among themselves, the bowmen began to pick the Carthaginians off one by one. As the third man fell, the others abandoned their attempt and dove overboard. The stern of the ship was already underwater. As the Macedonians watched, the bow lifted even

further, the bronze ram rising toward the sky, and
then the entire ship sank abruptly beneath the waves.

That scene was repeated all along the Macedonian
line: though the Carthaginian fleet more than equalled
the Macedonian ships both in numbers and in sea-
manship, Nearchus had caught them in the harbor
mouth, before they could maneuver to match his formation. The Carthaginians recognized the situation
and recalled their fleet, leaving three wrecks wallowing
in the wave-troughs. Nearchus had lost a ship as well;
he moved in to pick up its survivors, and then to
rescue any surviving Carthaginians. The first Carthaginian aboard did his best to knife the man who rescued
him, and was himself thrown back like a fish. The
Greek mercenaries were less fanatical, but after that
the Macedonians were less eager to rescue them, and
several hundred drowned.

As planned, Nearchus left half of his ships on station, where they could dominate the harbor entrance,
and sailed south and east across the bay to establish a
base for the rest of his fleet. From there he could
supply and refit the blockading ships and still respond
to any major threat of a breakout.

The rest of the fleet, escorted by a few quinquiremes
under the command of Pnytagoras of Cyprus, pushed
deeper on into the bay, landing some forty stadia to
the south of the city. There was no opposition waiting,
but Alexander drove his men hard, unloading the
ships and drawing them well up onto the beach, then
constructing a crude palisade to defend the new camp.
Only when the first rough walls were in place did
Pnytagoras put to sea again to rejoin Nearchus, leaving only a pair of warships to help defend the campsite.

The Carthaginians did not make a sortie against the
Macedonian camp until the following day, and by then
the Macedonians were ready for them. The Carthaginian
party was repulsed with heavy losses, which would
have been heavier had the horses been fit for the

pursuit. Alexander increased his own perimeter guard, even though that meant that it would take longer to unload the merchant ships, and sent the first scouting parties inland to assess the Carthaginian walls.

From the doorway of the king's tent, the assembled Friends could just see the first of the warships pulled up on the beach, its scarred paint bright against the dark line of trees that ringed the campsite. A gang of sailors were still working around it, some unloading the last of its cargo while others took aboard fresh supplies. The presence of the ships gave the camp a strange, Homeric look emphasized by the temporary palisade on the inland side.

The Homeric echoes made Hephaestion uneasy, and he was glad that most of the army would soon be abandoning the campsite. He waved away the bowl offered by an attendant page—the oily stew still turned his stomach—but accepted a half-loaf of bread from one of the other boys. Craterus glanced up from his own well-stocked plate and gave the cavalry commander a contemptuous smile.

The royal engineers, Charias and Diades, bent over the unbalanced table, comparing the notes scribbled on wax tablets in their own illegible abbreviated script. "I think this is all," one of them said at last, putting aside the tablets.

Alexander nodded. "And?" It was Diades who had spoken, though sometimes it was difficult to tell the two men apart. It was not so much that they looked alike—they were of similar height and build, but Diades was going bald, while Charias was missing two fingers since the siege of Tyre—but rather that they shared inflection and gesture, the similarities bred into them during their long apprenticeship under Philip's master engineer.

"The damage isn't as bad as we first thought." This time the speaker was Charias. The maimed right hand made an abortive movement, an eloquent gesture quickly suppressed. "Most of it we've been able to repair—"

"Though the wood here isn't of the best quality," Diades interjected, and his partner nodded.

"As for the catapults, we can take replacements from the fleet," Charias went on. "They throw a lighter weight than the ones we lost, but I think we can compensate. The biggest problem is the supply ships that were lost. About half the cast ammunition for the catapults—bolts and light darts—and most of the shaped stones for the larger machines are gone."

Alexander made a face. "And it's the stones we'll need to crack the walls," he murmured, half to himself. "How long will it take to replace them?"

Charias shrugged. "Five days to get a bare minimum, but ten would be better."

"Can you do it on the march?" The king's eyes were fixed on nothing, calculating.

The two engineers exchanged glances, then Diades said, "Not easily. But there's good material inland of here. We could quarry there, get a minimum supply, and then bring up more as needed."

Alexander nodded slowly. "All right. Hephaestion, Craterus, detail extra men for the garrison here, enough to protect the quarrying parties."

Hephaestion nodded his acknowledgement of the king's order, mentally reviewing the forces at his disposal. He had plenty of men to spare: the Companion Cavalry were of little use during a prolonged siege. Craterus said, his mouth full, "The garrison's already pretty strong, Alexander. I'd rather keep the rest with me."

The king shook his head. "And I want to protect our landing. Leave another hundred men, that should do it." He looked at the engineers again. "What about timber for rams?"

"Cut," Diades answered, "but we'll build the carriage and add the sheathing at the walls."

Ptolemy cleared his throat. "This is all well and good," he said mildly, "but what are we going to do when we get to Carthage?" It was the first time he had spoken in the day's council session. The rest of the Friends glanced in his direction.

"We'll know enough to make plans when the scouting parties return," Alexander said, rather sharply.

"Ptolemy's right," Craterus said. "There're a few things that ought to be decided now, before we get under the walls—and while we don't have any Romans present."

Ptolemy's eyes narrowed, and Alexander said, "What do you mean by that?"

"Who's going to be first over the walls?" Craterus said bluntly. "I say we send the Romans—and that snake Domitius for preference."

Simmias son of Andromenes, who had been given command of what had been Meleager's brigade, opened his mouth to voice a cautious protest, but Ptolemy spoke first.

"I have an obligation to them, you can't try to get them killed." Then he smiled with an effort, and said, "Besides, I'd have to go in with them. I am consul, remember?"

"If I send Domitius's men in first," Alexander said, "rest assured you won't go with them, Ptolemy." There was a new, bleak note in his voice that made the others look up sharply.

Ptolemy said, "You're seriously considering it, then."

"In Bactra, you told me to consider murdering the entire Sacred Band," Alexander said. "So did you, Craterus. This way, at least the Romans would have some chance." Then, like Ptolemy, he smiled tautly. "But we'll see what happens. It probably won't be necessary."

The scouting parties, when they returned, confirmed Eumenes's earlier information, and added a certain amount of unpleasant detail. As the secretary had reported, there was a triple wall stretching all the way across the isthmus; the outermost wall was of earth topped by a low wooden palisade, fronted by a ditch six feet deep and fifteen feet wide. The second wall was of masonry, perhaps twenty-five feet high and thirty feet wide, and it, too, was fronted by a broad ditch. The third wall was even taller than the others— the scouts estimated it variously as anywhere from forty-five to sixty-five feet high; they had not been able to get too close before being driven off by Carthaginian patrols—and capped at regular intervals by four-story towers. It was not particularly encouraging news, and Alexander sent messengers to Nearchus asking him to send a ship along the city's seaward walls to see if there were any likely points for an attack from the sea. There were none, in the admiral's considered judgment, and the king resigned himself to a long siege. It would be too costly to attempt to storm the triple walls without lengthy preparation.

The greater part of the Macedonian army left the landing site as soon as the engineers declared the siege train ready to travel, leaving only a slightly understrength mercenary brigade and six squadrons of cavalry to hold the camp. The army advanced slowly toward Carthage and the Carthaginian camp twenty stadia outside the walls.

Forty stadia from the triple walls, a scout squadron captured a Greek mercenary officer who claimed to carry a message to Alexander. When brought before the king, the Greek, who gave his own name as Cleomenes, swore that his commander, Deïmachus, was prepared, no, begged, to surrender to Alexander. The king, who disliked treachery even when it worked to his advantage, at first refused to listen, but both Ptolemy and Craterus pointed out that, if Deïmachus really were willing to betray his current employers, there was a chance that the Macedonians could take the walls without too great a loss of life. Alexander reluctantly agreed, and sent Balacrus, one of the scout squadron leaders, to negotiate with Deïmachus, keeping the mercenary officer as a hostage.

When Balacrus failed to return as planned, Alexander cursed the brigadiers and Cleomenes, and dispatched a squadrom of cavalry under a flag of truce to the Carthaginian camp, with instructions to buy Balacrus's return. The camp was gone. In its place stretched twenty stadia of smoldering farmland, extending almost all the way to the walls. Two tau-shaped wooden structures stood before the burned area, a shapeless bundle hanging from each. Hephaestion, already suspecting what he would find, rode forward warily. The bodies pinned to the wooden tau were almost unrecognizable, eyes gouged out, noses and ears hacked away. Hephaestion recognized Balacrus first by the faded scar that ran diagonally across his chest.

There were more bodies huddled on the ground beyond the crosses. Hephaestion, controlling the urge to vomit, ordered the squadron's senior trooper to free the suspended bodies, and dismounted to examine the other bodies. They all seemed to be Greeks, and probably mercenaries; most were at least partly armed, and had died fighting. Hephaestion shook his head, unable to make any further guesses, and walked back to join his men. The senior trooper, his face ashen, had freed the bodies; they lay, wrapped in cloaks, across the backs of the two most placid horses. The squadron rode back to the main army in silence.

Alexander received the news with cold fury, and the army halted for the night to let the fires burn themselves out. Cleomenes identified the second body as Deïmachus's, and the two bodies were burned on the same pyre. Overnight, a few more Greeks, survivors of Deïmachus's brigade, straggled into the camp, and from their stories it was possible to piece together what had happened. The Hundred, the Carthaginian oligarchs who controlled the Carthaginian senate and thus the city, had gotten word of Deïmachus's plan through one of the junior officers and had ordered the Carthaginian commander to attack at once. Deïmachus had been surprised in his tent and taken, with Balacrus; the rest of his brigade had done their best to fight back, but most of them had been killed or captured, only a few individuals managing to escape. The leaders of the Hundred had come in person to pass sentence on Deïmachus and Balacrus. Faced with the loss of Deïmachus's two thousand men, and uncertain of other mercenary units' reliability, the Hundred and the Carthaginian commander had jointly decided to withdraw to the safety of the wall, firing the last fields behind them.

Alexander listened to each of the survivors, and when they had finished, said simply, "It won't be safe enough." At dawn, the smoldering fires were out and the Macedonians moved forward through the ashy fields, to take up positions along the planned siege lines. Cleomenes and the other survivors of Deïmachus's brigade went with them: they had their own injuries to avenge.

Despite his anger, Alexander proceeded methodically with the siege, setting up his own lines to cut Carthage off from communication with her allies in the interior, then turning his attention to the city itself. The outermost of the walls was not strongly made, earth topped by a thin, wooden palisade, fronted only by a reasonably shallow ditch, and Perdiccas and Neoptolemus both volunteered to lead a direct attack. Alexander pointed out what each man should have known—that the first counterattack would pin them in the killing ground between the two walls, unable easily to retreat over palisade and ditch—and advised them to join the foraging parties.

The two engineers were in their element. While Diades concentrated on setting up the great stone-throwers where they could concentrate their fire on the towers of the innermost wall, Charias turned his attention to the aqueduct that supplied at least a part of Carthage's water. Working through the days and at night by torchlight, Charias managed to construct a crude cistern of his own, and then diverted the water from the aqueduct into it, supplying the army fully. Alexander had hoped to use the waterless aqueduct as a way into the city, but when that proved impractical, the engineers began dismantling it. By the end of Artemisios, it had almost vanished completely. Diades used some of the rubble as ammunition for his catapults, coating the stones with clay to make them fly true—he had still not been able to make up for all the stones lost in the sunk on merchant ships—and Charias took the rest of the rubble to begin filling in the first ditch. Files of Foot Companions sweated under the stifling protection of Charias's wooden penthouses, choking in the stink of the wet hide facings as they hauled yet another hundredweight of earth and stone up to the ditch. The catapults in the siege towers were manned day and night, and Ombrion's archers stood a constant guard against any sally from behind the wall.

Returning from leading yet another foraging party, Cassius Nasidienis sighed to see how slowly the work was proceeding. He glanced over his shoulder to where his own legionaries sweated over a half dozen carts, manhandling them and their protesting draft animals over the uneven ground. They brought barely a day's rations for the entire army, and he hoped the other foragers, the parties sent further west, had had better luck. The king had opened negotiations with some of the inland cities, cities that had no particular reason to love Carthage and every reason to fear and to placate Alexander, but nothing had come of that as yet. If— when, Cassius corrected himself firmly—the cities agreed, a regular supply system could be set up, and the army would not have to spend half its time foraging.

The first of the carts tottered on the brow of the hill. The legionaries who a moment before had been pushing frantically now clung to its sides to keep it from plunging out of control and overrunning the mules. A sweating centurion threw his weight against the cart's tail, grinning, teeth showing bright in his dirt-streaked face. Then the cart tipped forward, descended the hill in a barely controlled rush, legionaries yelping their delight. Cassius shook his head dubiously and nudged his horse forward, letting it pick its own way down the uneven slope.

Somewhat to the tribune's surprise, they managed to get all the carts down without overturning any of them, and without serious injury to man or mule. Of course, they might have sustained far worse injury during the foraging itself, but Alexander had insisted that his men pay for what they took.

The routine challenge at the camp's perimeter turned to a cheerful greeting as the Foot Companions saw the well-loaded carts. Cassius returned the greeting as cheerfully, wondering if the other foraging parties had done that much worse. Once inside the camp, Eumenes and a gang of his slaves came forward to take charge of the food. Cassius turned the carts over to him gratefully—he had been smelling his own sweat for three days, and thought longingly of a bath even in seawater— and turned his horse toward his own tent.

There was not much activity in the camp itself. A line of soldiers with buckets, working always out of range of the catapults on the city walls, brought seawater to dampen the hide facings of the towers and the low penthouses, protecting them against the fire arrows the Carthaginians fired off at random intervals. From the center of the camp came the sound of metal against metal: the armory slaves were hard at work.

"Cassius!"

The tribune turned slowly on his horse, recognizing the voice. "Yes, Domitius?"

"I need to talk to you," the other tribune said, catching at Cassius's foot. "Now. In private."

Cassius frowned, recognizing the urgency in the other's voice, and did not try to pull free. "What is it?"

"Not here," Domitius insisted. "But it's important, Cassius."

"All right," Cassius said. Domitius released his foot and stepped back a few paces. Cassius swung himself down from the horse and glanced around for a groom. Domitius grimaced, put two fingers to his mouth and whistled; a second later, a slave appeared to take the horse. Cassius relinquished the reins unwillingly, glaring at the other tribune.

"This way," Domitius said, and pulled back the door flap of his tent. Cassius ducked under the low doorway, then stood blinking while Domitius secured the tentflap behind them.

"What is it?" Cassius asked again, and Domitius waved him to a seat. Cassius sat carefully, composing himself to wait with at least outward patience for the other to come to the point, and glanced around him. He had never been in Domitius's tent before, but it was much as he had expected: plain, with only the most necessary of furniture—a low bed, two fragile folding chairs, a single table to hold the single lamp—and severely clean, the dirt floor still bearing the marks of the most recent sweeping.

Domitius took his place in the other chair, dragging it close and lowering his voice almost to a whisper. "I'll speak plainly," he began, and Cassius barely restrained himself from snapping at him.

"It's about Alexander's plans for the attack on Carthage," Domitius went on. "I have it on good authority that he plans to have us make the first assault—as soon as they make a breach, that is—and that he doesn't plan to support the attack. What do you say to that?"

"What do you expect me to say?" Cassius temporized. He realized he was whispering, too, and deliberately raised his voice to a normal level. "What proof do you have?"

"Proof enough," Domitius snapped. "The important thing is that your precious ally is trying to get us all killed."

"Nonsense," Cassius said. He glared at the other tribune. "Whatever else anyone has been able to accuse him of, Alexander has never broken his given word."

"Look at how he treated Thebes."

"Thebes betrayed him first," Cassius retorted. "Look at how he treated the Sacred Band. No one would've thought twice if he'd had them all killed, and they're holding Greece for him—"

"Is that the kind of power you want for Rome?" Domitius asked. "To be Alexander's watchdog in Italy?"

Cassius flinched and was furious with himself for doing so. Domitius had a gift for hitting the sore spots, emphasizing the parts of the alliance that galled most. And Cassius did not dare give him Fabius's answer, that Rome would still outlive Alexander, for fear Domitius would attempt to act on it. He took a deep breath, and said, "Show me your proof, then."

For the first time, Domitius's eyes wavered. "It's common knowledge among the Macedonians."

"When was soldiers' gossip ever evidence?" Cassius demanded. "Have you spoken to Alexander about it?"

"What good would that do?" Domitius said contemptuously. "He'd only deny it."

"Have you spoken to any of the generals?"

"No."

"Then how can you say you have any sort of proof?" Cassius said, with what he knew was false triumph. "For the gods' sake, Domitius. it's Carthage that's the enemy, not Alexander." He stood up without waiting for the other's answer and, reluctantly, Domitius rose with him, pulling back the tent flap.

The groom was still holding Cassius's horse, and the tribune snatched the reins impatiently from him, swinging irritably and ungracefully onto the animal's back. Only when he had settled his weight comfortably did he look back. Domitius was still standing stooped in the doorway of his tent, staring up at him, an odd, unreadable expression on his fine-boned face. Unaccountably disconcerted, and then angry with himself for being so, Cassius wheeled his horse away, heading at a trot toward the opposite end of the Roman camp.

But before he had covered half the distance to his own tent, he pulled the horse to a walk. It was possible Alexander was planning to sacrifice the Roman contingent as shock troops. From a Macedonian point of view—and Cassius could even name the specific Macedonian—such a move could be good policy, weakening Alexander's most dangerous ally even further. Cassius sighed deeply. The king was not a devious man, nor a particularly good liar: he had never had need to be. One way or another, in words or reaction, a direct question would get an honest answer—if the tribune dared to ask it. Cassius turned his horse again, skirting the edge of the Roman camp, and went in search of the king.

Alexander was standing in the shadow of one of the larger towers, staring thoughtfully at the gate it threatened. At his elbow, Diades said, "If you bring it closer, it does more damage, but it'll be harder to defend against a sortie."

The king nodded, and turned at the sound of hoofbeats behind him. "Cassius! How was the foraging?"

Cassius gave his reins to the page who appeared from nowhere to attend him, and dismounted rather stiffly to join the king. "The foraging went well enough, King Alexander," he said slowly, "but there's a thing I need to ask you."

Alexander frowned. "Ask," he said. Behind him, the engineers exchanged questioning glances.

Cassius took a deep breath. As far as he could tell, the king's puzzlement was genuine, at least this far. "It's come to my ears you're planning to send my people first into any breach that's made. We obey orders, of course—provided always that we'll be supported in the attack."

The balding engineer made a choked sound of outrage. Alexander silenced him with an outthrust hand. "I've made no firm plans," he said, with surprising restraint. "Yes, it's been suggested that Ptolemy's men be the ones to make a first assault, but we were talking mainly of his Foot Companion brigade, not your legion. Someone seems to have misunderstood."

Cassius studied the king dubiously, less reassured than he wanted to be. Then Alexander's face changed, and he added, "Even if I were in the habit of sending allies to their deaths, would I risk one of my best generals with them? Or have you forgotten Ptolemy's your consul?"

Cassius shook his head, his doubts fading. "No, King Alexander, nor did I truly think you intended our deaths. But when you make plans without us, it's no wonder these rumors get started."

Alexander smiled, rather grimly. "But I've made no plans for your people without your knowledge, I assure you. Nor will I—and you have my word on that."

"Thank you, King Alexander," Cassius said, and meant it. This was the Alexander he had hoped to see, the man of honor, one he would follow almost blindly. With that promise to back him up—and regardless of what Domitius did or said—he himself would keep the legion in line. "With your permission, then, I'll take my leave. It was a long ride, foraging."

Some version of the conversation had spread to every corner of the camp before sundown. Hephaestion, dining alone with the king that night, waited until the wine bowl had made its rounds before broaching the subject. Even so, Alexander grimaced angrily. "Gods below, is that all over the camp already?"

"I'm afraid so," Hephaestion answered.

Alexander grunted, staring into his wine. "I don't like lying," he said after a moment. "And I don't like having to lie."

Hephaestion frowned, uncertain of what the king meant—the informant had given the broad outline of the conversation, but no specifics. Alexander glanced at him, and smiled tightly. "Cassius asked me outright if I had planned to send his people over the wall without proper support, and I told him I would not."

"I don't see that that's a lie," Hephaestion began.

"He asked me," Alexander went on, still with that humorless smile, "if such a thing had been suggested. What could I say to that?"

Hephaestion nodded, but before he could say anything, the king went on, "And I have been thinking about it, at least about ways of getting rid of Domitius. If Craterus had just kept his mouth shut, it could have been arranged discreetly. But once it was mentioned in council. . . ." His voice trailed off in disgust.

Hephaestion eyed the other warily. That sort of solution was more like Philip than Alexander, the sort of thing that Alexander scorned to consider, calling it unworthy of him. Alexander knew it, too, and didn't like the change. Hephaestion said aloud, "We can deal with Domitius, Alexander. You don't need that kind of solution."

"I hope not," Alexander said, but his expression eased a little. "Because I will do it if I have to."

Hephaestion said, with all the confidence he could muster, "You won't."

The Macedonians took the first wall just after the full moon of Panemos. The attack had been well prepared, the ditch at least partially filled in places, and

spanned by portable bridges in others; the Carthaginians
made only a tentative counterattack and retreated behind the shelter of their second, much stronger wall.
In the meetings of the Hundred, it was declared that,
if it had taken the great Alexander three months to
break the weakest wall, the Macedonians would surely
starve before the city did. This was partially bravado,
and the more pessimistic oligarchs branded it as such:
Alexander had succeeded in setting up a regular trade
with several of Carthage's former allies, and was now
in no danger of starving. But if he was well supplied,
so was Carthage. The city's wells were deep, and
supplemented by massive cisterns that had not yet
been touched. The Macedonian fleet had been unable
to impose a complete blockade, and supplies still arrived, if irregularly, from the Iberian colonies. Already the new Carthaginian admiral, inspired perhaps
by the execution of his predecessor for his failure to
break out against the Macedonian fleet, proposed to
dig a second exit from the inner harbor, on the other
side of Cape Carthage from the main exit. The Hundred rejected the plan as currently unnecessary, but
looked favorably on the admiral for suggesting it.

Outside the walls, Alexander moved to consolidate
his gains. Parts of the earthen wall were demolished
and used to fill in the ditch; a few sections, notably
those nearest the gatehouse that guarded the main
road south, were left intact, though modified, to help
deter any sortie. It was a long, slow job, the soldiers
under constant fire from the inner walls. The engineers did their best to provide protection for them,
both by building more of the protective penthouses
and by maintaining a constant counterfire from the
siege towers, but neither could be completely effective. Losses mounted slowly.

The Carthaginians mounted a number of small-scale
sorties as well, slipping out from behind their walls to
attack the siege towers and the Macedonian fortifica-

tions. Each time the battalions detailed to protect the towers drove them back, but two days after the new moon of Loios, a determined party slipped out of the northern sea gate and made their way through the marshy ponds to attack the penthouses. Polyperchon's brigade, which had responsibility for that part of the siege line, was caught napping, and the raiders succeeded in setting fire to two of the structures before they were driven back. A third penthouse caught fire before the men of the neighboring brigades could douse the flames, and all three were badly damaged. Surveying the wreckage in the brilliant morning sunlight, Diades shook his head, doubting that he could salvage more than one.

In this timber-poor country, that was a hard blow. Alexander rubbed his stinging eyes and glared irritably at the distant walls. He had fought the fire with the rest of the army, first organizing a bucket brigade and then moving in to smother the last of the flames with his dampened cloak; he would bear an ugly scar on his left arm for some weeks, where a smoldering beam had struck him. "Do what you can," he said grimly, and moved on to arrange for a gang to go inland in search of wood for the repairs.

Despite Diades's pessimism, the engineers were able to make some repairs, and the search parties were able to acquire—everyone was careful not to ask for details—a wagon-load of cut timbers. The attack proceeded with only a week's delay, the soldiers beginning the monotonous, dangerous job of filling in parts of the ditch that fronted the second wall. They came under attack at once from the wall itself, and the catapults were unable to provide adequate covering fire.

If the siege towers were moved to point-blank range, the stone-throwers on the lower levels were powerful enough to rip the battlements right off the top of the wall itself—but point-blank range was two hundred feet further in toward the city, closer than any of the siege towers now stood, and less than three hundred feet from the ruined outer wall. The problems of protecting the towers from a determined assault were obvious, and it was equally obvious that, if the towers were to be moved in, the Macedonians would have to commit themselves to two or three specific points of attack. The Friends' agreement ended there, Craterus arguing for a further delay and perhaps a diversionary attack from the sea, the engineers pushing for a chance to demonstrate what their machines could do, the other infantry commanders demanding some sort of increased support for their men before proceeding with the attack. Alexander listened to everyone and then announced that the towers would be moved closer. He dissolved the council and walked to the siege lines to survey the possible points of attack for himself.

Caterus, seeing the king's intent, headed there himself, and others of the Friends copied him. By the time the king's party had reached the palisade and ditch that surrounded the camp just outside the two-stadia range of the Carthaginian catapults, the council had effectively reformed itself. Alexander gave them a sardonic look, silencing any attempts to renew the argument, and continued on toward the nearest tower, keeping its bulk between himself and the walls.

At the king's approach, Charias slid down the ladder from the tower's lowest floor and came forward to greet the king. He was unarmored, and nearly naked, his tunic falling loose from one shoulder: armor was unbearable in the heat of the enclosed tower.

"How goes it?" Alexander asked. The officers hung back a little, not quite out of earshot, unwilling to approach further without an invitation. They were careful, however, to stay behind the protection of the tower.

Charias shrugged, wiping greasy hands across his already filthy tunic. "Well enough, sire. A snapped cord this morning on one of the sixty-pounders, but we've got it back in service now."

As if to underline his words, there was a shout from within the tower, and one of the lower shutters rumbled open. That was followed almost at once by the unmistakable thrum and crack of a sixty-pound stone-thrower. Charias turned at once and shouted up at the tower, "Sighting, Philip?"

After a moment, a figure waved from the railing at the edge of the second story, then cupped a hand to his ear. Like Charias, he was nearly naked, his tunic clinging to his body.

"Sighting!" Charias shouted again.

"Just below the parapet!" The figure shouted back. "First wall! Raise it?"

Charias waved his agreement, and turned back to the king. "If we could come within a stadion of the wall," he began, "I could take that course of stones right off."

Alexander said, "So Diades said. You'll get your chance, don't worry. The question now is where to try to break through."

"With your permission?" Charias asked, suddenly formal. The king nodded. "I'd say the point where the aqueduct crossed the wall. They've torn down what was left of the watercourse, but no matter what they've done to strengthen it, that will be the weak point."

"That's very close to the main gate, isn't it?" Alexander asked, frowning.

"About a stadion to the north," Charias admitted. The king made a face, and the engineer added quickly, "But that will be the weakest point, sire."

"I'll take a look," Alexander said, and swung himself up the ladder onto the tower's lowest floor. The engineer followed nimbly, despite his maimed hand.

The interior of the tower was dark and stiflingly hot. The ceiling of the lowest floor was just high enough for the crew, who worked the capstan that turned the tower's heavy wheels, to stand upright. Part of the capstan crew, which also provided the water carriers and guards when the tower was stationary, sat or sprawled along the railing, their armor piled against the walls. The various units took it in turn to provide the tower crews: these were Romans who watched incuriously, unmoving in the heat.

Alexander stepped over and around the sprawled bodies and pulled himself up to the second level. There the ceiling was higher to accommodate the eighteen-foot height of the heavy stone-throwers, and more light leaked in around the edges of the shutters that covered the catapult ports between shots. A pair of Roman soldiers, sweating and sullen, had just man-handled a sixty-pound stone into the machine's sling. They stood aside while one of Charias's engineers checked the elevation of the slider, and then stepped forward again to throw their weight against the levers that drew back the slider. The king did not stay to watch but pulled himself up the next ladder to the final story.

The machines were smaller there, a pair of true catapults and a lighter ten-pound stone-thrower, each attended by a two-man crew. The supervising engineer—Philip again—turned to welcome the king, but his words were drowned by the prolonged rattle of the shutter opening on the floor below. The sixty-pounder fired, and the entire tower shivered.

"Welcome, sire," Philip tried again. "How may we serve you?"

Both the catapults were loaded and cocked, cords straining against the triggers. Alexander nodded to them. "Fire away, but then I want to take a look at the walls."

Philip nodded, and gestured to the Romans waiting at the back of the tower. "Raise the shutters."

Both troopers reached for the ropes that ran across the tower ceiling through a complex array of pulleys, and began to pull steadily. The shutters lifted slowly, and Philip said, "Hold."

The Romans hastily wound their ropes around handy cleats, and waited, breathing hard. Philip said, "Fire," and, as the sliders snapped forward against their frames, "Close." The Romans released their ropes, and the shutters slammed closed again.

Charias rested his good hand against the nearest wall, frowning, then moved forward to test the shutter. "This is too dry," he said, irritably. "What do you think you're doing, Philip?"

The younger engineer looked away nervously, and said, "There isn't much water left, sir. I was waiting. . . ." His voice trailed off under the Greek's stern gaze.

"Well, send for more," Charias said, after a moment. He gestured to the nearest Roman. "Inform your captain we need water."

The Roman said, almost insolently, "Right, captain," and dropped down the nearest ladder.

Alexander's eyes narrowed, and he said, "Have you had trouble, Philip?"

The younger engineer said, not quite truthfully, "No, sire."

The king eyed him dubiously, but said only, "Can you raise the shutter so that I can get a look at the walls?"

"Of course, sire." Rather than order the remaining Roman back to his place, Philip himself hauled open the shutter halfway, so that the king could see out without exposing himself fully to Carthaginian arrows. Alexander leaned against the sun-warmed frame, staring out at the distant walls.

It was impossible to miss the gates, one behind the other, or the points where the aqueduct had passed through both walls. The Carthaginians had entirely cleared the ground between the walls; there was no advantage to be gained by striking at other points, and

Charias could be relied on to know where a wall was weakest. Alexander gestured for Philip to close the shutter again—it fell with a resounding crash—and crossed to the railing. "Craterus! All of you, come up here."

The officers who had been milling about below entered the stifling tower reluctantly, crowding into the upper story. The shutter was raised for the various officers to take a look—this time by the Roman trooper, moving smartly under Cassius's censorious stare—and then Alexander said, "We'll make the main attack where the aqueduct was."

"That's close to the gates," Craterus said, and gestured for the shutter to be opened again, briefly. The unusual movements had attracted the Carthaginians' attention. A few seconds after the shutter closed again, several heavy catapult bolts rattled against the tower's side. The brigadier did not deign to notice. "But I grant the gate towers're no different from the others."

That was the only objection. Charias said, eagerly, "This tower's best sited to move in. We can bring the one to the south, too."

Alexander nodded. "Cassius, send for the rest of your men to help push."

The tribune looked away. "These are Domitius's men, Alexander. But I'll send a runner."

Domitius was unreasonably slow in responding to the king's summons. When at last his men did arrive, they grumbled as they took their places around the capstan and along the back of the tower. At the shouted order, the capstan groaned, but the wheels barely moved. Alexander's mouth tightened dangerously, and he said, "Can't your men do any better, tribune?"

Domitius said, "They're soldiers, not slaves."

"Slaves' work, is it?" Without waiting for the Roman's answer, Alexander pushed through the crowd of soldiers to the ladder, pausing halfway up it to shout,

"Come along, Domitius, if you think you can do a man's job."

Most of the legionaires had learned enough Greek to understand the king's words, and Alexander's voice had been pitched to carry. A ripple of laughter spread through the line and among the men on the capstan. Domitius flushed angrily and pushed his way in after the king. Cassius, swearing to himself, followed.

"Make a place for me," Alexander said, and the Romans circling the capstan shifted to make room, grinning both at the king and at their own officers. Alexander hastily stripped off his armor, then took his place along the long beam. Both tribunes copied him, Domitius with an air of distaste.

"Slave's work, Domitius?" Alexander asked again, and before the other could answer, shouted, "Now!"

The capstan turned then, very slowly at first, and then, as the men at the base of the tower threw their weight against it, more easily. With an almost human shriek, the tower's wheels began to turn, and the whole structure crept forward across the empty ground. The men on the capstan raised a breathless cheer, cut off abruptly when Cassius shouted, "Save your strength, men, we've a way to go yet."

Foot by foot, the tower moved ponderously to its new position. In the distance they could hear more shouting as the other towers got under way, moving in toward the new line. Cassius, gasping for breath in the airless chamber, lost count of the number of times he made the full circuit of the room, concentrating at last on the need to keep moving forward, to keep from falling under the feet of the men behind him.

At last, Charias shouted, "Enough!"

The men on the capstan stopped abruptly, stumbling against each other in sheer exhaustion. Cassius leaned forward against the bar, trying to gather the strength to climb down the ladder out of the tower, and was suddenly aware of Alexander leaning against the bar beside him. The king was soaked in sweat, hair plastered to his head, but his face bore an expression of savage pleasure. He fixed his eyes on Domitius, who had propped himself against the far wall, utter hatred transforming his face.

"King's work, Domitius," Alexander said, quietly, fiercely, and pushed himself away from the bar. "Come with me, Cassius."

Cassius dragged himself upright, unable to suppress a groan, and followed the king. Alexander paused at the tower railing, still breathing heavily, and said, "He had better mend his ways, Cassius."

He dropped down the ladder without waiting for an answer, leaving the tribune staring after him. Cassius stood at the railing for a long moment, taking deep breaths of the comparatively cool air, then, reluctantly, went back into the tower to talk to Domitius.

CHAPTER 12:

Carthage, late summer (Gorpiaios) to early autumn (Hyper-beretaios), 32 imperial (324 B.C., 429 A.U.C.)

The siege proceeded slowly. Once the siege towers had all been moved to their new locations, the engineers moved in to direct the building of field fortifications—staked trenches and sturdy palisades—to protect them. The penthouses once again moved forward to begin filling in the ditch outside the second wall, covered by fire from the siege towers and from Ombrion's archers, stationed along the palisade. The Carthaginians returned the attack as well, sallying twice against the penthouses when attack from the walls proved ineffective, but each time the archers held them until a relief force could arrive from the siege lines. The Carthaginians also turned their catapults against the siege towers themselves, but the heavy stone-throwers in the turrets along the inner wall proved useless against Charias's machines. Fire arrows were no more effective, and the hide-covered faces of the towers were soon streaked with long smudges where the arrows had burned themselves out. Under Charias's direction, the soldiers extended the ditch that protected the northeastern flank of camp and siege line all the way to the sea, angling it to bring the seawater almost up to the siege line itself. This made it easier to keep the facings of the penthouses and siege towers well soaked, and the water added another protection to the Macedonian fortifications.

The infantry units spent their time in fear or boredom, alternately working under the direction of the engineers, the noise of catapults, enemy and friend alike, loud around them, or standing guard along the various earthworks that defended camp and siege lines against an unexpected attack. The latter duty was tedious, unrewarding work, and provoked much grumbling, especially when the veterans were able to compare their lot with the cavalry's. The horsemen were responsible for foraging, and thus had a chance for loot. The Foot Companion brigadiers did their best to ignore the grumbling, knowing that it was not a serious problem, and knowing equally well that no commander who ever lived could have relieved all the soldiers' complaints. Only Domitius, still smarting from his brief, shaming encounter with Alexander, did his cautious best to fan the flames. His own century, handpicked for their loyalty to Rome, listened, and began to spread his words among the other Romans.

A Libyan captain, captured during one of the Carthaginian night-raids and promptly ransomed back to the city—Alexander had stated from the beginning that he had no desire to feed captives—overheard a few of the Romans' remarks and, when the Hundred questioned him closely about possible faint-heartedness, used those remarks to buy his release. The Hundred still had friends in Rome and knew that not all the city had approved of the treaty with Alexander. Some nights later, when the Romans had the southern perimeter watch, a Greek mercenary in Carthaginian pay slipped in among them, with Poppaeus Piso's name for his password. The Greek had been careful to choose one of Domitius's centuries for the attempt, though he had also demanded triple pay in advance, and his care paid off. The first legionary, rather than raising the alarm, brought him to the centurion of Domitius's own century, and the centurion, after some thought brought them both to Domitius. When the Greek evoked the name of Domitius's patron and implied that Poppaeus had sanctioned this contact, the tribune hesitated only briefly before agreeing. Slowly and cautiously, Domitius began to negotiate with Carthage.

As Charias had promised, at point-blank range the stone-throwers were capable of stripping the battlements from the walls. Once the engineers had gotten the range, they pounded the second wall unmercifully both along the section where the aqueduct had been and at a second spot two stadia to the north. When the upper wall had been knocked away, the soldiers were able to bring their penthouses right up to the ditch without fear of attack from above. The engineers turned their attention then to the stretch of wall between the two main points of attack. They were less successful there, the angle being more difficult for their engines, but soon the battlements began to show odd gaps. The Carthaginians did their best to repair them, but they were under constant fire from archers in the towers and along the siege line.

On the morning before the new moon that marked the beginning of Hyperberetaios, the monotony of the dawn watch was broken by a sudden shriek of trumpets from the Carthaginian walls. Amyntas son of Coenus, whose brigade had the watch, sent a runner back to the camp at once, and braced himself to defend the siege lines. The engineers, two of whom always slept in the towers, kicked their slaves awake and made an effort to man at least one catapult in each tower. Amyntas dispatched a battalion to help them, and waited. The city gates drew open and the Carthaginian troops poured out.

The rising sun threw a long shadow across the ground in front of the walls, stretching beyond the earthworks of the siege line. The Carthaginian troops moved in that shadow, their numbers momentarily obscured by it. Amyntas frowned, then cursed softly to himself. This was no ordinary sortie; the Carthaginians were out in force. He prodded his signaller, who stared open-mouthed at the approaching column.

"Sound the general alert," he ordered. The battalion commanders, all of whom had served with his father for many years, were waiting for orders. Amyntas took a deep breath, fighting down his own fear, and said, "I've sent for reinforcements. All we have to do, men, is hold on 'til they get here." He barely saw the grin, at once paternal and encouraging, on the nearest captain's face before he pulled down his helmet and moved to take his own place along the palisade.

The king had been awakened by the first sound of trumpets from the Carthaginian walls, and was already dressed and half-armed by the time Amyntas's runner appeared in the door of his tent. The other commanders were as alert, shouting for the file-leaders to rouse their men even before the general alarm had sounded. That signal turned the disciplined movement into organized chaos. Craterus and Perdiccas, whose brigades were closest to the oncoming attack, cursed and bullied their men out into the space behind the siege line, forming up as they ran.

The Carthaginians had already reached the siege line. Amyntas's men, spread thin along the defensive palisade, were hard pressed to hold on. A massive Carthaginian dragged heavily at the weakest section of the palisade. The timbers, set in loose ground, groaned and gave way. Cursing, a Foot Companion drove his sarissa through the man's body, but two more soldiers sprang to take his place. The short section of palisade collapsed, and the Carthaginians began to force their way through the gap. Neoptolemus, at the head of his hypaspists, saw the breach and raised the war cry, pointing. His men rushed forward to contain it.

Domitius led his centuries out through the northern gate of the camp, leaving a detachment to guard it, and spread out along the earthworks that backed the watery ditch. Menes, whose battalion had had the watch there, ran forward to meet him, saying, "They need you on the south wall, Domitius."

"Orders," the tribune answered soothingly, and as Menes slid to a halt beside him, still protesting, he drove his short sword neatly under the other's corselet. Menes fell in mid-word, a terrible look of surprise on his face. All along the palisade, Roman turned on Macedonian. Menes had already sent most of his men to shore up Amyntas's line: the remainder fell almost at once, their shouts drowned in the general noise of battle. Satisfied that he had not been seen, Domitius stepped up to the palisade and raised the legion's standard, once, then again. At once, the smaller northern gate opened in the Carthaginian wall, and more troops emerged.

Philotas, another of Amyntas's battalion captains, saw them first and shouted a warning. Alexander, mounted now to direct the defense, wrenched his animal around to face the new threat. The Roman troops were huddled against the walls waiting. . . . Then the king saw what they were doing and he yelled out in rage. Domitius's centuries gave a final shove, toppling a long section of the palisade so that its fallen timbers bridged the ditch, then wheeled to advance against the Macedonian flank. The Carthaginians advanced at the double, scrambling across the fallen palisade.

Alexander cursed them at the top of his voice and shouted for the fresh brigades of Foot Companions, Simmias's and Polyperchon's men, to follow him. He

would not be able, in this confined space, to use
numbers to his advantage, but neither would the
Carthaginians be able to deploy fully. He slid from his
horse and ran to his place in the line.

Inside the camp there was utter chaos. Cassius's
loyalists struggled with Domitius's men for control of
the gates while panicked engineers fought to subdue
the Carthaginians and Roman mutineers who had managed to penetrate the compound. Ptolemy, whose brigade was camped farthest from the palisade, swore
furiously, then lifted his voice to contradict his own
orders. He got his battalions moving in the right direction at last, and cursed them on their way, praying
that they would remember that some of the Romans
were on their side. He turned to follow them, and
found himself abruptly face to face with a trio of
Romans. Ptolemy hesitated, uncertain whose men they
were, and the leader jumped at him.

The brigadier leaped backward, shouting to warn
his men, and parried the attack with his shield. The
second Roman cut skillfully at his legs. Ptolemy twisted
away, but the blade cut deep into his thigh. He fell,
and rolled to his left, away from the Romans. A Roman javelin struck the ground to his right. Then a
dozen men rushed past him, half-armored Thracians
and Agrianians and even someone's kitchen slave,
cleaver in hand. The Romans gave way before them,
and the smallest turned to run. One of the Agrianians
spun his sling and the fleeing Roman crumpled. The
slave was on him in an instant, wielding his cleaver
with professional skill.

Ptolemy struggled to one knee, shield hand pressed
to his leg to stop the bleeding. One of the Thracians
dropped to the ground beside him, ripping at the hem
of his tunic. The brigadier waved him angrily on, but
the Thracian said, in barbarous Greek, "The Foot
Companions, sir, and the little Roman—they've closed
the gates again."

Ptolemy shook his head, unable to picture the precise chain of events, but reasonably sure it was good news, and submitted to the Thracian's rough medicine. The infantryman wadded the strip of cloth against the wound, then tore loose a second rag to hold it in place, knotting it securely as he said, "And they're holding the towers."

Ptolemy grunted—that was definitely good news—and started to lever himself to his feet. The Thracian helped him up, then yanked the javelin out of the ground, knocking off the iron head with a single swordstroke, and offered it to Ptolemy. The brigadier accepted it—it was just long enough to support him—and glanced quickly around to assess the situation. There were bodies on the ground but those were mostly Romans, killed in the light infantry's attack. Gritting his teeth, he limped forward to take command of his own people.

Along the siege lines, the Macedonians were holding their own. Neoptolemus and his men contained the first breakthrough and slowly drove the Carthaginians back. Amyntas's men sealed the gap behind them, and it was butcher's work in the space between the towers. Along the southern perimeter, Amyntas's spearhead battalion, strengthened by men from Perdiccas and Craterus's brigades, succeeded in pushing the Carthaginians from the walls. They retreated toward the city in good order, harassed by the Companion Cavalry.

The fighting was heavier to the north, where the Romans had pulled down the palisade, but slowly the Macedonians' superior postion took its toll. Simmias's and Polyperchon's men had been able to catch the mixed force of Carthaginians and Romans before they could deploy properly, pinning them against the water-filled ditch that ran north to the sea. Some of the Carthaginians sought to break through the gates to join up with their men inside the camp itself. Cassius's men, caught between that attack and Domitius's men inside the camp, were briefly hard pressed to hold. Then Simmias's own battalion came to their relief, driving the Carthaginians back into the staked ditch.

As soon as the northern attack was contained, Alexander fought his way out of the press, shouting for one of the pages to bring his horse. Miraculously, Theodatus appeared in seconds, leading the grey gelding. Alexander swung himself onto its back and headed back into the camp, shouting for the nearest troopers to follow him.

Ptolemy, limping behind his men as they pushed grimly toward the gate, swung 'round at the sound of hoofbeats, still supporting himself on the broken javelin. Alexander reined in before him, pushing back his helmet. His face beneath it was a Fury's mask.

"You're hurt," the king said. His eyes shifted, sweeping over the bodies still lying in the dirt. "And Clitus is dead, and Hector. Domitius?"

"Pinned against the gate," Ptolemy answered. "If he's not dead yet."

"Gods send he is," Alexander said. "For his sake." He swung 'round to survey the situation, then looked directly at Ptolemy. "No prisoners."

Ptolemy started to protest, then bit off the words. Alexander was right to be ruthless now, with everything at stake, and his ruthlessness would be a bloody lesson to Rome itself. "Yes, Alexander," he said, then turned awkwardly at the sound of another horseman, riding fast from the direction of the gate. Alexander recognized the distinctive Roman helmet before he recognized the rider, and lifted his lance.

"Wait, Alexander," Ptolemy shouted, and at the same moment the horseman cried, "Sire!"

Alexander let the sarissa fall, its point grounding harmlessly in the dust, and said, "And what do you want with me, Cassius Nasidienis?"

The tribune reined in, pushing back his helmet. He was on the verge of tears. "Alexander, I beg you. My men have no part in this, they're loyal—they're fighting their own countrymen for you. I beg you, spare my people."

Alexander's face changed, the taut, angry lines easing, and he said, almost gently, "I've done you an injustice, Cassius."

The tribune said nothing, eyes fixed on the king's face. After a brief instant, Alexander said, "Your people are spared, of course, and have my gratitude for their loyalty. What happened?"

Cassius took a deep breath. "Sire, somehow Domitius has made a fool's bargain with Carthage; I don't know why."

Alexander nodded, and said to Ptolemy, "Kill them." He turned his horse as though to ride away, and Cassius spurred forward to block his path, saying, "Alexander, no!"

The king reined in angrily, the gelding snorting as it fought the bit. "Why shouldn't they be killed, they've betrayed me—betrayed the treaty, as well."

The tribune was weeping now, the tears making a path through the dirt on his face. "Alexander, I beg you," he said again, fighting for words that the king would understand. "They're my people, my responsibility. Domitius has misled them—no Roman has any real love for Carthage—"

Alexander said, "But they love me even less."

"No!" Cassius paused. "Not all of them are part of this plot. I'm sure of it, sire." He stopped, then added, with a strange, cold pride, "And there are the lives of your men to consider. I can persuade a surrender. Please, King Alexander, let me try."

Alexander hesitated, moved in spite of himself by the Roman's appeal. "Very well," he said at last. "Persuade them to surrender, if you can, and I'll show mercy. But not to the organizers." Without waiting for an answer, he swung his horse away.

Cassius stared after him for a moment longer, then turned his horse back to the gate. The fighting had eased there: the mutineers had given up their attempts to break out through the encircling troops, and waited, sullenly, for the inevitable attack. Neither Ptolemy's nor Cassius's men had pressed the attack, and the waiting legionaries raised a cheer at their tribune's approach. Cassius called to the nearest, "Help me up onto the gate."

The legionary did as he was asked, and the tribune caught the top of the gatepost, pulling himself onto the narrow inner walkway. He balanced there, waiting for the first shock of a javelin, and shouted, "Domitius Mela!"

He was answered by derisive shouts from the mutineers, but, amazingly, no one fired on him. Cassius shouted again, and Domitius shoved his way through the Roman ranks, to stand staring up at the other tribune.

"What could you possibly want, Cassius Nasidienis?" he shouted back. "Come to ask us to surrender, to tell us Alexander offers mercy? We're not children, boy."

"No mercy to you," Cassius retorted promptly. "You're a traitor to Rome and a disgrace to your office." He raised his voice to carry to the Macedonian lines. "Yes, Alexander offers mercy, but only to those of you who deserve it, who weren't part of this—conspiracy."

There was a murmur of response from the listening Romans, uncertain, questioning, and Domitius shouted, "You're a liar, Cassius. Come down and I'll prove it—if you're not too much a coward."

Domitius was well known to be the better fighter. Cassius laughed, welcoming an open fight against an acknowledged enemy, and dropped to the ground in front of his fellow tribune. He landed heavily, and nearly fell. Domitius slashed blindly at him, putting his whole weight behind the blow. There was a shout of outrage from the Romans guarding the gate. Then Cassius was up, moving with unexpected grace, striking backhanded as the other tribune stumbled past him. Domitius fell forward, and Cassius struck again, nearly severing the other tribune's head.

There were shouts from both lines, and Cassius's men surged forward a few steps. Cassius held up his hands, not looking over his shoulder. "Romans," he called, "I ask you to surrender to my authority."

"Will Alexander show mercy?" someone shouted from the rear lines, and Cassius answered instantly.

"He has promised mercy for those of you Domitius misled, who didn't plan the mutiny. What more can you ask?"

There was more muttering from the Roman line, men shifting warily from side to side, glancing at their neighbors. Then, abruptly, an older man in the first rank threw down his sword. Slowly at first, then more quickly, the rest copied him, and someone shouted, "We've no love for Carthage, sir."

Ptolemy had been waiting for that moment. He waved his file leaders forward to move among the unresisting Romans, collecting their weapons and then herding them away. The brigadier himself moved to join Cassius, who looked bleakly at him, then down at Domitius's body.

"This should never have happened," the tribune said quietly. "Ptolemy, Alexander had better keep the word I've given them, or I will have to kill myself."

Ptolemy glanced warily at the younger man, but Cassius's face was oddly composed, showed no sign of after-battle hysteria. "He'll keep it," he said. "You did right."

"I hope so," Cassius said softly. "I pray so."

CHAPTER 13:

Carthage, early autumn (Hyperberetaios), 32 imperial (324 B.C., 429 A.U.C.)

It took some weeks for the camp to recover from the Carthaginian attack. First and foremost, in that climate, there were the dead to burn. Alexander made the sacrifices, his face set and angry, then returned to the camp perimeter to supervise the repairing of the palisade, seemingly oblivious to the thick smoke that swept from the pyres across the camp. Hephaestion, who had lost only two men in the raid—the cavalry had hardly been involved at all—made his own sacrifices, then retired to his tent, ordering his slaves to close all the tent flaps. Even with them all laced tightly shut, the smoke penetrated the tent. Hephaestion choked, dragging his blankets across his nose and mouth.

The wind shifted at last, blowing the smoke inland away from the tents, but he could still almost taste the stench. He sat up and fumbled in the darkness until he found the half-full wineskin, and drank eagerly. Even the good Macedonian wine was unable to erase the vileness; he spat the mouthful into the dirt at his feet, and collapsed back onto his cot, pulling his discarded tunic across his face.

By the time the last of the pyres had burned itself out, Cassius, aided by Ptolemy as consul, had begun the nasty job of weeding out the real conspirators among Domitius's men. Alexander, his first anger past, was inclined to be lenient, and Cassius did nothing to discourage him. The few active conspirators—centurions and junior officers all—were executed. The rest were formed into a special battalion, to earn the king's trust if they could.

Once the field fortifications were repaired and strengthened, the camp returned to the routine of the siege. The penthouses moved forward, filling in broad sections of the ditch while the stone-throwers once again bombarded the walls. Diades turned his attention now to the innermost wall, concentrating the fire of one siege tower on the tower that flanked the spot where the aqueduct had crossed the walls. Other engines attacked the wall itself, and by the end of the month, the inner wall was missing a long section of its parapet. One tower had been beaten into uselessness, and a second had fallen in a spectacular slide of stone and mortar.

Alexander watched the engineers' progress with satisfaction, and, after the tower's fall, ordered Diades to concentrate on the wall beneath it and the section of the outer wall in front of it. The year was growing old, and it was time to end the siege. The Friends agreed— the inland cities could only supply so much food—and gathered daily in the king's tent to plan the final attack. If a big enough gap could be made in the outer wall, a full brigade could be fed through the breach, and sambucas—engines that bore an enclosed scaling ladder—could be brought up to the inner wall, to get the army into the city. The two engineers considered the plan, murmuring to each other in half-sentences, then agreed that, yes, it could be done. Diades returned to his siege towers to supervise the aiming of the new bombardment, and Charias went inland again to collect timber for the sambucas and for battering rams.

As the engineers labored, Alexander summoned Nearchus from his camp opposite the harbor to join the rest of the Friends for a final conference. The king's plan was a dangerously simple one: to get most of his men into the city by means of the sambucas, and then drive directly for the Byrsa, Carthage's citadel. Craterus shook his head.

"I don't like it," he said bluntly. "We need a diversion."

Alexander nodded. "Such as?"

Craterus scowled, and Hephaestion hid a smile. Nearchus leaned foward suddenly, reaching for Eumenes's stained map of the city. "There's a sea-gate," the admiral said, spinning the map so that the others could see and pointing to a spot two stadia north of the Byrsa, "here."

The generals considered the map in silence for a moment, and then Ptolemy said, dubiously, "That's just below the steepest face of the Byrsa, isn't it?"

Nearchus nodded, and Perdiccas said, "That doesn't matter, if it's a diversion you want."

Alexander said, "We'll do it. Amyntas, your brigade and Cassius's troops will land at the sea gate." He glanced at the admiral, who answered promptly, "I have the ships."

"Good." Alexander studied the battered map a moment longer, and said, "Simmias, Ptolemy, Polyperchon, your men will defend the sambucas until they reach the innermost wall. Craterus, Perdiccas, your brigades—and the hypaspists, Neoptolemus—will be responsible for moving the sambucas to the wall, and making the first assault. I'll lead one battalion of hypaspists myself and take overall command of that first wave. Hephaestion, you'll take the mercenaries and secure our communications."

The cavalry commander nodded. His own men would not be of much use in this attack; he was merely grateful to be given any command.

There was not much more discussion. The generals reviewed the plan twice more, adding refinements here and there, but beyond that there was little more to do. One by one, they rose and took their leave, until only Hephaestion remained. He looked questioningly at the king.

"Stay."

The cavalry commander leaned back in his chair, gesturing for more wine. After the page had disappeared again, Hephaestion said, "What will you do when you've taken Carthage?"

Alexander sighed and looked away. After a long silence, he said quietly, "Destroy it."

Hephaestion waited, and then, when the king showed no signs of continuing, asked, "Why?" He could guess at any number of reasons for Alexander's decision— anger, hatred, revenge, strategy—but he could not see any one of them in the king's face.

Alexander said, "First, I can't arrange a lasting peace any more than I could with Tyre. Second, Carthage and its harbors can dominate this half of the Inner Ocean, and I still don't have the fleet to counter that. Third—" He glanced sideways at the cavalry commander and smiled wryly. "I haven't forgotten Balacrus."

Hephaestion nodded thoughtfully. The Carthaginians had been within their rights to kill the scout, but the memory of the mutilated bodies sickened him. Alexander still felt responsible for that death and always paid his debts: the destruction of the city would be suitable payment, regardless of the strategic considerations.

Reading his friend's thought, Alexander said, "No, that's not all of it. I don't want to spend the rest of my life scrabbling along the African coast—which I would; these people won't surrender—and I'm going to have enough problems holding together Persians, Medes, Macedonians, Greeks, and now Romans, without adding Carthaginians to the mix."

"And if we'd come to Carthage first," Hephaestion asked, "would we be sacking Rome?"

The king looked away again. "It didn't happen that way, did it? So why ask?"

"And after Carthage is destroyed?" the cavalry commander asked. "What next?"

Alexander said grimly, "We return to Alexandria in Egypt, and set my kingdoms in order." He saw Hephaestion's sidelong look and added, "No, we will not go east, into India; that's ended, I know." Hephaestion touched his shoulder in sympathy. Alexander rested his head against the other's hand. "I must leave that final corner of the world unconquered if I am to hold what I have. Ammon spoke truly: The die is cast." The king wept.

Hephaestion slipped from his chair to kneel beside the king, embracing him. He could guess most of the king's thoughts, and fought to find the words that would comfort him. At last he said, "Achilles wasn't a king, he could choose his death. And you are not Achilles."

There was no answer, but gradually the king's weeping eased. He leaned against Hephaestion's shoulder, saying "Be careful tomorrow, my friend. I will need you more than ever, now."

Hephaestion tightened his hold again. It was dangerous, even hubristic, to answer that, but he said anyway, "I'm always careful, Alexander. And I'll always be there."

It was enough. Alexander returned the other's embrace, then pulled gently away, visibly turning his attention to the next day's fighting. If Carthage was to

be the last of his great campaigns, he would end it
gloriously.

The sun rose very red the next morning. The army,
knowing perfectly well that they faced a hard fight,
chose to take that as a good omen, and the king was
careful to do nothing at the morning sacrifice that
might change their minds. After the ceremony, the
officers began chivvying their men into place behind
the sambucas or in the screening force alongside them.

Alexander crouched in the mouth of the first sambuca, bracing himself against the side and lip of the
compartment as a team of slaves worked the capstan.
The entire structure, essentially no more than a hollow wooden tube balanced on a wheeled carriage,
shuddered slowly upward, tilting to match the walls'
height as the counterweighting stones in the rear compartment overcame the weight of the ten men waiting
in the bucket. As the sambuca rose, Alexander caught
a brief glimpse of the soldiers waiting nervously in the
shelter of the siege towers: they would follow the first
wave to hold the breach and the ruined wall.

There was a warning shout from the engineers below, and the sambuca seemed to drop a few feet as the
ratchet locked into place. Alexander steadied himself
against the edge of the bucket and glanced back at the
men who shared the compartment with him. They
were all volunteers, of course, hypaspists of the spearhead battalion, chosen for their proven skill. Attarhias.
the sheep-nosed battalion commander, grinned back
at him and said, "We're ready, sire."

Alexander nodded and glanced back down the hollow column of the sambuca to the engineer crouching
among the gears and levers of the carriage. "Now!" he
shouted, and waved broadly. "Let's go!"

The figure—Charias—waved back and jumped down
off the carriage. Alexander turned back to face the
walls, bracing himself against the rim of the bucket,
and drew his shield across his body. The others did

the same, huddling behind their shields. The sambuca shuddered into motion, the bucket bobbing up and down against the ratchet despite the restraining blocks. Alexander dropped to his knees, clinging to an inner rib. The others did the same to keep from being thrown free or tossed back down the hollow tube to the carriage. The sambuca jerked abruptly, and tilted to the right, throwing one of the hypaspists against Attarhias's knees and nearly knocking him off his feet. Alexander risked a glance around the rim of his shield and saw that the sambuca's wheels were sinking in the imperfectly packed rubble that filled the first ditch. Below, Charias screamed orders and insults at the hypaspists, and with a superhuman effort the soldiers heaved the machine forward again onto solid ground.

The Carthaginians chose that moment to open fire from the final wall. Arrows, javelins, stones and heavy bolts from the catapults crashed like hail against the sides of the sambuca, and there were shrieks of pain from the men ranged along the side of the carriage, where its bulk offered no protection. A metal bolt ripped through the bucket, tearing open the hide facing between two of the reinforced beams, and lodged harmlessly in the wooden floor. There were letters stamped on its broad head, and one of the hypaspists stared at it, lips moving as he sounded out the words.

The Carthaginians fired again. It was a volley of arrows this time. Some of them left trails of smoke as they flew. Attarhias cursed softly, and the others looked uneasy. The sambuca had been wetted down before the attack began, but the wood would dry out quickly.

Alexander ducked as something flashed past his head and he turned just in time to see a hypaspist slam his shield down on a fire arrow, smothering its flame. "Well done," the king said, and the trooper grinned, but the others stared nervously back down the hollow beam, waiting to see if any of the other arrows would catch.

Then the sambuca reached the wall. A mass of Carthaginians balanced on the ruined parapet, one of them extending a long beam as though to fend off the sambuca. The beam was much too light to stop the massive engine, but a hypaspist lurched to his feet anyway, clutching a Roman javelin.

"Get down," Alexander shouted, "save your weapons."

The trooper ignored him, balancing against the last irregular movements of the sambuca, and flung his javelin wildly. Then Attarhias dragged him to his knees, and the lip of the bucket slammed against the wall. Alexander gave the war cry and swung his sword at the nearest Carthaginian. The roof of the bucket was in his way, shortening his stroke. He checked his next blow and pushed forward with his shield, shoving a Carthaginian off the parapet to the ground fifty feet below. The sambuca trembled, the lip of the bucket bouncing against the wall as the rest of the hypaspists swarmed up the ladder after them.

On the wall itself, the hypaspists locked shields and pushed forward, striking almost blindly at the Carthaginians crowding around them to clear a space for their fellows. Then the first of Neoptolemus's men reached the top of the sambuca and poured out onto the wall, driving back the Carthaginians. There was a cheer from further long the wall as the second sambuca reached it, and then the third was in place as well, hypaspists and Foot Companions streaming up the ladders and onto the wall. Gasping, Alexander steadied the next man who stumbled out of the bucket, and turned to look for the stairways that must lead off the wall. Neoptolemus, who had been in the second sambuca, made his way along the crumbling wall to join the king.

"Orders?" he asked, quite calmly.

Alexander pointed to the nearest stairway and the Carthaginian troops—Greek and Libyan mercenaries—

rushing forward to block the Macedonian advance. "As before. I want to reach the citadel by nightfall."

Neoptolemus nodded, studied the situation for a brief second, and was gone. Alexander hesitated a moment longer, glancing back over his shoulder at the dead ground between the walls. His own Greek mercenaries moved forward in good order, ready to hold the breach against any counterattack. The king smiled, satisfied, and headed down the nearest stairway to join his men.

The suburbs, pleasant villas set in well-tended garden land, stretched for some seventeen stadia between the main walls and the rising ground of the city proper. The Carthaginians fell back slowly among those now-abandoned villas, disputing each house in a series of bloody skirmishes. As the hypaspists faltered, taking heavy losses, the Foot Companion brigades moved forward to replace them, and made better progress as Perdiccas's men finally forced their way through the sea gate. Some time in the mid-afternoon, the Carthaginians fired the northernmost part of the suburbs, driving the few slaves who had not fled with their masters into the Byrsa out of their hiding places among the empty houses. They, and various valuable animals unaccountably left behind, complicated the Macedonians' efforts to deal with the fires. Hephaestion was hard pressed to send Alexander the reinforcements the king needed to keep the fire from trapping his men. By nightfall Alexander's men controlled about a third of the city, though they had not yet reached the city proper, and Perdiccas's men held most of Cape Carthage itself, below the Byrsa. But the cost had been high.

The king sat with his back to the ruin of someone's garden wall, wineskin at his feet, staring into the center of the bonfire the pages had built. His officers sat or sprawled nearby, soot-streaked faces blank with exhaustion. One of the pages brought a loaf of bread, but the king waved it away, too tired to eat. Neoptolemus was asleep, so wrapped in his cloak that he looked like a rug someone had rolled up and tossed away. Craterus sat beside him, helmet off, chewing methodically on a handful of olives. Across the fire, Hephaestion leaned against a broken pillar, gathering the strength for the dangerous journey back to his own men. Feeling the king's eyes on him, he smiled mechanically, but said nothing. Ombrion squatted by the fire, idly tossing bits of grass into the flames. Ptolemy and Charias sat together, the bodyguard rubbing methodically at his wounded leg as they talked in low voices.

"The thing now is to link up with Perdiccas," Alexander said, as though continuing an argument, "and then take the Byrsa."

Neoptolemus stirred in his sleep, and Craterus prodded him fully awake.

"I know your people took the worst of it, Craterus," Alexander went on. "But I need to make contact with Perdiccas."

The brigade commander nodded grimly. "They'll do," he said. "They'll do."

Alexander nodded. "Polyperchon, your men will link with Hephaestion and hold our lines of communication. Craterus, the rest of the Foot Companions are under your command; join with Perdiccas. Neoptolemus, the hypaspists will push on with me to the Byrsa. Charias, you said you brought the rams in already?"

Charias nodded. "And the men to mount them," he said, with some pride.

"What about prisoners?" Hephaestion asked.

Craterus sneered, and Alexander said, "I've no objection to taking prisoners—if they'll surrender."

"So that's the way of it," the cavalry commander murmured, then shrugged. "As you please."

Ptolemy said, "We've taken nothing but slaves and mercenaries. The rest don't seem to want to surrender." He looked quickly at Alexander. "Did you get a chance to speak to that old woman we found?"

The king nodded. The woman in question was an old, dirty, terrified slave, probably nurse to at least one generation of some noble family. A couple of Ptolemy's men—probably looking for loot if the truth were told—had rescued her from the cellar of a half-burned mansion, and in gratitude for her rescue she had babbled out some story of terrible things that were happening, or would happen, in the Byrsa. The troopers had brought her to their officer, and he in turn sent her on to the king. Alexander had listened to her story, but the woman was incoherent with age and fear, and the king had been able to make no sense of it. "All she said that made sense was that there was some trap being set in the Byrsa—though from her talk you'd have thought it was directed against her own people, not us."

"So we'll be careful," Craterus muttered.

Alexander nodded and stretched painfully. "Do that, all of you. Is everything clear, then?" He went on without really waiting for the others to nod agreement, "Polyperchon has the perimeter? Then let's get some sleep while we can."

The second day was no easier than the first. The Macedonians were awakened before dawn by an attack on the perimeter, which Polyperchon's exhausted men were barely able to contain. It took a good two hours' hard fighting before the Carthaginians were driven back again and the Macedonians regained the initiative. Craterus pressed forward grimly at the head of the Foot Companions, and finally, shortly after noon, made contact with Perdiccas and Cassius. The Carthaginians sallied a final time and were beaten back. By mid-afternoon, Alexander and the hypaspists had fought their way through the city proper to the base of the Byrsa wall, and Charias brought up the rams. The wall was a thin curtain of stone, with only a

light palisade; the engineer, bleeding along his cheek
where the stones from a falling house had grazed him,
promised he could have it down in an hour. The
hypaspists, who had suffered enough in the bitter
house to house fighting, manned the ram willingly.

Alexander stared up at the Byrsa. He could not see
any soldiers along the long wall, or on the tops of the
buildings, but the sporadic flights of arrows, the occasional thrown spear, proved that they were there.
There would be other people, too, in the citadel's
buildings, women and children. As the last wall began
to fall, he held back his men, waiting for the inevitable surrender.

There was no signal from the wall, no appearance of
the Hundred, and the king shrugged, motioning the
hypaspists forward. There would be good looting in
the inner treasury of Carthage: the troopers pushed
eagerly through the breach, elbowing each other a
little in their excitement.

Then Theodatus shouted from the rear, "It's on fire.
They're burning the city!"

Alexander turned rapidly. Great plumes of smoke
were rising from the Byrsa, and others from the twin
harbors, smoke that rose so quickly that the fires had
to have been deliberately set and extravagantly fueled:
the trap the old woman had spoken of. "Neoptolemus,"
the king shouted, "Get our men out of there."

Even as he spoke there was a shout from the citadel, and the Carthaginian troops plunged forward again.
The hypaspists, distracted by their thoughts of plunder, were slow to respond, and a hundred men died
before Neoptolemus and his officers could rally their
people. They retreated then, in good order, and the
Carthaginians, following recklessly, were cut down to
a man.

The buildings of the citadel were well afire now.
Alexander shaded his eyes, staring at the flames that
already broke from the roof of one low building, and

thought he saw, through the smoke a line of figures with raised arms silhouetted against the fire. He blinked, and the picture was gone, swallowed by the flames. The wind was from the sea, a strong, steady wind that would carry the fires well out into the suburbs; it was more than time to be gone.

Runners passed quickly along the Macedonian line. By the time the last one returned to the king, it was clear that the city was gone. The Macedonians withdrew cautiously, wary of further traps. One Roman century and a battalion of Perdiccas's Foot Companions pulled back along the length of Cape Carthage to protect Nearchus's waiting ships, the rest of the army fell back toward Hephaestion's men. As the army pulled apart, Carthaginian troops sortied for the final time, turning on the smaller group moving along the cape. Perdiccas held back, expecting them to ask for mercy, and so lost the initiative. The Carthaginians smashed into his hastily formed lines, driving him back in disarray. Cassius brought his own men up to reinforce the Foot Companion lines, and they held.

Alexander heard the sound of fighting even before a runner reached him from the rearguard; he took personal command of the hypaspists' spearhead battalion and two battalions of Ptolemy's Foot Companions, and turned back to take the Carthaginians in the rear. Outnumbered and surrounded, the Carthaginians still refused to surrender, fighting grimly until their officers were dead. Only then did the survivors dare to shout for mercy, and the Foot Companions, sickened and angered by the slaughter forced upon them, were not inclined to grant it. Only Alexander's personal intervention saved the last seventy or so Carthaginians for the slave markets. Perdiccas took them in hand.

The wind from the sea had carried the smoke and sparks from the burning citadel well inland, and parts of the suburbs untouched by the earlier fires were beginning to burn. The orderly Macedonian retreat became disorganized, the troopers first walking quickly, then jogging, and finally running hard to join up with Hephaestion's men before the fires cut them off. Alexander, in personal command of the rearguard, kept his men to a walk, making a final nightmare passage between two burning villas. Then at last he was back in the cleared space behind the broken inner wall, and Hephaestion came forward to meet him, escorting two unarmed strangers.

"These are the mercenary commanders who held the wall," the cavalry commander said steadily, his voice giving no hint of the relief he felt. "They wish to surrender, Alexander."

The king nodded. "Very well, we'll discuss terms later."

Hephaestion backed away, herding the mercenary officers with him. Alexander turned to stare up at the burning city. He had known since the night before that this was the last campaign, but it had seemed unreal then, less solid than his visions of Zeus Ammon. Now the reality of it was all too apparent, and he let that grief wash through him. This was the end of his dream of a world-empire. Now there was other work to be done, the less glorious task of melding all his disparate peoples into a common, lasting empire. Philip had excelled at that, had had the knack of government as well as the gift of command. Alexander took a deep breath. He had surpassed his father as a commander; he would set himself to be a better king as well. He shook himself, and walked back toward Hephaestion, framing the terms of the mercenaries' surrender as he went.

EPILOGUE:

Alexandria-in-orbit, summer (Loios), 1947 imperial (1591 A.D., 2344 A.U.C.)

The crew's quarters was a long cylinder, with sleeping bags suspended by a complicated system of elastic lines along its sides. Hector son of Amyntor flipped himself through the circular hatchway, aligning himself in the lack of gravity so that his feet pointed back toward the hatch, and pulled himself along the line of sleeping men until he reached the last one. Alexander Maiorian hung comfortably asleep, face turned into the bag's netting. One arm had worked free of the sleeping bag, and drifted limply in the faint current of air from the main compartment. Hector anchored himself to the nearest handhold and reached across to shake the drifting arm. Maiorian stirred, opening his eyes, and Hector said, "The commander wants you. Transmission in fifteen minutes."

Maiorian groaned and fumbled for the snaps of the bag. He freed himself in a single convulsive gesture and drifted out into the middle of the cylinder, wearing only the long underwear in which they all slept. Hector caught him as he drifted toward another sleeper.

311

Maiorian muttered something that might have been thanks, caught a handhold, and spun to reclose his sleeping bag, then hung in the center of the cylinder.

"Transmission?" he asked.

"To Alexandria—to your uncle the emperor," Hector said, patiently. Maiorian was not at his best immediately on waking. "It's Foundation Day, remember?"

Maiorian grunted. It was a sound that could mean either comprehension or complete rejection of the idea, and Hector eyed him dubiously, waiting for some more positive sign. Then Maiorian shook himself and pulled himself along the row of handholds toward the crew's private lockers. Hector watched his friend pull on the coveralls badged with the Air Companions' winged star, calmly retrieving the various belongings that threatened to drift away in the lack of gravity. Then Hector followed him into the second of the three main compartments that made up Alexandria-in-orbit.

About half of the station's staff was already there, floating in the central space among the panels that monitored the experiments that were the primary function of the station. Most panels bore the scarab-and-wreath stamp of the Universities of Alexandria-in-Egypt, but some carried the fasces of the Roman School of Engineering, and a few were marked with the symbols of schools in Hausa, Africa. A narrow band of bare metal encircled the middle of the cylinder and four thick portholes were spaced at equal intervals along it. Asander son of Proexes, the station's commander, drifted within easy reach of the grab bar beneath one portal and lifted one hand in lazy greeting.

Maiorian returned the gesture, pushing himself farther out into the chamber, and Asander asked, "Are you ready, then?"

Hector murmured, "Are you awake, that's the question."

Maiorian gave his friend a quick, malevolent glance,

and said to Asander, "As ready as I'll ever be." He snagged the bright-red guide rope that stretched across the compartment and flipped neatly to a stop, upright in relation to the commander. "Below" him, Stasanor of Augaea, the chief technician, finished making the final adjustments to the station's hand-held camera, and spun it expertly toward Lucius Mancinus, waiting by the hatch to the forward compartment. The younger technician caught it easily and hooked a foot through the nearest grab bar, using both hands to adjust the lens.

"Ready, Your Highness, sir?" he called.

Maiorian made a face—there were some thirty princes of the blood throughout the empire, enough to make any such title seem faintly ridiculous—but made no other response to the too-familiar teasing. "Go ahead."

Mancinus's face changed, and he said soberly, "Filming—now." Behind him, Stasanor flipped a series of switches, and a bank of lights flashed from yellow to green: the transmission was being beamed directly to Egyptian Alexandria, and from there to the borders of the empire and beyond.

Alexander Maiorian took a deep breath, looking directly into the camera lens, and began to speak. He was the first of his line to go into space, and part of the first crew to inhabit Alexandria-in-orbit; on this, the anniversary of the empire's foundation, he spoke of his own pride and responsibility, and of his desire—shared by the rest of the crew, and the emperor, and many others—to see this new Alexandria grow and prosper, as had the other Alexandrias, the cities of the great Alexander himself.

Hector, listening from the hatchway, felt a stirring in the air behind him, and moved aside to let the others of the crew float silently into the second chamber. They were as caught up in the words as he: somehow, despite a Hausa mother and a German grandmother, despite the generations that separated

Maiorian from his great ancestor, the gift had not been lost. Wrapped in his own desire, he could transmit that longing to others, binding them to his own plans: not of conquest, this time, but of exploration. As long as Alexander Maiorian spoke for it, this newest Alexandria would prosper, and form the basis, perhaps, for a further empire in the stars.